FRAGMENTS OF FOREVER

FRAGMENTS OF FOREVER

J. A. Springs

Dedication

To Christina Perri—

Your song gave me a question:

"What would it take to love someone for a thousand years?"

This story is my answer.

—J. A. Springs

"I embarked on this journey without a clear vision, searching for that elusive 'je ne sais quoi' that would give my work its essence. Along the way, I discovered something profound. As you delve into these pages, I invite you to uncover it for yourself, dear reader."

Author's Note

This narrative was deeply inspired by the timeless and evocative song *"A Thousand Years"* by **Christina Perri**. From the moment I heard the song, its haunting melody and poignant lyrics resonated with me, capturing the essence of a love that transcends time and adversity.

I heard a calling from my heart for that same type of love—and I wanted the world to experience it with me.

The song's theme of enduring love—waiting patiently, never giving up, and facing the passage of time with unwavering devotion—became the foundation upon which this story was built.

As I developed the main characters, **Constance** and **Tempus**, I often returned to the idea that their love, much like the one described in *"A Thousand Years"*, was both eternal and tested by the cruel hand of fate. The lyrics spoke to the longing and hope that defined their relationship, inspiring the shape of their journey—meeting, falling in love, being torn apart, and finding one another again.

The song's message of steadfast love informed not just the plot, but also the emotional core of the story. Every decision they made, every trial they faced, was influenced by the idea that love can endure anything—even when it seems impossible.

It is my hope that this narrative captures the same timelessness and depth that Christina Perri's *"A Thousand Years"* so beautifully conveys.

— **J. A. Springs**

Prologue

for those who've ever waited across lifetimes,
held their breath through silence,
cradled their tears in the palm of their hand,
existed through heartache,
and believed that love—real love—could survive anything.

i will take you through sorrow.
i will deny you relief or respite.
i will isolate you in silence when you expect verse.
i will withhold clarity when you expect prose.
i will confuse you, mislead you, and ask that you sit in discomfort.
but, i promise... if you stay...
i'll give you something whole.
i will give you a real love story.

Chapter 1 "Echoes of Florence"

Present Day - Atlanta, USA

A forgotten memory stirs.

In the labyrinthine depths of Atlanta's High Museum of Art's archive room, a sense of hushed reverence enveloped two young women at work. Though both held the title of curator, they were currently assigned to a special project: preparing an upcoming exhibition that traced the changing ways humans have captured and preserved images of people across time. From carved stone busts and oil portraits to early photography and industrial-era lithographs, the project required careful selection from the museum's vast and varied archive.

It was a welcome shift from the usual routine. Most days found Constance buried in climate-controlled galleries or lost in academic correspondences about provenance. But today, she was elbow-deep in dust, handling artifacts with the reverence of someone holding stories instead of stone.

She tapped her pen against a nearby box lid and glanced at the digital clock blinking 9:43. Across the room, Lynette hunched over a crate of framed prints, humming a slow jazz tune she claimed helped her focus. The rhythm of their working relationship was easy—Constance brought the precision, Lynette the spontaneity. Their shared sense of purpose grounded them, but this project had added a thread of excitement beneath the surface—curating a narrative of how we have tried to remember ourselves.

Their makeshift workstation stood in the middle of the archive, surrounded by neatly arranged tables strewn with stacks of lithographs, black-and-white photos, and weathered sketches. The soft hum of the computer provided a steady rhythm to their progress, punctuated by the occasional rustle of paper.

Constance stretched, rolling her shoulders. Boredom crept in easily, despite her passion. This was the job she had always wanted—but not every day in the dream was a masterpiece.

She reached for the next lithograph and paused. Her fingers lingered on its surface, as if coaxing something from the silence. A portrait. A man. Something about him... She leaned closer.

The man stood in partial profile, his head turned just enough to meet the viewer's gaze with sharp, knowing eyes. His features were refined yet timeless—a strong jawline softened by the faintest suggestion of a smile, high cheekbones casting elegant shadows across his face. Dark hair swept back from a widow's peak framed a pale, intelligent brow. He wore a long, buttoned coat with a high collar, something out of the late 18th century, yet his posture carried a quiet, confident defiance that felt oddly modern.

She couldn't shake the sensation that she had encountered his face before, perhaps in a dream or a life unremembered. Yet the image, striking as it was, held its silence.

"Constance, what have you found there?" Lynette's voice broke through the air, laced with curiosity.

Constance turned to her friend, her expression a mix of confusion and intrigue. "It's one of the lithographs for the upcoming exhibit," she explained, gesturing towards the portrait. "But there's something about him... I can't quite put my finger on it, but he feels... familiar somehow."

Lynette stepped closer, her eyes narrowing as she studied the image. "I see what you mean. He is handsome," she murmured, her gaze flickering between Constance and the portrait. "There's a certain intensity in his eyes, as if he's seen things beyond..." she trailed off before picking back up the thought. "I don't know. Like the scope of mortal understanding."

Constance nodded, her mind buzzing with questions. "I can't shake the feeling that I know him though... like I've met him before," she admitted, her voice barely above a whisper.

Lynette furrowed her brow, her expression thoughtful. "That's impossible," she replied with care. "This lithograph is centuries old. Whoever this man is, he would have been long gone by now."

Despite Lynette's logical explanation, Constance still couldn't shake the sense of familiarity that gnawed at her insides. She glanced back at the portrait, a silent plea for answers echoing in her mind. Knowing that no answers would readily appear, she absently placed the item aside.

The two friends returned to sorting through the collection of lithographs, old photos, and paintings, their conversation drifting to other topics as they worked. Yet Constance's thoughts kept returning to the mysterious man in the lithograph, his image haunting her like a ghost from the past.

It was then that Lynette's sharp intake of breath broke the silence once more. "Constance, come look at this!" she called out, her voice tinged with excitement.

Constance hurried to Lynette, her heart pounding; Lynette's urgent summons piqued her curiosity. As she peered over her friend's shoulder, her breath caught in her throat.

There, amidst faded paintings, a figure strikingly resembled the lithograph's man. Her heart skipped, but she pushed the feeling down. It was a trick of the mind, probably. People saw patterns in clouds, animals in inkblots. The man in the lithograph could have shared a dozen features with this one, and it still wouldn't mean anything.

The painting's composition and color palette suggested a much earlier period—likely the Renaissance. The man wore a velvet tunic with ornate gold trim and a wide lace collar, framed in a thick, dark wooden border that hinted at 16th-century craftsmanship. Unlike the formal pose of the lithograph, this version had a quiet dignity, with the man's hand resting on a globe and his gaze tilted slightly downward, contemplative yet intense. Yet the eyes—sharp, penetrating, and hauntingly familiar—were unmistakably the same.

"Who is this man?" Constance's fingers delicately grazed the image before her, her gaze fixed intently on the enigmatic figure. Everything else faded. The world became background noise.

Lynette looked over at Constance, noting her rapt attention. Lynette's brows furrowed in contemplation, and she offered a nonchalant shrug. "Please tell me that was a rhetorical question," Lynette asked, half serious. When Constance didn't respond, Lynette continued. "I don't know," she replied, turning the small painting to inspect its back.

Attached to the rear was an index number, a discreet marker used for identification purposes for all pieces within the museum. Constance knew from their meticulous cataloging process that such numbers corresponded to detailed entries in the museum's database, containing vital information about each piece's origin and history.

Lynette sought further details on the painting. Without hesitation, Lynette navigated to the nearby computer, swiftly inputting the reference number. Lines of text scrolled across the screen, and she read aloud the retrieved information.

"It says here that it's a painting by a Rufgalio Durstrsky," Lynette announced, her tone tinged with intrigue. She faced Constance, turning from her monitor. "He's not widely recognized, but his works are scattered across various museum inventories." She gave Constance a quizzical expression. "Oddly enough, there's no mention of the subject's identity."

Constance's curiosity stirred, a nagging feeling of connection to the mysterious man gnawing at her thoughts. A fleeting curiosity regarding the man's identity prompted a brief research consideration, but she gave up on the idea. She knew their primary task demanded attention.

With a resigned sigh, Constance pushed aside her intrigue. "Well," she began, a shrug punctuating her words, "I suppose it's inconsequential for now. Let's focus on sorting through the rest of these items."

Lynette nodded in agreement, returning to the table to resume their task. Together, they sifted through the remaining images, their conversation drifting back to the enigma of the unidentified man. Despite that, their dedication to their work remained steadfast.

But the mystery only deepened when Constance stumbled upon a black-and-white photograph from the 1800s, taken somewhere in Europe. Amidst the sea of historical records, Constance's gaze fell upon a faded photograph tucked away in a dusty corner of a box. With a gasp of surprise, she reached out to retrieve it, her fingers trembling as she held the aged photograph in her hands. That man, pictured again, looked remarkably similar to the figure that fascinated her.

'This is getting ridiculous,' Constance thought.

Three images, across centuries, and she was convincing herself they looked the same? Her brain must be chasing connection where there was none. Humans were wired to find faces—even when they weren't there.

In the photograph, he wore a dark waistcoat and tightly tied cravat, his posture rigid and unsmiling—hallmarks of the late 19th century's early photographic processes, likely a daguerreotype or one of its successors. The sepia tones and faint blurring at the edges of the image gave it a ghostly quality, but the face was unmistakable.

"This is really weird," Constance began, her brow furrowed in perplexity.

"What have you found now?" Lynette's voice echoed with curiosity as she turned to look over Constance's shoulder, her eyes widening in anticipation.

Constance's heart raced as she examined the photograph, her breath catching in her throat at the sight of the familiar face staring back at her from the worn paper. "Look," she whispered, her voice barely above a hushed tone, "it's him again."

"What?" Lynette's curiosity piqued, causing her to lean over from the precarious stool she occupied, nearly sending it toppling over.

Reacting with quickness, Constance extended a supporting hand to steady her friend and colleague, their laughter mingling with relief as the stool found its balance once more. With a shared chuckle, they refocused their attention on the matter at hand.

"It's that guy we saw in the lithograph, the one who bore a resemblance to the man in the painting?" Constance stated.

Lynette nodded, her interest clear. "Yeah, did you uncover something about him?"

Constance shook her head briskly. "No, not exactly." With a deft movement, she retrieved the small black-and-white photograph, presenting it to Lynette. "But look at this—it's another image that seems to resemble him."

Lynette's eyes widened in astonishment as she studied the image, her mind racing with questions. "But how...?" she began, her voice trailing off as she struggled to comprehend the significance of their discovery.

A vast time separated the creation of the painting and the lithograph, making it impossible for the same person to have created them both. However, the photograph was only a century old. The dating on the lithograph was already pressing the limits.

"Wow," Lynette breathed, her eyes widening in astonishment.

As Lynette studied the photograph, a furrow creased her brow. "This is getting stranger by the minute," she murmured, her voice tinged with uncertainty.

Constance nodded in agreement, her mind buzzing with questions. "It's like... He's everywhere we look today," she mused, her gaze fixed on the image before them.

She wanted to believe it was a coincidence. A fluke. But something gnawed at her, a whisper of familiarity too vivid to ignore. And that made it worse—because it meant she was starting to believe something she couldn't explain.

The two friends exchanged a meaningful glance, a silent acknowledgment of the inexplicable nature of their discovery. The mystery surrounding the painting—and its lack of identifying details—was mounting. Still, they searched for information about the photograph and the enigmatic figure it depicted.

They returned once more to the database, hoping to find information about the lithograph and the old black-and-white photograph. Unfortunately, their pursuit of an identity returned nothing, leaving them even less sure of what they believed was the same person.

"This can't be the same person," Lynette finally stated.

Constance, breaking her seemingly increasing fascination with the individual, turned to Lynette and said, "You're right. The years are too dispersed between each of these for it to be the same guy looking like he hadn't aged at all."

Constance and Lynette, bewildered by the pictures, sensed a peculiar, inexplicable collection of faces spanning time. Despite their efforts, a rational explanation eluded them.

Unable to make sense of it, they set the images aside, their thoughts already drifting toward finishing their work. Whatever secrets lay hidden within the depths of history, Constance and

Lynette would not find them in the records and archives contained on the computer.

With a shared glance filled with unspoken questions, they reluctantly set the images aside, their minds still buzzing with unanswered mysteries. They returned to sorting. The enigmatic figure, whose presence transcended time, lingered in their thoughts.

As Constance and Lynette continued to sift through the images, their focus distracted by the mystery before them, the sound of footsteps approached from the doorway.

"Connie, are you ready to go to lunch?" Sera's voice floated into the room, her presence bringing a welcome interruption to the weird atmosphere.

Constance turned to greet her twin sister, a smile lighting up her face. "Hey, Sera," she said warmly, momentarily forgetting the enigmatic images that had captivated her attention.

Sera's eyes swept over the room, landing on Lynette. "Hello, Lynette," she greeted with a nod, her expression curious.

Lynette returned the greeting with a smile, but before she could engage in further conversation, Constance's movement drew her attention. The images spread before Constance drew her back.

As she turned to show Sera the intriguing images, her sister stopped in her tracks.

Sera's gaze locked onto the photograph—then froze. Her shoulders tensed. A strange stillness settled into the room, like the moment before a storm hits. Constance noticed the subtle shift, a flicker of unease crossing her sister's features, but before she could speak, Sera winced and brought her hands to her temples.

"Sera, what's wrong?" Constance asked, concern lacing her voice as she rushed to her sister's side.

Sera pressed her hands to her temples, a sharp intake of breath escaping from her lips. "My head... it hurts," she muttered, her voice strained.

Constance's heart sank at the sight of her sister in distress, her immediate focus shifting from the images to Sera's well-being.

As Sera's affliction subsided, she looked up at Constance with a bewildered expression, confusion clear in her eyes.

Constance wrapped her arms around her sister, offering comfort and reassurance. "Are you okay, Sera?" she asked softly, her concern palpable.

Sera nodded, her gaze distant, as if lost in thought. Unbeknownst to Constance and Lynette, a flood of memories from past lives surged through Sera's mind, leaving her reeling with the newfound knowledge.

With a sense of foreboding lingering in the air, the trio exchanged uneasy glances, unaware of the profound revelation that Sera had just experienced. While they readied to depart, the man's enigmatic images faded away, eclipsed by the mysterious events taking place.

As they left the archive, Constance cast one last glance at the table behind them. The images remained where they had been laid out—silent, still, and ordinary. Yet something about them tugged at her thoughts like a thread she hadn't meant to pull. She told herself it was nothing. A coincidence. Just the human mind finding patterns in the chaos. Even as the door clicked shut behind her, the face remained.

The day's events had unfolded, as they always do, and Constance and Sera found themselves at home later that night. In the cozy living room, nestled on the sofa's soft cushions, Constance and Sera found comfort.

The room was all warmth and comfort. Plush sofas were arranged around a coffee table adorned with family photos and scattered magazines. Soft, ambient lighting cast a gentle glow over the space, creating an atmosphere perfect for relaxation after a long day.

Sitting side by side, their resemblance, while striking, was subtly distinct. Constance's features were slightly sharper, with high cheekbones and a determined set to her jaw. Sera's face, on the other hand, was softer, with gentle curves and a more contemplative expression.

Both women shared cascading waves of chestnut hair, but Constance's fell in sleeker, more controlled waves, while Sera's tumbled in loose, carefree curls.

Sera's feet rested in her sister's lap, her posture relaxed yet tense with internal turmoil. A furrow creased her brow, betraying the inner conflict she grappled with. Although she tried to hide her discomfort, the faint lines around her eyes betrayed her unspoken thoughts.

Constance's gaze was tender as she looked at her sister. Concern was evident in the depths of her eyes. With a gentle touch, she massaged Sera's feet, silently supporting her sister. It was in response to her sister's time of need because of the effects of the recent headaches. When she spoke, her voice was soft and soothing, a beacon of reassurance amid Sera's turmoil.

"Are you alright, Sera?" Constance's words were laced with genuine concern as she searched her sister's face for any sign of distress.

Sera hesitated just a second too long. Her answer came quickly after—but it was too smooth, too rehearsed. The kind of answer given when the truth was too heavy to say aloud.

She looked away, gaze flickering, lips pressing into a line. Whatever memories had returned, they weighed on her more than she would admit.

"How's William?" she asked, a forced lightness in her tone as she tried to smile. It was a subtle yet deliberate attempt to avoid confronting the uncomfortable truths lurking beneath the surface.

Constance's eyes shifted downward. A hint of sadness colored her response as she contemplated her relationship.

"He's good," she replied, her voice tinged with a hint of melancholy. She brought her hands together, touching her index fingers as she continued, "everything's good, really. But..." she trailed off, her words hanging in the air, unfinished and unspoken.

While looking at Sera's feet, Constance's gaze turned introspective, her thoughts drifting to the emptiness inside that gnawed at her. Despite having everything she ever wanted—a loving partner, a successful career, and material comforts aplenty—there was a nagging sense of incompleteness that eluded her grasp, leaving her feeling adrift in a sea of uncertainty.

She wasn't sure what she was looking for—only that it wasn't here. And maybe that was the problem. It seemed that it had always been present. Right there in her life. At the center of her being, it felt like something had been erased—an absence waiting to be filled. As she grew older, that feeling that something was missing only got more intense.

This intimate moment between sisters was thick with unspoken tension, mirroring the intricate nature of their relationship. As they sat together in quiet contemplation, each grappling with their own inner demons, the bond that united them remained unbreakable. They were each other's anchor.

Constance sighed, her brows furrowing in frustration as she turned to her sister.

"Sera, I just don't understand," she confessed, her voice tinged with uncertainty. "We're only just twenty-three. Why should I be unhappy when I have everything I need?"

Considering her sister's words, Sera's gaze softened with empathy. She knew more than she was willing to reveal at this moment, her mind awash with fragments of past lives and forgotten memories. But now was not the time for confessions. Instead, she offered a gentle reassurance.

"Maybe you're just confused, Connie," she suggested, her tone thoughtful. "Perhaps you need to give more attention to your relationship with William. Maybe changing the stakes of the relationship, like moving in together, could bring you the clarity you seek."

Constance's eyes widened in shock at her sister's suggestion.

"Move in with William?" she echoed, incredulous. "But Sera, I can't imagine my life without you by my side. You're my rock, my confidante..." her voice drifted off before she continued, saying, "I need you here with me."

Leaning closer to her sister, Sera chuckled softly, a knowing glint in her eyes.

"Oh Connie, you know I'll always be here for you, no matter what," she reassured, her voice filled with warmth. "But sometimes, change can be a good thing. And who knows? Living with William might just bring you the happiness you've been searching for."

Constance found the situation so absurd that she couldn't help but laugh, and the tension of the moment dissolved into shared amusement.

"You're being selfish, you know that?" she teased, nudging her sister playfully. "You just want the house to yourself."

Sera's smile lingered, but it didn't quite reach her eyes. It held there—delicate, performative—like something she was trying to believe herself. Still, warmth and light filled the room as Sera and her sister laughed together.

"Maybe I do," Sera admitted with a playful wink. "But deep down, I just want what's best for you."

Despite the comfortable camaraderie of sisterhood, doubts persistently gnawed at Constance's heart as she sat with her sister.

"I appreciate your advice, Sera," she began, her voice tinged with vulnerability. "But the truth is... I'm not sure if William is the one for me. There's something missing, something... undefinable."

As Sera reached out to squeeze her sister's hand, her expression softened with understanding.

"Go for it, Connie," she urged, her voice gentle yet firm. "You'll find your way. I know you will. And I'll be right here beside you, every step of the way."

Looking at her sister, Constance's gaze softened, a flicker of curiosity dancing in her eyes.

"You really think there's something worth exploring with William, don't you, Sera?" she asked, her voice laced with uncertainty yet tinged with hope.

Sera met her sister's gaze with a reassuring smile.

"I do, Connie," she affirmed, her tone filled with conviction. "I believe that there's potential for something special between you two. But you won't know unless you give it a chance." Sera kept to herself the quiet truth—that even she didn't believe what she'd just said.

Conflicting emotions swirled in Constance's mind as she nodded slowly. She trusted her sister's judgment without fail, knowing that Sera always had her best interests at heart. Yet, something in Sera's tone lingered in her thoughts. Not quite doubt, but a quiet sense that her sister's certainty came from somewhere deeper—somewhere Constance couldn't quite reach.

"Alright," Constance relented with a sigh, a small smile tugging at the corners of her lips. "I'll give it more time. Who knows? Maybe you're right, Sera."

As Constance spoke, Sera shifted on the sofa, her movements causing her t-shirt to ride up. Constance wondered if now was the right opportunity. One of their unspoken rituals after heavy talks was to break the mood—sometimes with laughter, sometimes with a ridiculous surprise. It was how they reset, how they reminded each other that things were still okay.

Seizing the opportunity for mischief, she launched herself at her unsuspecting sister, a playful grin on her face.

Sera let out a startled yelp as Constance landed on her with a playful thud, their laughter mingling in the air like music. "Connie, you scared the life out of me!" Sera exclaimed between fits of laughter, her cheeks flushed with mirth.

Constance grinned mischievously, her heart lightened by the shared moment of levity. "Sorry, Sera," she chuckled, bumping her forehead lightly against her sister's. "But I needed to keep you on your toes."

With laughter fading and sisterhood's comfort enveloping them, Constance silently vowed to heed Sera's advice, giving her relationship with William a deserved chance. With Sera by her side, guiding her every step of the way, she knew that whatever the future held, they would face it together.

A comfortable silence settled between Constance and Sera, their breathing slowing into a steady rhythm as they lay side by side on the cozy couch. The dim light filtering from the few lamps cast a soft glow over the room, cocooning them in a sense of peace and contentment.

After a few moments of quiet, Sera turned to her sister, her expression thoughtful. "So, are you really going to give it a try with William?" she asked, her tone gentle yet probing.

Constance shifted slightly, her gaze meeting Sera's with a mixture of determination and uncertainty. "I think so," she replied slowly, her voice tinged with hesitation. "At least I'm willing to give it more time and effort. Who knows? Maybe something good will come of it."

Sera nodded in understanding, a faint smile playing at the corners of her lips. "I hope so, Connie," she murmured, her voice soft with sincerity. Though she smiled, her eyes betrayed her troubled thoughts.

Curiosity piqued, Constance turned to her sister, a questioning look in her eyes. "Why are you so invested in my love life all of a sudden, Sera?" she asked, a hint of amusement coloring her tone.

Sera's expression softened, a fond glimmer in her eyes as she reminisced. "Oh, I don't know," she replied cryptically, a playful smile dancing on her lips. "Maybe it's because I've seen a few of your past relationships come and go."

As she spoke, Sera recounted a few of Constance's previous boyfriends, each accompanied by the duration of their relationship. "There was Bert, one year and three months; Thomas, two years and six months; and let's not forget Nathan, fifteen days."

At the mention of Nathan's name, both sisters erupted into fits of laughter. The absurdity of the short-lived romance bringing tears of mirth to their eyes.

When the laughter finally subsided, Constance leaned over to plant a tender kiss on Sera's cheek, a silent expression of gratitude and affection.

With a contented sigh, Constance rose from the couch, stretching her limbs lazily. "I think I'll turn in for the night," she announced, casting a warm smile at her sister. "And Sera, I promise I'll give it a try with William."

Sera returned her sister's smile, her heart warmed by Constance's willingness to embrace the unknown.

"Goodnight, Connie," she whispered softly, her voice filled with love.

As Constance slipped away into the shadows of the hallway, Sera lingered on the couch, her mind meandering through the labyrinth of potential futures awaiting her sister.

She yearned to guide Constance away from the treacherous paths that threatened to ensnare her in a fate she dreaded. A fate she could sense pressing closer, like an unnamed, unseen shadow. Yet, amidst the maze of uncertainty, one immutable truth stood firm—the unyielding bond between two sisters, bound by threads of love, laughter, and the precious moments they shared.

Chapter 2: "Childhood Bonds"

12th Century - Florence, Italy

In the heart of Renaissance.

Florence was a magnificent city in a magnificent era, its sunlit streets alive with the vibrancy of 1168. The scent of blooming jasmine and the distant melody of church bells permeated the summer air. Noble families and merchants bustled through the narrow, cobbled alleys, their voices blending with the hawkers' cries in the market square. The Arno River glistened under the midday sun, its waters reflecting the terracotta rooftops and the grandeur of the Cathedral of Santa Maria del Fiore.

Far away were the conflicts occurring within the Italian peninsula. Emperor Frederick Barbarossa laid siege to the city of Alessandria in Piedmont, which was founded by the Lombard League in 1168 as a defensive measure against the Emperor.

Leonardo Auerelius and his lineage had their home in San Marino. Another local that was far from the fighting in the Holy Roman Empire. Here, Leonardo had put down roots with his family. Long enough to see that his enterprise did well. A small goods and import export business that suited the area and was bound to succeed. Once that was completed, he planned to return to San Marino, a richer man.

Leonardo adjusted the wide-brimmed hat, shielding his eyes from the blazing sun. As he strolled through the Piazza del la Signoria, he marveled at the newly constructed Palazzo Vecchio, its tower reaching ambitiously towards the heavens.

"Remarkable, isn't it?" Giovanni Fiorianzo, his long-time friend and confidant, appeared at his side, a grin spreading across his tanned face. "Hard to believe they built it in our lifetime."

Leonardo nodded, a smile playing on his lips. "Florence never ceases to amaze me. The city breathes ambition."

Giovanni laughed heartily. "And you, my friend, are one of its most ambitious souls."

They walked in companionable silence for a moment, the lively chatter of merchants and townsfolk enveloping them. Leonardo's thoughts drifted, contemplating the bustling life around him. He had seen Florence grow from a modest town to this flourishing city-state during his many visits from his family home in San Marino. Florence's prosperity reflected in the opulence of the buildings and the richness of its culture.

"Do you remember when we were boys?" Giovanni's voice broke into his reverie. "We'd run through the streets like these brats..." Giovanni began before playfully swatting at one boy running between the two of them. "Dreaming of adventures beyond the walls of our town."

"How could I forget?" Leonardo chuckled. "You always spoke of distant lands and great deeds. I was content just imagining the next day."

Giovanni's expression softened, his eyes reflecting a shared past.

"And now look at us," Giovanni continued. "You basically ran from San Marino. You've traveled more than most could ever dream, and I've settled into the life of a merchant. Funny how things turn out."

A sudden burst of laughter drew their attention. A group of children chased each other around a fountain, their carefree joy a stark contrast to Leonardo's reflections. He envied them, their innocence unburdened by the passage of time and the secrets he harbored.

"Giovanni," he began, his voice barely above a whisper, "have you ever wondered if we are mere pawns in a grander scheme? That our lives, no matter how grand, are just fleeting moments in the tapestry of time?"

Giovanni looked at him thoughtfully. "I believe we make our own paths, my friend. Florence itself is a testament to human endeavor and spirit. And you, more than anyone, have shaped your destiny."

Leonardo smiled, though his thoughts remained troubled. Giovanni could never understand the true extent of the pain he carried after receiving word from home. But here, in the heart of Florence, amidst the summer's warmth and the city's relentless heartbeat, he felt a momentary peace.

They continued their walk, the conversation shifting. The marketplace came alive around them, with vendors offering everything from silk to spices, the air thick with the promise of new possibilities. Leonardo breathed deeply, savoring the mingling scents and the warmth of the sun on his face. He had to tell his friend the news at some point. He wondered if it would hit Giovanni just as hard.

"Giovanni," Leonardo began hesitantly.

Having caught Giovanni's attention by the tone of address, the man stopped walking and peered at his friend. As he sharpened his focus on the lines of worry on his friend's face, doubt and worry crept into his own mind.

Giovanni's voice pierced through the bustling noise of the city. "What's wrong, Leonardo?" he asked, his concern palpable.

Leonardo felt the weight of the moment approaching, yet he forged ahead.

"Alphonse..." His voice trailed off, emotion constricting his throat, threatening to spill over into tears.

"What about Alphonse, Leonardo?" Giovanni's question was gentle, his hand finding Leonardo's shoulder in a comforting gesture as he drew nearer.

Leonardo met Giovanni's gaze, uncertainty flickering in his eyes. Would confiding in Giovanni solidify the reality of the news? Would it make it more permanent? His hand rose instinctively, covering his mouth to stifle the sob threatening to escape.

Sensing his friend's distress, Giovanni moved closer, his touch firm as he guided Leonardo away from the crowded thoroughfare and into the relative privacy of a nearby alley.

"What is going on, Leonardo?" Giovanni's concern was clear in his voice.

Leonardo steadied his breath, lowered his eyes slightly—people expected grief to have a shape. And then he spoke.

"Alphonse is dead." The words rushed out, unplanned and raw. Leonardo couldn't help but wonder if he was overplaying his grief, masking emotions that didn't exist. Despite their shared blood, he had never been particularly close to Alphonse—a truth he'd kept from Giovanni all these years.

Leonardo paused, unsettled by the hollowness within. '*Should I even be mourning him?*' He searched for something—anything—that resembled sorrow and came up short. His own self-interest had always outweighed any sense of brotherhood.

'*Did I care about him at all? What was he to me?*'

After a long silence in his thoughts, he settled on a word—*family*. But not in the way people meant when they said it with affection. Not loyalty, not love—just *blood*. A connection by birth and nothing more.

He frowned. '*Shouldn't I feel more than that?*'

He tried to conjure a memory—a shared childhood laugh, a moment of true closeness—but each one felt thin, like echoes without a source. He could picture Alphonse's face, but not how it had ever made him feel. And in that *absence*, something almost like shame flickered—then passed.

The status quo had always favored Alphonse. Though they were twins, it was Alphonse who was named heir to the Auerelius family fortune. And now, with his death, Leonardo saw what he had long coveted suddenly within reach.

Giovanni recoiled slightly, his expression one of shock as he absorbed Leonardo's words. He listened with a sense of detachment as Leonardo recounted the tragic fate of his brother- and sister-in-law, caught in the turmoil surrounding Alessandria in Piedmont.

It took some time for Giovanni to regain his composure, his features reflecting a mixture of sympathy and disbelief.

"He was a good man," Giovanni murmured, more to himself than to Leonardo. "And a better friend than I deserved."

Leonardo maintained his facade, ensuring his distress appeared genuine, even though inwardly he harbored conflicting emotions. He understood the importance of preserving his public image, aware that any hint of insincerity could tarnish his reputation. Despite the weight of his newfound freedom, Leonardo recognized the need to tread carefully in the aftermath of his brother's demise.

For now, he would embrace this moment; this day in the ever-changing, ever-beautiful city of Florence. Tomorrow, his journey would continue, but today, he was simply a man among men, lost in the splendor of a magnificent era.

Florence, being situated in a valley surrounded by hills and close to the Arno River, experienced morning mists, especially during certain seasons or weather conditions. This morning, following their walk in the city, found Leonardo and Giovanni as they walked their tired horses back towards the stables.

Morning mist lingered in the valley, rolling softly between trees and open fields. It blurred the edges of buildings, casting the world in a gentle haze that dulled the city's sharp lines and turned the familiar into something ethereal. Softening stone, blurring rooftops, turning Florence into a dream of itself.

A heavy silence hung between Leonardo and Giovanni like the fog. Each lost in their own thoughts, they were merely shadows of the camaraderie they once shared.

Giovanni's mind wandered back to happier times, memories of Alphonse flooding his thoughts like a relentless tide. He missed the jovial laughter, the shared adventures, the brotherhood they once had. It pained him to think that Alphonse's death weighed on Leonardo too, though they hadn't spoken of it much at all since the day prior.

Leonardo, meanwhile, thought of none of these things. He couldn't shake the anticipation of the final word on the family financial affairs. The prospect of gaining control over the fortune tantalized him, promising freedom from the suffocating grasp of his wife's extravagant demands.

His wife, the niece of Emperor Frederick Barbarossa, had driven them to the brink of ruin with her lavish desires. Leonardo couldn't help but harbor resentful thoughts towards her, imagining darkly humorous ways to solve their financial woes.

As they neared the stables, a burst of youthful energy shattered the somber atmosphere. Tempus, Leonardo's only child, greeted them with unabashed joy. His innocent enthusiasm brought a flicker of warmth to Leonardo's heart, momentarily distracting him from his troubles.

"Yo, Tempus," called out Giovanni before Tempus's own father could greet him.

Giovanni smiled over at Leonardo, knowing he had preempted his friend, before returning his gaze to Tempus.

The young boy looked up at the man with adoration. "Zio, can you teach me to ride a horse like you?" he asked, tugging at Giovanni's sleeve after finally coming to a stop beside him.

The quick sprint left a glow on Tempus's skin. His breathing seemed none the worse for wear, despite the sprint from where he was at the stable gates to where he had spotted his father and Giovanni.

Giovanni's face softened at the boy's request, a faint smile playing on his lips. He glanced at Leonardo, silently acknowledging the bond they shared with the young boy. Despite their own burdens, they both cherished Tempus and the innocence he represented.

With a gentle pat on Tempus's shoulder, Leonardo mustered a smile. "Of course, my boy," he replied, his voice tinged with a hint of warmth. "Giovanni will teach you everything he knows about riding," Leonardo started. But there was a caveat. "He can't teach you this morning. Important tasks require our attention this afternoon; ensure your presence at the front by noon."

"Yes, father," said Tempus, his brows knitting together as his smile dimmed.

Leonardo smiled down at him. He hated having to disappoint his son. "I guess you can ask your Zio if he can take you out after that is done."

Tempus beamed with delight, his eyes sparkling with anticipation. Unaware of the weighty thoughts weighing on the two men's minds, he regarded them both with unwavering admiration.

As they led the horses into the stables, the burden of their troubles was momentarily lifted, replaced by the simple joy of a shared moment with family. In that fleeting moment, amidst the hay-scented air and the soft nickers of the horses, they found that it was easy to be in each other's company.

Later in the afternoon, Tempus stood in the entry hall to the villa, fidgeting beside his mother. He tugged at the collar of his shirt, then the cuffs of his sleeves. Lady Aurelia shot him a warning glare, and he quickly folded his hands behind his back. His father didn't notice. He rarely did.

Tempus had learned early not to expect warmth from his father. Leonardo's affection, if it could be called that, came in measured silences and sharp expectations—not kindness. It wasn't cruelty, exactly. Just an absence where something should have been. He hadn't been asked to be here—he'd been ordered. And in Leonardo's world, presence was obedience. Nothing more.

He pondered why they were waiting to greet someone in the villa's hall. As far as he knew, there had been no indication that they would have visitors today. Not before his father had told him to be at the door at this hour.

As the grand doors of the Auerelius family estate opened, Constance and Sera stepped hesitantly into the vast, echoing hall, their grief hanging around them like a heavy cloak. Tempus's parents awaited them—Lady Aurelia standing with impeccable grace, Lord Leonardo beside her, his expression unreadable. Their smiles were performative, brittle at the edges.

Aurelia's gaze swept over the girls like a merchant appraising goods. Her eyes, cold and calculating, belied the warmth in her voice.

She was every inch the noblewoman: refined posture, deliberate movements, and an aura honed in the courts of power. Born into the imperial circles of Frederick Barbarossa, she had grown up expecting more—more stature, more access, more meaning. Her marriage into the Auerelius family had secured the right name but little else. Florence was not the empire. And Leonardo was not an emperor.

What power she couldn't claim through marriage, she seized within the home. Through discipline. Appearances. Influence. If nobility could not be expanded by title, then it would be asserted by force of will.

These girls, she saw now, were not family. They were opportunity.

"Welcome, Constance, Sera," Lady Aurelia cooed, her voice dripping with false sweetness as she took in their appearance. "Such pretty girls, aren't they, Leonardo?"

Lord Leonardo nodded curtly, his gaze lingering on the sisters with the disinterest one might afford a piece of unwanted correspondence. "Indeed, my dear," he replied, his voice flat, habitual—a response more automatic than engaged.

"They resemble their mother," Aurelia muttered under her breath, her tone dry, wholly disdainful. The words weren't meant to be private—just quiet enough to feign civility while delivering the insult squarely. Her eyes scanned the girls like one assessing flawed merchandise.

She didn't envy the girls—she envied their youth. That raw, unshaped potential. If molded correctly, they could become something valuable. If not, well... Florence had no place for softness. People were potential to Aurelia—assets to be refined, hardened, presented. She didn't see tragedy in their arrival, only opportunity. And she would shape them, with or without affection.

Leonardo watched her from the corner of his eye, catching the gleam she didn't bother to hide. He knew that look. It was the same one she wore at court years ago, when status hung on a glance and futures were written in whispers.

She'd married beneath her expectations, and he knew it. What she hadn't gained through title or blood, she clawed for through appearances—control of the home, of perception, of people.

Let her play her games. If it made their household look more polished, more enviable, more powerful... then it served him just fine.

He didn't care how she did it. Where she manipulated, he maneuvered. She groomed; he brokered.

Different means. Same result.

Children. Wives. Wards. All were pieces. All were strategy. In Florence, the ones who played best survived.

Leonardo had to agree, though. The resemblance to his brother's wife was obvious, and to him, unfortunate. There was nothing of the Auerelius blood in their features, but that was to be expected—after all, the girls had been born during her first marriage.

As Leonardo continued to gaze at the two young girls, he had to admit that they were indeed a beautiful pair. "Beauty alone won't secure their future," Leonardo stated plainly.

Constance and Sera exchanged uneasy glances, sensing the undercurrent in the air that left them ill at ease. They felt like commodities being evaluated for their market worth rather than grieving orphans seeking refuge.

Lady Aurelia continued, her tone veering towards business-like efficiency. "We must consider how to best utilize their presence in our household. They could be of great benefit to us if we play our cards right, Leonardo."

Leonardo grunted in response. His concern for the girls ended where their avoidance of him began. He had only reluctantly taken them in, considering that they had no other living relatives, to save his own face.

"Whatever," Leonardo mumbled.

Constance bit her lip, feeling a surge of indignation rise within her at the callousness of their words. She tightened her grip on Sera's hand, silently vowing to protect her sister from whatever the future had in store.

Sera's eyes narrowed slightly, her intuition telling her that their relatives had ulterior motives. But she remained composed, masking her unease behind a facade of politeness.

As Lady Aurelia and Lord Leonardo continued their discussion in hushed tones, oblivious to the discomfort of the girls, Constance and Sera exchanged a silent vow to stay vigilant and navigate the waters of their new reality together.

The Auerelius household entryway framed Constance and Sera, their safe world destroyed by tragedy. Just days ago, they had been a happy family, their parents doting on them with love and affection. But now, their home lay in ruins, their parents stolen from them by the merciless hands of conflict between the Emperor and the Holy Roman Empire.

With nowhere else to turn, they had sought refuge with the relatives of their late step father, the Auerelius family. The lesser branch of the family, headed by Tempus's parents, was known for their wealth and influence in Florence. But Constance and Sera belonged to the main branch, their family fortunes now tied to those before them.

The girls stood in the grand foyer, their nervous gazes flitting over the unfamiliar surroundings. Sera's grip on Constance's hand tightened in silent reassurance.

Tempus lingered in the shadows, watching Constance and Sera. His gaze settled on Constance, captivated by her quiet strength. Though he tried to remain unnoticed by his parents, Tempus couldn't tear his eyes away from the scene unfolding before him. Something about Constance, a spark of determination in her eyes, captivated him.

Tempus remained discreet, not bringing attention to himself. His thoughts were swirling with questions and uncertainties. This marked his initial awareness of the two girls. Little did he know, the arrival of Constance and Sera would irrevocably change the course of his life, setting into motion a series of events that would bind their fates together in ways they could never have imagined.

As Lady Aurelia and Lord Leonardo discussed their plans for the girls, their voices barely above a whisper, Tempus continued to observe as the two girls looked around at their surroundings, their inspection unnoticed by Tempus's parents.

"We can't simply turn them away, Leonardo," Lady Aurelia murmured, her brow furrowed with concern. "They are family, after all."

Leonardo, his tone authoritative, made it clear that the girls were of little use. "What are we to do with these two?" he asked only to himself. He walked closer to the two and leaned down to peer at Constance.

Lady Aurelia seemed to have an idea that she presently gave to Leonardo. "Should we marry them off?"

"How old are you two, child?" Aurelia asked Constance, as she was the nearer of the two.

Constance cleared her throat. "We're thirteen."

Tempus blinked. '*Same as me,*' he thought. It struck him strangely—how different they seemed despite sharing an age. He didn't feel young, not anymore. Not in this house.

Leonardo's sharp gaze flicked over them, his mind immediately assessing their value within the rigid expectations of the era. According to the Catholic Church, twelve was the minimum age for girls to be eligible for marriage. Technically, they were of an age where they might begin to attract interest, but eligibility alone did not make them suitable candidates—especially for noble families. Leonardo knew that more was required: refinement, education, and physical maturity.

"They're hardly marriage material at their current age," he stated bluntly. "Neither their minds nor their bodies are prepared for what would be expected of them."

His eyes lingered on their posture and the way they carried themselves. They lacked the polished bearing of girls raised with the intention of securing advantageous matches. He imagined their lives thus far had been devoid of the rigorous education noble daughters received—instruction in household management, courtly manners, and the art of subtle conversation. Without these skills, no nobleman would consider them worthy of his lineage.

Moreover, Leonardo noted with clinical detachment that the girls still had the appearance of youth. Their frames lacked the signs of physical maturity necessary to assure any potential suitor that they could bear children, the ultimate measure of a wife's value in their society. At this stage, they were little more than children themselves, and any proposition of marriage would be laughable.

The pressure of finances returning to him, Leonardo sighed, his thoughts momentarily drifting to the extravagant spending that had driven them dangerously close to ruin, and the arrival of these girls was yet another potential burden. Still, he couldn't entirely dismiss their potential usefulness. If properly trained, they might one day secure alliances or provide some form of leverage. But for now, they were simply mouths to feed and responsibilities to bear.

With a dismissive wave, he sighed again. "Let us hope they prove more useful in the future," he added, his tone laced with pragmatic detachment.

Aurelia's lips thinned as she observed the girls. Her initial instinct was to reject them outright, to send them to a convent or some distant relative willing to take them in. But such a move would be seen as heartless by their peers, a mark against the Auerelius family's reputation. She knew Florence thrived on appearances, and the slightest misstep could invite scandal or diminish their standing.

Still, the girls posed a complication she had not anticipated. They reminded her of her own youth, a time when she too had felt displaced and overlooked, striving to prove her worth in a household that valued status above all else. But unlike her, these girls had no family legacy to lean on. That made them both a liability and an opportunity. If she played her cards right, Aurelia could mold them into assets for the family.

With a curt gesture, Leonardo turned to Aurelia. "Take them into our home, Aurelia. Ensure they are clothed and fed. They'll need every advantage we can provide if they're to become anything more than burdens." His voice carried the finality of a man accustomed to obedience, leaving no room for argument.

Aurelia nodded, though a flicker of hesitation lingered in her expression. She glanced at Constance and Sera, their small hands clasped tightly together, their wide eyes betraying their fear and uncertainty. For a moment, Aurelia softened, imagining what these girls might become with the right guidance. But just as quickly, she steeled herself, knowing that sentimentality had no place in their world.

"Of course, Leonardo," she replied, her tone carefully neutral. "I'll see to it immediately."

Constance and her sister followed Aurelia as she led them deeper into the villa. Aurelia's mind churned with calculations, weighing the cost of their upkeep against the potential benefits they might bring. She resolved to test their capabilities in the coming days, to see if they had any skills worth honing. And if not, well, there were always other ways to secure the family's future.

As Leonardo watched them leave, he found himself once again consumed by thoughts of the family's precarious position. His wife's connections to Emperor Frederick Barbarossa had once seemed a blessing, but her relentless pursuit of luxury had turned their fortune into a fragile facade. The arrival of these girls added another layer of complexity to his already strained calculations. Still, he reminded himself, fortune favored those who adapted. Perhaps these girls would prove to be the unforeseen advantage he needed.

He turned away, his gaze settling out the opened door to the distant hills beyond Florence. The city thrived on ambition, and he would do whatever it took to ensure his family remained among its elite. For now, the girls were a gamble, but one he couldn't afford to ignore.

Sensing his father's imminent departure, Tempus silently withdrew, his footsteps light as he moved down the corridor.

He hadn't meant to overhear—hadn't even wanted to. Tempus clutched his belly. Listening to them discuss the girls like burdens had left a sourness in his stomach.

His presence hadn't mattered anyway. Neither of his parents had acknowledged him once. Frustrated that his time with Zio had been stolen, and that these two strangers had upended his day, Tempus slipped away, unnoticed and unmissed.

His father's earlier instructions were unnecessary; his presence hadn't been required. They hadn't even acknowledged his presence during the entire encounter. Frustrated at the interruption in his life causing him to miss out on spending time with his Zio, and the fact that the two girls were relative strangers to him, Tempus slipped away unnoticed.

As Leonardo and Aurelia exited the foyer, their voices fading into the distance, Tempus breathed a sigh of relief. As Tempus left, he cast a final glance back over his shoulder at where the two girls had been.

"They were pretty," he mumbled to himself before turning and disappearing.

Despite lingering unease, he recognized his life irrevocably changed upon Constance's and Sera's arrival.

The garden had become their refuge.

In the quiet hours before dinner, Constance and Sera often escaped the suffocating hush of the villa to walk the gravel paths, the sound of their steps swallowed by leaves and birdsong. It was the only place that still felt like it belonged to them.

They weren't the same girls who had arrived months ago. Florence had stripped them of certainty—but not each other. That had to be enough.

Sera wandered a few steps ahead, her fingers trailing through the hedgerow as though searching for something she couldn't name. Lately, everything felt still—too still. She missed the noise of their old life, the color. She missed feeling seen.

"Do you ever wonder if they'll send us away?" she asked, her voice low.

"Every day," Constance answered. "But we haven't given them a reason yet."

Sera kicked at a stone. "I don't want to be quiet all the time."

"Then don't," Constance said, though her own voice was a practiced hush. "I'll cover for you."

Sera grinned, mischief returning. She always walked a step ahead, tugging Constance into her pace. Constance let her—half laughing, half watching for danger.

Their bond was their anchor. The tasks they performed in the villa were done with diligence and grace, but outside, under the open sky, they could be girls again. Constance carried her duty quietly; Sera resisted it with a smile.

Sometimes, Constance caught herself wondering what their mother would think of them now. Would she be proud of how well they'd adapted, or ashamed of how much they'd changed?

"Sometimes I forget," Constance whispered. "What it felt like before."

Sera didn't answer. Her gaze had drifted upward, toward the upper floor of the villa. She squinted, a grin slowly spreading across her face.

"He's watching us again," she murmured.

"Who?" Constance followed her sister's gaze.

There he was. Tempus. The quiet boy who said little, who never sat with them, but whose eyes always seemed to hold a world she couldn't name.

"Did you see that, Constance?" Sera whispered, her voice alight. "I think someone's intrigued by our little garden adventure."

Sera's heart jumped—not in fear, but in something else. Something brighter. Tempus never spoke much at dinner, but she'd caught him glancing her way more than once. She wasn't sure if he meant anything by it. Still, the thought of it made her grin widen.

Constance laughed, amused, but her smile faded slightly as she looked again. She hadn't really noticed him before—not like this. Not until Sera pointed him out.

"Let him watch," she said, brushing dust from her lap. But she didn't look away.

From above, Tempus didn't move. He leaned against the glass, watching as the sisters disappeared into the hedgerows. A sigh escaped him—soft, uncertain. There was something about Constance he didn't yet understand.

As the sun dipped behind the hills, casting long shadows across the courtyard, he stayed at the window, thoughts drifting toward the girl who had become impossible to ignore.

In the days that followed, the atmosphere in the Auerelius household shifted subtly but perceptibly. What had once been wary civility gave way to something more strained. There was no single moment that marked the change—only the accumulation of glances that lingered too long, silences that weighed heavier than before, and a sense that the walls themselves had begun to listen.

Constance and Sera felt it first in the kitchen, where a servant who had once smiled now avoided eye contact. Then in the corridors, where conversations ceased as they passed. They had long grown used to being overlooked by their hosts, but now they felt observed—not by Tempus, whose glances were different, almost unsure—but by the household itself.

No one told them what they had done to warrant suspicion. Perhaps it wasn't any one thing. Perhaps it was merely the fact of their continued presence.

The change had started, Constance suspected, after a visit from one of Lord Leonardo's associates—a man with a hard voice and a softer smile, who had met privately with Leonardo and Aurelia for the better part of an hour. After that, things grew colder.

Dinner became an exercise in discomfort. That evening, seated at the long dining table beneath the glittering chandelier, the girls tried to pretend nothing had changed. But the air was tight with something unspoken.

At the far end of the table, Lord Leonardo and Lady Aurelia exchanged hushed words between bites, their expressions carefully neutral. Constance couldn't hear the words, but she saw the way Aurelia's brow arched, the way Leonardo's fingers tapped restlessly against his wine glass.

Tempus sat apart from it all, his arms folded and his gaze fixed somewhere just beyond the table. He said nothing, but his posture betrayed a quiet frustration. He hadn't looked at the girls once since they sat down.

Sera leaned close to Constance, her whisper barely audible over the clink of cutlery. "Something doesn't feel right."

Constance nodded, keeping her expression blank. She followed Sera's glance toward their hosts and caught a flicker of cold amusement in Aurelia's eyes. "They're planning something."

Tempus stirred slightly at the sound of their voices, his jaw tightening, though his gaze remained averted.

When the meal ended, they were dismissed with polite indifference. As they walked the dim hallway back to their room, neither spoke until the door closed behind them.

"Do you think they'll send us away?" Sera asked.

Constance paused, her hand on the edge of her bed. "I think they're deciding what to do with us. That's worse."

Neither of them slept easily that night. And neither of them noticed the way the lanterns in the hallway stayed lit long after the rest of the house had gone dark.

In the dimly lit corridors of the Auerelius estate, a shadowy figure lurked, his intentions dark and sinister. Marcus, a household servant with a cunning glint in his eye, had grown bold. The Lord and Lady's indifference toward the twins had not gone unnoticed—and he mistook neglect for permission.

As Constance and Sera made their way through the maze-like halls, they sensed nothing untoward. Unaware of Marcus's twisted intentions, they continued on their path, their laughter masking the stifling feeling that they felt within the household almost continuously.

Suddenly, Marcus emerged from the shadows, his gaze predatory as he cornered the unsuspecting girls, his intentions unclear. Constance's heart raced with fear, her instincts screaming at her to flee, but she found herself rooted to the spot, paralyzed by terror at his sudden appearance.

Sera, sensing the danger, moved to shield her sister from harm, her eyes flashing with defiance. "What do you want, Marcus?"

Marcus didn't respond, only continued to stand, blocking their way forward.

"Leave us alone, Marcus," she commanded, her voice trembling but resolute.

But Marcus only laughed, his twisted grin sending chills down their spines. "You two are pretty. Would you mind spending time with me this evening?"

Sera looked back at Constance in shock.

"You're overstepping your bounds, Marcus. Know your place as a servant," said Constance.

Marcus wasn't going to be easily blown off.

"You think you're safe under this roof?" he sneered. "You're nothing."

His voice hit them like thickened, virulent oil.

Sera's foot glided back half a step from the impact.

He slinked closer.

He was close enough that his breath didn't waft—they felt it.

Thick and foul.

A humid rot that pressed against their faces, clinging like mildew.

Constance glanced down at the gooseflesh rising on her arm. She shivered.

"Tucked away in fine rooms like that—you think it makes you off-limits? No one even looks your way at dinner. Not even the Lord and Lady."

With nowhere to run and no one to turn to, Constance and Sera braced themselves for the worst, their minds racing with fear and desperation. But just as Marcus reached out to grab them, sudden footsteps echoed through the halls, drawing his attention away.

In the moment that ensued, Tempus burst onto the scene, his presence commanding and authoritative as he confronted Marcus, his eyes blazing with fury. "What are you doing here, Marcus?" he asked as much as commanded, his voice brooking no argument.

Caught off guard by Tempus's intervention, Marcus hesitated, his cowardice overpowering his thirsty desire. He attempted to retreat into the shadows, muttering, "Excuse me, young master. I was just asking if the young ladies needed an escort to their room."

Tempus moved to stand between Marcus and the girls, subtly shifting his position to block Marcus's view. "I'll escort them. You can leave now, Marcus," he said firmly.

Marcus, tight-lipped and defeated, slithered away into the obscurity of the vast home, seeking a place far from Tempus, Constance, and Sera.

As the danger passed and the adrenaline ebbed, Constance and Sera clung to each other, their hearts still pounding. Gazing into each other's eyes, they silently acknowledged the narrow escape, realizing the peril they had avoided thanks to Tempus's timely intervention.

In the days that followed, with Marcus gone and the shadow lifted, the estate felt lighter. Conversations grew less formal. Walks stretched longer. And Tempus—once little more than a ghost at dinner—began to linger. Sometimes he'd appear in the garden without a word. Other times, he'd speak only to ask if they were comfortable. But he was there.

Sera noticed it first.

It wasn't the way he looked at Constance—though she saw that too. It was how her own thoughts returned to him, uninvited. How she began to notice his voice. The way his presence changed a room. She tried to keep it quiet. Even from herself.

But Constance... Constance didn't notice.

She thanked Tempus politely. Smiled when he approached. Spoke to him without hesitation—but never lingered. To her, he was a kindness in a cruel house. Nothing more.

Sera said nothing. But sometimes, at night, she would lie awake and wonder what it would be like—if only he looked at her the way he looked at Constance.

As they navigated the complexities of their newfound dynamic, the trio found themselves drawn into a delicate dance of emotions, each one grappling with their own desires and insecurities. And as the bonds between them grew stronger, they could only wonder what the future held in store.

As the days turned into weeks, Constance and Sera found themselves caught in a delicate balancing act—teetering between obedience and quiet resistance.

Gone were the days of idle leisure and music lessons under their mother's watchful eye. In Florence, they rose before dawn to scrub corridors not their own, mend linens they'd never sleep in, and polish silver they'd never touch at dinner. Under Lady Aurelia's exacting eye, perfection was demanded but never praised.

Their new responsibilities weren't cruel, but they were relentless. Silent expectations pressed down like a weight on their backs—elbows straight while serving, heads bowed while speaking, voices trimmed to whispers. And always, the unspoken reminder: you are guests here, not family.

It wore on them in different ways. Sera, ever restless, chafed at the invisible leash around her freedom. She spoke out too loudly, laughed when she should have curtsied, and earned glares for the trouble. Constance, by contrast, folded inward. She carried herself with rigid grace, performing each task with care, but in her eyes was the haunted look of someone trying not to be noticed.

Yet even in their discomfort, their bond remained unbroken. Shared glances during chores. Silent jokes passed while clearing the sitting room. A brief touch of hands beneath the tablecloth at dinner.

They had learned to adapt—but not to belong.

And as they began to dream of more—of freedom, of feeling seen—the world around them reminded them of its terms. One wrong word, one misstep, and the fragile peace they had built could vanish.

One afternoon, as they wandered through the ornate gardens of the estate, their footsteps echoing against the polished marble pathways, Constance's thoughts drifted back to the confrontation with Marcus, the malevolent servant who had threatened to shatter their fragile world.

"I can't believe he had the audacity to approach us like that," Constance muttered, her voice tight with lingering frustration.

Sera nodded. "It was terrifying. I still feel like I can't breathe when I think about it."

Their conversation was interrupted by the distant sound of raised voices drifting from the direction of the main house. They exchanged a glance. It wasn't the first time they'd heard this.

As they crept closer, they caught Tempus mid-argument with his parents. This conversation—this fight—had happened more than once since the Marcus incident. But this time, it sounded sharper.

"You know what Marcus was trying to do," Tempus said, his voice calm but edged with steel. "And you both stood by. If you'd treated them like relatives—or at least respected guests—this wouldn't have happened."

"You're jeopardizing our standing," Leonardo snapped. "Marcus may have... misstepped—but he was useful. Losing him cost this household more than you know."

"Useful doesn't excuse him," Tempus countered. "You keep talking about scandal. You should be scandalized that he ever thought he had the right."

"We are scandalized," Aurelia cut in, her tone sharp. "But your continued defiance is worse. This is the third time you've dragged this up. How long must we keep revisiting it?"

Tempus's shoulders stiffened. He held her gaze a second too long—then faltered, dropping his eyes. The heat behind her glare was too much to bear.

Aurelia turned to Leonardo. Her eyes turned cold. "And what of the girls? What value do they hold if they're tainted by rumor?"

"They weren't tainted," Leonardo said evenly.

"They're human. And they're under this roof because you let them be," Tempus interjected. Emboldened once more by his anger.

"Enough!" Leonardo slammed his hand on the table. "I will not be lectured about how to run my household."

Silence.

"Marcus was competent," Leonardo said bitterly. "Efficient. Quiet. One of the few we didn't have to worry about—until now. His absence leaves a gap, and you created it."

As Constance and Sera watched from the sidelines, a sense of dread settled over them. They knew that without Tempus's intervention, they could have fallen victim to a fate far worse than they dared to imagine.

In the aftermath of the confrontation, Tempus's parents relented, reluctantly agreeing to inform the staff of the status of the two girls as family. But the damage had been done, their trust in their son shaken by his defiance.

As Tempus stormed away, his shoulders squared with determination, Constance and Sera exchanged a silent vow to repay his kindness in any way they could. They found in Tempus not only a protector but also a beacon of hope in a world overshadowed by darkness.

Later that evening, Tempus found himself sitting alone in the garden, his thoughts swirling like a tempest within him. He idly kicked at the ground beneath his feet, seeking an outlet for the turmoil he felt. He couldn't fathom allowing anything to happen to the girls under their roof. It baffled him that his beloved parents could act as if they didn't care for one of their own. Blood ties aside, they all shared the same last name now.

Tempus wanted to curse aloud, but his reverie was interrupted by hushed whispers emanating from behind one of the nearby hedges.

"Come out. I know you're there. I can hear you," Tempus said softly. His anger had abated somewhat, now that he knew the identity of the intruders encroaching on his solitary moment.

Constance and Junie emerged from behind the hedge, bickering quietly as they approached. Though the words of their reprimands weren't clear, their intent was evident.

As they stopped a few feet away from Tempus, they stood in joined silence, their gazes downcast to avoid his scrutiny. Their positions within the house had left them skittish, hesitant to speak freely to anyone.

To Tempus, they seemed as delicate as bunny rabbits, ready to flee at the slightest provocation. His hand clutched his chest. He couldn't help but feel a pang at the sight of their unease. It hurt to see them on edge, especially knowing that the girl he was growing fond of felt the need to act this way in his presence, fearing his reaction.

Tempus exhaled slowly, his eyes still closed. "Sit, you two," he called out softly, patting the stone bench beside him.

Neither girl moved, which puzzled Tempus until Constance spoke up.

Her voice was hesitant, soft. "You're not mad at us, are you?" she asked cautiously.

Tempus cocked his head to the side, wondering if she was serious. Even their fear must have its limits. Her inquiry regarding his anger tested his patience.

"Are you asking about spying on me?" Tempus sought clarification, seeing no reason to be angry at all.

Sera shook her head, her eyes clenched shut, making her appear more childish. "No," she uttered softly. "We mean for having to stand up for us against your parents."

Tempus shifted his gaze from Sera to Constance. Constance nodded once, affirming her agreement with her sister's sentiment.

After a moment, Tempus waved a dismissive hand, and the tension seemed to ease from the girls. As he spoke, he noticed them becoming more at ease.

"My parents are at fault for what happened to you. You two should feel safe in your own home," Tempus stated firmly.

Constance stepped forward, a hint of urgency in her movement. "You really mean that?" she asked quickly.

Taken aback, Tempus involuntarily shifted backwards. He cleared his throat, intending to speak, but closed his mouth abruptly when he realized he couldn't give Constance a definitive answer. It wasn't because he didn't grasp her question; it was precisely because he did. Her query touched on multiple layers of significance. Was she asking about his parents being at fault or about feeling safe?

Tempus's hand rose—not to stop her, but as if to pause the moment itself. He wasn't sure what to respond to first: the question, the weight behind it, or the way it had landed so differently than he'd intended. "Wait. What... exactly are you asking?" he said, though part of him already feared the answer. He scratched his head next, the movement buying him a moment to process, to look away, to think.

Constance's expression remained serious. "About this being our home," she clarified.

At first, Tempus was confused, but then the realization dawned on him. It wasn't just about the words he had spoken; it was about what those words meant to them, a powerful affirmation of their belonging. The impact wasn't lost on Tempus.

"Yeah. Yeah... I meant that. This is your home too," Tempus affirmed with a smile.

He shifted over on the bench to make room for the girls. They quickly accepted the invitation and joined him. Together, they sat in silence as the early evening unfolded, watching as the stars twinkled into existence above them before eventually retiring for the night.

Interlude: "Almost?..., or Something Like That"

Then - Atlanta, USA

Trying had never meant falling.

Pause.

This matters—not to the plot, but to the people.

The first time William brought her soup, Constance had the flu and hadn't told anyone. He'd noticed—because he noticed everything—and showed up at her doorstep with three kinds, just in case. She hadn't asked. He hadn't asked if she needed help. He just helped.

They weren't dating then. Barely more than acquaintances. But that moment stuck with her.

Later, when things were quieter in her life—after the last failed almost-something with someone more exciting—she let herself think: *'Maybe this is what love looks like. Not fire, but warmth.'*

Sera had stayed silent when Constance mentioned him the first time.

"He's nice," Constance had said. "He doesn't make me feel much, but he never makes me feel worse, either. That's something, right?"

Sera hadn't answered. That silence still lingered.

But William stayed. Steady, earnest, full of small gestures and open doors. When she reached for him, he was always there. She liked that. Maybe she even needed it.

One night, he walked her home in the rain. No umbrella. No rush. He didn't try to make it romantic. He didn't try to make it anything. Just walked beside her, coat soaked, saying little.

She started to notice how often he checked in—never with pressure. Never hovering. Just a quick text: Got home safe? or Coffee before class?

She didn't always reply. He never made her feel guilty when she didn't.

'When did this start? Was it in college?'

Once, when he kissed her cheek and asked if she wanted to stay over, she nearly declined.

Not because she didn't trust him, but because she didn't want to be unkind.

Because she knew what she'd be giving him wouldn't match what he'd be offering.

But she didn't pull away. Not that night.

She tried. Earnestly. Quietly. Because part of her wanted it to be enough.

Because part of her hoped it might grow into something real if she just gave it time.

She told herself: '*I don't know if this is what I wanted. But for now, it's enough. It has to be. This might not be passionate, but it's safe. And that might be enough for me.'*

Pause.

Why is this here?

You're going to see this fall apart soon.

So remember this moment, this version of her, when it does.

Chapter 3: "A Love Remembered"

Present Day - Atlanta, USA

Throes of Indecision.

As the weekend dawned upon Atlanta, the city's bustling streets seemed to slow their pace, granting its inhabitants a moment of respite from the usual chaos of urban life. Several days had passed since Constance and Lynette had been sorting through items at the museum, marking the passage of time with each tick of the clock.

On this tranquil day in Midtown, however, the vibrant energy of the city was palpable. Locals and visitors alike took to the streets, embracing the warm sunshine and gentle breeze. The aroma of freshly brewed coffee wafted from cozy cafes lining the sidewalks, mingling with the scent of blooming flowers adorning lush green spaces.

Families leisurely strolled through Piedmont Park, laughter echoing as children played on the playgrounds, while couples shared intimate moments by the serene lake. The eclectic mix of shops and boutiques on Peachtree Street buzzed with activity, offering unique treasures and delectable treats to curious passersby.

In the quiet ambiance of a cozy cafe, Constance and Lynette found themselves seated at a small table, their cups of steaming coffee cradled in their hands. The warm aroma of brewed java mingled with the soft murmur of conversation, creating a serene atmosphere conducive to contemplation.

Constance fidgeted with her cup, her thoughts consumed by the enigmatic man from the photograph that had captured her imagination. She couldn't shake the unease that had settled in her core, the inexplicable pull towards a stranger she had never met, defying all logic and reason.

Lynette couldn't bear the prolonged silence any longer, its weight pressing down on her nerves. "What's bothering you?" she finally asked, genuine concern lacing her words. It was unusual for Constance to be so withdrawn, and it stirred Lynette's worry, prompting her inquiry.

Turning to her trusted friend, Constance hesitated before confiding in her about the recurring thoughts plaguing her nights, each one haunted by the image of a mysterious man. "It's like he's following me," she murmured, a hint of apprehension coloring her voice.

Lynette furrowed her brow, studying Constance's tired expression and the faint shadows beneath her eyes with growing concern. "Who are you talking about?" she asked, scanning their surroundings as if expecting to see the man lurking nearby.

Constance realized her friend's misunderstanding and clarified, "The guy from the photo, lithograph, and painting."

"Oh," Lynette breathed out in understanding, though she couldn't fathom why this man held such sway over Constance. The timelines didn't align; the man depicted in the various artworks couldn't possibly be the same person. The math didn't add up, and the age of the black-and-white photo alone suggested he was long deceased.

"You've been under a lot of stress lately," she remarked gently, her tone laced with sympathy. "Maybe it's just your subconscious playing tricks on you."

But Constance found herself unable to shake the feeling that there was something more to it, a nagging sense of urgency that gnawed at her insides. "I need to know who he is," she confessed, her voice tinged with determination.

Lynette nodded in understanding, her mind already racing with potential solutions. "We could use facial recognition software to try and identify him," she suggested, her eyes alight with curiosity. "We just need to scan the images into the computer and see what we find."

Before Constance could respond, her phone rang, interrupting their conversation with its insistent tone. With a sigh, she glanced at the caller ID, her heart sinking at the sight of William's name flashing on the screen.

"I have to take this," she murmured apologetically. Her lips twisted downward slightly. She rose from her seat with a sense of reluctance. "I'll catch up with you later, okay?"

Lynette watched in silence as her friend slipped away, her own thoughts swirling with concern for Constance's obvious distraction. With a resigned sigh, she acknowledged there was little she could do until Constance reached out again.

Meanwhile, as Constance hurriedly exited the cafe, a sense of guilt tugged at her conscience. Despite her intentions to spend the morning with Lynette, her promise to Sera weighed on her mind, a constant reminder of the intricate emotions entangling her heart.

"I need to give it my all with William," she mused inwardly, feeling obligated to fulfill her commitment to her sister. "I did promise her I'd try."

Stepping onto the sidewalk, Constance held her phone to her ear. She greeted William with a soft, "Hello?"

William's warm voice returned her greeting on the other end. "Hey, Constance," he said. "I was wondering if you're free this morning. I'd love to see you and maybe grab breakfast together."

Constance's heart sank at the invitation, the irony not lost on her. Moments ago, she had been sharing coffee with Lynette, and now she found herself torn between her sister's wishes and her budding relationship with William. With a bitter laugh, she replied, "Sure, William. Breakfast sounds great. Where should we meet up?"

Without hesitation, William suggested their usual spot near the downtown library. Constance agreed with a nod, though realizing her nod was futile over the phone, she quickly confirmed, "I'll meet you in twenty minutes?"

"Perfect," William replied eagerly. "I'll see you then, Constance."

As Constance ended the call, an unsettling feeling settled in the pit of her stomach, a nagging sense of guilt gnawing at her conscience. There was no apparent reason for her to feel this way, no justification for her internal conflict regarding her loyalty to William. Their relationship was stable, devoid of any betrayal or wrongdoing.

Yet, it wasn't about William. It was about something deeper, something that eluded her grasp. It was the haunting presence of the man from those images, invading her thoughts once more without invitation. There was an inexplicable connection between her and this enigmatic figure from the past, a bond she struggled to comprehend. Her true feelings remained elusive, her heart torn between conflicting forces beyond her control.

Taking a deep breath to steady her nerves, Constance made her way through the bustling streets of the city, her mind consumed with thoughts of the mysterious man from the photograph. It seemed as though his presence haunted her every waking moment, his image etched into her mind like a ghost from a forgotten dream.

Shaking her head in an attempt to dispel the shadowy thoughts clouding her mind, Constance chose to focus on the road ahead, ensuring safe navigation to her destination. Despite the bustling weekend traffic of the inner city, the journey was swift, aided by the proximity of her previous attempt at breakfast with Lynette.

Pulling up to the quaint restaurant where she'd agreed to meet William, Constance spotted him waiting at a table near the window. His warm smile beckoned. Yet as she drew closer, a sense of unease settled upon her.

Her emotions felt hollow, devoid of the warmth and excitement she had anticipated. She had seen countless portrayals of loving couples reuniting, felt the energy of their affectionate embraces. But with William, it felt mundane, ordinary. There was no spark, no special connection that stirred her heart. Confusion clouded her thoughts as she grappled with these unexpected feelings, unable to comprehend their origin.

"Hey, Constance," William greeted her with a kiss on the cheek as she settled into the seat opposite him. "I'm so glad you could make it."

William's unexpected return from his travels caught Constance off guard. She had expected his arrival today, but not this early, and she silently scolded herself for feeling a pang of frustration at his unannounced return, knowing it interrupted her morning with Lynette.

He'd been away for work again—something about hospital networks he helped design systems for—beds, monitors, the things no one thinks about until they stop working.

"Thanks for inviting me," Constance replied, forcing a smile despite the inner turmoil. "I was having breakfast with Lynette that I had to cut short after your call."

Although she intended her words to be informative, not accusatory, William interpreted them as a rebuke. He felt a pang of guilt for not informing her of his premature return. His intention to surprise her with his unexpected arrival had backfired.

"I get it if you're upset," William said gently, reading more into her words than she'd meant. "I should have let you know I was coming back early. I just thought... I don't know, maybe you'd be happy to see me."

When Constance's reaction didn't align with what he expected after his apology, he pressed gently, "Is everything alright?"

Constance hesitated, grappling with how to respond. How could she make clear that her statement wasn't intended as criticism, given how it came across? And then there was her promise to her sister, adding pressure to an already tense situation. As she sat across from William, she couldn't escape the feeling that something essential was missing from their relationship. A certain indefinable quality.

"Everything's fine," she lied, forcing herself to meet William's gaze. "I've just been feeling a little... overwhelmed recently."

William's brow furrowed in concern, his hand reaching out to cover hers in a gesture of comfort. "You know you can talk to me about anything, right?" he said softly. "I'm here for you, Constance. Alway."

The sincerity in William's words only served to deepen Constance's sense of guilt. Here was a man who loved her unconditionally, who would do anything to make her happy, and yet she found herself unable to reciprocate his feelings in the way he deserved.

"I know," she replied. "And I appreciate that more than you know."

For a moment, the two of them sat in silence, the unspoken words hanging in the air between them. It was moments like these that Constance found herself questioning everything, wondering if she was making the right choices or if she was simply deluding herself into believing that she could ever be happy with someone like William.

Constance found herself drifting—not toward memories of past lovers, but the quiet ache that followed them. A connection she'd never quite reached.

She glanced at William and smiled, though it felt more like habit than feeling.

As they sipped their coffee in silence, that yearning stirred again—faint but insistent. A forgotten kind of love, still smoldering somewhere in the dark.

She tried to focus on the man in front of her, but the past held tight, its grip quiet and unrelenting.

But as the morning wore on and the sun rose higher in the sky, Constance found herself drawn back to the present, to the man who sat before her with a look of unwavering devotion in his eyes. And though she couldn't deny the pull of the past, she hoped that her future lay with William. She hoped that her heart would finally be at peace with the choices she had made.

With a sigh of resignation, Constance set aside her doubts and fears, intertwining her fingers with William's. "I love you," she confessed, her voice carrying a newfound sense of conviction.

Her declaration was meant to feel earnest but instead, felt hollow. She refused to admit to herself that it felt like she'd said, 'I care about you,' instead of 'I love you.' She wanted it to be real, even when it wasn't.

William's brows furrowed in confusion. He was taken aback by the sudden declaration. "Why say that now?" he queried, his tone tinged with surprise.

Constance withdrew her hand, leaning back in her chair as she met William's gaze squarely. "I just wanted to reassure you," she explained earnestly. "I didn't want you to doubt my feelings or think I don't appreciate you. If I've given you that impression, I'm truly sorry."

A smile spread across William's face, relief evident in his eyes. "I love you too, Constance," he responded warmly, tightening his grip around her hand. "And you do make me happy. I've never doubted your love for me."

Yet, as William's certainty washed over her, Constance couldn't shake a growing discomfort. His unwavering faith in their relationship only highlighted her own internal conflict. She knew there was something missing, an elusive connection she couldn't ignore. Despite her fondness for William and his admirable qualities, she couldn't deny her own feelings—or lack thereof. She felt her silence like a heavy burden, knowing she wasn't being entirely truthful with him. It was unfair, both to William and to herself, to continue hiding the truth.

Constance leaned forward abruptly, capturing William's hands and pressing a tender kiss to his fingertips. She thought of how safe he made her feel—his steadiness, his care, the quiet way he never asked for more than she could give. He offered her something rare: a life with fewer unknowns.

And still, she couldn't love him the way he loved her.

Not because he lacked anything—but because something in her still felt unfinished. Like a puzzle with the center piece missing. She didn't know what it was, only that it wasn't here.

But she wanted to want him. And that counted for something, right?

In that moment, she made a silent vow to herself: to push past the fog of doubt, to try—not because of guilt, but because he deserved that much honesty. Because maybe trying was a kind of love too.

William's smile widened as he reached out to gently caress her cheek, his expression radiating warmth and affection. He was reassured by Constance's gesture, finding solace in the subtle yet profound way she expressed her feelings.

As they sat together in the warm embrace of the morning sun, Constance couldn't help but feel a sense of peace wash over her, her heart finally at ease with the decisions she had made. And though the memory of the man from the past lingered in the back of her mind, she knew that as long as she had William by her side, she could face whatever the future held with courage and grace.

As the warm morning sun bathed the cafe in golden light, Constance and William continued enjoying a leisurely breakfast, lost in conversation and laughter, when suddenly, William grew serious, his gaze fixed on Constance with a mixture of nervousness and determination.

"Constance," he began, his voice tinged with emotion, "there's something I need to ask you."

Constance felt her heart skip a beat as she met his gaze, a flicker of apprehension stirring in her mind. She had sensed a shift in William's demeanor.

"What is it, William?" she asked.

William took a deep breath, his hands trembling slightly as he reached into his pocket and produced a small velvet box. Constance's breath caught in her throat as he opened it, revealing a brass key nestled within.

Constance blinked, her breath escaping in a rush as she glanced around, cheeks flushed with relief. She had braced herself for a proposal, expecting William to present her with a ring and ask for her hand in marriage. The surge of relief she felt at the absence of such a grand gesture mingled with a pang of shame for her reaction.

William's voice interrupted her thoughts.

"Constance," William said, his voice trembling with emotion, "I love you more than words can express. Will you move in with me?"

He meant it. Every word. He loved her stillness, her honesty, the way she never tried to be anything but herself. She wasn't flashy, wasn't easily impressed—and never once made him feel like he had to be more than he was. She was one of the few people who didn't just see him—she steadied him.

Time seemed to freeze as Constance stared down at the key in his hand, a whirlwind of thoughts and feelings swirling within her. Panic surged through her veins, her heart pounding with uncertainty. While this request was certainly less daunting than a sudden proposal, it still carried immense weight in her mind.

"William, I..." she started, her voice faltering as she struggled to articulate her thoughts.

But before she could form a coherent response, William gently pressed the key into her palm, his eyes locking with hers in a silent plea. The other patrons in the cafe glanced over, their curiosity sparked by the unfolding scene.

She looked down at the key.

He'd brought her soup once. Walked her home in the rain without a word.

And still, her heart hesitated.

"Constance," William said, his voice trembling with emotion, "I want to marry you eventually. I think we should move in together. What do you think?"

Constance felt her cheeks flush with embarrassment as all eyes turned to her, their whispers echoing in her ears like a chorus of disapproval. She glanced around the cafe, acutely aware of the attention they were drawing, and felt a surge of panic rise within her.

"William, please," she whispered, her cheeks burning with embarrassment. "Not here."

But William appeared oblivious to her discomfort, his gaze locked onto hers with unyielding intensity. "Constance, I love you," he continued, his voice brimming with sincerity. "I could ask you to marry me now," he added with a playful grin, misinterpreting her reaction as overwhelming joy rather than the mix of emotions she truly felt.

Caught off guard by his sudden proposal, Constance felt her heart race with uncertainty. She opened her mouth to speak, but no words came out, her mind a whirlwind of conflicting emotions.

"Constance?" William's voice broke through her thoughts, his brow furrowed in concern. "Are you okay?"

Panic surged through Constance's veins as she realized she couldn't give William the answer he was waiting for.

Not here.

Not now.

Not like this.

"I... I need some time," she stammered, her voice barely above a whisper. "Please, just give me some time to think."

With that, Constance rose abruptly from her seat, her cheeks burning with embarrassment as she fled the cafe, leaving William sitting at the table.

As she made her way through the crowded streets, her mind in turmoil, Constance's thoughts turned to her sister, Sera. She needed someone to talk to, someone who understood the complexities of her heart and soul.

Constance, her heart burdened by her indecision, pulled out her phone and called up her sister.

"Sera," she called out when her sister answered, her voice trembling with emotion. "I need to talk to you."

Sera sensed the distress in her sister's voice as she answered the call.

"I'm still at home. We can talk there when you get back." Her tone was calm, but beneath it, Sera already knew.

Sera, sitting in their shared, safe space, clutched her chest reflexively. She realized her sister was deeply troubled and needed to talk face-to-face. They were so attuned to each other, after all.

As Constance stepped into their cozy home, she found Sera waiting for her in the living room, a concerned look etched on her face.

"Hey," Sera greeted as Constance closed the door behind her. "You okay?"

Constance sighed, sinking down onto the couch beside her sister. "Not really," she admitted, her voice heavy with emotion.

Sera placed a comforting hand on her shoulder, her eyes filled with empathy. "What's wrong?" she asked gently.

Constance took a deep breath, gathering her thoughts before speaking. "It's William," she began, her voice trembling slightly. "He proposed we move in together."

Sera's eyes widened in surprise, a mixture of shock and concern crossing her features. "Oh, Constance," she murmured, her heart going out to her sister.

Constance let out a bitter laugh, the sound tinged with frustration. "Yeah, that was pretty much my reaction too," she admitted, running a hand through her hair in agitation.

Sera studied her sister intently, her brow furrowed in concern. "Aren't you happy about it?" she asked, with a light tone.

Constance shook her head vehemently, her lips pressing into a thin line. "Hell no," she replied, her voice sharp with emotion.

Sera's eyes softened with understanding as she reached out to take her sister's hand in hers. "Why not?" she asked gently.

Constance let out a weary sigh, her shoulders slumping in her uncertainty. "I told you I would give him a fair chance," she said, her voice tinged with frustration. "But that doesn't mean I'm ready to move in together, let alone married."

Sera nodded in understanding, her expression sympathetic. "I get it," she breathed. "It's a big decision, and you shouldn't feel pressured into anything you're not ready for."

Constance felt a wave of relief wash over her at her sister's words, grateful for her unwavering support. "Thanks, Sera," she said, offering her sister a small smile. "I don't know what I'd do without you."

Sera returned her sister's smile, squeezing her hand gently. "You'll figure it out," she said reassuringly.

They sat together in the comfort of their home. Constance's uncertainty began to lift, replaced by a sense of clarity and determination. And as they talked late into the night, their bond grew stronger than ever, a beacon of hope guiding them through the uncertainties of the future.

Sera sat on the edge of the sofa, her mind swirling with conflicting emotions. She wanted so desperately for things to work out for her sister—not just because William was kind, but because he was steady, present, safe. A man rooted in the real world. The kind of man who might tether Constance to a life untouched by fate.

But now, with William's unexpected proposal that they move in together, those hopes seemed to have been shattered. Instead of bringing them closer together, it threatened to drive a wedge between them, pushing Constance further away.

As she forced a smile, a pang of disappointment tugged at her heart. She couldn't afford to reveal her distress to her sister, especially when Constance was already grappling with her own inner turmoil.

She told herself that protecting Constance meant guiding her toward something stable, something that couldn't be taken away. But deep down, she feared that nothing in this life could hold against what was already in motion.

Yet, as the minutes ticked by, the weight of her emotions became unbearable. They triggered a flood of memories, returning with such intensity that they ignited a pounding headache.

With a wince, Sera pressed her hand against her temple, trying to ease the growing ache. "These damn memories," she muttered under her breath, the words slipping out. She spoke without realizing what she had said.

Beside her, Constance turned, concern etched on her features. "What did you say?" she inquired, her brow furrowing with worry. "Are you alright? You seem to be rubbing your head."

Waving off her sister's concern with a forced smile, Sera replied, "I'm fine," though her voice carried a hint of strain. "Just a headache, nothing serious."

Observing her sister's skeptical glance, Constance opted not to delve deeper. She possessed an innate understanding of Sera's moods, recognizing when something troubled her, yet she also valued her sister's privacy. Instead, she offered a reassuring squeeze of Sera's hand, a silent display of solidarity between siblings.

"You're returning to the set tomorrow, right?" Constance inquired, her concern clear in her tone as she contemplated her sister's well-being and professional commitments.

Sera responded with a complex smile, partly to reassure her sister of her capability, but also to mask her own apprehensions regarding Constance. It amused her that Constance fretted over her ability to perform on set the next day, oblivious to the intricacies of their intertwined lives that Sera struggled with whether or not to disclose.

"Yeah, I'll be fine," Sera affirmed. "We're starting the final scenes tomorrow, so shooting should wrap up within another month or so."

Sera shifted to sit up beside her sister, her expression reflecting concern. "Enough about me. What's your plan with William?"

Constance paused, weighing her options. The decision ahead loomed large, with implications not only for her own life but also for William's. And then there was the matter of their relationship's future.

As she contemplated, Constance's words spilled out, almost unbidden, revealing her inner turmoil. "I don't feel that kind of love for him. I sense that someone else, someone I'm meant to love, is on the horizon," she revealed, her voice tinged with uncertainty.

Turning to gauge her sister's reaction, Constance was taken aback by the shock evident on Sera's face. She hadn't expected her own admission, and for a moment, she struggled to recall her exact words, finding nothing but a blank space where her thoughts should have been.

"What did I just say?" Constance asked Sera, her voice tinged with confusion.

Sera returned her gaze with a blank expression, her mind racing as she processed Constance's words. It took her a moment to formulate a response, the weight of their implications sinking in. The thought that "It's too late now" reverberated through her head, sending shivers down her spine.

Shaken to the core, Sera struggled to maintain composure, the fear of an unavoidable fate gnawing at her. With a conscious effort, she banished the blank look from her face, replacing it with a forced smile. Rising from her seat, she stretched, attempting to disguise the turmoil brewing within her.

"You didn't say anything," she replied with a smile, her words laced with reassurance. She couldn't burden her sister with her own fears, couldn't reveal what she knew. Leaning down, she placed a gentle kiss on Constance's forehead. "I'm heading to bed. Early start tomorrow, so I'll be gone by the time you wake up. I love you, Connie."

With those words, Sera left, retreating to her room for the night, leaving behind a bewildered Constance in her wake.

Sera's early morning drive took her to the film studios near Lakewood in Atlanta. She had left home early, accounting for the minimal weekend traffic. The sun had barely crested the horizon, casting a soft light over the tree-laden city as it slowly woke up. As Sera navigated the highway, her thoughts mirrored the city's stir, filled with the flood of memories she had recovered in the past few days.

These memories spanned multiple eras, encompassing lives in different cities, societies, and communities. The sheer volume was overwhelming. Her head throbbed with the mental strain, but she pressed on, knowing she couldn't ease the ache.

It felt like a switch had been thrown, inundating her mind with these newfound memories. Sera's world had shifted dramatically, and she was far from pleased. These memories jeopardized her primary goal: keeping her sister safe. The resurgence of past events made that nearly impossible.

Determined, Sera focused on what she could control. She needed to handle immediate concerns while finding ways to mitigate unforeseen challenges. It was a monumental task. The past loomed large, with too many events that had happened and could easily recur. What weighed heaviest was the potential fate she and her sister faced at the age of 25, just two years away.

Her thoughts inevitably circled back to one person—the person she dreaded might reenter their lives. She hoped with all her heart that this time, he would stay away. Sera prayed for a chance at happiness for herself and her sister, free from his shadow and the capricious whims of fate.

Sera's attention snapped back to the present as she pulled up to the gates of the facility. She presented her identity card and was granted entrance. Taking a deep breath, she shook the tension from her slight frame, stepped out of the car, and made her way into the bustling set.

The film set hummed with activity as actors rehearsed lines and crew members adjusted lighting and props. Sera walked through the chaos, her mind weighed down by resurfacing memories of past lives. She pored over the script in her hands, trying to redirect her thoughts. She wasn't paying much attention to her surroundings, focusing instead on her lines to forget the fear of the future threatening to engulf her.

As she approached the wardrobe area, something about the costumes caught her eye. Suddenly, memories of a small 14th-century villa in Europe surged into her mind. The film's setting matched this period, and the details resurfaced unbidden. She didn't choose to remember; the memories came on their own, and she reacted instinctively.

"Wait, stop," she called out, her voice cutting through the clamor. The room fell silent as everyone turned to look at her. Alexander, the film's director, stepped forward, a puzzled look on his face.

"What's wrong, Sera?"

She hesitated for a moment, her heart pounding. "Dammit," she muttered under her breath, frustrated that she had spoken on instinct. Now she was committed. "The costumes... they're not accurate," she began, her voice gaining confidence. "These styles are off by at least a century. The fabrics and cuts are all wrong for the period we're portraying."

Alexander frowned, glancing at the costume designer, who looked equally confused. "Are you sure?"

Sera nodded. "Absolutely. For this era, the fashion was much more understated. Subtle changes can make a huge difference in authenticity." She walked over to a rack of clothes and pulled out a dress. "See these sleeves? They should be narrower, and the fabric should be more subdued. This bright color wouldn't have been used."

The crew paused, exchanging impressed looks. Sera's unexpected expertise was evident, and the room buzzed with whispers. Alexander, still taken aback, couldn't shake the suspicion that there was more to her knowledge than met the eye.

"That's... incredible," he finally said. "How do you know all this?"

Sera's mind raced. She couldn't reveal the truth—not yet. "I've always been a history buff," she lied, forcing a smile. "I guess I've just picked up a lot over the years."

Alexander studied her, his curiosity piqued. "Well, you've just saved us from a major authenticity blunder. Thank you."

"No problem," Sera replied, but inside, her thoughts were turbulent. How much longer could she keep her past lives a secret?

Sera walked away as Alexander consulted with the costume designer and manager to verify her claims. By the end of the day, word reached her that they had confirmed what she pointed out. Although Sera should have been pleased that her insights ensured the film's accuracy, she wasn't. She wanted no more attention than she already had. With too many worries on her mind, the last thing she needed was additional scrutiny.

Chapter 4: "Desperate Measures"

12th Century - Florence, Italy

A desperate bid for love amidst societal turmoil.

They had been in Florence for two years now, ever since the death of their parents. At fifteen, the girls stood on the precipice of womanhood—no longer children in the eyes of society, but not yet fully claimed by the roles that awaited them. Tempus had watched them grow since they first arrived, quiet and unsure, into something luminous and complex. In the eyes of Florence, they were nearly of age to be married.

For Tempus's family, that meant plans.

Arrangements.

Legacy.

The sun cast a golden glow over the bustling streets of Florence as Tempus strolled alongside Constance through the lively market. Sera flitted ahead, her curiosity piqued by the array of goods on display at each stall.

Tempus had been about to speak to Constance when his attention was abruptly drawn to Sera as she collided with a much older, rather imposing man. His protective instincts kicked in as he stepped closer to the girls, ready to intervene if necessary.

"What's this, now," the man called out. His gaze lingered on Sera, his eyes narrow with scrutiny. "You look even more beautiful than my own daughters. Maybe even my wife," he remarked gruffly, his voice heavy with age.

Sera's discomfort was palpable as she shifted uneasily under the man's gaze, her instincts warning her of impending danger. His next words only served to confirm her fears as he brazenly asked if she was married and if she would consider marrying him.

Repulsed by the man's audacity, Sera instinctively moved to hide behind Tempus, seeking refuge from the unwanted advances.

Tempus's expression hardened as he stepped forward, placing himself between the girls and the man.

"These girls are under my protection," Tempus declared firmly, his voice carrying a note of authority. "You would do well to remember that."

A handful of passersby paused in their tracks, their attention drawn to the unfolding scene. Among them, a couple stood close, murmuring softly to each other, hands strategically placed over their mouths to prevent their conversation from drifting to unintended ears.

"Isn't that Tempus Auerelius?"

The older man's demeanor shifted at the mention of Tempus's affiliation with the Auerelius family. His contemptuous expression softened slightly as he glanced at the insignia adorning Tempus's clothing, a silent acknowledgment of the power and influence wielded by the Auerelius name.

With a muttered curse under his breath, the man hastily retreated, his earlier bravado replaced by a palpable sense of unease. As he disappeared into the crowd, Tempus breathed a sigh of relief, grateful that he had been able to protect the girls from harm.

Turning to Constance and Sera, Tempus offered them a reassuring smile. "Are you two alright?" he asked, his concern evident in his voice.

Constance nodded, her gratitude evident in her eyes. "Thank you, Tempus," she said softly, her voice filled with genuine appreciation.

Sera offered a shaky smile, her nerves still rattled by the encounter. "Yes, thank you," she echoed, her voice trembling slightly.

Tempus gently rested his hand on Sera's shoulder, a silent promise of unwavering support. Sera felt her heart quicken beneath his touch, its rhythm escalating beyond even the intensity of their previous exchange.

As they continued on their way through the market, the memory of the encounter no longer lingered in the air, fading away from the world beyond the three of them on their foray from home.

As they continued weaving through the market, the vibrant colors and lively chatter dispelled the unease that lingered in the air after their encounter with the older man. Constance and Sera remained close to Tempus, their steps slightly hurried as they moved from stall to stall, their laughter tinged with a hint of nervousness.

Tempus couldn't shake the feeling that the girls were even closer to him now than they had been before, especially Sera, who had initially been a bit more adventurous in exploring the market. He felt their trust in him, their unspoken reliance on his protection.

Because of Constance's proximity, Tempus couldn't help but notice how easily he could slip his hand into hers if he dared to reach out. The thought sent a shiver down his spine, a stark reminder of the growing complexity of their relationship as they transitioned from carefree teenagers to young adults.

As they paused to admire a display of handcrafted jewelry, Tempus's mind drifted to his parents' plans for the twins. The mere thought of it made his stomach churn with disgust. He couldn't bear the idea of the girls being forced into a loveless marriage for the sake of securing the Auerelius family's legacy.

Lost in his thoughts, Tempus didn't notice Constance's concerned gaze until she gently touched his arm, drawing him out of his reverie. "Is everything alright, Tempus?" she asked, her voice soft with concern.

Tempus forced a reassuring smile, masking the turmoil brewing within him. "Just shaken up by that unpleasant encounter," he replied vaguely, unwilling to burden Constance with the weight of his worries.

Constance studied him for a moment, her intuition telling her that there was more to his unease than he was letting on. However, she respected his privacy, guessing that he would share his concerns with her when he was ready.

With a nod, Constance turned her attention back to the jewelry, her mind racing with questions and uncertainties. But amidst the chaos of their emotions, one thing remained clear – whatever challenges lay ahead, she was sure that Tempus would be there with her to help her navigate the troubled waters.

Tempus observed the girls interacting with the boy running the stall, noting the intense interest he seemed to have in Sera. The boy's unwavering attention on her didn't escape Tempus's notice as Sera examined the jewelry on display. Giggles and laughter filled the air as the girls tried on earrings and draped necklaces around their necks, playfully modeling the pieces.

Determined to bring joy to the girls, Tempus called out to the stall owner, inquiring about the prices of the jewelry. The sudden interruption caught the girls off guard, causing them to turn towards Tempus in unison. Meanwhile, the stall owner, still entranced by Sera, seemed startled by Tempus's question, prompting him to repeat it. Eventually, Tempus received a satisfactory response.

Despite Tempus's intention to purchase something for them, the girls politely declined his offer, expressing their gratitude but refusing to accept anything. With a shared glance, they turned away from the stall, walking off as the boy continued to gaze fixedly at Sera.

The sun dipped lower on the horizon, casting a golden hue over the sprawling city below as the trio savored their simple meal from the food stall. With satisfied stomachs, they wandered along the boulevard until they found themselves on a path leading up a hill, offering a picturesque view of the city bathed in the warm glow of the setting sun.

As they reached the crest of the hill, they spread out on the grass, each lost in their own thoughts, the gentle breeze a soothing balm against the heat of the day. Conversations ebbed and flowed, filled with dreams and aspirations for the future.

Sera lay on her back, arms flung wide like she could hold the sky in her palms. "I'll marry a man with a crooked smile and a dog that hates me," she declared with mock solemnity. "We'll live above a bakery, and I'll grow bitter from city air and write sad poems about birds."

Constance chuckled beside her. "That sounds miserable."

"Not at first," Sera replied, grinning. Then, quieter: "Or maybe I'll just find somewhere no one can find me. Just once. Before life decides who I'm supposed to be."

The silence that followed was tender—shared rather than heavy. Then Constance, brushing a blade of grass between her fingers, added, "I want a life of my own. Not arranged, not expected. I'd live by the sea, maybe. Sell painted fans or strange little sculptures no one wants but everyone remembers. Something useless. But mine."

Tempus listened intently, marveling at the intricate plans the girls spun for themselves. Their voices carried possibility, not certainty. Their optimism was contagious—and heartbreaking.

He couldn't bring himself to interrupt them—not while they dreamed. But in his mind, another truth quietly unfolded:

'They smile as they spin futures they'll never live; as if the telling might make the lie feel true.

Not because they believe it; but because it hurts less than saying nothing at all.

Because silence makes it real. And they aren't ready for real.

But the truth won't wait.

There would come a point when their tears no longer flow— no matter what is felt.'

He tried to imagine them that way—free, untethered, choosing joy instead of survival. He failed. Miserably. Even their laughter felt edged with longing.

In the quiet moments that followed, Constance turned her gaze toward him.

"What about you, Tempus?" she asked, her tone light, almost teasing. "What do you see in your future?"

Tempus hesitated, his hand instinctively rising to shield his eyes from the fading sunlight. He knew what his parents expected. What the Auerelius name required. And he knew that if he spoke too much of it, the moment would disappear.

Slowly, he clenched his hand into a fist, a silent vow forming in his mind.

"I'll make you my wife," he murmured.

The words slipped from his lips before he could stop them. And then they hung there—unclaimed, irreversible.

He froze, his heart pounding in his chest as the implications struck him like thunder.

Constance and Sera sat up, their expressions a mix of shock and confusion as they turned to look at him. Tempus's cheeks flushed crimson with embarrassment as he met their gaze, his mind racing to find an explanation for his slip of the tongue.

"I... I mean..." he stammered, his voice trailing off as he struggled to find the right words to convey his thoughts. But no words came, leaving him to face the stunned silence that hung between them, his heart heavy because of his unintended confession.

The atmosphere shifted abruptly as Sera suddenly bolted upright and dashed away, leaving Tempus and Constance behind. Constance's eyes widened in surprise, her heart skipping a beat as she watched her sister's retreating figure. She could see the telltale signs of tears glistening in Sera's eyes before her face was lost to sight, leaving Constance shaken by the sudden turn of events.

Tempus, his brow furrowed with concern, turned to Constance, his voice laced with worry. "What's wrong with Sera? Why did she run off like that?" he asked, his eyes searching Constance's face for answers.

Constance shook her head, her mind racing as she tried to make sense of Sera's sudden departure. "I don't know," she admitted, her voice tinged with anxiety. Without hesitation, she scrambled to her feet, her heart pounding in her chest as she made a split-second decision to chase after her sister.

Tempus rose more slowly, his gaze following Constance as she darted down the path in pursuit of Sera. "Wait for me!" he called out, his voice echoing in the quiet stillness of the hilltop. With a sense of urgency, he hurried after Constance, determined to find Sera and unravel the mystery behind her distress.

As the night enveloped them in its dark embrace, Constance and Tempus continued their search for Sera, their footsteps echoing softly in the quiet stillness of the evening. Despite their best efforts, Sera remained elusive, her absence casting a shadow of worry over the pair.

Tempus, his demeanor calm and collected, sought to reassure Constance, his voice a steady anchor amidst the storm of her emotions. "We'll find her, Constance. I know we will," he said, his words a soothing balm to her frazzled nerves.

Constance, her anxiety palpable in the tense lines of her face, struggled to contain her panic. She clung to Tempus's words like a lifeline, drawing strength from his unwavering presence by her side.

As they trudged through the darkness, their conversation turned to the unexpected confession Tempus had made earlier. Constance, her heart filled with uncertainty, broached the subject tentatively, seeking clarity amidst the chaos of their surroundings.

"Tempus, earlier... were you talking about marrying me?" Constance asked, her voice barely above a whisper, her eyes searching his for answers.

Tempus, caught off guard by the directness of her question, hesitated for a moment before offering a vague response, his words carefully chosen to evade the truth. "I... I don't know, Constance. It's... complicated," he stammered, his gaze flickering away from hers.

But Constance, undeterred by his evasion, pressed on, her determination unwavering. "Do you love me, Tempus?" she asked, her voice tinged with vulnerability as she waited for his answer.

Tempus, his heart pounding in his chest, took a step closer to Constance, his hands reaching out to gently cradle hers in his. He met her gaze, his eyes brimming with emotion as he confessed his deepest truth.

"Yes, Constance. I do love you," he admitted, his voice barely above a whisper, his words carrying a lifetime of longing. "I think... I think I've loved you from the moment you and Sera walked into my life."

Caught off guard by Tempus's confession, Constance felt a jumble of conflicting emotions swirling inside her. She couldn't bring herself to meet his gaze, her heart racing with uncertainty and fear. Despite her inner turmoil, she found herself unable to pull away from Tempus, his touch anchoring her in the midst of her turmoil.

"What... about you," Tempus asked hesitantly.

"I think..." her voice thinned to silence.

Turning away from Tempus, she continued, saying, "I think we should find my sister," Constance mumbled, her voice barely above a whisper, her words a feeble attempt to divert the conversation away from the tumultuous revelation hanging between them.

As Tempus released her hands, Constance felt a pang of regret wash over her, a nagging sense of longing to keep the touch of his hands ongoing lingering in the space between them.

Tempus desperately wanted to know how Constance truly felt about him, but fear of rejection stifled his longing to learn Constance's true feelings, leaving him paralyzed with indecision.

In the pregnant silence that followed, Tempus braced himself to voice the question that was on his mind anyway, despite the fear. But before he could utter a word, Constance held up her hand, a silent plea for him to wait. A call for silence.

Misinterpreting her gesture as a sign to keep his feelings hidden, Tempus hesitated, his heart sinking with disappointment. But then, to his surprise, Constance turned abruptly and began to move down the alley, her sense of urgency palpable in the air.

Tempus called out to her, his voice tinged with concern, but Constance didn't pause. Instead, she spoke over her shoulder, her words cutting through the darkness like a beacon of hope. "I heard crying. I think it's my sister," she said, her voice trembling with emotion.

Tempus followed, but something about her sudden certainty nagged at him. There hadn't been any sound—at least, none he could hear. And yet Constance moved with such purpose, as if she simply knew where her sister was.

It didn't take long to find her. Constance had gone the only route that Sera could have taken. That's how Tempus justified it.

The reality of it didn't matter. Constance quickened her pace as she caught sight of Sera sitting in the shadow of a few crates. Her back against the wall of the alley, her tears glistening in the dim light.

As Tempus stood beside Constance and Sera, relief washed over him as he watched the sisters embrace. He couldn't help but feel a pang of frustration at the same time, knowing that the answer he longed for remained just out of reach. Yet, in that moment, the safety and well-being of Sera took precedence over his own desires.

Constance lowered herself beside her sister, their arms intertwining in a tight embrace. Concern etched across her face, she gently probed, "Why did you run off, Sera? What's wrong? Is it about the man in the market earlier?" Her voice was soft, filled with genuine care and worry for her sister's well-being.

Sera turned her head slightly, casting a glance towards Tempus, who stood a few steps away. Inwardly, she couldn't help but feel a twinge of guilt, knowing that her thoughts were tangled up with the young man beside them. Sera discreetly acknowledged to herself that a man from the marketplace had indeed upset her, but the individual occupying her thoughts was none other than the young Tempus. But she kept her musings to herself, burying her head in her sister's shoulder as she murmured, "It's okay now. I feel better. Can we go home?"

Her words were muffled against Constance's shoulder, but her relief was palpable. With a nod from Constance, they rose to their feet, Tempus falling into step beside them as they made their way back home. Though the questions still lingered in Tempus's mind, for now, he pushed them aside, focusing instead on the safety and comfort of the two girls he had come to care for so deeply.

As they walked, the noise of the evening crowds swallowed up their footsteps. Constance kept her arm loosely wrapped around Sera, the two of them close enough to share warmth. But in her chest, Constance still carried an uneasiness she couldn't quite name.

She glanced sideways at her sister. "Sera... you really scared me back there," she said quietly. "You ran off so fast. I thought—"

She shook her head. "Was it just that man in the market?"

Sera didn't answer right away. She cast a glance toward Tempus, who walked a few paces behind them, then looked down at her hands.

"He upset me," she said softly. "But not in the way you think."

Constance studied her for a moment. "You're not... afraid you'll end up married off to someone like that, are you?" she asked, only half-teasing.

Sera gave a faint smile, but her voice was quieter than usual.

"A fat noble who smells of wine and doesn't know your name?" She forced a shrug. "I try not to think about it."

Constance sighed. "I guess we don't get much say, do we."

"Maybe just enough to regret it later," Sera murmured.

They walked a few more steps before Sera changed the subject, asking what they'd do for supper when they got home. Constance followed her lead, though the question still lingered at the edge of her mind:

What had truly made Sera run?

She didn't press it. Not yet

Several days had passed since the incident at the market, and the atmosphere in the Auerelius household remained tense with unspoken issues. In the secluded tranquility of the back garden, Constance and Sera found a moment of respite from the chaos of their surroundings. The soft breeze carried the faint scent of flowers, mingling with the distant chatter of birdsong as they settled into their seats, a sense of calm settling over them.

Tempus had excused himself from their presence a short while ago, promising to fetch a servant to bring refreshments for them. Left alone in the dappled shade of the garden, Constance and Sera exchanged glances, their thoughts circling the unspoken complexities of their situation.

As they sat together in the tranquil confines of the garden, the gentle rustle of leaves overhead providing a soothing backdrop, Constance broached the delicate topic with her sister.

"Sera, can I ask you something?" she began, her voice soft with uncertainty.

"Do you think Tempus might have feelings for you?"

Constance didn't ask to uncover a truth about her sister. Nor was she trying to understand Tempus better. She wasn't even sure why the question came.

It had risen from somewhere murkier—a place tangled with guilt and longing. Maybe it was her own feelings she was trying to untangle.

Something in her heart had gone quiet and strange since that night—since he said those words.

Maybe she was hoping her sister would give her permission to feel something back. Whatever the reason, she hadn't meant to hurt Sera. But somehow, she had.

The question, gentle as it sounded, had become a kind of cruelty—soft on the surface, but cutting all the same.

At the mere mention of Tempus's name, Sera's heart fluttered with a mix of emotions, her thoughts swirling in a tumultuous whirlwind.

She assumed Constance had seen through her—had noticed the lingering looks, the way her voice softened around him.

Maybe this question was her sister's quiet way of offering grace. A way to let Sera speak her feelings without judgment.

That thought, more than anything, made it harder to answer.

"I... I'm not sure," Sera replied carefully, her words laced with a hint of hesitation. "But you know how he is, always so protective and caring towards both of us."

Constance nodded, though her thoughts lagged behind the gesture. Something felt off. Like the ground beneath her was shifting—quietly, insistently—and she wasn't sure where to place her feet.

It hadn't really answered anything. Not for Constance.

She'd told herself that if Sera had shown a depth of feeling—something certain, something undeniable—then maybe she could have stepped aside. Maybe she would have.

But Sera's hesitation had left everything muddled. It opened no doors and closed none.

And in that space between clarity and silence, something fragile in Constance began to fray.

She glanced at her sister, searching for certainty in her expression.

Instead, she found softness. Kindness.

And that only made her feel worse.

"I suppose you're right," she said, the smile she offered feeling too light for the weight in her chest.

"But it's just... I can't help but wonder sometimes."

Sera reached out, her hand resting gently on Constance's arm. "Constance, whatever happens... we'll figure it out together," she said. Her voice didn't shake. It was steady, loyal—everything Sera believed she needed to be in that moment.

But inside, the storm hadn't passed.

If Tempus didn't love her—fine.

If he... loved Constance more...

She would carry that quietly.

As the hush between them settled, tender but tense, Sera made a promise to herself: She would protect Constance. Even if it meant stepping away from the one person she thought she might love. Even if it meant never knowing whether he might have loved her back.

Sera then questioned everything she had resolved herself to do.

'I should do that... right?'

The thought came quietly, like a whisper she didn't want to hear—but couldn't unhear.

Meanwhile, Tempus ventured through the corridors of the grand estate, his mind was consumed by a whirlwind of conflicting emotions. He couldn't shake the sense of unease that had settled over him since the incident at the market, the memory of the encounter with the older man still fresh in his mind.

As he approached the servants' quarters, Tempus's thoughts turned to Constance and Sera. He couldn't deny the growing bond he felt with the two sisters, a sense of protectiveness driving him to ensure their safety and well-being.

Entering the bustling hub of activity, Tempus scanned the room for a servant to assist him. Spotting a familiar face among the throng, he made his way over to the young maid, a sense of urgency guiding his steps.

"Excuse me, Maria," Tempus greeted the maid with a nod of acknowledgment. "Would you mind fetching some refreshments for the ladies in the back garden?"

Maria's eyes widened in surprise at Tempus's request, her curiosity piqued by the unusual task. "Of course, Master Tempus," she replied with a quick nod. "Right away."

As Maria bustled off to fulfill his request, Tempus's thoughts drifted back to Constance and Sera. Despite his efforts to maintain a facade of composure, he couldn't shake the nagging sense of concern that gnawed at his insides.

With a heavy sigh, Tempus turned on his heel and made his way back to the garden, his heart heavy with uncertainty. Little did he know, the fateful conversation unfolding between the two sisters would only serve to deepen the complexities of their entangled destinies.

Tempus was almost out of the inside of the vista when he encountered his father in the halls. As they stood face to face in the dimly lit corridor, Tempus braced himself for the inevitable confrontation. Things had been getting steadily worse with his relationship with his parents as he observed their treatment of the two girls.

"Father," Tempus greeted him with a forced politeness, his voice laced with tension.

His father's cold gaze bore into him, sending a shiver down Tempus's spine. "I've noticed you spending quite a bit of time with those girls," his father remarked, his tone laced with disapproval.

Tempus felt a surge of defiance rising within him, but he fought to keep his emotions in check. "They are under my protection, Father," he replied evenly, his voice steady despite the turmoil swirling inside him.

His father's lips curled into a grin, a glint in his eyes.

A voice from the adjacent corridor caught Tempus's attention. His mother, spoke softly. "They won't be under your protection for long, son," she said. "I've already begun arrangements for scouting potential marriages. It's time they fulfilled their duty to the family."

Tempus's heart sank at his mother's callous words, the realization of the girls' impending fate sending a surge of anger coursing through his veins. "But Mother, is it necessary?" he protested, unable to hide the desperation in his voice.

His father's expression hardened, his eyes narrowing into slits as he fixed Tempus with a steely gaze. "The needs of the family outweigh the needs of the individual," he retorted, his voice dripping with disdain. "Sons are promises of a future. Daughters have always been assets to be placed—nothing more."

Tempus's blood boiled at his father's words, his fists clenching at his sides as he fought to contain his rage. "That's not true, Father," he argued, his voice tinged with defiance. "Women deserve to be treated with respect and dignity, not as mere objects to be discarded at will."

His father's face twisted into a mask of fury at Tempus's insolence, his hand lashing out in a swift, punishing slap across Tempus's cheek. The sting of the blow sent shockwaves through Tempus's body, but he refused to back down, his gaze locked with his father's in a silent challenge.

For a moment, they stood locked in a tense standoff, the air thick with unspoken animosity. Then, with a curt nod of dismissal, Tempus's father turned on his heel and stalked off down the corridor, leaving Tempus alone with his mother.

Tempus turned to her. He should have known better than to expect consoling from her. She had never really been the mothering type to him at all. He had always been closer to his father and to his Zio Giovanni. At this moment, he wished his Zio was there to guide him.

His mother regarded him with cold eyes a moment longer before she turned and left as well.

As Tempus nursed his throbbing cheek, he couldn't help but feel a sense of unease gnawing at him. Despite his father's admonishments, he knew he couldn't stand idly by and watch as the girls' futures were decided for them. And as he met his father's retreating gaze with a steely stare of his own, he silently vowed to fight for what he believed was right, no matter the cost.

The evening sun cast long shadows across the Auerelius estate as Tempus approached his parents' study. He braced himself, knowing the gravity of what awaited behind those imposing oak doors. The urgency in his heart drove him forward; he needed to apologize for his earlier behavior and plead for the girls' future, particularly for Constance, whom he loved dearly.

Upon entering, the incongruous atmosphere struck Tempus. A small gathering of nobles highlighted the looming specter of arranged marriages for Constance and Sera. His parents stood by the large arched stone portal leading to the veranda, with Giovanni, his Zio, beside them. The presence of these nobles heightened Tempus's unease, though Giovanni's presence was a small comfort.

As Tempus neared, he noticed Giovanni's unsettled demeanor. His parents were engaged in a hushed conversation with Giovanni as they moved toward the veranda, clearly separating themselves for privacy. Tempus trailed after them, positioning himself just outside the veranda, far enough to remain unnoticed.

"What is this about?" sputtered Giovanni, gesturing towards the nobles. "I've heard you're seeking marriage partners for your nieces."

Leonardo turned away dismissively and let out a humph. After a few steps, he turned back, saying, "Those two girls are not my nieces."

Giovanni recoiled. "How can they not be?"

Leonardo's slow, measured words cut through the air. "They are not my blood."

"Your late brother was recognized as the father of those two girls. They share the same family name as you," Giovanni retorted.

The tension thickened, the air shimmering with unspoken conflict. Before it could escalate, Aurelia smoothly intervened, her voice like silk. "Giovanni, you're right—they share our name, but Leonardo is correct. They are not of his blood."

Aurelia moved to the veranda railing, her smile calculated. "We've fulfilled our duty by giving them shelter—but we're not beholden to them forever. Arranging suitable marriages is simply... practical. For their good. For ours."

Giovanni took a moment to consider her words. What she said made sense in one way or another. Even if he didn't agree with what Leonardo and Aurelia were doing, he couldn't argue against their rationale. To Tempus, it looked as if his Zio might capitulate to their schemes.

Tempus took a deep breath, his resolve firm. He stepped forward, out of the shadows of the veranda's edge and into their line of sight, inserting himself between the nobles and his parents.

"Mother. Father," he began, his voice steady despite the turmoil behind it. "I cannot stand by and watch as you use the girls to bolster our family's standing."

His father cut him off, cold and authoritative. "Enough, Tempus. You have done enough by caring for them. Do not overstep your bounds."

Desperation tinged Tempus's voice. "But Father, I love Constance. I can't bear to see her married off for politics."

His parents exchanged a cold glance. "The girls' worth lies in their marriage prospects," his mother declared. "They will fulfill their duty, whether you like it or not."

Aurelia turned slowly to regard her son, the barest lift of her chin casting her gaze downward as though even looking Tempus in the eye would grant him more importance than he deserved. Her expression was unreadable—practiced indifference draped in civility. She said nothing to him.

But she knew the room, such as it was—the gathering, the air between glances and silence—had begun to shift.

Giovanni's posture had grown tense, his jaw clenched as his gaze swept between the nobles and the girls' names spoken like bargaining chips. The conversation was growing heated—not dangerous, but unsavory. And Giovanni had never had much patience for unpleasantness.

Before either man could erupt, Aurelia softened her voice just enough to carry a thread of reason.

"It's for the girls' good," she said smoothly, eyes now on Giovanni. "To have partners who can provide for them. That's all we're seeking."

Giovanni's furrowed brow eased slightly—not with agreement, but with the temporary satisfaction of a response that acknowledged his presence. Aurelia stepped nearer to her husband, her gaze never once returning to Tempus.

Tempus's heart sank. "At least let me marry Constance. We can keep Sera as her lady-in-waiting. The girls stay together, and I can be with the woman I love."

Giovanni's face lit up. "That's a good idea," he said, clapping Tempus on the back. "Doesn't that sound like a solution?" But his words faded as he saw Leonardo and Aurelia's horrified expressions.

"You will not marry either of those girls," Aurelia hissed. "Their purpose is to secure a beneficial marriage."

Aurelia brushed past Tempus, nearly knocking him over, her footsteps echoing ominously. Tempus looked to his father for support, but Leonardo only turned his back, staring at the darkening skyline. Tempus's heart shattered, realizing his pleas were in vain.

Giovanni, torn between comforting Tempus and reasoning with Leonardo, hesitated. His hand reached out but dropped as Tempus turned away, defeated.

As Tempus prepared to leave, he glimpsed Sera in the doorway, her eyes wide with shock. Before he could speak, she fled, her footsteps echoing down the empty corridor.

Tempus's heart ached at the sight of her retreating figure, thinking that his parent's words had caused her pain. But as stood there, his mind consumed by turmoil, he couldn't shake the gnawing sense of despair that threatened to consume him whole.

"Tempus," Leonardo called out, stopping his son in his tracks. His voice, firm and authoritative, contrasted sharply with his turned back.

Tempus regarded his father's rigid stance with a mix of defiance and resentment. Leonardo Auerelius was a man who commanded respect and obedience, yet his recent actions had only deepened Tempus's feelings of rebellion.

"We have guests for dinner tonight," Leonardo stated, his tone brooking no argument.

Tempus frowned, fully aware that this was no ordinary gathering. "And who are these guests, Father?" he asked, striving to keep his voice neutral. He knew the answer but felt obstinacy was the only safe way to express his frustration.

Leonardo turned slowly to regard his son, his eyes narrowing slightly. He knew Tempus was acting out but chose to ignore it, feeling that succumbing to his rising anger would serve no purpose. "They are potential suitors for the girls, as you well know," he replied, his words hanging heavy in the air.

Tempus felt a surge of anger rise within him. His first instinct was to defy his father, to tell him he was wrong. But he stopped himself, the memory of the stinging slap from their last argument still fresh in his mind. The rejection of support from his parents still ached in his chest.

"Do tell the girls to get presentable for this dinner," Leonardo continued, his tone sarcastic.

A gust of wind flitted across the cold stone veranda. The sheer curtains at the open doors behind him stirred, lifting and drifting inward. The fading light spilled from outside into the candlelit space within.

It was dusk—and Tempus couldn't remember a time the house had felt so hollow.

Tempus nodded curtly, swallowing his objections. He turned on his heel and made his way to the girls' quarters, his heart heavy with the task ahead.

He walked away not because he agreed—but because there was nothing left to say that wouldn't cost more than he had left to give. Words had stopped working. Maybe they never would have. Only now did he finally understand: he had never had parents.

Not really.

Not the kind that held you when you were scared, or fought for your joy like it was their own.

Not in the way the *word* was meant to feel.

What he had were pillars—cold, towering, and unmoving—foundations of a house that reeked of rot. They were facsimiles—hollow shapes dressed in duty—caricatures.

Besides, he needed to check on Sera. She hadn't looked well when she ran off. Tempus had seen the tears streaming down her face.

Sera's chest tightened with a dull ache, compelling her to clutch it desperately. Within her, conflicting emotions clashed like warring factions; her love for her sister battled against the overwhelming surge of feelings she held for Tempus.

Tempus's unexpected words echoed in her mind, shattering her expectations. He had asked for Constance, not her. It wasn't the first time she'd heard him say it. She'd overheard it once before—softly, almost as if he hadn't meant it. But tonight he had said it clearly, firmly, in front of their family. There was no mistaking it now. No space for Sera's hopes to live.

This was the confirmation—not just the first time she heard it.

The realization pierced her heart, leaving her reeling. Leaning against the smooth stone walls of the hall, she paused in her retreat, doubled over and gasping for air. A foul taste lingered in her mouth, a bitter reminder of the truth she had just learned.

Aware that lingering in the hallway would serve no purpose, Sera summoned her dwindling strength and pressed forward. Eventually, she reached the sanctuary of her room. With trembling hands, she pushed open the door to the shared space she inhabited with her sister, her thoughts swirling in a tumultuous storm of conflicting desires.

'*Not yet. Not when the pain was still so fresh, and the hope hadn't died quietly,*' her thoughts screamed.

Constance, ever perceptive to her sister's distress, immediately rose from her seat as Sera entered the room, concern etched into the lines of her face. "Sera, what's wrong?" she asked, her voice gentle and soothing.

Sera thought something kind, something familiar, but now tainted it with resentment and sadness.

She wanted to tell Constance everything. She always did. But this time, the truth had claws. It would scratch them both if it got out.

She reached for the edge of Constance's sleeve and held it, not to be reassured—but to remember what she still had.

She curled her fingers against her own palm, nails biting skin, as if she could squeeze her feelings into something small enough to hide.

Constance's arms wrapped around her, warm and familiar. It should have helped. It always had before.

But tonight, it felt like leaning on something that couldn't support her at all. Like leaning on the leaves of a tree branch instead of the trunk itself. Sera stayed still, grateful—but hollow. She buried her face in Constance's shoulder to hide the truth from both of them.

They held each other like they always had—but Sera's arms didn't tighten the way they used to. The love between the sisters still existed, but it wasn't synchronous anymore.

She wanted to speak. To say what she'd heard. To scream what she felt. But even now, she knew her pain would only become her sister's.

Sera couldn't find the words to respond. If Constance knew—really knew—that Tempus had asked for her hand... she might say yes.

And what would Sera become then?

Not the loved one. Not the chosen. Just the girl who overheard it all and said nothing.

Just the shadow of the story.

The thought made her stomach churn again.

She hated herself for thinking it. Hated herself more for believing it might already be true.

How could she tell Constance the truth without it causing her pain in return for the telling? How could she bear to see the look of betrayal in Constance's eyes if her sister did indeed feel the need to reciprocate Tempus's wishes for marriage?

Sera grappled with the dilemma. The truth clawed at her chest, but giving it voice would only wound them both. She wanted to confess—needed to—but even that desire felt selfish. The risk of being understood, and still unwanted, was more than she could bear.

Constance was always the gentler one. The wiser one. And maybe that's why Tempus loved her. Sera hated that she could think that. Hated it more that it might be true.

Constance pulled back just slightly, brushing Sera's hair behind her ear. "You're not yourself today. Is it about the suitors?"

And Sera lied.

"Yeah."

Sera nodded, tears falling freely as she collapsed into her sister's arms. Constance held her close, murmuring words of comfort and reassurance, her touch a balm to Sera's fractured soul.

"Are you sure?" Constance asked.

Sera nodded without speaking. Let her believe it. Let her fix the wrong heartbreak. That was safer.

The crack was widening, not because of absence of care, but because of misunderstanding rooted in love.

Sera had always thought there would be nothing they couldn't say to each other. But now, silence felt like mercy. She clung to Constance like she always had, and it hurt more because of it. This embrace had once meant home—now it felt like standing in the doorway, too afraid to step all the way in.

She felt herself pulling away, and couldn't stop it. Some part of her was already retreating, even as she clung tighter. She didn't want to let go—yet something inside her already had.

In that moment, as the warmth of her sister's embrace enveloped her, Sera found herself grappling with the weight of her own emotions. She knew she couldn't keep the truth from Constance forever, but the thought of confessing her feelings filled her with dread.

As they clung to each other in the dim light of their room, Sera's heart ached with the knowledge that she was teetering on the edge of a precipice, her every choice fraught with consequences she couldn't bear to face. But for now, all she could do was surrender to the comforting embrace of her sister's love, seeking solace in the fleeting respite it offered amidst the storm of her emotions.

"You're shaking," Constance whispered. "Do you want me to stay close tonight?"

Sera nodded, grateful—and not. She didn't want to be alone. But she also didn't want to be seen.

They were still bound. That much hadn't changed. But something inside the bond had begun to crack—not enough to break, just enough to echo.

Sera realized a fracture was beginning to form between she and her sister. Subtle, emotional, quiet—that felt organic, not driven by jealousy alone, but by the deeper ache of being "almost chosen" but not.

There was her helplessness. Her isolation. Her desire to change her fate. Her love for both her sister and Tempus, which put her in conflict with herself.

All of this with no room for more. Too much baggage for a single person to reasonably carry. Sera's heartbreak wasn't just pain—it had now become motive. She didn't want to destroy anything—she wanted to preserve what she had. The tragedy was that in trying to keep what she loved, she was unraveling it at the same time.

There *had* to be a way to change it. A way to fix what hadn't been broken—*yet?*...

There just had to be.

She'd find it.

As Sera nestled in her sister's comforting embrace, her mind drifted back to the haunting image of Tempus's surprised expression when their paths had crossed outside their parents' study. The memory gnawed at her, stirring a tumultuous whirlwind of emotions within her chest.

She couldn't shake the feeling of vulnerability that had washed over her in that moment, the raw intensity of Tempus's gaze searing into her soul like a branding iron. How could she face him again after revealing her heart's deepest desires?

With a heavy sigh, Sera buried her face deeper into her sister's shoulder, her thoughts spinning like a whirlpool of uncertainty. She couldn't find the words to articulate the turmoil brewing within her, the fear of rejection and the overwhelming surge of longing that threatened to consume her whole.

But despite the tempest raging inside her, Sera remained silent, her lips pressed tightly together as she wrestled with the complexities of her emotions. She couldn't burden her sister with the weight of her own heartache, couldn't bear to see the pain reflected in Constance's eyes if she were to confess the truth.

So she kept her thoughts locked away, hidden behind a mask of stoic composure, even as her heart cried out for release. In the stillness of the moment, with only the rhythmic beat of her sister's heart to anchor her, Sera surrendered to the quiet anguish that gripped her soul, praying for the strength to face the challenges that lay ahead.

Tempus's mind churned like turbulent sea foam, thoughts crashing against each other in a relentless storm. He yearned for a moment of clarity, a respite from the chaotic whirlwind in his head. Shaking off the confusion, he pressed forward toward the girls' room. Softly, he rapped on the door, and Constance's warm greeting beckoned him inside.

"Tempus," Constance's smile faltered as she detected the tension in his demeanor, her concern replacing the initial warmth. "What's troubling you?"

Sera lifted her gaze from the bed, her eyes a mix of curiosity and wariness, attempting to conceal the turmoil within her heart. "Yes, Tempus, what brings you here?"

Tempus hesitated, unsure of where to begin. Glancing at Sera, she appeared composed now, unlike the defeated figure he had witnessed fleeing from his parents' study earlier. The memory churned his stomach.

Gathering himself, he took a deep breath, searching for the right words. "Father has informed me that we have guests for dinner tonight. He expects both of you to dress appropriately and be presentable."

Constance exchanged a glance with Sera, their expressions mirroring each other's apprehension. "Why is this dinner different?" Constance asked, her voice tinged with nervousness.

Tempus hesitated, not wanting to burden them with the truth but knowing he couldn't lie to them either.

"The guests are potential suitors," he admitted reluctantly. "Father and Mother are... arranging for you both to meet them."

The room fell silent, the weight of his words sinking in. Sera's face paled, and Constance's eyes widened with a mix of fear and disbelief.

"Potential suitors?" Sera echoed, her voice barely above a whisper. "Does that mean...?"

"Yes," Tempus said softly. "Father intends to see if there are any suitable engagements. He will eventually marry you off to these men to strengthen the family's standing."

A beat passed before Constance spoke—her voice thin, trembling. "We don't even know them. What if we're separated? They're strangers we don't love."

Sera's voice followed quietly. "We've already lost our parents. This... this feels like losing our lives too."

Constance's eyes filled with tears, and she took a step toward Tempus. "I don't even know what I'm supposed to do? I don't want this."

She didn't know what she meant by it—only that something inside her recoiled. Like a bird trapped in a cage it never knew it was in.

Tempus's heart ached at the sight of their distress. He reached out, taking Constance's hands in his, and looked at both of them with earnest determination.

"I don't agree with what Father is doing," he said firmly. "I'm trying my best to look out for you both, I promise."

Sera's eyes softened, a glimmer of hope shining through her fear. "Thank you, Tempus," she said, her voice filled with gratitude.

Constance squeezed his hands, her tears falling freely now.

Tempus pulled her into a comforting embrace, his heart breaking for the sisters he had come to care so deeply for.

"I know," he whispered. "But it's not like they're saying it is definite that you'll be engaged anytime soon. I'm still trying to get them to stop this."

Sera nodded in agreement, her heart fluttering with uncertainty. "Yes, I suppose we must find strength," she murmured, casting pleading eyes toward her sister. Despite her efforts, she struggled to maintain composure.

Constance moved to her sister's side, enfolding her in a comforting embrace. "We have to face this. We've gotta get through it," she stated, her voice gentle and reassuring.

Tempus offered them an encouraging smile. "I'll go prepare myself," he announced.

There followed an awkward silence that had settled over the room like a heavy fog. The tension was palpable, stretching on uncomfortably. Tempus turned to leave. With a hesitant glance back, he left the sisters to their thoughts, retreating from the suffocating atmosphere.

Tempus stepped out of the room, his mind racing with the upcoming dinner. He knew the battle was far from over, but he was determined to protect Constance and Sera from whatever schemes his parents had in store. The evening ahead would be challenging, but with the strength of their bond, he believed they could face anything.

In their room, Constance and Sera began to prepare for the dinner, their hands moving mechanically as they selected their finest dresses. The atmosphere was heavy with unspoken fears and hopes.

"Do you think Tempus can really help us?" Sera asked, her voice barely above a whisper.

Constance paused, looking at her sister with a mixture of determination and sorrow. "I believe he will do everything in his power," she replied. "But we have to be strong, Sera. Let's try not to be afraid."

Sera nodded, drawing strength from her sister's resolve. "You're right," Sera agreed, although in her heart she was already afraid. She was afraid because the love that she hoped for was now definitely directed at her sister and not her. She kept her feelings bottled up and continued to get ready.

As they finished dressing, they exchanged a silent vow to face whatever came their way together. No matter what their futures held, they would stand by each other.

Back in the dining room, as the evening progressed, the atmosphere grew festive—on the surface. The long mahogany table gleamed under the soft flicker of candlelight, lined with polished silverware and crystal goblets that caught the light like scattered stars. Velvet drapes muffled the noise from the street outside, wrapping the gathering in a kind of insulated grandeur.

Roughly two dozen guests filled the space—nobles, merchants, their jeweled wives fanning themselves as servants glided between them with practiced silence. Laughter rose in waves, shallow and performative, a fragile veneer over the real business of the evening.

Of the guests, two men stood out from the rest: both tall, poised, with an air of entitlement that seemed to radiate from the fine embroidery of their doublets. They stood off to the side beside Leonardo, as if above mingling. Leonardo introduced them to Tempus as Signore Ludovico and Signore Marcello—men of considerable wealth and influence in Florence, though their reputations whispered of arrogance more than honor.

With reluctance, Tempus offered his respects to the two men, his mind wandering to distant places he'd rather be.

Coming their way, Baron Ricci, a stout man with a bushy mustache, glanced around the room before his gaze settled on Tempus. "Ah, this must be your son, Lord Auerelius. Fine young man," he remarked, though his tone was more appraising than complimentary.

Another man beside him, Count Moretti, tall and thin with a hawk-like nose, nodded in agreement. "Indeed. I hear there are two young ladies we are to meet tonight?"

Lord Auerelius's smile widened. "Yes, my wards, Constance and Sera. Lovely girls, both of them. I'm sure you'll find them... suitable."

Tempus's jaw tightened at his father's words, but he held his tongue, knowing any outburst now would only make things worse. Scanning the room for a familiar face, his gaze settled on his Zio. Seeking approval, Tempus sought permission from his father before discreetly making his way towards his uncle.

Leonardo greeted the men warmly, his eyes gleaming with the potential alliances they represented. "Signore Ludovico, Signore Marcello, I hope you enjoy dinner," he said, gesturing to the lavishly set table. "Please, make yourselves comfortable."

Ludovico, a portly man with a neatly trimmed beard, nodded appreciatively. "Thank you, Leonardo. Your table is as grand as ever."

Marcello, a tall, thin man with sharp features, glanced around the room with a calculating eye. "Indeed, it is a pleasure to be here," he added, his gaze lingering on Constance and Sera as they entered the room.

As the girls arrived, the room seemed to hold its collective breath. Aurelia, noticing the unexpected silence, glanced around. She had her back turned to the doorway through which the twins had entered, but the sudden lack of response from her companions prompted her to turn and see what had caused the shift in atmosphere.

The twins entered the room, their radiance instantly drawing the eyes of everyone present. Their beauty outshone that of most other women at the gathering, prompting many wives to glance at their husbands' reactions. As if by silent agreement, a wave of animosity emanated from the women in the room, all directed at the twins. Aurelia, noticing this, turned her nose up disdainfully before making her way towards Leonardo.

"Ah, here they are," Lord Auerelius announced, gesturing for the twins to join the table. "Baron Ricci, Count Moretti, may I present Constance and Sera."

The baron and count stepped forward, their eyes roving over the girls with undisguised interest. Both men were well into their forties—perhaps even fifties—seasoned by decades of privilege, their graying temples and lined faces stark against the youthful glow of the girls not yet seventeen.

"Enchanting," Baron Ricci murmured, his gaze lingering on Constance. "Absolutely enchanting."

Count Moretti nodded in agreement, his eyes fixed on Sera. "A pleasure to meet you both," he said smoothly. "You are even more lovely than I had heard."

Moretti's fingers twitched as if to reach out—and then curled back into a fist, as though remembering the room was still watching.

Tempus's heart sank as he noticed the lecherous gazes of the men fixed on the girls. His fists clenched involuntarily, and he found himself moving towards the twins, driven by a protective instinct. However, Giovanni's presence halted his advance.

Giovanni placed a restraining hand on Tempus's arm, preventing him from acting on his temper.

"Zio?" Tempus questioned, his eyes searching his uncle's face.

Giovanni shook his head slowly. "Not now. They are in no danger here. Just be patient, young Tempus."

Tempus gritted his teeth, his head snapping back toward the twins. He had to endure this for Constance and Sera's sake. He noticed the twins had drawn even closer together, an impressive feat given how closely they were already standing. Their proximity underscored their mutual support in the face of the crowd's scrutiny.

The twins' eyes scanned the dining room in unison, searching for something familiar, an anchor amidst the sea of unfamiliar faces. Their gazes locked onto Tempus, standing across the room. Both girls gave him a faint smile, and an invisible pull seemed to draw them all toward one another. The girls sought protection; Tempus aimed to provide it. He had already resolved that if Giovanni tried to stop him again, he would have to use much more force than he had previously.

However, before Tempus could make any progress, his parents interceded.

"Come, girls," Aurelia said, her voice firm yet smooth. "You're to sit here beside me." She guided them to seats opposite where Tempus was to sit.

Though somewhat reassured that the girls would be safer next to his mother, Tempus reluctantly moved to take his seat at his father's right hand.

As the guests took their seats, Constance and Sera scanned the room, their faces composed but their eyes betraying their anxiety. Tempus's heart ached as he watched them, their beauty and grace evident despite the circumstances.

Dinner was served, and the conversation flowed, though it was tinged with the underlying tension of the evening. The baron and count spoke at length about their estates and titles, barely masking their true intentions.

As the dinner began, Ludovico and Marcello wasted no time in making their intentions clear. Ludovico leaned forward from where he was seated at the table, his eyes fixed on Sera. "Leonardo, you have truly raised two beautiful daughters," he said with a sly smile. "I must say, Sera's beauty is unparalleled. She would make a fine addition to any household."

Leonardo made no mention of correcting his relationship to the girls. He cared not if others mistook him for their father if he could capitalize off of that mistake. As for Tempus's mother, Tempus noticed that she seemed to act indifferent to anything being said about the twins as long as Leonardo was content.

Marcello, not to be outdone, turned his attention to Constance. "And Constance, such grace and elegance. I can see why you are so eager to find suitable matches for them."

Baron Ricci leaned towards Lord Auerelius, his voice carrying across the table. "You have raised them well, my lord. They will make fine additions to any noble household."

Count Moretti nodded, a predatory gleam in his eyes. "Indeed. Such beauty and grace are rare. They will bring great honor to their husbands."

Tempus's blood boiled at their lecherous looks and insincere compliments. He could bear it no longer. He slammed his fist on the table, causing the silverware to clatter and the guests to look at him in shock. These men were treating Constance and Sera like prizes to be won, completely disregarding their feelings and autonomy. He couldn't stay silent any longer.

"These are not just 'suitable matches,'" Tempus said sharply, his voice cutting through the room. "Constance and Sera are not objects to be bartered. They are human beings with their own dreams and desires."

Leonardo's face darkened with anger, but before he could speak, Ludovico laughed dismissively. "Oh, Tempus, you are still young. You will learn that in our world, alliances and marriages are tools for power and influence."

Marcello nodded in agreement. "Indeed. It is not about love or dreams, but about securing a future for the family."

Tempus's eyes blazed with fury. "You speak of securing a future, but at what cost? Using people as tools is not a future I want any part of."

"Tempus," Giovanni interjected, his tone stern. "Be respectful!" Though he shared Tempus's misgivings, he would not tolerate such outbursts.

Baron Ricci and Count Moretti exchanged glances, clearly taken aback by Tempus's defiance. "Young man, you should mind your place," the baron warned, his tone condescending.

Count Moretti nodded. "Respect for one's elders is a virtue," he added, his voice oily with false sincerity.

Simultaneously, Leonardo's patience snapped. "Enough, Tempus!" he shouted, slamming his hand on the table. "You will not disrespect our guests. This is the way of our world, and you will learn to accept it."

Tempus stood up, his chair scraping against the floor. "No, Father, I will not accept it. I will not stand by while you use Constance and Sera for your own gain."

The room fell into a tense silence, Tempus's defiance causing ripples in the air. Tempus's hands shook with suppressed rage. Constance and Sera exchanged worried glances, their hearts pounding with a mix of fear and admiration for Tempus's courage.

Leonardo's face turned red with rage. "You insolent boy! You have done enough. Sit down and hold your tongue."

Tempus took a step back, his resolve unwavering. "No, Father. I will not sit down, and I will not hold my tongue. This is wrong, and deep down, you know it."

The tension in the room was palpable, everyone holding their breath, waiting to see what would happen next. Leonardo glared at Tempus, his eyes filled with fury. "You will respect your elders, Tempus," he growled. "And you will respect the needs of this family."

Tempus met his father's gaze, his voice steady and calm. "Respect is earned, Father. Using people as pawns is not something I can respect."

Leonardo's eyes flickered with a mix of anger and something else—perhaps a hint of unease. But he quickly masked it, his expression hardening. "Don't regret this, Tempus," Leonardo warned.

Tempus turned to Constance and Sera, his eyes filled with determination. "Come on, let's go."

Leonardo cast a withering glance at the twins, causing them to stay rooted in place. They lowered their eyes to their laps, trying to shrink into obscurity amidst the attention now fixated on them from everyone in the room.

Leonardo turned back to his son. "The novelty of your presence at this dinner is finished. We will speak later, you and I. For now, you are dismissed."

An awkward, pregnant silence followed as those gathered waited to see what course Tempus would choose. He fought the conflicting emotions and thoughts battering him. He didn't want to give in to his father's command, but more importantly, he couldn't leave the twins to fend for themselves in this quagmire of a dinner. The eyes still on him made him acutely aware of his precarious position.

A soft clearing of a throat caught everyone's attention. Aurelia sat demurely beside her husband, seemingly fixated on her plate as she fiddled with her utensils, plainly bored with the entire affair.

"Let them go, Leonardo. Everyone has seen the girls. Let the adults dine and talk while the children leave," she said, emphasizing the word "children" and staring directly at Tempus. Her words cut him deeply. Referring to him as a child in front of everyone seemed to diminish his stance, casting it as a childish outburst rather than a principled stand.

Reluctantly, Leonardo waved his hand dismissively, including the girls in the gesture. Tempus felt a surge of frustration but forced himself to remain calm. "Thank you, Mother," he said, his voice laced with controlled defiance. He deliberately acknowledged his mother's dismissal, pointedly ignoring that it was his father's permission that actually allowed them to leave.

Turning to Constance and Sera, he offered them a reassuring nod. "Come on, let's go."

With one last look at his parents, Tempus led the twins out of the room, his heart aching from his mother's words. He refused to give them the satisfaction of seeing him cry, though it was a struggle. Tears misted the corners of his eyes, but he was determined to protect the twins, regardless of the personal cost.

As he left the dining room, the tension remained thick in the air. Tempus knew that the battle was far from over, but he was prepared to fight for Constance and Sera's freedom.

Constance, her heart pounding, quickly rose from her seat and followed him. She was followed hurriedly by Sera. They found him on the veranda, staring out at the night-time city skyline, his shoulders tense with anger.

"Tempus," she called softly, approaching him hesitantly. "Are you alright?"

He turned to face her, his expression softening at the sight of her. "No, Constance," he admitted, his voice heavy with emotion. "I can't stand what they're trying to do to you and Sera."

Constance stepped closer, taking his hands in hers. "Thank you for standing up for us," she said, her voice filled with gratitude and affection. "It means more than you know."

Tempus squeezed her hands gently, his eyes meeting hers. "I did it because I love you, Constance," he confessed, his voice barely above a whisper. "I can't bear the thought of you being forced into a loveless marriage."

Constance's breath caught at his words. She looked down at their intertwined hands, her heart racing. "I..." she began, but faltered. "Tempus, I..." she wanted to admit it. Her voice trembling.

'*Saying it out loud... it makes it real,*' she thought.

When the words failed to materialize, Tempus pressed on for her. "You don't have to say it."

His fingers slipped from her. He turned away and took a small step. Not large. Not far. But the chasm that formed... it was wider than a sea. Far enough that the roar of the storm tossed waves could be heard for miles.

Constance's hand still hung there. Abandoned. She pulled it into a tight fist and tucked it against her chest. Her head hung low. Not knowing what else to do, she turned and left.

Unbeknownst to them, Sera stood a few steps behind, watching from a distance. Her heart ached with the confirmation of what she had suspected. Tempus loved Constance, and Constance...? she didn't know how Constance felt. Tears filled her eyes as she turned away, slipping back to the room she shared with her sister, her own feelings a tumultuous storm inside her.

The afternoon sun slanted through the windows of their shared room, catching on the dust in the air like the memory of something already fading.

Sera sat at the edge of her bed, hands folded, gaze distant. Constance, brushing out her hair near the mirror, glanced toward her sister's reflection. She could feel the question before it came.

"Have you thought about what he said?"

Sera's voice was light—too light. Practiced casual. A question like a stone thrown sideways.

Constance blinked at the mirror. "What who said?"

Sera didn't turn to look at her. "Tempus."

A pause.

Constance shifted her brush to her other hand. "Oh."

That was all. Just "oh."

Sera exhaled softly. "You don't have to talk about it." She stood and crossed the room to the small table where a pitcher sat. "I just... wondered."

Another pause, longer this time.

Constance lowered the brush, her voice barely audible. "I haven't really... I don't know what I think."

"You should know," Sera said gently. "He's waiting."

Constance turned. "Have you thought about it? What you would have said if he'd said that to you?"

That froze Sera—just for a heartbeat.

Constance told herself the question was for Sera.

But some deeper part of her knew—it was really for her. She wanted permission. She wanted to know if the path was clear.

But asking that way... it was cleaner. It didn't make her guilty. Just curious.

"I'm not the one he confessed to," she said, pouring water into a glass, her back still turned.

Constance looked down. "No. I guess not."

Sera handed her the glass. Their fingers touched, but neither lingered.

There was a knock at the door. Tempus, from the other side. "Would you both like to walk?"

Constance looked to Sera, who was already shaking her head.

"I think I'll stay in," Sera said quickly. "You go."

"You sure?"

"I'm sure." Sera's gave a smile. It was a little off beat, arriving after it naturally should have. "I'm a bit chilly anyway," she finished, waving her hand at her sister.

Constance hesitated. She could feel something was off—Sera's tone too soft, her gaze a little too careful. But she didn't question it.

She nodded and turned toward the door.

Behind her, Sera whispered, "Just... tell me how it feels. After."

It was late afternoon when Constance found Tempus waiting by the garden gate.

They had spoken little since the night of the hilltop. Since Sera's tears. Since the confession neither of them had really addressed.

But there he was, standing beneath the arch of flowering ivy as if he had been there all along, as if waiting for her to arrive had always been part of the day.

The garden was quiet.

The kind of quiet that invited thoughts you didn't mean to have.

He didn't ask if she wanted to walk. He didn't need to. She simply nodded once, and they began down the winding path in silence, the gravel crunching softly beneath their feet.

Tempus walked beside her, his hands clasped behind his back, commenting on the strange shape of a cloud or the scent of the late-blooming hyacinths. She answered like a well-trained echo—pleasant, appropriate, and completely borrowed.

The hedge rows loomed tall and manicured, neat in the fading light. Constance could smell the rosemary and mint brushing against her skirt as they passed.

"I think the lilies might bloom late this year," Tempus said, gesturing toward the beds lining the eastern wall.

"Mm. Maybe," Constance replied. Her eyes followed the rows of green stems. She had no opinion about lilies. But it seemed like the right sort of thing to say.

She knew he was waiting for her to say something. Something more.

And the longer she didn't answer him, the more the space stretched into something else. Something tight and pressing and quiet. Something that whispered: he's still waiting.

She didn't know how to fill the silence. Or even if she wanted to.

Instead, she wondered if Sera had meant what she'd said. Or if that moment had been a goodbye in disguise.

Other things drew her twirling thoughts in.

There had been a time—before Florence, before the estate, before the Auerelius name loomed over everything—when she might've said she wanted to be loved. When she imagined love as something like what Sera dreamt of: poems, mischief, someone who saw you clearly.

But here she was, beside someone who did love her. Someone who'd said so.

And she had felt... nothing? No, not nothing. But not what she thought she should. Not what stories said she would.

He hadn't mentioned it. And she had let the moment pass—like breath caught in the throat, never released. The silence had grown so familiar, it sat between them like a shadow neither of them dared disturb.

Why hadn't she said anything?

She turned that question over in her head like a coin she couldn't spend. It sat between them like an unopened letter.

He didn't press. He never would.

And that, somehow, made her feel worse.

She told herself she wasn't ready—but for what, she had no idea. Only that readiness sounded better than absence.

It wasn't that she didn't care.

But she didn't know how to care like he did. Not with certainty. Not with shape.

She didn't even know what she wanted—not from him, not from herself. All she had were reactions, polite ones. Behaviors learned from corridors and tutors and table settings. She had no answers, only the echo of things others thought she should be.

Did she want to love him? Maybe. Did she already? Maybe. But how could she tell if what she felt was love... or habit?

Tempus slowed near the fountain and glanced her way. "Would you like to sit for a moment?"

"No, I think I'd like to walk a little longer," Constance said, almost surprising herself.

"You seem tired today," he said gently.

"It's nothing," she replied.

And it was nothing.

That was the problem.

Sera was always feeling something. Wanting something. Fighting some imagined future.

Even when she was confused, she moved.

But Constance? Constance reacted. She agreed. She smiled. She asked how others felt and held their hands when they cried.

She was kind.

That was all anyone ever said of her.

Tempus gestured toward a trellis overtaken by vines. She nodded again.

She found herself watching the way he moved—gentle, cautious, like he was giving her space she hadn't asked for but wasn't ready to lose.

They passed beneath an arbor draped in ivy. The path turned, and the light shifted. Dapples of gold spread across the stones.

"I heard they're hosting another feast at the ducal estate this week," Tempus said lightly. "Another celebration of nothing in particular, I suspect."

"Florence does love its excuses," Constance replied, polite, almost amused.

But she wasn't really listening. Not because she didn't care. But because her mind had slipped somewhere quieter. Somewhere less rehearsed.

And even in his stillness—his patience—she felt like a vase slowly filling with water. Quiet. Pressurized. Inescapable.

They rounded a corner by the lilacs. The shade felt cooler here.

Constance's gaze dropped to the stones beneath her feet.

"I love gardens. What about you?" Tempus asked, gesturing to the hedgework. "Do you like gardens like this?"

"They're tidy," she replied.

"Is that a compliment or a complaint?"

"I'm not sure," she said honestly.

Tempus gave her a dubious look.

"They make sense," she said. "Even when nothing else does."

He chuckled, and they kept walking.

She didn't speak again. Not because she had nothing to say. But because something inside her was finally beginning to form—a feeling, raw and indistinct, that she wasn't finished becoming. Not yet.

And until she understood herself, how could she offer anything real in return?

The scent of lavender and rosemary drifted around them.

She didn't know what she liked. That thought settled over her like the sun slipping behind a cloud. Not in a tragic way. Not self-pitying. Just—true.

She had never chosen anything. Not really.

Dresses. Tutors. Manners. Paths.

Love.

She loved Tempus, didn't she?

Or did she simply not know how to respond to being loved?

Was that love? Or habit?

She blinked, suddenly unsure why her chest felt tight.

Tempus said something about the vines overtaking the trellis, and she nodded again, not hearing a word of it. Her thoughts spiraling to that hilltop.

He had said the words—and she had said... nothing. Not rejection. Not acceptance. Just absence.

Not because she didn't care. But because she didn't know how to meet the weight of it. Not then. Not now.

The late afternoon light skimmed across the garden path, pooling gold between the hedgerows and dappling the stone benches with patterns of shadow. Constance walked slowly beside Tempus, the hem of her dress whispering against lavender and rosemary as they passed.

Her mind had slipped somewhere else—somewhere quieter. Somewhere less rehearsed.

Tempus was still waiting.

Not on the food.

Not on the conversation.

On her.

She'd spoken. But not with meaning. Not with the part of herself he was waiting to hear from. And he hadn't pressed her. That was how he was.

But even the stillness of his waiting made her feel like she was standing in a room filling with water. Slowly. Inescapably.

"We should host something of our own," Tempus said idly. "For your birthday, perhaps. Something small."

"Maybe," Constance murmured, fingers brushing the tips of the hedge.

What did she want?

Not in the future. Not as escape. Just here. Just now.

And why was it so hard to answer that question?

She had no dreams. Not ones that belonged to her. And until this very moment, she hadn't even noticed their absence.

That was the worst part. Not that she was lost—but that she hadn't realized she was wandering.

They passed a fountain. Birds chirped in the branches. A soft mist drifted across the hedge line.

"I think I'd like to sit," she said suddenly, gesturing toward a bench half-shadowed by cypress.

Tempus nodded, no questions asked. He followed her to the bench, and they settled in side by side.

A servant's laugh drifted faintly from the courtyard. Somewhere nearby, the faint splash of a fountain marked time.

It's quiet. Twilight settled. A thin mist rises from the garden hedges. The scent of cypress and rose hangs heavy. Lanterns have just been lit around the perimeter, casting the paths in soft gold.

"It's always quieter here at dusk," Constance said, fingers trailing along the edge of the hedge. "Like the garden's holding its breath."

"I like the quiet," he said.

"So do I." She paused. "But sometimes I wonder if I like it because it lets me avoid saying anything."

He glanced at her. "What would you say, if the quiet didn't take it from you?"

She smiled faintly, eyes still on the path. "I don't know. That's the problem."

The silence returned. Quieter than usual, even with the breeze stirring the hedges and the distant clang of the estate's wrought-iron gate being closed for the night. But not unkind.

"You're quiet tonight," Tempus said.

Constance glanced up, smiled slightly. "So are you."

A pause.

"Do you think," she began, her voice barely louder than the breeze, "that people always know who they are?"

Tempus looked at her.

"I don't mean in the grand sense," she added quickly. "Just... do you think they notice when something is missing from inside themselves?"

He was quiet for a moment longer than she expected. Then:

"Sometimes I think people only notice what's missing once they see someone who has it."

Constance nodded, slowly. "That sounds like envy."

"Or awe," he said.

She stopped walking. Looked up at the sky. "Sera talks about the life she wants. Her own house. A strange husband. Sad poetry."

He chuckled gently.

"But I don't know if I've ever thought about what I want," she said. "Not in that way. I always assumed my life would... arrive. That it would be given. And I'd say 'thank you,' and step into it. Like a dress you wear on a wedding day."

She turned to him. "Is that strange?"

Tempus looked as if he wanted to say yes. But he didn't. "I think it's how most people live. Until they don't."

Constance looked away. "I think I'm afraid I'm only real when someone looks at me. When someone needs me. If no one did... I don't know who I'd be."

She felt like she ought to say something. But nothing that came to mind felt... real. Everything felt rehearsed. Like answering a question she hadn't asked herself yet.

"It's lovely out tonight," she said finally, and hated herself for the uselessness of it.

Tempus offered a small smile. "It is."

Another silence.

"Did you mean what you said?"

The question made her pulse jump, but she didn't flinch. If anything, she felt proud for asking. That was something.

"About... love?" Tempus's voice was gentle. He didn't sound regretful. Just cautious.

She nodded.

Tempus hesitated, then said, "I don't know. Maybe I did. Maybe I didn't."

Constance punched him in the arm. Tempus laughed lightly.

"I haven't answered you," she said quietly, after a long pause. "That night... when you said what you said."

Tempus didn't look at her. "I wasn't waiting for an answer," he lied gently.

She turned her head. "But I was. I've been waiting for one from myself. I just didn't know it."

A silence.

"After our parents died... everything just moved," she said. "We were told what to wear. What to say. Where to live. And I kept doing the next thing. Because it was expected. Because it was easier than falling apart."

She touched a flower beside the bench.

"I didn't stop to think about what I felt. I didn't ask myself what I wanted. I didn't know I was allowed to."

Another silence.

"And then you said those words. You said you loved me. And all I could think was..."

She faltered.

"Why didn't I feel ready to answer you? Why did I feel like I was caught in someone else's dream?"

Her eyes met his.

"I care about you, Tempus. Truly. But I'm only just realizing I don't know how to... return something I never learned how to hold."

She looked away again.

"I think I've lived a life of being loved. Not of loving. Not with understanding. Not with intention."

She swallowed.

"That's not a rejection. It's just... the first honest thing I've said about love. And maybe the first honest thing I've said about myself."

They sat in quiet.

Not comfortable.

Not broken.

Just... quiet.

And in that thought, she realized: She thought she was saying no. But maybe she'd just never seen what yes looked like.

Constance folded her hands in her lap, gaze distant.

'I will answer him. Not today. Not yet. But soon. And when I do—it will be real. Because I will know what I'm offering. And what I am not.'

And in the weight of that thought, she found something she hadn't felt in a long time:

A beginning.

Not of love.

Of self.

They started back to the main house in comfortable quiet.

Then, Constance said, "Sometimes I think it's easier to be wanted than it is to want."

Tempus tilted his head slightly. "What do you mean?"

She laughed, soft and strange. "I mean I've never asked myself how I feel—not really. People love me. That's always been enough. So I just... let them."

She wasn't sure why she'd said it. Maybe because it was dark. Maybe because he wouldn't push.

Maybe because it felt like the first thing she'd said that was entirely her own.

Tempus reached out and gently brushed a stray wisp of hair from her cheek. "You don't have to answer anything now."

"That's just it," she said quietly. "I don't know what I'd say if I did."

Then, as they neared the white arbor, Constance turned and smiled at Tempus. She walked a little farther, hands clasped behind her. Head held high.

Her mind raced with the thought that her story was her own. For now.

"I'll tell you my answer," she said, half-smiling, "when ivy grows in the moonlight."

Tempus imagined the smile he knew was on her face. The one he'd barely caught a glimpse of before she turned away. Her laughing softly with a sound like little bells.

He walked into the kitchen to find her sitting there. Comfortable. As if there was more time left in this minute than there had been when a minute had first been envisioned. There were no extra seconds, but you couldn't tell her that.

Despite that, she looked comfortable. A cup of coffee was in her hands. Her jeans fit just right. Maybe they had been measured, cut, and sewn specially for her, even though they came off the rack. Her top? A simple t-shirt. Plain. Unadorned. Reminding him much of how she cherished the idea of makeup to beautify. Not necessary.

Her hair was pulled back in a bun and her features set. Not stone like. Soft still. But not welcoming. Not that she was refusing company, just not actively inviting it.

Any other day, she would have been dressed more comfortably. One of his shirts, maybe. Definitely. Nothing else but what was necessary for modesty beneath it.

A small line. A crack. It seemed to be just there at the corner of her chin. A slight thing.

How long had it been there, he wondered. He closed his eyes. He shook his head to dismiss the sight. The line was gone when he opened his eyes again.

The thought that this was something new occurred to him briefly.

He was paused at the doorway while he stared. A moment more, he was seated beside her at the kitchen counter. She glanced at him. A passing thing. Not critical, more of an acknowledgement. His own features appearing worn in to her. His contenance looking as if grief had set in to stay permanently. A new home. Bought. Paid for. A tenant refusing to leave.

"You told me..." he began. His voice trailed off.

She, in her manner, shifted in her seat and leaned over to kiss him on the cheek. He slipped away. The distance not great, but enough that the affection missed. It landed... somewhere, where it did. But not where it was supposed to.

Without feeling slighted, she stood. Stretched. She headed to the door to leave, taking the feeling of her warm presence with her. When she got to the door, she looked back. Once. Briefly.

Her mouth moved. She was saying something. He could see the shape of the words. He just couldn't hear them. He watched as her lip's spread wide, pursed together and opened again once more.

He could barely hear her. It was too loud. The AC compressor on the refrigerator kicked on. The microwave beeped. The static on the flickering TV at just the right decibels.

He didn't need to hear the words. He knew what had been said lovingly.

The line now presented by her lips formed what should have been a ritualistic expression she'd always shown. The sorrow of that smile showed through the lie it told of being happy.

When the door closed behind her, he sat there. Still. Unmoving. The air of the apartment felling into the stillness and staleness that could no longer be masked.

Now, this was right now.

He looked down at the dusty cup that had been left behind. It was empty, of course. Dry. Debris collected in the well because it had been left neglected. He hadn't wanted to put it away.

He started. His hands came to his face. His body shook.

"You told me you were coming back. You lied to me. You said you'd never leave."

That door hadn't opened in a long time.

Chapter 5: "Shadows of Pursuit"

Present Day - London, England

Fleeing from relentless pursuit, a perilous journey unfolds.

Tempus awoke to the muted hum of London's early morning traffic filtering through the large window of his lavish hotel room. Sunlight, softened by sheer curtains, painted gentle patterns on the lacquered wooden floor. Without thinking, his hand drifted to the nightstand, fingers brushing the cool surface of an old locket.

He picked it up, the metal warming in his palm, and slowly opened it to reveal the faces of two identical women, their stunning beauty frozen in time. Twins. Memories flooded back—laughter, love, a life he could never return to. A life lost to the sands of 12th-century Florence. His heart ached with longing and regret, a sharp reminder of what once was and what could never be again.

Tempus lay there, the locket open in his hand, staring at their faces. Questions of existence and purpose swirled in his mind. What did his life mean now? Was there a purpose to this endless march of days, haunted by the ghosts of his past? He sighed deeply, feeling the familiar melancholy settle over him like a shroud.

After what felt like an eternity, he reluctantly closed the locket and placed it back on the nightstand. "Just another day," he whispered to the empty room, the words hollow and unconvincing. Slowly, he swung his legs over the side of the bed and pushed himself up.

In the bathroom, his reflection greeted him with tired eyes, mirrors to the soul suppressed by centuries of the human condition. Guilt and betrayal, anger and jealousy, hatred and fear. "You can't change the past," he reminded himself, his voice barely more than a murmur as he brushed his teeth. "But you can control today."

He rinsed his mouth, the routine motions offering a small semblance of normalcy. Yet, as he stared at his reflection, he knew today would be no different from the countless yesterdays. Still, he went on, driven by the hope that perhaps one day, the seemingly infinite string mornings might finally stop.

As he dressed in his tailored suit, one of many hanging in his closet, he couldn't help but feel hollow inside. To him, it felt like his clothes draped a hanger still, only passing over his form in a perfunctory manner that seemed ill-fitting despite the immaculate cut.

This day, being like any other in a long list of days, seemed to be no different from the onset. Tempus sighed. His feet shifted mechanically to propel him on his way to sameness.

By noon, Tempus found himself at his favorite café, a small, tucked-away spot in Soho. The barista, an older woman named Margaret, greeted him with a warm smile.

"Morning, Tempus. The usual?" she asked, already preparing his black coffee.

"Morning, Margaret. Yes, please," he replied, scanning the room out of habit. Eons of living had ingrained a deep sense of vigilance in him.

Margaret placed the steaming cup in front of him. "You look tired. Everything alright?"

Tempus managed a faint smile. "Just didn't sleep well. Too much on my mind, I guess." He yearned for someone to understand his burden, but he wasn't willing to risk it. Not again.

Margaret nodded sympathetically. "Well, take care of yourself, dear. Life's too short to spend it worrying."

The irony of her words wasn't lost on Tempus. She, with her brief lifespan, couldn't fathom just how interminable life could become—almost to the point of losing meaning.

He thanked her, refraining from sharing his bleak perspective, and carried his coffee to a secluded corner table. There, he pulled out a worn journal and began to jot down notes. Yet, an unsettling sensation lingered. He felt eyes on him, an invisible gaze that kept him on edge. He glanced up occasionally, his eyes darting to the entrance and scanning the windows.

Just paranoia, he tried to convince himself, though his instincts suggested otherwise. Centuries of existence had taught him not to ignore such warnings.

As the day ebbed away, Tempus retraced his steps towards the hotel he presently called home. The streets bustled with the evening rush, a symphony of hurried footsteps and distant chatter. Despite the throng, Tempus maintained a measured pace, his eyes vigilant, scanning his surroundings.

The sense of unease lingered from earlier, a nagging intuition that refused to dissipate. His gaze caught a utility van, inconspicuous to most, yet glaringly out of place to him. It wasn't just a vehicle; it felt like a warning sign in the urban landscape, a signal of impending danger.

"Damn," he muttered quietly, his jaw tightening. He paused briefly, assessing the situation, before resolutely turning away and striding in the opposite direction.

But evasion proved futile. A shadow in a dark suit materialized behind him, matching his pace with an eerie precision. Tempus's heart remained steady, a testament to his seasoned composure. This wasn't the first time he'd felt the weight of someone's gaze on his back.

"Stay calm," he coached himself inwardly. "It could be nothing." Yet, deep down, he knew better than to dismiss the signs of impending trouble.

While he clung to hope for a better outcome, Tempus recognized the falsehood in his optimism. He refused to succumb to anger, though the situation grated on him. To be discovered yet again after so many years, forcing him to abandon his current life and begin anew elsewhere, was a bitter pill to swallow. Yet, acceptance was his only recourse, a means of preserving his safety by keeping his distance.

Turning a corner, he increased his pace, stealing a glance over his shoulder. The figure persisted, now accompanied by another. Definitely not nothing.

Tempus slipped into an alley, hastening his steps without resorting to a full sprint. The echoes of pursuit reverberated behind him, the thunderous footfalls of his pursuers seemingly closing in.

Though he knew it was a mere trick of his mind, the illusion served as effective motivation. It spurred him to leave the streets behind, seeking refuge in the alleyways to gather his bearings.

Navigating the labyrinthine alleys of London, Tempus moved with purpose, his surroundings blurring into a whirlwind of motion. His stride was swift enough to create distance from his pursuers, yet cautious enough to evade attracting unwanted attention. This wasn't his first dance with danger; he'd dodged their grasp twice before already during this pursuit, each time elongating the interval before their inevitable reunion.

As he pressed forward, their voices became discernible, barking commands in pursuit. His mind raced, strategizing his next move with calculated precision.

Emerging onto an open street, he weaved through the bustling traffic towards the nearest subway entrance on the opposite side. The clamor and commotion of the station offered a fleeting refuge. With practiced nonchalance, he navigated the turnstiles and descended onto the platform just as a train pulled into the station.

Slipping inside, Tempus pressed against the carriage wall, watching intently through the window as his pursuers stormed onto the platform, their frustration palpable amidst the throng of commuters.

Tempus exhaled, a fleeting sense of relief washing over him. Yet, he remained acutely aware that this was just one victory in a protracted struggle.

As the train rumbled through the city, his thoughts drifted to Constance. What would she make of his tumultuous existence? Would she comprehend the decisions he was forced to make?

His reverie was shattered by the insistent buzz of his phone, yanking him back to reality. An ominous message from an unknown sender flashed across the screen: "You can't run forever, Tempus. Ridge will find you."

His fingers tightened around the device. "I can try," he countered softly, a defiant spark igniting within him. Glancing around the carriage, his eyes settled on an open window, a narrow portal to freedom. Without hesitation, he slipped the phone through the gap, severing the digital tether that bound him.

There was little point in pondering how they had acquired the phone number. Engaging in such speculation would only lead to fruitless circles of thought. If they had managed to uncover his current identity after all these years, obtaining his phone number likely posed little challenge.

With a sigh, Tempus retrieved the locket from his pocket, its weight a comforting presence in his hand. He clicked it open, revealing the image of the women within. A wistful smile tugged at his lips as he gazed at the familiar faces, his memories woven into the delicate metal.

With a soft click, he closed the locket, returning it to its place. Leaning his forehead against the cool glass of the window, he turned his attention to the passing scenery outside, seeking solace in the fleeting moments of tranquility amidst the monotonous chaos of his existence.

As the train approached the next station, Tempus prepared to disembark. His journey wasn't over. The shadows of pursuit were always close, but so was his determination to stay out of their reach.

Stepping off the train, he melted into the crowd. For now, it was enough to know he had survived another day.

It was well into early evening as Tempus made his way back to the café, the familiar glow of its lights beckoning him like a beacon in the gathering dusk. Margaret greeted him with a warm smile as he approached the counter.

"Evening, Tempus. Back for another cup?" she asked, her eyes reflecting genuine concern.

Tempus returned her smile, though it didn't quite reach his eyes. "Actually, Margaret, I need to borrow your phone for a moment. It's urgent."

Margaret's brow furrowed in concern, but she nodded, reaching for her phone beneath the counter. "Of course, Tempus. Here you go."

Tempus dialed a number from memory, his expression grave as he waited for the call to connect. When the line finally clicked, he wasted no time getting to the point.

"I need to initiate the scheduled contingency plan," he said tersely. "Where do I pick up my new items?"

The voice on the other end responded with an address, and Tempus nodded in acknowledgment before ending the call. He turned back to Margaret, a somber look in his eyes.

"I have to go," he said, his voice heavy with resignation. "But before I leave, I owe you a new phone."

Margaret's eyes widened in surprise, but before she could protest, Tempus pressed a wad of bills into her hand.

"Consider it a thank you for everything," he said softly, his gaze lingering on her for a moment longer before turning towards the door, her phone still in hand.

As he reached the threshold, he deposited Margeret's phone into a nearby pitcher of water.

Margaret gasped in shock, her mouth forming a silent 'O' as she watched Tempus exit the café without looking back. She was left speechless, unsure how to react to the unexpected turn of events, but a sense of unease lingered in the air long after he was gone.

Tempus stood outside an unassuming restaurant on the outskirts of the city, the address from the call leading him here. The area was moderately affluent and bustling, with the distant hum of traffic and the occasional chirp of a night bird filling the air. He took a deep breath, steeling himself before pushing open the door.

The maître d' looked up from his podium. "Will you be dining alone, sir?" he asked perfunctorily.

Tempus's expression remained neutral as he glanced past the man into the restaurant's interior. Despite it being dinner time, the place wasn't crowded, likely due to it being the middle of the week.

"I'll have a table by the back window and the steak tartare," Tempus said.

The maître d's eyes widened slightly before he came around from behind the podium. "This way, sir," he said, guiding Tempus past the regular dining area and into the back of the establishment. He led Tempus to a small, dimly lit room that served as a combination office and storage space.

Inside, the office was dimly lit, shadows flickering in the corners. A single lamp illuminated the desk, casting a warm glow over the cluttered surface. Tempus's eyes quickly adjusted to the gloom as he navigated past a row of stacked crates and crowded shelves before taking the only chair in front of the desk.

In the center of the desk, under the pool of light, lay a new identity package: passport, credit cards, a phone, keys to a new car, and keys to a safe house.

Behind the desk sat Elias, an older man with a stern but familiar face. Elias was the one responsible for Tempus's contingency plans in this area.

"You're late, sir," Elias said without preamble, his voice echoing slightly in the confined space.

"Got held up," Tempus replied, his gaze drifting over the items on the table. "Is everything here?"

Elias nodded. "Everything you need for the new identity, sir."

Tempus's jaw tightened at the mention of a new identity. This wouldn't have to keep happening if I'd just kept my damn mouth shut in the past, he thought to himself. He sighed, pushing the self-reproach aside.

"Thanks for your hard work," Tempus said softly, reaching out to inspect the items. The passport felt crisp and new in his hands, a stark contrast to his weary soul. The credit cards were sleek and unmarked, and the phone was a model he hadn't used before.

Elias handed him a folder. "This has all the details of your new life. And here," he pointed to a small duffel bag on the floor, "are some essentials to get you started."

Tempus took the folder, flipping through the documents inside. His expression was a mix of anger and resignation. He was weary of the constant need to run and change his identity, a never-ending cycle of reinvention.

"Thanks, Elias," he said, his voice tinged with bitterness.

Elias nodded before getting up and taking his leave. Tempus watched the man go. That was just the nature of Tempus's life.

Tempus sighed, his mind racing with thoughts of his past. He could have easily hired individuals to keep him safe; that wouldn't have been an issue at all. He had the means.

Some men sought power. Some men sought wealth. Tempus had an overwhelming abundance of both. It was enough to leverage influence over a small country like San Marino. From this country, acting as a member of its consulate staff, he had access to resources just about anyone would dream of having.

Despite all that, it was impossible for him to hire others to help protect him. First off, he'd never be able to adequately explain why their employer never seemed to age. That single point was the very reason he was being chased in the first place.

"You have the resources, Tempus. You could disappear completely, start fresh somewhere new. Why not take that chance?" Tempus asked himself aloud.

Tempus shook his head. "It's not that simple. No matter where I go, they'll find me. They always do. It's my burden to bear."

Tempus picked up the duffel bag and slung it over his shoulder, feeling his new life pressing down on him already. The bag was full of clothing. It would suffice until he could rebuild his wardrobe.

As Tempus turned to leave, he paused at the door, glancing back at the dimly lit office. The desk, now clear, reminded him of how it looked when he first entered, laden with his new items. He sighed, the weight of his past and future pressing heavily on him. "Maybe one day, I'll be able to stop running," he murmured to himself.

With that, he stepped out into the cool night air, the folder and duffel bag in hand. The city stretched out before him, a maze of possibilities and dangers. He knew the path ahead wouldn't be easy.

Before he'd taken a dozen steps down the sidewalk, a shiver ran up his spine. A sense of dread washed over him. He looked up at the new moon, just beginning to make its presence known. A new sense of purpose drove him forward now. That shiver—it was familiar, an old acquaintance that signaled fate had placed its hand squarely upon him.

He reached into his pocket and pulled out the locket, flipping open the cover to reveal the familiar faces inside. "I guess that means it's time we met each other again, Constance," he whispered, a mix of acceptance and resignation in his voice.

With reluctance to face the future, Tempus continued down the street. Above him, the sky darkened, a foreboding promise of impending rain.

Upon reaching his new abode, Tempus navigated the unfamiliar layout to the bedroom with weary feet. Dropping his duffel bag to the floor, he shed his outer layers. He slipped into bed, grateful for the furnished room and the solace it offered.

As he lay beneath the covers, exhaustion consumed him, dragging his eyelids shut. The rhythm of the rain against the windowpane lulled him into a fitful slumber, his mind swirling with fragments of past and present.

The dream unfolded with eerie simplicity, transporting Tempus to a dimly lit office that stirred a sense of unsettling familiarity within him.

As he gazed out through the discolored and uneven glass, he beheld the sights of an early evening, raindrops dancing against the windowpane in a melancholic rhythm. Tempus found himself thrust back into the Victorian Era, though the precise date eluded his grasp amidst the fog of memory.

A surge of resentment coursed through him, mingling with the weariness that had long since settled around his heart like an impenetrable barrier. The monotony of endless days melding into nights had left its mark, eroding his once vibrant spirit and leaving behind a hollow shell of discontent.

His body felt leaden, burdened by the weight of his perpetual existence, while his senses dulled under the oppressive specter of time. In that moment, Tempus longed for nothing more than an escape from the relentless cycle of repetition that had come to define the totality of his existence.

Tempus sat across from Harlan Ridge, surrounded by stacks of papers and the faint scent of cigar smoke lingering in the air. They were business partners, their collaboration spanning years of shared successes and failures.

Harlan, was a sharp-eyed man with a calculating demeanor. He leaned forward in his chair, his gaze fixed intently on Tempus. "I can't help but notice, Tempus, that despite the passage of time, you still look remarkably young. How do you explain that?"

Tempus hesitated. He had kept his secret hidden for so long, but the lonesome burden of immortality grew heavier with each passing tic of the clock. And now, faced with Harlan's probing question, he felt an overwhelming urge to confide in someone, to share the truth that had been locked away inside him for far too long.

There was a moment where he considered what it might mean to share his burden with someone else. Maybe, if he dared, he could have someone to share the loneliness with. At least for a while.

"I am immortal," Tempus said, his voice barely above a whisper. "I've walked this earth for centuries, cursed with a life that knows no end."

Harlan's eyes widen in disbelief, his mind struggling to comprehend the enormity of Tempus's revelation. "Immortal?" he repeated, his voice tinged with incredulity. "Surely you jest, Tempus. Such things belong in the realm of fantasy, not reality."

Tempus maintained a resolute expression, his gaze steady and unwavering. "I speak the truth, Harlan. My existence is a perpetual jest, subject to the caprices of fate and liberated from the constraints of mortality."

Harlan struggled to comprehend Tempus's assertion. "Surely, immortality would be a gift, wouldn't it?"

"How so?" Tempus countered, his tone grave. "It's a curse imposed upon me by forces beyond my control."

"But the prospect of eternal life..." Harlan trailed off, still grappling with disbelief. Though he couldn't entirely dismiss Tempus's claims; after all, he had known him for years, yet the passage of time seemed to leave no mark on the man. Meanwhile, Harlan keenly felt the toll of years, exacerbated by the incessant rain drumming against the windowpane.

"Are you being earnest with me?" Harlan pressed, a note of urgency creeping into his voice, craving validation.

Tempus nodded solemnly, confirming his sincerity.

As the truth sunk in, Harlan's disbelief gave way to a different emotion—an overwhelming desire to defy the natural order, to transcend the limitations of mortality and seize the power of immortality for himself. The heft of Tempus's revelation bore down on Harlan, igniting a tumultuous storm of thoughts within him. The mere notion of immortality sparked a fervent desire, kindling a flame within him. Yet, to some observers, it wasn't a flame of ambition but rather the repugnant mask of greed. Though Harlan didn't openly express it, the twisted contours of his features betrayed the grotesque allure of his newfound obsession.

"You must reveal the secret, Tempus," Harlan insisted, urgency lacing his voice as he leaned forward across the desk, threatening to disturb the neatly arranged papers.

Tempus was taken aback by Harlan's demand. It was certainly not the reaction he had anticipated. In response, he shifted uneasily in his seat, fixing Harlan with an intense gaze. "What secret?" Tempus countered, his tone edged with disbelief. "I have no clue how this came to pass. Who would desire to endure an eternity, witnessing all they hold dear crumble to dust?"

"You can't keep such knowledge from me. Think of what I..." Harlan paused, then leaned back in his chair, slowing down his pace of speech. "...what we could achieve together, the power we could wield if only I knew the truth," he corrected, his tone veering from eager to contemplative.

Tempus recoiled at Harlan's words, the weight of his burden pressing down upon him like an insurmountable weight. "I cannot grant your request, Harlan," he replied, his voice heavy with regret. "My immortality is not a gift to be shared, but a curse. Something I've endured alone."

Harlan's desperation grew with each passing moment, his obsession with Tempus's secret consuming him like a flame devouring dry tinder. He couldn't fathom why anyone wouldn't want to live forever. The ability to accumulate wealth indefinitely, to gain unparalleled power over others, to indulge in every conceivable pleasure—these thoughts made his mouth water. His mind raced with fantasies of eternal nights filled with intimate encounters, a life where nothing ever ended.

A slimy smile crept across his face, desire twisting his features into something grotesque. "You've lived forever? For how long? When were you born?" Harlan's questions came in rapid succession, each one more insistent than the last. He was driven by a fervent need to uncover what he felt Tempus was unjustly withholding from him. The thirst for immortality consumed him, brushing aside all remnants of reason.

"I tell you, Harlan, living forever is not as wonderful as you think. In the end, nothing remains but you, alone," Tempus said, trying to quell the growing desire he saw in his friend's eyes.

"You're lying. You just want to keep the knowledge to yourself," Harlan accused, his tone sharp and accusatory.

Tempus couldn't believe his friend would slander him like that. He had never lied to Harlan, trusting him implicitly in all matters regarding their business. He had hoped for the same trust in return.

"I swear to you, I know nothing of how this came about. But I tell you now, it's a gift I would give my life to rid myself of," Tempus insisted, his voice heavy with sincerity and regret.

Harlan rose from his seat, his hands dropping heavily onto the dense wooden desk between them. "I thought better of you, Tempus. You have this wonderful gift, and you won't share it with me?"

He stood up straight, holding out his hands for Tempus to see. "Look at this," he declared, displaying the age spots. His hands began to tremble. "I can't even pick up a quill and write properly because of the shaking. Your immortality can save me. It can make me never grow older, and you won't tell me how you came about this?"

Tempus's mouth opened and then shut, his heart breaking. He had tried to confide in someone to alleviate the torment of the loneliness brought on by his unwanted longevity, only to be accused of lying. He had hoped it wasn't too much to ask fate for a shoulder to lean on, someone to confide in, a confidant to give him support. But it was too much to ask.

Harlan pleaded and cajoled, his words growing increasingly frantic as he sought to extract the secret of immortality from Tempus. Desperation etched his face as he tried to break through what he perceived as Tempus's unwillingness to share.

But Tempus remained steadfast. His decision was made; he would forever have to bear this burden alone, relying on his own strength. With a heavy heart, he rose from his chair and made his way to the door, leaving Harlan behind in the dimly lit office, consumed by his obsession.

As Tempus stepped into the damp night air, his soul felt even heavier. The rain had slowed but still persisted, quickly dampening his hair. Small rivulets ran down his cheeks. Tempus wanted to lie to himself that it was just rain trickling from his head. He wanted to lie—but he didn't.

The next day, Tempus awoke but did not head down to the office he shared with Harlan. The memory of their encounter lingered like a ghost, haunting his thoughts and casting a pall over his soul. He spent most of the day sitting in his home, lost in his troubled thoughts.

In the afternoon, a group of men appeared at his door. After a brief exchange, Tempus learned they were in Harlan's employ. Harlan had sent them to collect him and bring him back.

As if from a distance, Tempus heard the faint sound of his own voice, calling out in the darkness, pleading for release from the nightmare that plagued him.

With a start, Tempus awoke from his troubled sleep, his heart pounding in his chest as he struggled to shake off the lingering remnants of his dream. The room was bathed in darkness, the only sound the soft patter of rain against the windowpanes.

Tempus's fingers found the small lump of metal resting on his chest, its chill seeping into the warmth of his palm. Its weight served as an anchor, grounding him in the reality of wakefulness. With a firm grip, he affirmed his consciousness, drawing strength from the tangible connection to his past.

As he forced his eyes to open, the remnants of dreams faded into the recesses of his mind. Yet, the weight of his reality remained, pressing against his chest like an unyielding burden. Despite his efforts to calm his racing heart, Tempus knew the nightmare was far from over. Harlan's relentless pursuit of his secret continued unabated through his progeny, a threat that loomed over Tempus like a shadow, waiting to consume him whole.

Chapter 6: "Confessions"

Present Day - Atlanta, USA
Unveiling buried memories, a revelation brings forth inner turmoil.

Constance led the way with purpose, striding down the sidewalk as the early evening crowd thinned, making their path to their destination clear. Sera trailed behind, her steps hesitant, her mood not quite aligning with the idea of a dinner date for the girls.

Glancing back, Constance offered her sister a warm smile seemingly in a cheerful mood, despite her own reservations about where her relationship with William was heading. Though Sera tried to reciprocate her sister's energy, she couldn't mask her unease as effectively. Unlike Constance, she couldn't simply push her concerns aside.

Still, for her sister's sake, Sera managed a cautious but willing smile, hoping not to dampen Constance's spirits with her own worries.

"Come on, slowpoke," Constance called back teasingly. "Lynette just texted me; she's waiting at the door."

"Oh, great," Sera muttered dryly, lacking any hint of enthusiasm.

Constance halted abruptly, almost causing a collision with her sister. Sera stopped short, peering at her sister with a questioning expression.

"Are you alright? You seem a bit distant," Constance inquired, concern flickering in her eyes.

Sera waved her hand dismissively. "Just some career thoughts swirling around," she fibbed, forcing a smile. "Nothing to fret over."

She made a concerted effort to conceal her concerns, linking her arm with her sister's and forging ahead towards their destination. "Let's go. I'm famished."

Constance scoffed. "Consider yourself lucky we're dining out tonight. Otherwise, we'd be facing another one of your culinary experiments, and I'd have to play savior again just so we can eat something edible."

As they reached the restaurant door, Lynette, having caught wind of their banter, greeted them with a warm smile and a hug.

Resuming their earlier conversation, Sera glanced at Constance. "My cooking isn't that bad."

"Yeah, if you enjoy a trip to the ER," Lynette chimed in, eliciting giggles from both her and Constance.

Sera, wearing an expression of mild irritation, stepped up to defend her culinary prowess. "My food is at least edible."

"Barely," Constance interjected, her tone teasingly skeptical. "And that's being generous."

Sera's hands found their way to her hips, her lower lip jutting out in a gesture of defiance as she let out an exasperated sigh.

"Let's not debate it further," Lynette interjected with a chuckle, looping her arms through those of the other two women and guiding them into the restaurant.

They were swiftly ushered to their seats, menus in hand, eagerly awaiting the waiter's arrival to take their orders.

"Man, look at these prices," Lynette exclaimed, eyeing the menu incredulously.

"At least they're transparent about it," Constance remarked. "If they weren't, we'd be running for the nearest fast-food joint."

Sera, seemingly detached from the conversation, chimed in with a disinterested tone, reassuring her sister and friend, "I invited you both out. Don't worry about the cost. It's on me."

"Ah, look at the generosity from 'Miss Thing' here," Lynette teased, her voice dripping with theatricality. "Big shot now you got a major motion picture under your belt, huh?"

Constance chuckled lightly, but Sera felt a pang of guilt as she realized she hadn't been fully engaged in their banter. She chided herself for the oversight. Lately, she had been increasingly preoccupied with resurfacing memories, struggling to reconcile her past with her present reality.

"That's not it. It's..." Sera began, her voice trailing off. She didn't want to delve into the memories, not yet, especially not with Lynette. This was a matter for her and Constance alone. Sensing that she had paused too long, she swiftly changed the subject. "The final scenes for the film will be shot in the next few weeks. I thought we could celebrate before production wraps up and moves into post-production."

"That's fantastic news, kiddo," Lynette exclaimed, her enthusiasm palpable. Then, turning to Constance, she added, "Speaking of disappearing acts, you vanished during our breakfast the other day. What gives?"

Constance's demeanor shifted, her festive mood dampened by memories of more recent events. She had not only left their breakfast abruptly but had also walked out on William afterward, leaving their relationship in uncertain territory.

"William asked her to move in with him," Sera revealed, breaking the tension.

Lynette's jaw dropped in surprise, her eyes wide with astonishment.

"Sera," Constance interjected, her tone a mix of exasperation and amusement.

"What?" Sera shrugged. "It's not like it's a state secret."

Constance felt a pang of guilt. Sera was right; she hadn't intended to keep William's proposal under wraps, but she hadn't fully processed it herself. Now that Lynette knew, she knew there would be questions.

"So, spill the beans," Lynette prompted, propping her chin on her hand, her elbow resting on the table. She fixed Constance with an intense gaze, making her feel like she was under interrogation.

Constance began to respond, but her thoughts were interrupted by the arrival of the waiter. She silently thanked whatever stroke of luck had brought him at that moment. It was a welcome reprieve, giving her a chance to collect her thoughts before facing Lynette's inquiries again.

As the waiter retreated, Constance exhaled a silent sigh of relief, grateful for the momentary distraction. However, her respite was short-lived as Lynette leaned in, her eyes probing.

"So, spill it, Constance," Lynette demanded in a low voice, her curiosity palpable. "What's the deal with you and William?"

Constance fidgeted with her napkin, her mind racing. She didn't want to delve into the complexities of her relationship with William. But Lynette's persistence left her little choice.

"It's nothing, really," Constance deflected, her words lacking conviction as she glossed over the details. "He just asked me to move in with him out of the blue. I'm still figuring things out."

Lynette's expression softened, her tone gentle. "Hey, it's okay to take your time, Constance. These things aren't easy. Just trust your instincts."

As they finished their meal, Sera's distracted demeanor didn't go unnoticed by either Constance or Lynette. She kept glancing over her shoulder, eyes lingering on the bar. Her unspoken worries crowded the space between them, casting a shadow over their evening.

"Are you alright, Sera?" Constance asked, concern etching her features.

Sera forced a smile, though it didn't quite reach her eyes. "I'm fine, just tired."

Sensing that Sera needed space, Constance and Lynette exchanged a knowing glance. It was clear that Sera wasn't fully present.

"We should call it a night," Lynette suggested gently, rising from her seat. Constance followed suit shortly thereafter.

"You're right," Constance agreed, turning her attention to her sister who remained seated. "Ready to head out, Sera?"

Caught off guard, Sera paused mid-turn, her brow furrowing in confusion. Shaking off her distraction, she pieced together her sister's question. "I'll grab a shared ride home, Connie," she replied, though her response sounded more automatic than intentional.

Worry flickered across Constance's features as she glanced at Lynette. The concern mirrored in Lynette's expression spoke volumes—they both knew something was amiss with Sera. Yet, neither dared to broach the subject, opting to wait for Sera to confide in them when she was ready.

"Are you sure?" Constance pressed gently.

Sera shook her head. "I'll stay a bit longer," she asserted, her voice distant. "I'll catch up with you guys later."

Concern etched on their faces, Constance and Lynette reluctantly bid Sera farewell, watching as she made her way to the bar.

Seated alone on a stool at the bar, Sera's thoughts churned, her mind consumed by the returning memories. A silent question lingering in her mind. When would she tell Constance the truth? With a heavy heart, she ordered a strong drink, seeking solace in the comfort of oblivion.

Lost in her own tumultuous thoughts, Sera sought solace in the numbing embrace of alcohol. As she drowned her inner turmoil, she absentmindedly scrolled through images of exotic flowers on her phone, the vibrant colors a stark contrast to the dimly lit bar.

Startled by a familiar voice that pierced through her haze, Sera nearly toppled off her bar stool. She turned abruptly to face the source, only to find herself locking eyes with Alexander.

"Hi," Alexander greeted with a warm smile, sliding onto the bar stool beside her. "I called out to you earlier, but you seemed lost in thought."

Sera blinked, her thumb frozen mid-swipe on her phone screen as she held it limply in her hand.

"You know, you always manage to surprise me," Alexander continued, his gaze fixed on her. "I feel like I'm getting to know you more and more with each encounter."

Sera struggled to keep pace with the conversation, her senses dulled by the alcohol coursing through her veins. Alexander's sudden appearance only added to her disorientation, making it difficult for her to form a coherent response.

"What are you talking about?" Sera asked, her confusion evident as she turned to face him. In the close quarters of the bar stools, their legs brushed against each other, drawing Alexander's attention to the exposed skin beneath her miniskirt.

"I was just saying how I've noticed your diverse interests and knowledge," Alexander elaborated, sensing Sera's confusion. "You seem to have a wide range of passions, like with the costumes on set and now with botany."

Sera's brows furrowed, her expression skeptical as she tried to piece together his words amidst the haze of her thoughts.

Sera felt utterly adrift in the conversation. "Why do you think I'm interested in botany?" she asked, her confusion evident in her voice.

In response, Alexander gestured towards her phone, where her thumb still hovered over the screen. Sera followed his gaze, her eyes landing on the images of flowers displayed on the screen.

"Oh," she murmured, comprehension dawning. "I'm just searching for a particular flower," she confessed. "I've been trying to find one like the original I received ages ago, but no luck so far."

"That's interesting," Alexander replied, his tone genuinely intrigued.

A sense of relief washed over Sera as she shared her secret with Alexander. His easy acceptance and understanding seemed to lift a weight from her shoulders, temporarily easing the burden of her worries and returning memories. She found herself drawn to Alex's easy smile, the warmth of his demeanor melting away some of her anxieties.

"I dabble in amateur botany myself," Alexander offered, breaking the silence with a casual remark. "When I'm not directing, I'm usually trying to breed orchids."

"How's that going?" Sera inquired softly, turning back to face the bar but keeping her attention on Alexander.

Before Alexander could respond, he lifted his hand to catch the bartender's eye, placing a drink order. As he waited for his order to arrive, he turned his focus back to Sera. "Let's just say I'm not winning any orchid competitions anytime soon. If I want to eat, I'd better stick with producing and directing," he chuckled.

Sera found herself chuckling along, the tension easing from her shoulders despite her earlier mood. When Alexander's drink arrived, they engaged in easy conversation, discussing the film they were working on and various other topics. A sense of camaraderie settled between them as they sat together, sharing drinks and laughter.

As the crowd dwindled in the restaurant, Sera glanced around before turning her attention back to Alexander, a question bubbling up in her mind. "So, why are you here, Alex? Stalking me?" she teased, a playful glint in her eyes.

Alexander's laughter filled the air, his easy demeanor evident as he shook his head. "No, not at all," he assured her, gesturing between them with a dismissive wave. "I've been staying in this hotel since we started filming on location here in Atlanta."

Sera chuckled at her own joke, feeling a touch embarrassed for even entertaining the notion of Alexander stalking her. With the tension broken, their evening resumed its comfortable rhythm of banter and laughter.

As Alexander continued to converse with Sera, he found himself increasingly intrigued by her. Not only was she a talented actress, but she also possessed a captivating presence that drew him in. Since working together on the film, he had come to know her beyond her on-screen persona.

There was something magnetic about her, something that held his attention long after the cameras stopped rolling. And after witnessing her handling of the wardrobe mishap, he found himself paying even closer attention to the woman behind the character. Her authenticity was striking, making her even more compelling in his eyes.

But something bothered Alexander about Sera. Over the last few days, he couldn't help but notice the subtle changes in Sera's behavior. She seemed more withdrawn, often lost in thought, her usual spark dimmed by an unseen weight. On set, she maintained her professionalism, but off camera, she was distant.

Sera nursed her drink, her gaze unfocused, while Alex watched her with growing concern.

"Sera," he began gently, "I've noticed you've been different lately. Distant. Is everything okay?"

She sighed, swirling her drink before taking a sip. "It's complicated, Alex. There are things about me, about my past, that I've never told anyone."

Alexander's expression turned earnest. "Then I guess I better not pry," he jested, a playful glint in his eyes.

Sera met his gaze over the rim of her raised glass, contemplating his words. Setting her glass down gently on the bar top, she took a deep breath before speaking softly. "Do you know what the greatest lie ever told was?" she asked Alexander, her voice barely above a whisper.

Sensing that Sera might be opening up, Alexander leaned in attentively, ready to listen. Though he wasn't sure where she was headed with her question, he was certain it would lead to a deeper conversation.

"No, I have no clue. Fill me in," he replied with a warm smile, encouraging her to continue.

Straightening up on her stool, Sera began to speak, her voice steady. "The greatest lie ever told was that we have control of our own lives and fate doesn't play a role in it."

Alexander absorbed Sera's words, pondering the validity of her statement. Whether or not it held true mattered less than the fact that she believed it did.

Not expecting a response from Alexander, Sera returned her attention to her phone, scrolling through the images of flowers once more.

Curiosity piqued, Alexanderr leaned in closer, glancing at the pictures she was browsing. "Is there a particular flower you're searching for? Do you know its name?"

Sera shook her head, a hint of wistfulness in her voice. "No, I've only ever seen one of its kind in my life. I've never encountered it again."

"That seems rare," Alexander remarked, genuine curiosity coloring his tone. "So, how do you know what you're looking for? Do you remember details about its appearance?"

Pausing in her scrolling, Sera glanced at Alexander, silently assessing his sincerity. The earnestness in his expression convinced her he wasn't just engaging in idle conversation. With a nod, she refocused her attention on her phone, closing the app she had been browsing. After a moment, she located a picture and handed the phone to him.

"This is the flower I've been searching for," she explained softly. "I can't seem to find it anywhere."

Accepting the phone, Alexander examined the image closely, his thumb and forefinger deftly pinching the screen to zoom in on the intricate details of the painting.

"Where did you get this painting?" Alexander asked, clearly taken aback by its beauty. He looked up at Sera, awaiting her response with genuine curiosity.

Sera smiled softly. "I guess you've stumbled upon another one of my talents," she replied modestly, her tone devoid of ego. "I painted that."

"It's an incredible piece," Alexander remarked, turning his attention back to the photo. After a moment, he passed the phone back to Sera. "Unfortunately, I've never seen a flower like that. If those colors are true to life..." he trailed off, his expression contemplative.

Sera nodded in confirmation.

"Yeah, just what I thought," Alexander continued. "That kind of flower seems like something out of a fairy tale. It can't possibly be that vibrant in real life, can it? It's too surreal to be true."

Again, Sera nodded, her gaze drifting as she recalled a distant memory. "I was given this flower as a child," she revealed softly. "I lost it, and I've been searching for one like it ever since."

She hesitated to divulge the full truth—that the flower had been given to her in the 12th century—but she knew Alexander would have a hard time believing such a fantastical tale. After all, she would have doubted it herself if she hadn't experienced it firsthand.

Seeing that Sera was willing to open up further, Alexander chose to respond with a nod, indicating his readiness to listen whenever she was ready to continue.

The alcohol had begun to erode Sera's usual barriers, prompting an overwhelming urge to unburden herself. "You might find this hard to believe, but I need to tell you the truth," she confessed, her voice trembling with emotion. "It's about who I really am and a curse that has plagued me and my sister for lifetimes."

Though taken aback by her solemn tone, Alexander remained silent, offering her a supportive space to share her story. And so, Sera embarked on the daunting task of recounting her tale, the words pouring forth as she laid bare the burden she had carried alone for so long. She spoke of Tempus, the curse that bound them, and the relentless cycle of death and rebirth.

As Sera spoke, Alexander listened intently, his respect and admiration for her growing with each revelation. "That's... a lot to process," he murmured softly when she finally finished. Her story forced him to suspend disbelief, challenging him to consider the possibility of a reality far beyond his comprehension. If what she said was true, it was a staggering burden to bear.

For nearly an hour, Sera spoke uninterrupted, her words punctuated by sips of alcohol. By the time the bartender announced last call, both she and Alexander were well beyond inebriated. As he processed Sera's revelations, he realized how profound her revelations were. He assessed her anew, feeling that she transcended the ordinary and went well past the boundaries of extraordinary.

The morning sun beamed through the partially drawn curtains, casting a glow squarely across Sera's face. She grimaced and a hand went to cover her eyes as they squinted reluctantly open. Her head throbbed and she felt like she had a mouth full of sand. Taking a moment to orient herself, she recalled following Alex up to his room in the hotel, too drunk to even find a ride share to take her home safely.

It all rushed back to her as she looked over at Alex's seemingly serene face, glowing in the morning sun. She looked down at herself, noting she was fully dressed, and realized that Alex was essentially one of the good guys.

Sera was feeling sorry for herself, nursing a bad hangover. While she rested her head in her hands as she sat still on the corner of the bed, her memory returned to a time before all of this, to a different lifetime.

It was the 12th century in Florence, Italy.

As Sera walked through the dimly lit streets of the town, her mind was in turmoil. She couldn't shake off the image of her sister, Constance, confessing her love for Tempus. It felt like a dagger to her heart, twisting with every step she took. Lost in her thoughts, she wandered aimlessly, the streets growing darker with each passing moment.

Eventually, Sera found herself standing in front of a quaint cottage, a flickering lamp casting a warm glow on the door. Desperate for some direction, she hesitated for a moment before mustering the courage to knock.

The door creaked open, revealing an elderly woman with kind eyes and a gentle smile. "Good evening, child," she greeted warmly. "What brings you here at this late hour?"

Sera hesitated, feeling a rush of emotions welling up inside her. "I... I'm lost," she admitted, her voice barely above a whisper. "I was hoping you could help me find my way back home."

The old woman nodded understandingly, stepping aside to allow Sera into the cozy interior of her cottage. "Come in, dear. You must be freezing out there," she said, her voice laced with concern.

As Sera stepped inside, she couldn't help but notice the comforting aroma of herbs and spices that filled the air. It felt like a soothing balm to her troubled soul. Settling into a chair by the crackling fireplace, she glanced around the room curiously, taking in the shelves lined with jars and bottles containing various concoctions.

The old woman, whom Sera now knew as Hellena, bustled about the room, preparing a steaming cup of herbal tea. "Here, child, this will warm you up," she said, handing Sera the cup with a reassuring smile.

Sera took a hesitant sip, feeling the warmth spread through her body. "Thank you," she murmured gratefully, her eyes meeting Hellena's wise gaze.

Hellena sat across from Sera, her expression filled with empathy. "Now, tell me, child, what troubles you?" she asked gently, her voice soft but firm.

Sera hesitated, unsure of where to begin. "It's... complicated," she admitted, her words catching in her throat. "I... I overheard something tonight, something that has left me feeling lost and confused."

Hellena nodded encouragingly, urging Sera to continue. "You can trust me, child. Whatever it is, I'm here to listen," she reassured.

Taking a deep breath, Sera recounted the events of the evening, from Constance's confession of love to her own conflicted feelings for Tempus. Tears welled up in her eyes as she spoke, the weight of her emotions finally spilling over.

Hellena listened intently, her face a mask of compassion. "Love can be a complicated thing, child," she said softly, reaching out to pat Sera's hand comfortingly. "But remember, true love is worth fighting for, no matter the obstacles that stand in your way."

Sera looked up at Hellena, her eyes searching for answers. "But what if... what if I've already lost the one I love?" she whispered, her voice trembling with fear.

Hellena's gaze softened, her eyes filled with understanding. "Sometimes, fate has a way of leading us down unexpected paths," she said cryptically. "But that doesn't mean all hope is lost. Sometimes, all it takes is a little courage to change our destiny."

Sera's brow furrowed in confusion. "But how? How can I change what's already been set in motion?" she asked, her voice tinged with desperation.

"I don't want to be forced to marry. I don't want to be torn from Tempus. I don't want to hurt my sister but..." she paused, staring down into the now lukewarm mug caught between her fingers. She looked up at Hellena with determination in her eyes after a moment. "I want to change my fate. Is there a way to do that?"

Hellena's smile held a hint of mystery as she reached for a small wooden box perched on the shelf beside her. "You'd be surprised, child, at the power that lies within you," she said enigmatically, flipping open the lid to reveal a collection of dried herbs and flowers. With a practiced hand, she sifted through them until she found what she was looking for—a plucked flower with a stem barely an inch long.

The vibrancy of the flower seemed to defy its state, as if it were still alive, never separated from its stalk. A soft effervescence emanated from it, infusing the cozy cottage with an air of enchantment.

Hellena held up the small flower, its fragrance mingling with the herbal scents around them. "This," she continued, her voice low and melodic, "is something my mother gave me many years ago, when I was just a girl like you. It's a promise of sorts, one that holds the power to change fate itself. With this, you should be able to find what you're looking for."

Sera's eyes widened in astonishment, her heart racing with anticipation. "Can it... can it really help me?" she asked eagerly, her voice quivering with hope.

It seemed implausible that such a small flower could possess the power to change fate. After all, it was just a collection of plant matter, albeit arranged in a beautiful form. Yet, there was an undeniable aura of significance surrounding it. Sera couldn't shake the feeling that there was more to this flower than met the eye. If it had survived all these years since Hellena's childhood, it must hold some extraordinary power.

Hellena nodded solemnly, her expression a blend of gravity and compassion, as she handed Sera the pouch with a gentle smile. "Take it, child, and use it wisely," she advised. "Place it under your pillow on the night you decide you want your fate changed. But remember, the choices you make from here on out will shape your destiny. Trust in yourself, and in the power of love, and you may just find a way to rewrite the stars."

Taking the flower with trembling hands, Sera felt a surge of determination coursing through her veins. "Thank you, Hellena," she said earnestly, her voice brimming with gratitude. "I won't forget this."

"I'm sure you won't," Hellena replied gently as she stood. Offering a hand to Sera, she helped her to her feet. "Now, let's get you sorted out."

With Hellena's guidance, Sera made her way to the door of the cottage. Hellena provided explicit directions to lead her back to the town center. Assuring Hellena that she could find her way home from there, Sera stepped out into the cool evening air,

With a nod, Sera bid Hellena goodbye, her heart lighter than it had been in days. She felt a newfound sense of purpose guiding her steps. Her mind was buzzing with the possibilities that lay ahead. With the flower clutched tightly in her hand, she set off into the night.

As the memory drew to a close, Sera leaned forward, her face resting gently in her hands. "You lied to me. My fate only got worse," she said softly.

As the morning sun crept higher in the sky, Sera sat on the edge of the bed, her thoughts still heavy with the weight of her memories. She glanced over at Alexander, who was stirring awake beside her. With a sigh, she ran a hand through her disheveled hair, wondering how she could face another day after the emotional whirlwind of the previous night.

Alexander blinked sleepily, his gaze focusing on Sera's somber expression. Concern flickered in his eyes as he sat up, rubbing the sleep from his own eyes. "Morning," he greeted softly, his voice rough with sleep. "You okay?"

Sera offered him a faint smile, though it didn't quite reach her eyes. "Yeah, just... processing, I guess," she replied, her voice barely above a whisper.

Alexander shifted closer, reaching out to gently squeeze her hand. "You know, if you need someone to talk to or just... be with, I'm here," he offered earnestly. "We don't have any crucial shots today. I can take the day off if you want."

Sera's brow furrowed in uncertainty, torn between her desire to be alone with her thoughts and the comfort of Alexander's presence. She knew he had his own responsibilities as the director of their film, and she didn't want to burden him with her troubles.

"But the film..." she began, her voice trailing off as Alexander shook his head, cutting her off.

"Forget about the film for today," he insisted gently. "Your well-being is more important than anything else right now. We can take a day to recharge, clear our heads, and come back stronger tomorrow."

Sera hesitated, feeling the weight of Alexander's offer settling over her like a warm blanket. She knew he was right—that she needed this time to gather herself and find some semblance of peace amidst the chaos of her thoughts.

"Okay," she relented, her voice barely audible. "Okay, let's spend the day together."

A small smile tugged at the corners of Alexander's lips as he squeezed her hand reassuringly. "Great," he said softly. "Let's start with breakfast. I know a little cafe nearby that serves the best pancakes."

As they got ready for the day, Sera felt a sense of gratitude washing over her. Despite the heaviness of her heart, she found solace in the simple act of being with someone who cared for her well-being. And as they stepped out into the bright morning sunlight, she felt a glimmer of hope stirring within her—a belief that perhaps, with Alexander by her side, she could forget the uncertainties of her past for a while and just focus on the moment.

Sera found herself nodding in agreement as Alexander mentioned pancakes, a faint smile tugging at her lips. "Pancakes sound perfect," she admitted, feeling a flicker of anticipation at the thought of indulging in a comforting breakfast.

As they made their way to the cafe, Sera couldn't shake off the heaviness that lingered in her chest. Yet, with each step, she felt the burden of her worries easing ever so slightly, replaced by a sense of warmth that emanated from Alexander's unwavering support.

The aroma of freshly brewed coffee and sizzling pancakes greeted them as they stepped into the cozy cafe. Sera breathed in deeply, the familiar scent bringing a sense of comfort and nostalgia. Finding a table by the window, they settled in, their conversation flowing effortlessly as they awaited their orders.

When the waitress set down their plates piled high with steaming pancakes, Sera's spirits lifted even further. She dug into her breakfast with gusto, savoring each bite as if it were a small victory in itself.

"These are amazing," she exclaimed between mouthfuls, her eyes twinkling with delight as she glanced at Alexander.

He chuckled, a warmth spreading across his features. "Told you they were worth it," he replied, his own plate nearly empty. "Glad you're enjoying them."

As they finished their meal, Alexander leaned back in his chair, contemplating their plans for the day. "So, what do you say we head to Stone Mountain?" he suggested, his tone casual but hopeful. "I've heard so much about it, but I've never had the chance to visit. It'd be a shame to leave Atlanta without experiencing it firsthand."

Sera considered his proposal, the idea of exploring a new place offering a welcome distraction from her thoughts. "That sounds like a great idea," she agreed, a spark of excitement igniting within her. "I've been there a few times, but I haven't gone hiking on the trail in ages. It could be a nice way to clear our heads."

Alexander smiled, pleased by her enthusiasm. "Exactly," he agreed. "And who knows? We might discover something unexpected along the way."

With their plans set, they settled the bill and made their way out of the cafe, the promise of adventure beckoning them forward. As they stepped into the warm embrace of the morning sun, Sera felt a renewed sense of optimism blooming within her.

As they navigated through the bustling city streets, Sera couldn't help but notice the heavy traffic slowing their progress. Cars honked impatiently, their engines rumbling in frustration as they inched forward. Sera's shoulders sagged, a hint of disappointment clouding her expression at the unexpected delay.

However, Alexander refused to let the traffic dampen their spirits. With a mischievous grin, he reached for the radio dial, flipping through stations until he found a lively tune that filled the car with upbeat rhythms. Soon, they found themselves singing along to the music, their voices blending in harmony as they laughed and joked, momentarily forgetting the chaos outside.

As they finally broke free from the city's grip and made their way towards Stone Mountain, Sera found herself reminiscing about her last visit to the park. She recalled the excitement of exploring the trails with Constance, their laughter echoing through the forest as they embarked on their adventure.

However, a pang of uncertainty gnawed at her as she remembered the arduous journey back down the mountain. The memory of her exhaustion lingered, casting a shadow over her enthusiasm for the hike.

Sera recalled the last time she had been there. She had gone with her twin sister Constance on a school field trip. While she wasn't a couch potato, she wasn't a fitness freak either. With this combination, she wasn't adverse to some physical endeavor but her memory of having to walk back down the trail from the top of the mountain didn't bring back pleasant feelings of the end result.

Sera turned to Alexander and said, "we've got a choice of taking the cable car up and walking down. Walking up and taking the cable car down, or just walking both ways." She paused and waited for Alexander to make a decision.

As she waited, it eventually dawned on her that he wasn't considering giving any input. "I'm not sure I want to walk both ways," she finally added.

Sensing her hesitation, Alexander reached out to squeeze her hand reassuringly. "Hey, it's gonna be fine," he said softly, his eyes filled with understanding. "We'll take it slow, enjoy the scenery, and before you know it, we'll be at the top."

Sera mustered a weak smile, grateful for his unwavering support. "I'm just worried about keeping up," she admitted, her voice tinged with uncertainty.

But Alexander wouldn't hear of it. With a playful grin, he leaned in closer, his eyes twinkling with mischief. "Come on, where's that adventurous spirit of yours?" he teased, nudging her gently. "Besides, think of the view from the top. It'll be worth every step."

Sera couldn't help but be swayed by his infectious enthusiasm. As they arrived at the base of the mountain, she found herself nodding in agreement, a sense of determination rising within her.

"Alright," she conceded with a soft sigh, a reluctant smile tugging at her lips. "Let's do this."

With Alexander leading the way, they set off along the trail, their footsteps echoing in harmony as they ventured deeper into the wilderness. As they climbed higher, the air grew crisper, the scent of pine mingling with the earthy aroma of fallen leaves.

Despite her initial doubts, Sera found herself losing herself in the beauty of their surroundings. The verdant canopy stretched out before them, dappled sunlight filtering through the branches overhead. With each step, she felt the weight of her worries melting away, replaced by a sense of peace and tranquility.

As they reached the halfway point, Sera couldn't help but glance back down the trail, marveling at how far they had come. Yet, the sight of the steep incline ahead filled her with a twinge of apprehension.

"Are you sure about this?" she asked, her voice tinged with uncertainty as she turned to Alexander. "Maybe we should just take the cable car back down."

But Alexander shook his head, his eyes gleaming with determination. "We've come this far," he said firmly, his tone leaving no room for argument. "And besides, where's the fun in taking the easy way out?"

Sera hesitated, torn between her desire to reach the summit and her fear of exhaustion. Yet, as she met Alexander's gaze, she saw a flicker of something in his eyes—a silent plea, a longing for adventure.

With a resigned sigh, she relented, a small smile playing at her lips. "Alright," she conceded, her voice soft but resolute. "Let's finish what we started."

And so, with renewed determination, they pressed on, their laughter mingling with the rustle of leaves as they ascended the mountain. Each step brought them closer to their goal, their bond growing stronger with every shared moment.

As they reached the summit, Sera couldn't help but be overcome by a sense of awe. The panoramic view stretched out before them, a breathtaking tapestry of colors and textures that seemed to stretch on for eternity.

And as she stood there, hand in hand with Alexander, she realized that sometimes, the most rewarding journeys are the ones that push us beyond our comfort zones—the ones that challenge us to rise above our doubts and fears and embrace the unknown with open arms.

Sera found herself caught off guard by the unexpected closeness with Alexander. As they approached the overhang for a better view, he instinctively wrapped his arms around her, a protective gesture that she surprisingly welcomed. It dawned on her, not until later, the significance of this moment. In all her past lives with her memories of Tempus intact, she couldn't recall ever allowing another man to be so close. It struck her how effortlessly Alex had broken through her defenses.

Glancing back at him, she met his smiling gaze, feeling her cheeks flush with warmth. Quickly averting her eyes, she hoped to conceal her blush, but Alexander's teasing remark only made it worse. "If you're trying to hide your blushing, you should take your hair down and let it cover up your ears too," he chuckled.

Embarrassed yet oddly comforted by his presence, Sera shrugged, her shoulders hunching slightly. She didn't move away from Alexander's embrace, finding a sense of security in his arms despite the rush of emotions swirling within her.

'*What the hell*,' Sera mused to herself, momentarily attempting to steal a glance over her shoulder at Alexander, almost needing confirmation that this wasn't a figment of her imagination. Yet, Alexander seemed oblivious, his attention focused on the distant horizon. Instead of meeting her gaze, he drew her closer, enveloping her in his embrace.

'*I've always desired this moment, to finally be with her without the shadow of our past lives hanging over us. To be able to love her freely, without the curse tearing us apart. And now, here we are, but the truth is still there, waiting to be revealed,*' thought Alexander.

Sera's heart pounded in her chest, her mind consumed by the suddenness of the moment. For that fleeting instant, everything else faded away, leaving her with the realization that this unexpected closeness felt strangely right, and perhaps, she didn't want it to come to an end.

As they began their descent down the mountain, Alexander's question interrupted the tranquil atmosphere. "Are you still worried about the curse?" he inquired, his voice gentle but probing.

Sera's thoughts momentarily scattered at the mention of the curse, a reminder of the heavy burden she carried. Surprisingly, she realized she had completely forgotten about it until Alex brought it up. A wry thought flitted through her mind, '*Who the hell can think of a curse when they've got a guy like you holding them so damn close?*'

Lost in the moment and the warmth of Alexander's presence, Sera hardly noticed the passage of time as they made their way down the mountain. The serenity of the surroundings seemed to seep into her being, overshadowing any lingering worries.

It wasn't until they reached the bottom of the mountain that Sera became aware of something peculiar. She glanced down, her eyes widening in realization. Without even realizing it, she had allowed Alexander to hold onto her hand for almost the entire descent. The realization sent a thrill through her.

Sera quickly pulled her hand away, stepping back to create what she deemed appropriate personal space. But Alexander wasn't having it. He swiftly bent down and scooped her up into his arms.

Sera let out a surprised yelp, flinging her arms around Alexander's neck for support. "Put me down, you beast!" she exclaimed, her face flushing with a mix of embarrassment and something she couldn't quite name.

Alexander chuckled, his eyes twinkling with amusement. "I kind of like this," he said, holding her close.

"Put me down," she insisted again, though her voice lacked conviction.

Alexander looked at her kindly. "Only if you promise not to run away."

Sera turned her gaze away from his deep eyes, realizing that agreeing was her only way back to solid ground. But part of her wasn't sure she wanted to end this moment just yet. The confusion of her feelings mingled with an unexpected desire to linger in his embrace a little longer.

"Alright, you win," she said softly, her voice tinged with reluctant acceptance.

Alexander hesitated a moment before deciding to put her down. Sera guessed he was gauging whether she was serious about not pulling away from him. To make his thoughts clear, he cleared his throat and spoke softly, "I like hanging out with you. Do you want to do it again sometime?"

Sera felt a mix of uncertainty and curiosity. She wasn't sure if she wanted to risk him intruding on her personal space again, but she was open to the idea of spending more time with Alexander. "I can't make any promises. But, we'll see," she offered.

Alexander took that as a definite yes and smiled, confident in his assumption. "Good then. I'll drop you off at home and see you on set tomorrow. We can figure out what we want to do later so you don't feel rushed," he said.

"What do you mean?" Sera asked, puzzled by his comment about her feeling rushed.

Alexander decided to be direct. "Sera, the first time I met you, I was interested in you. I tried to keep it professional since we were working on the film. I didn't want things to get confused or complicated. But that all changed when you told me your story last night."

Sera looked at Alexander in astonishment, sensing where this might be heading. She was tempted to turn around and pretend she hadn't heard anything, but Alexander gently took hold of her forearm, preventing her from escaping the moment.

"Sera, please listen," he said, his voice sincere. "I've been trying to ignore how I feel, but I can't anymore."

He waited until he was sure she was paying full attention. "Look, Sera, I'm not asking for a commitment right now. I believed every word of your story, and if it's true, I can't afford to take my time. I need to be upfront and honest with you. I want you to know how I feel. I wanted you to know that I love you. I'm not expecting an answer immediately. Just think about it."

Sera nodded, a small smile playing on her lips. As they walked back to the car, she felt a strange blend of being overwhelmed, anticipation and comfort. She wasn't entirely sure where things were heading, but for now, she was content to let them unfold because she had no way to stop anything while she was trying to still process it herself.

She had just managed to push aside the turmoil of her returning memories, and now Alexander's confession had brought everything crashing back. The ride back into town was more subdued than their earlier trip, and the tension was palpable.

'Now Alexander says he loves me. How can he feel that way when we've only known each other for a few months? We've hardly gone on dates or spent that much time together, apart from work and today at Stone Mountain. I'm so confused. It doesn't make sense,' thought Sera.

Her thoughts continued to churn. *'But then again, love rarely makes sense, does it? I've been haunted by a curse for so long, one that promised nothing but pain and loss. Even if I were to let myself feel something for Alexander, the curse would only tear us apart. It's what it does. It's all it knows.'*

'He doesn't understand the depth of this curse. He doesn't know what it's like to live and die over and over again, each time losing the people you love. How can I bring him into this cycle? How can I subject him to the same fate that has caused me so much suffering?'

Sera's thoughts continued on in this manner until Alexander interrupted her, asking for where to drop her off. She gave him directions to her home and he dropped her off she was still reeling from his revelation. As she watched him drive away, she couldn't shake the whirlwind of emotions and thoughts now swirling in her mind.

'I don't deserve his love. I don't deserve anyone's love. I've caused so much pain, so much harm. Constance and Tempus have suffered because of me, because of my selfish wish. How can I ever atone for that?'

'*Yet, there's a part of me that longs for what Alexander is offering. A chance at love, at happiness. But I'm terrified. What if accepting his love only leads to more heartache? What if the curse strikes again, and I lose him too?*'

With events being too much for her to deal with, Sera eventually turned away from the driveway and went into the house.

Chapter 7: "The Black Death I"

14th Century - Paris, France

Fated reunion within the confines of a tragic age.

In the chambers of the University of Paris Medical School, Tempus had enrolled to educate himself on the complexities of the human system, those things that could afflict man and cause harm. By this time in his life, Tempus had already lived well past 175 years. Any normal man would have long been dead of old age by then, his bones returned under the weight of years to dust and ash. Yet, Tempus lived still. He had no idea why he could enjoy such longevity when others around him succumbed to father time's touch. He had hoped to learn more about his condition here in the medical school but now his talents were being called for another reason.

Amidst the solemnity of the school, Tempus found himself immersed in the turmoil of a world plunged into chaos and suffering. His enrollment came just before the biggest outbreak of disease that had ever impacted Europe. The continent reeled under the impact of the disease. The somber atmosphere bore witness to the relentless grip of the Black Death.

Within these hallowed halls, adorned with ancient tapestries and scholarly tomes, a sense of foreboding hung palpably in the air. The once-vibrant hub of learning now echoed with hushed whispers of fear and uncertainty, as students and faculty grappled with the harsh realities of the epidemic that ravaged their world.

Tempus sat in the lecture hall, his mind drifting as the Maître Gaston Reynolds, the instructor droned on about humors and the virtues of bloodletting. The words seemed to blur together, lost in a haze of monotony. He absently traced patterns on his parchment, barely registering the scratching of quills and the shuffling of papers around him.

Suddenly, the sharp voice of the instructor pierced through Tempus's reverie. "Mr. Tempus," the instructor called out, his tone laced with disapproval. "Perhaps you can enlighten us. What are the four humors and their corresponding elements?"

Tempus blinked, momentarily startled by the directness of the question. He hesitated, weighing his options, before deciding to take a different approach. "Forgive me, sir," he interjected, his voice carrying across the room. "But may I pose a question of my own?"

The instructor's brow furrowed in annoyance, but he reluctantly acquiesced. "Very well, Mr. Tempus. What is your question?"

"Why do most physicians not move the sick away from those who are not ill?" Tempus queried, his gaze unwavering as he met the instructor's stern glare.

The instructor's face flushed with indignation. "Mr. Tempus, it seems you were not paying attention," he admonished sharply. "The spread of disease is caused by foul air and miasma, not by proximity to the sick."

Tempus's jaw tightened, a flicker of defiance sparking in his eyes. "With all due respect, sir," he countered, his voice firm, "I believe there may be other factors at play. Perhaps we should consider alternative theories."

A murmur of dissent rippled through the room as the other students exchanged incredulous glances. "Always the contrarian, that one," someone muttered under their breath. "He'll get himself expelled one of these days."

Ignoring the murmurs of his classmates, Tempus squared his shoulders, prepared to defend his unconventional beliefs against the weight of tradition and authority.

Tempus took a deep breath, steeling himself for the inevitable confrontation. "Sir, with all due respect," he began, his voice steady, "I am merely discussing ideas put forth by a reputable physician in the field. His research suggests that isolating the sick may indeed have a beneficial effect in preventing the spread of disease."

Maître Reynolds's lips curled into a sneer of disdain. "Ideas? Research?" he scoffed derisively. "Mr. Tempus, you would do well to focus on the teachings of this esteemed institution rather than indulging in flights of fancy."

"But Maître Reynolds," Tempus persisted, his tone growing more insistent, "the physician's paper suggests that there may be a correlation between isolating the sick and reducing the transmission of illness. He points to observations of fewer sick individuals in households where isolation measures are implemented."

Gaston's patience wore thin, his face contorting with irritation. "Poppycock!" he exclaimed, his voice rising in frustration. "If... if... if you cannot be bothered to pay attention to my lecture, perhaps you... you... you would be better served lea... leaving this classroom!"

Tempus met the instructor's gaze with unwavering determination, his resolve unshaken by the threat of being put out of class. Without a word, he gathered his belongings and rose from his seat, the eyes of his classmates following his every move. With a decisive nod, he strode out of the lecture hall, leaving behind a stunned silence in his wake.

As the door closed shut behind Tempus, he let out a smile. Hearing Maître Gaston Reynolds stuttering had been worth it.

Tempus sat at his desk in the dimly lit room, lost in thought as he pondered the events of the day. The door creaked open, and his roommate, Alexander Grayson, sauntered in with a knowing smirk on his face.

"Well, well, well," Alexander said, his tone tinged with amusement. "Look who's become the talk of the campus. Seems hardly a day goes by without some new tale of your antics making the rounds."

Tempus chuckled wryly, shaking his head. "Infamous, am I?" he replied, arching an eyebrow. "I suppose Maître Reynolds won't be inviting me to his lectures anytime soon."

Alexander chuckled, taking a seat across from Tempus. "Reynolds, huh? Heard he's as stubborn as they come," he remarked. "Wouldn't know progress if it smacked him in the face. Still clinging to the teachings of Galen and Hippocrates like they're gospel."

Tempus nodded in agreement. "Exactly. But there can be no change without a shift in perspective," he mused, his gaze distant. "We must be willing to challenge the status quo, to question what we've been taught, if we ever hope to advance our understanding."

Alexander raised an eyebrow, a grin spreading across his face. "Well, as noble as your crusade may be, my friend, you'll find it hard to test out your grand ideas if you don't graduate," he pointed out, a hint of teasing in his voice.

Tempus chuckled, a twinkle of mischief in his eyes. "Ah, but where's the fun in making it easy?" he replied, sharing a laugh with his roommate. "Besides, who needs a diploma when you have the pursuit of knowledge at your fingertips?"

Alexander's expression turned serious as he leaned forward, his tone somber. "You know, Tempus, it's not just here in Paris. The devastation caused by the Black Plague spreads far beyond these walls. I've heard reports from Lyon, Marseille, even as far as Avignon. Entire communities decimated, families torn apart. That's not even including what is occurring in England and other countries."

Tempus's gaze flickered with a mixture of concern and frustration. "And what difference can I *possibly* make in the face of such overwhelming tragedy?" he questioned, his voice heavy with doubt.

Alexander sighed, his shoulders slumping slightly. "I wish I had an answer for you, my friend," he admitted. "But one thing's for certain: doing nothing won't help. Even if you're not sure how, even if it seems hopeless, we have to try. We owe it to those who are suffering, to those who have already been lost."

Tempus nodded slowly, his mind racing with conflicting thoughts and emotions. Despite the uncertainty that loomed ahead, a flicker of determination sparked within him. "You're right," he said, his voice firm. "We may not have all the answers, but we can't let that stop us from trying. We have to do something, anything, to make a difference."

Tempus's mind drifted to thoughts of his own immortality, a burden he had carried for centuries. He had come to the University of Paris Medical School in search of answers, hoping to uncover the secrets that set him apart from ordinary mortals. Yet, instead of enlightenment, he found himself ensnared in a nightmare of epic proportions.

Could he, an immortal being, succumb to the ravages of the Black Plague? It was a question that gnawed at his mind, a chilling reminder of his own mortality despite his unnaturally long lifespan. He had cheated death for so long, but could fate finally catch up with him in the form of a deadly epidemic? He had doubts.

Alexander's voice broke through Tempus's reverie, drawing him back to the present. "What's on your mind, Tempus?" he asked, concern etched in his features.

Tempus hesitated, his thoughts too tangled to unravel in words. Instead, he offered a noncommittal shrug. "Just thinking about the last few classes before graduation," he replied, his tone casual. "Trying to figure out whose lectures I haven't managed to offend yet."

Alexander chuckled wryly, a hint of amusement in his voice. "I'd wager that list is shorter than the list of instructors you've managed to piss off," he remarked, a teasing glint in his eye.

Tempus couldn't help but crack a smile at his friend's jest. "You may have a point there," he conceded with a chuckle. "Seems I have a knack for rubbing people the wrong way."

"Well, what can I say? It's one of your many talents," Alexander quipped, his tone lightening the mood. "But hey, at least you keep things interesting around here."

Tempus nodded, a sense of camaraderie warming his heart. Despite the challenges and uncertainties that lay ahead, he was grateful for the steadfast friendship of Alexander.

Alexander's smile faltered momentarily as a faint flush colored his cheeks. He cleared his throat with a subtle cough, his attempt to downplay the sudden discomfort evident.

"Everything alright there, Alex?" Tempus asked, a note of concern creeping into his voice as he noticed his friend's pallor.

Alexander waved a dismissive hand, mustering a weak smile. "Ah, just a bit of indigestion, I think," he replied, his tone casual. "Must have been something I ate earlier."

Tempus studied Alexander's features intently, a flicker of unease tugging at his heart. The onset of symptoms, however mild, sent a shiver down his spine. Could it be the first sign of the dreaded plague, lurking just beneath the surface? He pushed aside the thought, choosing instead to focus on comforting his friend in his moment of discomfort.

"Maybe you should try to get some rest," Tempus suggested gently, his concern deepening as he observed Alexander's pallid complexion. "Rest might help settle your stomach."

Alexander nodded weakly, offering a grateful smile. "Thanks, Tempus. I'll do that," he replied, his voice strained with effort.

With a reassuring pat on Alexander's shoulder, Tempus rose from his seat, a sense of urgency propelling him into action. "I'll be back later to check on you," he promised, his gaze lingering briefly on his friend before he turned to leave.

As Tempus stepped out into the hallway, a knot of worry tightened in his chest.

As Tempus wandered through the corridors, his mind swirled with thoughts of the day's events. He was on his way to the common kitchen, hoping to find something to satiate his hunger. His restless spirit had once again clashed with the staunch traditions of academia, leaving him poorer for it. Lacking the necessary credits to graduate, he was left trying to formulate a plan to find a professor willing to let him attend their lectures. Discontent lingered within him, and with events cascading out of control, his hopes of understanding his condition seemed even farther away.

There were only a handful of instructors he could possibly approach, but his first choice was also his last: his advisor. Just then, snippets of conversation drifted from an adjacent room, piquing Tempus's curiosity. He paused, his ears attuned to the voices within. Presently, he recognized Maître Laurent Dubois and Maître Henri Rousseau, engaged in earnest discussion, their tones hushed yet animated.

"...family of nobility, requesting my presence," Maître Dubois was saying, tinged with a hint of resignation. "They believe the head of the household is exhibiting mild symptoms of an unknown illness, but they fear it may be the plague."

Tempus's interest was instantly piqued. The mention of the Black Plague sent a chill down his spine, a reminder of the reality that loomed over Europe.

"I'm afraid I can't go," Maître Dubois continued, a note of regret evident in his voice. "My duties here at the university demand my presence, and I cannot simply abandon my post."

Maître Rousseau sighed sympathetically. "I understand, my friend," he replied. "But what will you do about the family's request? Your two families are friends. They are counting on your expertise."

Tempus's mind raced as he listened to their conversation. An opportunity presented itself before him, a chance to put his knowledge to the test in the real world. Without hesitation, he stepped forward, clearing his throat to announce his presence.

"Excuse me," Tempus interjected, his voice steady yet tinged with eagerness. "I couldn't help but overhear your conversation, Maître Dubois. If you're unable to go, perhaps I could offer my assistance in your stead."

Both instructors turned to regard Tempus with surprise, their expressions a mix of curiosity and intrigue.

"You?" Maître Rousseau asked, his brow furrowing in uncertainty. "You're just a boy. A mere student."

Maître Rousseau was one of the many instructors who didn't particularly welcome Tempus into their lecture halls. Tempus didn't mind; he considered the man an imbecile anyway. '*I may look young, you fool, but I'm old enough to have been your great-grandfather's father,*' Tempus thought to himself.

Outwardly, Tempus nodded and smiled pleasantly, masking his true thoughts with practiced ease. Centuries of experience had taught him to conceal his emotions well. Despite Maître Rousseau's skepticism, Tempus remained undeterred.

"True, but I am eager to learn and willing to help in any way I can," Tempus replied earnestly.

Maître Dubois regarded Tempus as a fine student, often disregarding the negative opinions of his colleagues. He admired Tempus's determination and ability to master any task he set his mind to.

Stepping forward, Maître Dubois placed a welcoming hand on Tempus's shoulder. "I'm not sure if you're suited for this task, Tempus. If I allow you to do this, and you make an error, the harmony between their family and mine could suffer."

Tempus placed a reassuring hand on the forearm of Maître Dubois. "I take my responsibilities seriously. Plus, this would be an excellent opportunity for me to earn the few credits I am short of graduation."

Eager to rid the prestigious school of Tempus, Maître Rousseau quickly crossed the distance between them, clasping both of Tempus's shoulders. His primary thought was to get this troublesome student out of the institution as quickly as possible. Normally inclined to deny Tempus's requests out of hand, Maître Rousseau now found himself openly supporting the boy's proposal.

"Monsieur Dubois, I'll support young Tempus. I can vouch for him. He'd be a great asset," Maître Rousseau blurted out, almost stumbling over Tempus in his haste.

Maître Dubois looked dubiously at Maître Rousseau, knowing full well his dislike of the boy. He was suspicious of the support being given to Tempus from him.

"Are you sure?" Maître Dubois questioned.

Maître Rousseau's head bounced up and down as he hurriedly spoke. "I'm certain, Monsieur. Give him a chance. I'm sure you will be pleased," Maître Rousseau endorsed enthusiastically.

Tempus was a bit surprised himself, being fully aware of the extent of Maître Rousseau's animosity towards him. The instructor's willingness to support something he would normally reject, just to get rid of Tempus, was revealing.

Tempus shifted his gaze from Maître Rousseau to Maître Dubois, his eyes silently pleading for permission.

"If you could provide me with the necessary information and instructions, I would be honored to represent you in this matter, Maître Dubois," Tempus said earnestly.

Maître Rousseau exchanged a meaningful glance with Maître Dubois before turning back to Tempus with a smile.

Maître Dubois looked at Tempus and said, "If you can succeed in this, I'll make sure you get your credits."

Tempus nodded. "I'll do my best, Maître Dubois. You won't regret it."

"Well, it seems we may have found a solution after all," Maître Dubois said, his tone warm with approval. "I will provide you with a letter of introduction and detailed instructions on how to proceed. You have my gratitude, young man."

With a sense of purpose coursing through his veins, Tempus accepted the letter and instructions from the instructor, his heart pounding with anticipation. This was his chance to get away from the school and its stifling environment and put to practice what he had learned so far. He felt that what he could learn from the instructors at this point amounted to little and he would be better off on his own, learning and practicing instead of listening to theory.

As he made his way back to his room, Tempus couldn't contain his excitement. Bursting through the door, he found Alexander lounging on his bed, a book in hand. Alexander looked no worse for wear and Tempus felt a little relieved that Alexander didn't look as pale as he had earlier.

"Alexander!" Tempus exclaimed, his voice alive with exhilaration. "You won't believe what just happened."

Alexander looked up, his curiosity piqued by Tempus's animated demeanor. "What is it?" he asked, setting aside his book.

Tempus took a deep breath, his words tumbling out in a rush. "I've been chosen to represent Maître Dubois on a mission of utmost importance," he explained, his eyes shining with excitement. "The De Montford family in Versailles has requested assistance for their ailing patriarch, and I have been entrusted with the task of assessing his condition and rendering some treatments if needed."

Alexander's eyes widened in surprise, a grin spreading across his face. "That's incredible, Tempus!" he exclaimed, sitting up in bed.

Tempus regarded his friend thoughtfully. He knew that Alexander, like himself, struggled to fit in at the school. However, while Tempus openly defied the status quo, Alexander made a concerted effort to not let his aversion to the staff and certain students hinder his ability to learn something valuable during his enrollment.

An idea sparked in Tempus's mind—one that would not only give him a companion on the journey but also provide Alexander with a much-needed break from the stifling school environment.

"Why don't you come with me. I'll talk to Maître Dubois and have him allow you to work with me," Tempus suggested.

Alexander's eyes narrowed. "I'll come with you as your assistant, then?" Alexander asked, surprised.

"That's about the gist of it, yeah," Tempus replied.

"Consider me in then," Alexander smiled. "Together, we'll make a formidable team."

Tempus's heart swelled with gratitude for his friend's support. "Thank you, Alexander," he said, clasping his friend's hand in a firm handshake. "With you by my side, I'm sure we can handle whatever lies ahead."

With their plans set and their resolve steeled, Tempus and Alexander prepared to embark on their journey to Versailles and the château of the De Montford family.

The next day was bright, the sun rising to meet Tempus and Alexander as they prepared to leave. As they rode in the carriage towards the De Montford château, the countryside unfolded before them in a patchwork of fields and forests. The rhythmic clip-clop of the horses' hooves provided a steady backdrop to their journey, the gentle swaying of the carriage lulling them into a sense of tranquility.

Tempus leaned back against the plush cushions, his gaze drifting over the landscape. But instead of the idyllic scenery he remembered from years past, he was met with a sobering sight. The roads were noticeably quieter, devoid of the usual bustle of travelers and merchants. Where once there had been a steady stream of people going about their daily lives, now there were only sparse clusters of travelers, their faces drawn and weary.

His keen eyes caught sight of carts trundling along the road, their wooden frames laden with a grim cargo. Tempus's heart sank as he realized what they carried. It was a sight he had become all too familiar with in recent years: carts filled with the dead, pulled out of the city to be buried in mass graves beyond its walls.

But what struck him the most was not just one cart, but multiple. A somber procession of death, winding its way through the countryside like a macabre parade. Each cart bore silent witness to the toll of the plague, a reminder of the devastation that had befallen the land.

Tempus turned to Alexander, his expression grave. "Do you see that, Alex?" he murmured, gesturing towards the carts. "The plague has taken its toll on this land. It's as if death itself rides alongside us."

Alexander's gaze followed Tempus's gesture, his features drawn with concern. "I've heard tales of the plague's devastation, but to see it firsthand like this is..." he trailed off, unable to find the words to express the magnitude of the scene before them.

Tempus nodded solemnly, his thoughts weighed down by the gravity of their surroundings. "It's a harsh reality we face," he said quietly. "But we must press on, Alex. There are lives to be saved, even amidst such despair." Tempus was also concerned about learning more in order to figure out his own circumstances of living forever.

As the sun began its leisurely descent, painting the landscape in a warm golden hue, Tempus observed that nightfall would soon shroud the land. The realization dawned upon him that they would probably have to dine on the road, a prospect that didn't entirely displease him, considering the somber sights they had encountered along their journey. Moreover, the current circumstances had made finding a suitable dining place nearly impossible. Hence, he and Alexander had wisely prepared modest provisions for the journey to be consumed en route.

The rhythmic clatter of the carriage wheels and the steady clip-clop of the horses' hooves provided a soothing backdrop, lulling Tempus and Alexander into a reflective silence. Tempus gazed out the window, his thoughts far from consuming food with his subdued appetite. His mind drifted between memories of the past and the grim reality of the present. The once-bustling roads were now eerily quiet, with only the occasional traveler passing by, their faces etched with weariness and fear.

Alexander, seated opposite Tempus, seemed equally absorbed in his thoughts. His usual jovial demeanor had given way to a more contemplative mood, his eyes distant as they flicked over the passing scenery.

The silence was broken only by the occasional creak of the carriage and the soft murmur of the wind. Tempus couldn't help but notice the stark contrast between his memories of the countryside and the current desolation. Where once there had been lively farms and vibrant villages, now there were empty fields and abandoned homesteads.

Tempus, his expression somber, spoke softly to himself. "It's hard to believe how much has changed," he remarked.

Meanwhile, within the grandeur of the De Montford château, the dining hall buzzed with the melodic interplay of subdued conversations and the gentle clinking of silverware, all bathed in the soft, flickering glow of candlelight that danced upon the faces of the gathered guests. Seated gracefully at the table, Sera traced the intricate patterns etched into the silverware, her mind swirling in a whirlwind of conflicting emotions.

Beside her, Constance wore a forced smile, her restless eyes darting between the distinguished guests who vied for their attention. To Constance, these men were nothing more than boys, despite their shared youth in their early twenties.

She harbored no interest in any of the noble sons who had come to visit. Sera keenly sensed her sister's distaste lingering in the air as they delicately navigated the social intricacies of the occasion. While Sera chose to gracefully ignore their presence, Constance couldn't help but voice her disdain for their self-aggrandizing tales of glory meant solely to impress the two girls.

Seated at the head of the table was Luviet De Montford, positioned near her father-in-law, Gerot De Montford. Her husband, Pierre De Montford, occupied the seat beside her, his attention drifting away from his father's evident discomfort as he grappled with stomach cramps and a mild fever.

Pierre entrusted the care of his ailing father to Luviet, acknowledging her capability in providing better care than himself. Left to his own devices, Pierre might have simply hired someone to look after his father, his concern for his wellbeing overshadowed by the desire to avoid his wife's potential nagging about the matter. With his attention diverted elsewhere, Pierre's focus lay in mingling with the other nobles present at the gathering.

"Monsieur LaPravey, your son's exploits are truly remarkable. Is it indeed factual that you tracked down a six-point buck in the woods within a single day?" Pierre inquired, his tone filled with genuine curiosity.

Henri LaPravey's chest swelled with paternal pride at his son's achievements. "Indeed, he brought down that buck with a single shot," he affirmed proudly.

His son, Jacques LaPravey, mimicked the action of drawing a bow to its full extent and then theatrically releasing the tension. "The creature stood a towering eight hands high from huff to horn. A truly magnificent beast. It's a pity you couldn't join us, Monsieur DeMontford," Jacques remarked, his tone laced with admiration.

A derisive huff from Constance diverted everyone's attention toward her. "And you find pride in taking down an innocent creature that couldn't defend itself?" Constance's accusatory tone sliced through the air, casting a momentary silence over the room.

Pierre intervened, his throat clearing as he attempted to restore the conversation's flow. "She means no offense. Please, carry on," he urged, though his gaze bore a stern warning that Constance gracefully ignored.

Jacques exchanged a puzzled glance with his father. He had expected his tales of hunting prowess to impress the young ladies, particularly Sera, whom he favored due to her typically agreeable disposition. Despite their identical appearances, Jacques felt a stronger connection with Sera in that moment. Not out of affection, but simply because she hadn't openly challenged his manhood in front of everyone.

Encouraged by his father's silent prompt, Jacques forged ahead with his story, seamlessly picking up where he left off as if Constance's interruption hadn't occurred.

Meanwhile, Sera's thoughts drifted elsewhere, consumed by her own desires. She oscillated between longing to be elsewhere and admiring her sister's assertiveness. A slight headache tugged at her attention, diverting her focus from the conversation. However, Jacques's reaction to Constance's interruption elicited a smile from Sera, prompting her to nudge her sister gently with her elbow.

"You should try to be nicer," Sera prompted Constance in hushed tones.

Constance glanced at her sister as if she had told her to stand on her head while wearing her dress. "That's ridiculous. Why should I entertain such drivel?" Constance asked in a quiet tone.

Both girls smiled and laughed behind raised hands before returning their attention to the others.

Amidst the ongoing conversations among the dinner guests, two distinguished men seated at the table directed their attention to Pierre.

Aluver Pliant, positioned farther down the table, exuded an air of authority with his tall stature, chiseled jawline, and penetrating gaze. "Ah, Monsieur De Montford," he began, his voice dripping with feigned charm. "Such a pleasure to be here. Your daughters are even more beautiful than I had imagined."

Beside him, Gustav Minomiet, characterized by his portly figure and oily smile, nodded in agreement. "Indeed," he interjected, his voice laced with insincerity. "I must say, Pierre, you've outdone yourself. These girls will undoubtedly make splendid additions to any noble household."

Maintaining a carefully neutral expression, Pierre inclined his head in acknowledgment. "Thank you," he responded, his tone polite yet guarded. "I'm certain that my daughters find your comments complimentary." Internally, he bristled at the thought of anyone eyeing his daughters. While he might not openly express emotion towards his wife or concern for his ailing father, his daughters were a different matter altogether. Suppressing his displeasure at the men's comments, he struggled to maintain composure.

Aluver's gaze fixated on Constance, a glint shimmering in his eyes like a predator assessing its prey. "Tell me, Pierre," he began, smoothly redirecting his attention to the patriarch, "have you begun contemplating potential matches for your lovely daughters? Allow me to assure you, my family boasts an illustrious lineage, one perfectly suited for a young lady of such grace and refinement."

Gustav, his gaze flitting between the two sisters, licked his lips in anticipation, his demeanor exuding a palpable sense of greed. "And what of the other one?" he inquired, gesturing towards Sera with a subtle nod. "While perhaps not as outspoken as her sister, she possesses the requisite qualities of womanhood. She could prove to be quite... beneficial."

"Now, see here," called out Henri. The sudden interruption cutting through the tense atmosphere, drew the attention of all present. It was evident that Henri had hoped for a different turn of events, aiming for Jacques to forge a connection with the twins, thereby paving the way for a potential marriage alliance between the families.

Pierre, keenly aware of Henri's underlying motives, had anticipated a different line of conversation from the other guests, not talks of marriage. As Henri's outburst disrupted the unfolding dialogue, Pierre swiftly raised a hand, signaling for calm.

Pierre's smile appeared strained, the tension palpable in the rigid set of his jaw. "We haven't delved into such considerations," he replied, his voice betraying a hint of unease. "But be assured, when the time comes, we'll weigh all suitable matches for our daughters. However, their choice will ultimately prevail, not mine."

Aluver's smile widened, his eyes lingering on Constance with a predatory gleam. "Splendid," he cooed, his tone dripping with false congeniality. "We eagerly anticipate hearing their perspectives. I'm certain they'll reach a... mutually beneficial decision."

Constance shot a withering glare at Aluver. "I'm afraid the sty outside might better suit your tastes," she retorted, her disdain evident in her curled lip.

"Constance," her mother, Luviet, interjected with a reproachful tone.

Before Luviet could continue, Sera seized the opportunity to speak her mind. "She's not entirely wrong, Mother," she chimed in.

"If they value appearances over substance, they might well find what they seek outside, perhaps around the barn."

Before another word could be uttered, the twins rose from the table. The sisters bid their parents goodnight, leaving behind a maelstrom of shock, surprise, and confusion. Jacques cast a perplexed glance at his father, silently questioning what to do now that the objects of his attempts at impressing had prepared to abruptly depart. Henri shrugged in confusion.

Pierre, his jaw clenched with suppressed anger, could barely contain his fury as he watched them go. Yet, his ire was not directed at his daughters but at the discomfort they had endured. As they left, Pierre took a deep breath, almost welcoming their departure as a means to diffuse the charged atmosphere in the room. This moment of calm allowed him to rein in his anger, preventing him from confronting the two men, or worse, challenging them to a duel of honor. He chuckled inwardly, realizing that his daughters' cutting remarks had effectively put the presumptuous men in their place.

As the evening progressed, the tension that had simmered beneath the surface, exacerbated by Constance and Sera's departure, slowly dissipated. Pierre remained vigilant against any further discussions of suitors for his daughters throughout the remainder of the night.

As dinner drew to a close, Pierre stood, the soft scrape of his chair against the marble floor accompanying his movement. The other guests followed suit, and eventually, Pierre escorted them to the door to bid them farewell.

Henri hesitated momentarily, torn between his desire to broach the topic of his son marrying one of Pierre's daughters and his awareness of Pierre's protective nature. Yet, as their eyes met, Henri detected a shift in his old friend's demeanor, a return to familiarity. In the gleam of Pierre's eyes, Henri recognized a rekindled spirit, a sign that Pierre had transitioned from his earlier anger back to his usual self, making him more approachable.

"Join me for a brandy," "Pierre called out, gesturing invitingly.

Henri nodded, welcoming the chance to unwind with his friend after dinner. The prospect of sitting and chatting in a relaxed setting was appealing at that moment.

Henri instructed his son, Jaques, to take their carriage home, trusting that Pierre would arrange for his return later. Together, the two men traversed the expansive home and eventually settled into a cozy room just off the main hall. Nestled in comfortable, high-backed leather chairs, each with a tumbler in hand, they prepared to relax.

"You were quick to anger back there, Pierre," Henri observed.

Recalling the earlier events, Pierre felt a surge of temper before quickly suppressing it. "Humph," he began. "You seemed quicker to voice your outrage," he chuckled, pointing out Henri's swift defense of his daughters before he, as their father, could intervene.

Henri rose from his seat, crossing the room to stand by the hearth, where the light played on the fabric of his suit. His intentions were sincere; he hoped to see their families united. Despite acknowledging his son's flaws, Henri held onto the hope that something meaningful might blossom from the union of their children.

Turning to face his friend, Henri prepared to broach the subject, but Pierre preempted him. "I know, Henri. You needn't say it. I understand your interest in Jacques potentially marrying one of the twins. As I mentioned earlier at the table, it's their choice, not mine," Pierre interjected.

Henri's smile softened, and a light chuckle escaped him as the tension eased from his body. "You're quite progressive, Pierre, giving your daughters the freedom to arrange their own affairs," he remarked before returning to his seat. "I admire your courage."

Pierre appreciated the compliment but remained intent on clarifying his stance without jeopardizing their friendship. "I'd like to believe that one of my daughters might develop an interest in Jacques in the future," he ventured.

Henri stifled a laugh. "You and I both know that my son is an insufferable bore. He too might have better luck picking from your barn than waiting for one of the girls to take notice of him."

Sharing laughter, they found solace in the bond of their friendship and the common challenges of parenthood. Their conversation carried on, weaving a tapestry of shared memories and renewed connections, stretching into the late hours of the evening. When it was time for Henri to depart, Pierre arranged for transportation, bidding his friend farewell at the doorstep. As Henri's carriage rolled away into the night, Pierre retired to his chambers, grateful for the cherished moments spent in the company of his dear friend.

The next morning, Constance and Sera wandered through the corridors of the De Montford château, their footsteps echoing softly against the polished marble floors. Sunlight filtered through the tall windows, casting warm beams of light across their path as they made their way towards their mother's chambers.

Upon reaching Luviet's door, they found her already seated at her vanity, a serene expression gracing her features as she carefully arranged her hair. She looked up as her daughters entered, offering them a warm smile.

"Good morning, my darlings," Luviet greeted, her voice soft and melodious. "How did you find the dinner last night? Did you enjoy the company of our guests?"

Constance exchanged a quick glance with Sera before replying, "It was... tolerable, Mother. Though, I must say, the company left much to be desired."

Sera nodded in agreement. "Yes, Mother. Some of the guests were rather... insufferable."

Luviet arched an elegant eyebrow, her curiosity piqued. "And what of Jacques LaPravey? He seemed quite taken with both of you."

Constance's lips curled into a slight frown. "Jacques is... not our cup of tea, Mother. He may boast of his hunting exploits, but beneath that bravado lies a rather shallow and self-absorbed individual."

Sera nodded in agreement. "Indeed, Mother. We found his constant need for validation and his tendency to exaggerate his accomplishments rather off-putting."

Luviet listened attentively to her daughters' assessments, a thoughtful expression crossing her features. "I see," she murmured, her gaze drifting towards the window. "And what of your own plans for the future, my dears? Have you given any thought to what you wish to pursue?"

Constance and Sera exchanged uncertain glances, their previous confidence faltering slightly. "Well, Mother," Constance began slowly, "we... we haven't quite decided yet. There are so many possibilities, and we want to ensure that whatever path we choose is the right one for us."

Sera nodded in agreement. "Yes, Mother. We want to explore our options and find something that truly resonates with us, something that we're passionate about."

Luviet smiled understandingly at her daughters, her eyes shining with pride. "Of course, my darlings. Take all the time you need. Your happiness and fulfillment are what matter most to me."

As Luviet finished attending to her hair, she gracefully rose from her seat, her movements fluid and composed. "Whatever you girls decide, don't concern yourselves with the needs of the family," she advised, completing her preparations for the day with practiced ease. "Now, let us go and greet your father," she declared, her tone firm as she led the way out of the room. "He's arranged for a family friend to visit and assess your grandfather's condition."

The gravity of the situation was not lost on the twins, their expressions mirroring a mix of concern and apprehension. "Could it be the plague? Is that why he's feeling unwell?" they both voiced simultaneously, their words overlapping in a chorus of worry.

"This..." Luviet began, her voice trailing off as she considered her response. Her gaze shifted downward, briefly betraying her own uncertainty before she composed herself, meeting her daughters' eyes with a reassuring smile. "We cannot be certain, but there's no need for alarm," she asserted, her voice tinged with conviction as she pushed aside her inner doubts. "Once the physician arrives, we'll have a clearer understanding. Now, come along, girls. We mustn't keep your father waiting," she urged, gesturing for them to follow as she guided them towards the door.

As they made their way down the corridor, Sera suddenly halted, her hand instinctively reaching out to the nearby wall for support as a wave of discomfort washed over her. Clutching her head with her other hand, she doubled over, clearly in distress. The headache that had plagued her the night before had returned with a vengeance.

Luviet reacted quickly, extending a supportive arm to her daughter and offering a reassuring presence. Concern etched her features as she observed Sera's sudden bout of pain, her motherly instincts kicking in.

"Are you alright, Sera?" Luviet inquired, her voice laced with worry as she studied her daughter's bewildered expression.

Sera's response came in a muttered whisper, barely audible as she grappled with the sensation overwhelming her. "Tempus," she muttered, her voice strained with uncertainty. Pausing, she struggled to articulate the strange feeling stirring within her. "Saying it out loud... it feels... real," she mumbled, her thoughts muddled by doubt. She couldn't shake the nagging feeling that the name held some significance, even if she couldn't quite place it.

Before she could delve further into her thoughts, Constance interjected, breaking the sudden silence and redirecting their focus.

"Sera?" Constance's voice, soft yet filled with concern, broke through her sister's thoughts. She approached Sera hesitantly, her eyes wide with worry. "Are you alright?"

Turning to face her sister, Sera's expression still betrayed the pain she was feeling, though it softened somewhat in response to Constance's presence. Though she wanted to confide in her sister, Sera opted to keep her true feelings to herself. "I'm fine," she eventually confessed, her voice trembling with barely suppressed emotion.

Constance reached out, her fingers gently brushing Sera's arm before she firmly grasped her hand. "Let's get you back to the room and into bed," she suggested quietly, her concern evident in her tone.

Sera's grip on Constance's hand tightened slightly, a steely resolve flickering in her eyes. "I'm fine," she insisted, her voice low and intense. "I just got dizzy, that's all."

Acknowledging Sera's words with a nod, Constance recognized that her sister wasn't being entirely truthful. However, she respected Sera's desire for privacy and decided not to press further. Determined to look out for her sister, Constance resolved to keep a watchful eye on Sera for the remainder of the day. Glancing down at their intertwined hands, her mind raced with concern and uncertainty. "Alright," she agreed. "Let's go say good morning to Father."

As the first light of dawn filtered through the dense canopy of trees lining the winding road, the carriage carrying Tempus was guided towards the looming silhouette of the De Montford château. Having traveled far and long, Tempus had foregone the chance to rest his weary bones during the night due to the circumstances of the black plague. Encouraging the carriage driver to press on, he now found himself nearing the end of his journey, the imposing façade of the De Montford family home standing before him.

The carriage rumbled through the ornate gates, the driver urging the horses forward with a resigned sigh, their hooves echoing against the cobblestone path. Despite the relative tranquility of the scene, Tempus felt a sense of unease wash over him, a vague apprehension that lingered at the edge of his consciousness. He had volunteered to tend to the ailing patriarch of the De Montford family in Maître Dubois's stead, confident in his ability to diagnose the elder De Montford's condition. There should have been no reason for him to feel unsettled, and yet, the feeling persisted, nagging at him like a persistent whisper in the back of his mind.

As they stepped out of the carriage, Tempus stretched his weary, aching bones, feeling the relief of movement after the long, cramped journey. He turned and watched Alexander exit the carriage, noting with concern the slight coughing fit that overtook his companion. Alexander's pallor seemed unusually washed out, prompting Tempus to voice his worry.

"It's just the cramped travel and the long hours," Alexander reassured him, brushing off Tempus's concern with a dismissive wave. Despite his words, the strain was evident on his face. Tempus opened his mouth to press further, but Alexander cut him off with a smile. "I'm fine, really."

Straightening up, Alexander clasped Tempus's arm firmly and led him up the stairs to the manor's imposing door. Tempus allowed himself to be guided, though he couldn't shake the lingering concern about his friend's health.

Tempus and Alexander were met at the door by a servant, who ushered them into the grandeur of the De Montford château. Stepping into the opulent study, Tempus's eyes swept over the lavish furnishings and ornate decor that spoke of wealth and prestige. Despite his earlier unease, the welcoming demeanor of Pierre De Montford seemed to alleviate Tempus's apprehension.

Handing Pierre the letter of recommendation he had received from Maître Dubois, Tempus introduced himself and Alexander with a courteous nod. Pierre accepted the letter, scanning it briefly before setting it aside in disinterest. Satisfied, Pierre turned his attention back to Tempus and Alexander, his expression one of polite interest.

"Welcome, Monsieur Tempus, Monsieur Alexander," Pierre greeted, extending a hand in greeting to them both in turn. "I trust your journey was not too arduous?"

Tempus nodded respectfully, his discerning gaze studying the older man before him. "Thank you, Monsieur De Montford. The journey was indeed lengthy, yet manageable. I am genuinely honored to be of assistance to your family."

"My wife arranged for our family friends to send aid, not I," Pierre interjected softly, revealing a glimpse of the family dynamics within the De Montford household.

Tempus acknowledged Pierre's words with a respectful nod, though he remained unsure about the intricacies of the family's inner workings. It struck him as surprising that Pierre appeared to be relatively unconcerned, especially given his lack of mention about when they would attend to his father's condition.

Pierre's demeanor softened, a sense of gratitude shimmering in his eyes. He motioned towards a pair of sofas and settled into one, gesturing for Tempus and Alexander to do the same. A small table between them held a pot of tea and a few cups. "Would you care for some tea?"

Tempus welcomed the offer. Their journey had not allowed time for breakfast, and while tea and biscuits wouldn't fully satisfy his hunger, they would curb his appetite until he could have a proper meal later.

As Tempus glanced at Alexander, he noticed his companion looking a bit pale, his hand covering his mouth and the other clasped at his belly. Sensing Tempus's concern, Alexander spoke up. "I'm just a bit queasy from the carriage ride. Probably a bout of motion sickness, nothing more," he explained, offering a weak smile that Tempus returned.

Pierre seemed ready to continue the conversation, but the unexpected arrival of his wife and daughters interrupted them.

The sofa upon which Tempus and Alexander sat faced away from the door, preventing them from seeing the ladies as they entered. They were first alerted to their presence by the sound of Luviet's voice addressing her daughters.

"Your father should have greeted our guests by now," she said, speaking over her shoulder to her trailing daughters. "Please do be on your best behavior."

"Yes, Mother," both girls responded in unison.

Pierre's attention shifted from Tempus and Alexander to the entrance of his wife and daughters. He stood, prompting Tempus and Alexander to do the same.

"Ah, here they are, my lovely daughters," Pierre announced, his voice filled with pride. He seemed more pleased by his daughters' presence than that of his wife.

Tempus turned, initially surprised that Pierre hadn't mentioned his wife, but his surprise quickly turned to shock.

"Tempus?" Sera said, confusion evident in her voice.

Constance glanced at her sister, puzzled as to how Sera could know this man's name before they had been introduced. Luviet also looked at Sera with a similar curiosity.

Alexander's mouth hung open, enraptured by the beauty of the twins and their mother. There was no doubt they were related. His surprise was as genuine as anyone else's in the room.

Tempus, however, could only stare in shock, fear, and overwhelming surprise at the sight of Constance and Sera, two women he thought he would never see again in his immortal years.

"Constance? Sera? What..." Tempus began, his voice trailing off into abrupt silence.

Constance, drawn to the sound of Tempus's voice, first registered it as someone speaking before a deeply forgotten memory surfaced, causing her eyes to widen in shock. Her hand pressed against her mouth as she stifled a gasp, and she began to slide to the floor as her legs gave out from under her. Sera swiftly caught her sister by the arms, helping her to retain her balance, her eyes never leaving Tempus.

Pierre's eyes darted between Tempus and his daughters, concern etched on his face. He was bewildered by the situation unfolding before him. As far as he knew, this was the first time Tempus had been to his house and the first time he had met his daughters. Yet, the three of them displayed an unworldly familiarity with one another.

"What's going on here?" Pierre asked, his confusion evident.

Tempus began to open his mouth to respond, but Sera cast him a withering glance, shaking her head ever so slightly to signal him to remain silent. The movement was subtle enough to go unnoticed by the others in the room.

"Nothing, Father," Sera said smoothly, helping Constance to stand up straight. "Constance isn't feeling well. I'll take her back to her room."

The gathered family watched as Sera gently guided a numbed Constance out of the room. As they exited, Sera cast one last look over her shoulder at Tempus, her eyes filled with a mix of confusion and urgency. She then hurried her steps, ensuring that she and her sister were swiftly out of the study.

Alexander, witnessing the strange interaction, remained silent but couldn't hide his confusion. The tension in the room was palpable as everyone tried to comprehend the uncanny recognition and the mysterious bond between Tempus and the twins.

"I... I don't know what to say," Pierre muttered, sinking heavily back into his seat.

Luviet hesitated, torn between her desire to follow after their daughters and her duty to care for her husband. Deciding that the girls could look after each other for now, she moved to Pierre's side, gently dabbing the slight sheen of sweat from his forehead with a handkerchief.

"You need to explain this immediately," Pierre demanded, brushing his wife's hands away. He stood and faced Tempus directly. "How do you know my daughters?"

Tempus, still grappling with his own shock, quickly offered an explanation. "Monsieur, I have just arrived at your home. I recall hearing the names of your wife and children from the servant as he led us to your study," Tempus lied.

Pierre scrutinized Tempus, skeptical of his words but lacking any alternative explanation. He squinted, as if trying to pierce through the surface to find the truth. When this proved insufficient, his anger subsided slightly, giving way to more measured thoughts. He decided he would verify Tempus's claim by questioning the servant later in the day.

As Pierre calmed down and resumed his seat, both Tempus and Alexander followed suit, the tension in the room easing just a fraction.

Luviet retrieved a tumbler with a dash of water and liquor from a hutch, hoping it would help calm her husband despite the early hour. Pierre accepted the drink perfunctorily, not acknowledging her care.

Attempting to steer the meeting back on track, Luviet asked after Tempus and Alexander. Pierre gruffly pointed to the letter of introduction on his desk. Luviet read it, familiarizing herself with the situation.

Turning to Tempus and Alexander with a calming smile, she said, "We are in dire need of your expertise, Monsieur Tempus. My father-in-law's condition has worsened, and we fear the worst."

Tempus's brow furrowed with concern. "I understand, Madame De Montford. Rest assured, I will do everything in my power to alleviate your father's suffering."

Tempus turned his attention to Pierre, hoping for more information about the issue at hand. However, Pierre appeared unconcerned, clearly leaving the matter entirely to his wife. Disappointed, Tempus refocused on Luviet, who gestured for him to follow her to the elder De Montford's room.

As Luviet led Tempus through the grand corridors of the château, he couldn't shake the feeling of shock gnawing at his insides. The sight of the twins had stirred a profound sense of déjà vu, reminding him of the centuries-old memories of burying them with his own hands. This unexpected connection left him unsettled, but he steeled himself to concentrate on diagnosing the elder De Montford.

Tempus stole a glance at his hands, noticing their imperceptible yet uncontrollable trembling. With a steadying breath, he refocused on the path ahead, determined to maintain his composure.

Aware of Pierre's proximity behind him, Tempus felt the weight of the man's gaze on the back of his head. It was evident that Pierre harbored suspicions about Tempus, likely related to his unexpected encounter with the daughters.

Swallowing hard, Tempus couldn't shake the feeling of disquiet, particularly concerning the presence of the girls. How had they ended up here? Why now, of all times? Was it mere coincidence, or was fate at play? They should have been long gone from this world. He was certain of that.

As tempting as it was to dwell on these questions, Tempus knew it would yield no answers. He would have to wait for an opportunity to speak to the girls alone before he could unravel the mystery surrounding their reappearance.

A tap on Tempus's arm snapped him back to the present. Alexander's gaze, brimming with unspoken questions, prompted Tempus to refocus on their surroundings. Instead of voicing his inquiries, Alexander subtly nodded in the direction they were headed, a silent reminder for Tempus to stay attentive.

Luviet stood ahead of them, her demeanor a blend of concern and anticipation. "He is just through here," she murmured softly, opening the door for Tempus to enter.

Stepping into the sickroom, Tempus's attention was immediately drawn to the frail figure of Gerot De Montford, his visage etched with pain and weariness. The weight of the situation settled heavily on Tempus's shoulders as he braced himself to assess the old man's condition.

"What the hell, Sera? What's going on with us?" Constance asked quietly, her voice barely above a whisper. She sat at her desk, hands pressed against her face, her eyes fixed on her palms, but her mind elsewhere, grappling with the bewildering reality before her.

This wasn't 12th-century Florence in the Auerelius household. This was France. This was the 14th century.

Constance turned slowly, her gaze sweeping across the room from her hands to finally settle on the face of her younger twin sister. "What happened to us? We..." Constance began, her voice trailing off. She couldn't find the words to articulate the confusion and disbelief swirling within her. To her knowledge, she was Constance De Montford, but now, at the same time, she was Constance Auerelius. It didn't make sense. None of it made sense. She recalled growing up in San Marino, and then when her parents died, she and her sister moved to Florence to live with... "Tempus," she whispered.

Sera hesitated for a moment, torn between the love she felt towards her sister and the burgeoning memories she recalled of the two of them, Constance and Tempus. She wondered about her own feelings for Tempus. Was it real or not.

But as Sera met her sister's gaze, she saw the flicker of determination burning bright within her eyes, and she knew that she, at least, had made her choice. Constance was committed to finding out what had happened to the three of them.

"We need to find a way to get past father and talk to Tempus," declared Constance.

"How can we?" Sera interjected. "There's no way father is going to let us speak to Tempus alone. It's not going to happen." Sera exhaled, turned, and walked over to the window to look out. She was frustrated and she wanted answers as well. Without being able to speak to Tempus, she realized that they wouldn't get the answers that they wanted. The years that had passed seemed to have dimmed the fire.

Chapter 8: "Fate's Bind"

An immortal's resolve is tested as he intervenes to safeguard his homeland.

Tempus awoke in yet another unfamiliar room, a stark contrast to the lavish hotel suite where he had first settled upon arriving in London years ago. Back then, maintaining a low profile had been challenging amidst such opulence. With his eyes still closed, he reached across and grasped the small locket on its delicate gold chain. This morning, he didn't open it to gaze at the familiar renditions inside. Not photographs, but a fragile jade engraving. He knew every detail by heart—the small crack at the corner of the engraving, the discolorations from time. Each imperfection was etched into his memory, a piece of his past that made up his present burden.

He handled the locket gently, as if it were made of fragile glass that could shatter and cut him with the slightest mishandling. Tempus sat up slowly, his head drooping low toward his chest. He inhaled deeply, a breath to center himself. Another breath followed, preparing him for the relentless march of days, the unending succession of years, the seemingly eternal passage of centuries.

Every breath was a step in his enduring journey, a way to brace himself for the challenges of his existence, an existence that stretched on endlessly.

He ran his hand through his hair, fastened the necklace around his neck, and got out of bed to face the day. Slipping into an exquisite suit, he stepped out into the morning sunlight. By midmorning, he was seated at a charming bistro, enjoying a coffee and a croissant while leisurely reading the newspaper.

As part of his daily routine, he pulled out a tablet. Over the centuries, managing multiple identities had become a necessity, leading him to establish an organization dedicated to consolidating his vast network of contacts. This organization, loyal only to him, ensured that his wealth was always accessible, regardless of which identity he was currently using.

Additionally, this network kept him informed about matters of personal interest, chief among them the small enclave of San Marino. This tiny nation within a nation was not just a point of curiosity; it was his ancestral home, the thread that wove through the tapestry of his long life and gave him a sense of purpose through the endless march of centuries. It was this connection to San Marino that fueled his resolve and kept him moving forward.

The burden of the twins' fate weighed heavily upon him, the ceaseless cycle of rebirth, reunion, and eventual demise haunting his every thought. Alone in his longevity, he bore the weight of their recurring destinies, waiting for the inevitable repetition of the cycle. His grip tightened around the locket, a physical manifestation of his emotional turmoil, as he grappled with these fleeting thoughts that lingered in the recesses of his mind.

Among his correspondences, he came across an article from a newspaper detailing accusations leveled against the Henderson Shipping Corporation for overcharging. Despite the allegations, the corporation adamantly denied any wrongdoing. For San Marino, a nation with limited resources, reliance on this particular transportation company was a necessity, especially for a specific product crucial to the country's economy. However, this reliance left San Marino vulnerable, with little recourse for enforcement or investigation into the allegations. Any action would require involvement from the British Government, given that the corporation was based in the United Kingdom.

Intrigued by the situation, Tempus felt compelled to intervene in the conflict, not out of loyalty to any specific individual, but rather out of a deep-rooted concern for his homeland. With resolve set in his mind, he concluded his brunch and made his way to the headquarters of the Henderson Shipping Corporation, conveniently located in London, where he currently resided. Prior to departing, he had made a brief phone call, requesting the presence of a certain individual at their destination.

Arriving promptly at the designated location, Tempus found his associate waiting on the sidewalk in front of the imposing building. He couldn't help but marvel at how Elias managed to beat him there, considering he should have been occupied elsewhere.

"You're late, sir," Elias remarked, his voice resonating slightly in the open space, a hint of reproach evident in his tone.

"Got held up," Tempus replied nonchalantly, their customary exchange falling into place effortlessly.

"Were you close by?" Tempus inquired, gesturing toward the other tasks he had assigned to Elias.

"Not far from here, all things considered," Elias responded cryptically.

Tempus understood the implications behind Elias's words. The recent discovery of his last identity by Victor had thrown a wrench into their plans, prompting a pursuit through the bustling streets of London's BOHO section. Thankfully, the pursuit had been ineffectual, allowing Tempus to slip through the net unscathed.

Elias gestured casually over his shoulder, indicating the imposing building behind him—the headquarters of the Henderson Shipping Corporation. "You need to get in there?" he asked calmly.

"Yep. That's the place," Tempus affirmed with a nod.

Without another word, Elias turned and strode off, his purposeful steps leaving no room for hesitation. Tempus followed closely, falling into step behind him, his movements mirroring those of the slightly larger man. Elias's stride was precise, a testament to his military background and tactical training—smooth, silent, and swift, driven by singular determination.

As they entered the building, Elias made a beeline for the security and reception desk, engaging in conversation with the seated guard. Meanwhile, Tempus found a seat at one of the small tables scattered around the lobby, his demeanor outwardly disinterested. His gaze wandered idly as a man in a suit emerged from a nearby office and approached the desk where Elias was in conversation with the security guard. After a brief exchange, all three men glanced in Tempus's direction, their attention momentarily drawn to him before returning to their discussion.

It all unfolded in a matter of minutes—a mere smattering of time, fleeting yet seemingly endless. The man in the suit, unmistakably the security manager, trailed behind Elias as they approached Tempus's location. Elias stood at a comfortable distance, a silent sentinel, while the security manager hovered uneasily, as if seeking solace in Elias's imposing presence rather than meeting Tempus's gaze directly.

"You should have no problem now, sir," Elias stated matter-of-factly. "I'll be going then."

Tempus observed Elias's departure with a brief nod before shifting his focus back to the security manager, who remained in his company. The man's patience was palpable, waiting for Tempus's acknowledgment before venturing to speak.

"Is there anywhere in particular you'd like to go?" the man inquired nervously.

Tempus gestured upwards, towards the towering ceilings. "Up," he replied succinctly. The security manager understood the implicit directive, promptly turning on his heel and leading the way with a deferential, "This way, sir." Together, they navigated the interior of the building, making their way towards the office of the company's President.

Nigel strode briskly down the polished hallway, his footsteps echoing against the marble floor. He was deep in conversation with his secretary, Mary, a meticulous woman who was always at the ready, filled with Nigel's packed schedule and an array of important notes in her head.

"Make sure the quarterly reports are finalized by Thursday, Mary. We need to be prepared for the board meeting," Nigel said, his tone clipped and businesslike.

"Of course, Mr. Highgarden," Mary replied, her fingers dancing over her tablet as she made a note of his request.

As they approached Nigel's office, he glanced at Mary, ensuring she was up to date on all necessary matters. Pushing open the heavy wooden door, he stepped inside, mid-sentence.

"And also, we need to review the—" Nigel stopped abruptly, his words hanging in the air as he noticed an unexpected figure seated in the chair before his desk. The man's back was to him, and Nigel's brow furrowed in confusion.

"Mary, was I expecting anyone for a meeting?" he asked, his voice lowered but tinged with irritation.

"No, sir, Mr. Highgarden. You weren't supposed to have a meeting right now," she replied, "Let me just double-check."

Mary, equally perplexed, swiftly checked the tablet in her hands. She scrolled through Nigel's appointments, her eyes narrowing as she meticulously reviewed his schedule.

Nigel waited, his impatience mounting. After a few moments, Mary looked up, shaking her head.

"No, sir, Mr. Highgarden. There's no appointment scheduled," she confirmed, glancing up briefly before returning to her search.

Nigel dismissed her with a curt nod. "Thank you, Mary. That will be all for now."

As Mary exited the office, closing the door softly behind her, Nigel took a deep breath. He adjusted his tie, trying to compose himself before confronting the intruder. Clearing his throat loudly, he stepped closer to the desk, hoping to assert his authority.

"Excuse me, can I help you?" Nigel asked, his voice steady but edged with annoyance.

The man in the chair turned slowly, revealing a calm yet resolute expression. He was impeccably dressed, his demeanor composed and professional. Nigel felt a flicker of uncertainty.

"Good morning, Nigel," the man said smoothly. "My name is Tempus Vincitore. I'm with the San Marino Consulate here in London."

Nigel's eyes narrowed slightly as he studied Tempus. "And what brings you to my office unannounced, Mr. Vincitore?"

Tempus leaned back slightly in the chair, his gaze unwavering. "I'm here to discuss some serious discrepancies we've found in your recent export documents to San Marino."

Nigel's initial irritation gave way to a defensive stance. "Discrepancies? I'm not aware of any issues. All our transactions are handled in compliance with the law."

Tempus nodded, seemingly unperturbed by Nigel's response. "Regardless, that's precisely what I'd like to discuss though. The invoices for certain goods show charges for Italian import taxes, which, according to our bilateral agreements, should be exempt. This has resulted in substantial overcharges."

Nigel's expression tightened, his features betraying his growing apprehension. Before he could formulate a response, Tempus deftly pulled out his phone and tapped out a quick text message. The atmosphere in the room grew palpably tense, a heavy silence settling between them like an unwelcome guest.

"What are you doing?" Nigel demanded, his patience wearing thin as he broke the uneasy silence that hung over them.

Tempus responded with a calm smile. "Just wait," he replied cryptically, his tone betraying a quiet confidence. No sooner had the words left his lips than Nigel's office phone rang sharply, the piercing sound cutting through the thick quietude like a knife.

"It would be better that you answer that," Tempus suggested calmly.

Nigel eyed the phone warily, his confusion mounting. Bracing himself, he answered the call, his gaze flickering between Tempus and the device in his hand. "Yes, Nigel Highgarden speaking," he greeted cautiously, wondering how a call got forwarded directly to him without being screened by his secretary. Only important individuals had access to this direct line to him.

The voice on the other end boomed through the receiver, loud enough for Tempus to catch fragments of the conversation. "Nigel, this is Director James McGinny from Her Majesty's Revenue and Customs," the voice announced, its authoritative tone leaving no room for doubt. "We've received a serious complaint about your company's trade practices. If you're found in violation of customs regulations, the consequences will be severe. You better have a damn good explanation for this, and you better cooperate fully. Do you understand?"

Nigel's mouth went dry, his heart hammering in his chest as he struggled to process the gravity of the situation. "I don't know what you're talking about, sir," he stammered out, his voice tinged with disbelief at the realization that the actual director of HMRC had personally called him.

The scene played out like a surreal nightmare, defying all expectations and norms. Typically, the Chief Executive of HMRC wouldn't directly intervene in such matters, delegating them to senior officials within the organization. Yet, the urgency and severity of the issue had prompted this unprecedented action, leaving Nigel reeling in disbelief. It was as if witnessing the sun rise from the west—a rare and inexplicable occurrence that defied the laws of nature.

"What is this all about?" Nigel demanded, his gaze darting between the phone and Tempus with growing unease.

"You bloody well know what this is about, you ass!" James's voice thundered through the earpiece, his anger palpable even from several feet away. The force of his words reverberated in the room, leaving no doubt about the severity of the situation.

The HMRC, responsible for tax collection, customs administration, and ensuring compliance, wielded considerable authority. Their ability to audit companies, impose fines, and initiate legal action meant they held significant sway over business operations. Nigel realized with mounting dread that if HMRC became involved, his company could face devastating consequences.

Nigel's complexion paled, his voice faltering as he attempted to respond, but the call abruptly ended, leaving him trembling with shock. Concern for his company paled in comparison to the overwhelming sense of influence emanating from Tempus. Nigel's thoughts gravitated towards Tempus like a planet caught in the gravitational pull of the sun.

"Who are you?" Nigel's voice was barely a whisper, his eyes wide with disbelief.

Tempus leaned forward, his gaze unwavering. "I'm someone who ensures that justice is served, Nigel," he replied, his voice carrying a weighty resolve. "Now, let's get to the bottom of this."

Nigel's desperation to rid himself of Tempus's presence was palpable. In just a few short moments, Tempus had disrupted the tranquility of his office—not with spoken words, but with a simple text message. Nigel couldn't shake the suspicion that Tempus had bypassed intermediaries and directly contacted the Director himself, given the swift response.

Tempus wasted no time in outlining a plan for Nigel to salvage the situation. "Right now, you need to hang up the phone and call whoever you need to call in San Marino to make this right," he instructed firmly.

Before Nigel could even formulate a response, Tempus rose from his seat and headed for the door, displaying little concern over whether Nigel would comply with his directives. To Tempus, it seemed inconsequential. Nigel, on the other hand, felt as though he were under divine mandate, compelled to heed Tempus's words as if they were divine decrees.

Within the hour, Nigel had devised a preliminary course of action to address the issues with San Marino. It involved arranging a face-to-face meeting and conducting an audit of the company's transactions with the small nation—a plan set in motion by Tempus's commanding presence and unwavering guidance.

As dusk settled over the city of London, Tempus occupied a secluded corner within the confines of a dimly illuminated bar. The amber hue of his ale swirled languidly within its vessel, mirroring the ebb and flow of memories that danced through his mind like spectral apparitions. Amidst the bustling streets of Mayfair, this modest pub served as Tempus's refuge, a sanctuary where he could momentarily escape the burdens of eternity, blending seamlessly into the shadows that enveloped him.

Having sampled the local fare earlier, Tempus now indulged in the lingering flavors of his ale, savoring each sip as if it were a fleeting moment of respite from the relentless passage of time.

Yet, as he sat there, a solitary figure amidst the ambient chatter of the bar, Tempus's thoughts inevitably gravitated towards Constance and Sera. He pondered their whereabouts, contemplating the possibility of crossing paths with them once more in their current incarnations. With a sigh, he closed his eyes, allowing his mind to wander back to some of the distinct moments when Constance had reentered his life, each memory etched vividly in his consciousness like scenes from a forgotten play.

In Paris, the year was 1895, and the Eiffel Tower loomed proudly over the cityscape, its lights casting an ethereal glow upon the cobblestone streets below. It was there, beneath the towering structure, that Tempus and Constance had shared an embrace, their souls entwined in a timeless dance of familiarity.

"I feel as though I've known you forever," Constance had whispered softly, her voice a melodic refrain in the night.

"You have, my love. In every lifetime, we find each other," Tempus had replied, his words tinged with both joy and melancholy, a reflection of the bittersweet nature of their eternal bond.

Years later, in the tumultuous year of 1938, Tempus found himself in Vienna, a city teetering on the precipice of war. It was there, amidst the chaos and uncertainty, that he had encountered Constance once more, her presence a beacon of familiarity in a world consumed by chaos.

"Do I know you?" Constance had inquired, her gaze searching yet somehow knowing.

"More than you can imagine," Tempus had responded with a wistful smile, his heart heavy with the weight of countless lifetimes spent in her company.

As Tempus sat ensconced within the hushed ambiance of the bar, the weight of bygone days hung heavy upon his spirit, the faint echoes of memories resonating within the depths of his being.

Returning to the present, Tempus blinked away the shadows of reverie, his gaze clouded with a profound sorrow tinged with determination. The phantom sensation of Constance's touch lingered, her delicate fingers entwining with his in moments of reunion, only to be wrenched apart by the cruel hand of fate. The anguish of losing her, not once, but countless times, gnawed at the core of his being, a relentless cycle of anguish that threatened to engulf him whole.

The resolve within Tempus hardened like steel as he contemplated the prospect of enduring another cycle of heartache. To break free from the relentless cycle of suffering, he must sever the ties that bound them together. Only in Europe, where the memories of the lives of the three of them, haunted him at every turn. Only here in Europe had they inevitably met again and again.

Their love, tempered in the crucible of tragedy. With each cycle of reunion and separation, the tendrils of destiny seemed to bind them tighter. The notion of losing her again, of witnessing her demise in this lifetime as she had before, loomed over him like a dark omen, a perennial wound etched into the fabric of his soul.

"I must go to the States," he resolved, his voice a whisper.

The thought of losing Constance once more, of watching her slip through his fingers like sand, that pierced his heart with an anguish beyond measure. He wanted to avoid that fate and avoid Constance having to die once more. That was the drive behind his decision to leave Europe.

Tempus's melancholic reverie was abruptly interrupted by the approach of an unexpected presence. A woman, radiating warmth and curiosity, stood before him. Introducing herself as Lila, she asked to join him, her eyes alight with a gentle intrigue that suggested he had already piqued her interest. Tempus nodded and offered a faint smile, welcoming her company, if only temporarily.

"Hi, my name is Lila. Is it alright if I sit here?" she asked, her voice soft yet steady.

"Tempus. Of course," he replied, gesturing to the empty chair beside him.

They exchanged pleasantries, and Lila quickly sensed the profound depth in Tempus's demeanor—the kind of depth that comes from living through more than a lifetime of experiences. Her interest in him deepened.

"What brings you here tonight?" she asked, attempting to pierce through the veil of his quietude.

Tempus took a sip of his ale, his eyes distant. "Just passing through," he said. "Finding solace in familiar places."

Lila tilted her head, intrigued. "You speak like someone who's seen a lot. What's your story?"

Tempus chuckled, a sound tinged with both amusement and sorrow. "My story is long and complicated. But tonight, I'm more interested in the stories of others. Tell me about yours."

Lila leaned in, undeterred. "I think your story is worth hearing. Sometimes talking helps."

Tempus sighed, the weight of his centuries pressing down on him. "Alright," he began slowly. "How about I tell you a story from my home? Are you interested in hearing that?"

Lila welcomed the idea wholeheartedly, finding Tempus far more intriguing than the other men in the bar. Their crude pick-up lines had driven her to seek out a more interesting and safer conversation. Her girlfriend had stood her up after she'd already arrived and ordered a round, so going at it alone wasn't an option.

"Let's say I want to hear your story. Is it going to be good? Memorable? Entertaining?" Lila smiled, her curiosity piqued.

Tempus, unperturbed, began his tale. "Imagine living through countless eras, watching everything and everyone you know fade away while you remain. The world changes, people come and go, but you... you stay the same."

Lila listened intently, sensing the gravity in his words. "That sounds... lonely," she said softly.

"It is," Tempus admitted. "But that isn't the point of the story. Mortals have the luxury of finality. Their lives are short but intense, filled with beginnings and endings. They cherish moments because they know they're fleeting. For an immortal, everything becomes a blur of endless continuation."

He put his mug down, allowing his words to settle in Lila's thoughts before continuing. "Mortals live with a sense of urgency, an appreciation for each fleeting moment. For someone who remains unchanged, those moments lose their significance. Imagine loving someone deeply, knowing that you'll outlive them, watching them fade while you remain the same. That's the story I've heard."

Lila's eyes softened, her initial curiosity deepening into genuine empathy. "That must be incredibly hard."

Tempus nodded, appreciating her understanding. "It is. That is the fate of a city that is born to endure forever." Tempus made it out that he was talking about the place of his birth and not his own circumstances.

He glanced at Lila through lidded eyes. Aware that he had captivated her attention but he wanted to change the subject and steer their conversation away from his worries, if only for a moment. "Now, I'd rather hear about you. What brought you here?"

Lila leaned back, still processing his tale. "Honestly, I was supposed to meet a friend, but she stood me up. So here I am, listening to an intriguing story. It's turning out to be a much more interesting evening than I anticipated."

Tempus smiled faintly, a spark of connection bridging the gap between their vastly different lives. "Then perhaps this night holds more promise than either of us expected."

"Back to the story. This immortal loved and lost someone dear to him many years ago. Her name was Isolde." Tempus paused, the name lingering in the air like a haunting melody. "She died of what you might call a broken heart. And the immortal, with all his time, could do nothing to stop it. He watched her fade away, powerless. Her loss is just one of many, yet it stays with him, a reminder of the impermanence that he is denied."

Lila's eyes softened with empathy. "That sounds horrible, Tempus. It must be hard, watching people you care about disappear from your life."

"It would be indeed," he nodded. "But what makes it harder is knowing that no matter how many times it happens, you will never follow. You are bound to witness the end of everything except your own."

Lila reached out, placing a hand gently on his arm. "Wouldn't an immortal still have the capacity to care, to feel? That's something. Maybe that's what keeps you human."

Tempus looked at her, a mixture of gratitude and sorrow in his eyes. "Perhaps you're right, but I would consider such an individual as unfortunate, as they can never erase the pain. An emotionless immortal would fare far better, wouldn't they?" he asked.

"I don't think so," replied Lila. "If you're an immortal and you have no emotions, then you'd have no reason to live at all. You'd never find joy in anything, even the fleeting moments. I guess that would be even more sad."

Tempus considered her words, a faint smile playing on his lips. "Perhaps you're right," he said softly. "Perhaps the capacity to feel, even in the face of endless loss, is what keeps one truly alive."

Lila returned his smile, sensing the depth of his understanding. "And maybe," she said gently, "sharing those stories, those emotions, is what makes life, immortal or not, worth living."

Tempus nodded, feeling a connection form between them. In this fleeting moment, amidst the dim lights and hum of the bar, he found a glimmer of solace in Lila's presence.

Tempus nodded. "I agree with you. It's the connections we make that give us purpose, even if they're fleeting. Sometimes, talking to a stranger in a bar can make all the difference."

Lila smiled, her presence a comforting anchor amidst his eternal turmoil. "Then let's make this moment count," she said. "Tell me more about Isolde. What's the moral of the story?"

Tempus took another sip of his ale, feeling an unexpected sense of relief wash over him. For the first time in a long while, he felt understood, even if she didn't know he was speaking about himself. In that fleeting moment, he found a glimmer of solace in the shared understanding of a stranger.

He shrugged nonchalantly. "There isn't much more about Isolde in this particular tale. The setting was merely to frame one question."

Lila waited for him to continue, but Tempus's attention had shifted back to his mug. He took another slow sip, his silence growing more pronounced. Impatient, she gave the table a playful slap. "You beast!"

Tempus chuckled, his mood lifting. "The question is this," he said slowly, his voice taking on a more serious tone, "Would you want to live forever?"

Lila pondered his question, reflecting on the points he had made. She wasn't sure she could fully grasp how someone would feel after losing everything and everyone they loved repeatedly. "I'm not certain. What would you answer?" she finally asked.

Tempus looked at her, a mixture of sorrow and wisdom in his eyes. *I've lived long enough to know that immortality is both a gift and a curse. The pain of loss never dulls, but the moments of joy, however fleeting, makes it bearable. I wouldn't wish it on anyone, but I've learned to find meaning in the transient connections I make,'* Tempus thought to himself.

"Who wants to live forever?" Tempus eventually asked with a sad smile on his lips. "There's no time for a relationship. Not saying that finding love is impossible. It's just that the time spent would be but a mere moment in a never-ending blur. There's no place for a lasting relationship in that kind of existence."

Lila sat still, absorbing Tempus's words. The thought of never dying had initially sounded appealing, but as she pondered it further, the allure began to fade.

"You can't build dreams with anyone because time slips away. The other grows older while you stay the same." Tempus paused for effect, watching his words impact Lila.

She'd originally sat next to him because he seemed like the safest option in the room, but now he had her questioning the idea of living forever. Her initial thought had been, *'Hell yeah, I want to live forever,'* but now she wasn't so sure.

"This world grants only one moment to mortals. That moment defines and proves our existence. The impact our passing leaves behind is our legacy. So, who wants to live forever? Who dares to love forever? I don't think anyone can," Lila finally admitted.

She was looking down into the depths of her glass. She stayed like that a while before looking back up at Tempus. Lila leaned closer, her curiosity deepening. "So, it's the fleeting moments that matter most?"

Tempus smiled, noting the somber expression on Lila's face. "You're right. It's just a story, though. It's not true. Mortals like us can live for today as our forever. Today never ends. It's like that saying, 'wherever you go, there you are.'"

"I guess you're right," Lila admitted.

"Yes," Tempus replied. "It's the fleeting moments that make life, immortal or not, worth living. They remind us that even in an endless existence, there is beauty in the temporary."

Lila's eyes softened, and she nodded in understanding. "Then let's make this one of those moments."

Tempus smiled, feeling a rare sense of peace. "Thank you," he whispered, more to himself than to her, as the night continued to unfold around them.

Having resolved some personal doubts, Tempus continued their small talk for another hour before parting ways. Tempus returned to his temporary home, feeling a rare sense of peace. By morning, he had packed his few possessions into a duffel bag and set out to leave Europe, hopefully leaving behind any chance of reconnecting with Constance and Sera in this lifetime. He was unaware that fate had other plans for him.

Chapter 9: "Chasing Shadows"

Present Day - Atlanta, USA

An eternal struggle for love in the modern world.

The post production of the film had concluded and this freed up some of Sera's time. The day after she went to Stone Mountain with Alex was kind of odd for her. Alex never mentioned anything that happened the day prior and they worked until finishing the final scenes,

A few days later, as part of the post-production work, Alex had called her in to perform some voice-over work for certain scenes. They met early that morning at a recording studio in downtown Atlanta, not far from where her sister worked at the High Museum of Art.

Despite her efforts, Sera struggled to focus, her mind preoccupied with recent resurfaced memories. She was amazed she could function at all, knowing that if Tempus reentered their lives, there was a certainty that their lives would be cut short.

Determined to stay present, Sera found it increasingly difficult to engage with her tasks. She needed frequent reminders and felt her concentration slipping.

"Is there a problem?" Alex's voice crackled over the intercom from the control booth.

Sera sighed, removing her headphones. She peered through the double-layered window separating the sound booth from the control room.

"I think I just need to take a break," she admitted, realizing she wasn't giving her best effort. Continuing now would be futile. Perhaps a break would help her refocus.

"That's probably for the best," Alex agreed.

The tone of disappointment in Alex's voice was unmistakable. Since his declaration of love, Sera had become acutely aware of his feelings. Though that confession lingered in her mind, she noticed Alex seemed unbothered by her lack of response three days later. It irked her that he could act so nonchalant, as if his emotional bombshell hadn't unsettled her completely. While she was a wreck, he remained composed and focused on his role as the film's director.

Sera decided to let it go. She took a deep breath, removed the headphones from around her neck, and placed them on a nearby stand. As she exited the sound booth, she felt Alex's eyes on her, tracking her every step with apparent interest.

His gaze made her nervous. Her stomach churned, and she instinctively grasped it. "This sucks," she muttered under her breath.

"What did you say?" Alex's voice came through the intercom.

Sera cursed inwardly, realizing the microphone had picked up her comment. "Nothing. Just said I'm stepping into the lounge to get a drink," she lied.

She was relieved when Alex let her lie slide, merely nodding instead of calling her out. Sera offered him a weak smile, tightening her grip on her stomach as she left the sound booth. Determined to avoid further slips, she resolved to keep her mouth shut unless she was sure no one could overhear.

A few minutes later, Alex found Sera in the lounge, staring intently at her cell phone. He approached quietly and stood beside her, waiting patiently. His presence prompted her to shift her focus from the phone to him.

After a long pause, Sera finally broke the silence. "Is there something you need, Alex?"

Alex smiled and leaned back against the counter, his hands supporting him. "Not really. Just wondering if you've got something on your mind."

Sera felt a flush rise to her cheeks, quickly followed by a wave of frustration. "You've got some nerve."

"What do you mean?" Alex asked, feigning innocence.

"You know exactly what you did," Sera shot back, her hands finding their way to her hips. "It's been three days and you haven't even mentioned the bombshell you dropped on me."

"That's bothering you?" Alex seemed genuinely surprised. "I thought you were more worried about this curse, given how you've been acting."

Using one finger, she gestured in the air. "That and this are two different things," Sera declared.

"I'd think the curse would be way more important than my confession," Alex began. He shifted, no longer leaning on the counter, and moved closer to Sera, stopping just a handspan away from her. He looked down into her eyes. "I know I'm more worried about that curse."

Sera could understand his perspective. If the curse resurfaced, it could tear her away from him. She wasn't entirely sure how she felt about Alex, but the idea of leaving this world without exploring their potential together didn't sit well with her.

Unable to continue looking into his eyes, Sera turned from Alex. "You shouldn't worry about that," Sera said softly, turning back and waving a hand dismissively. "I don't even know what *I'm* supposed to do right now, so *your* worrying isn't necessary."

Alex reached out and gently stopped her from moving away. She looked over her shoulder into his eyes and felt her resistance fade, no longer wanting to distance herself from him.

"I am worried though. I'm worried enough that I've done my own digging into this curse," said Alex.

Sera's eyes widened. "How?" she asked, shocked and confused. "How could you even find anything out about a curse you know so little about?"

"I know one thing," Alex replied.

Skeptical, Sera sought clarification. "And what is that?"

Alex pointed at the phone still in Sera's hand, its screen filled with images of flowers she had been researching. "That," he said simply. "I know about that."

Sera turned fully to face him, having been halfway turned when he stopped her. "You can't possibly know of this. I've been searching over multiple lifetimes for this flower and never found it."

"I asked a professional botanist friend of mine. I described the flower in every detail to him, and he said he knew of it," Alex revealed.

Sera bolted forward, closing the distance between them until it felt to Alex as though she was almost within his skin. He reeled back involuntarily, startled by her sudden closeness.

"Does he know where we can find it?" Sera asked anxiously.

Alex held up a hand, signaling for Sera to wait a moment. He encircled her waist with his other arm, holding her close. He wasn't sure how his news would be met, and he wanted to prevent her from fainting or bolting.

"Look, it's not that easy. He said he knew of the flower but that it was extinct," Alex said slowly.

Sera looked crestfallen, her shock evident as her mouth hung open. "Don't say that. It can't be true. Does he know where it grew?"

"He knew where it grew. He said there was a legend associated with the flower that eventually caused its extinction."

"What legend? Where did it grow?" Sera asked desperately.

Alex's concern for Sera was clear in his eyes. He knew this news would be hard for her to hear, but he had tried to deliver it as gently as possible. "The legend spoke of the flower having mystical properties, which led to its over-harvesting. It used to grow in a remote valley in San Marino, but no one has seen it for decades."

Sera's eyes filled with determination despite the disappointment. "We need to find that valley, Alex. There has to be a way."

Cognizant of her distress and need, Alex continued sharing what he had learned from his friend.

"There's a legend that the flower would lead you to the person you were meant to be with. No matter the time or distance, it would guide you to them. Because of this, many people sought it out, and eventually, the flower became extinct," Alex explained.

Sera hadn't protested being in Alex's embrace. In fact, she hadn't even noticed that he had drawn her in, too fixated on learning what he knew about the flower. She felt like crying, and she did. Slowly at first, a tear slipped down her cheek.

Gently, Sera pushed out of Alex's embrace. She turned away and walked a few feet to sit at a nearby table. Her shoulders rose and fell rhythmically as she took deep breaths to calm her nerves.

Alex watched her with concern, understanding the weight of what he had just revealed. "We'll figure something out, Sera. There has to be a way," he said softly, hoping to offer some comfort.

Sera nodded, wiping away her tears. "I just... I don't know what to do," she admitted, her voice trembling.

"All this time I've been searching. Now you're telling me it's all for nothing? I won't find what I'm looking for? I can't break free from this curse that I've caused?" Sera's voice was soft, barely audible as she questioned herself.

"It's alright, Sera," Alex said, kneeling beside her and placing a comforting hand on her knee. "It's not your fault."

Sera's eyes blazed with a fire as she looked at him. Misplaced anger surged within her, and she lashed out at Alex before she even realized it.

"What do *you* know? It was *my* fault. I found that flower and I used it, thinking I could change my fate. Not knowing it would cast me and my *sister* into the sands of time, to be born and die over and over again." Her hand pushed out, causing Alex to stumble back, falling onto his butt.

"*I* did this to my sister, thinking I loved a man I'm not even sure I *care* about anymore. It took all this time to realize it was *infatuation*, but I've *cursed* my sister with my own selfishness," Sera said, her anger palpable.

"You didn't know," argued Alex, standing and brushing off his pants, his gaze fixed on Sera. There was more that he wanted to say but — he couldn't. Not now. Not yet, anyway.

"You weren't there! How could you know? I selfishly desired a love that I couldn't have, to the point where I ended up causing a curse on *me*, my *sister*, and *Tempus*," Sera shouted.

Her raised voice drew the attention of a passing technician. He paused, peering into the lounge, observing the two of them—one seated at the table, the other standing nearby. Concern creased his brow, evident in his lingering gaze, noticing the tears streaming down Sera's face.

Alex glanced at the technician and offered a half smile. "It's alright. Just a little disagreement."

The technician looked at Sera, silently asking for clarification, ready to intervene if needed. Sera met his gaze briefly before turning away, arms crossed over her chest. Finding no immediate need for intervention, the technician slowly walked away, his gaze lingering on them as he left.

"What was that all about?" asked Alex, already feeling drained from the mental strain of their disagreement. This wasn't what he had anticipated. He might not have known what to expect, but this was far from it.

"Just leave. I need some time alone. I've got to think," said Sera.

Alex reached out hesitantly, but Sera remained partially turned away, unaware of his hand hovering near her shoulder. It was clear she didn't want to speak with him, let alone be in his company. Yet, she made no move to leave, seemingly waiting for Alex to depart, which he eventually decided was the best course of action. Giving her space seemed to be the only right choice in that moment, as far as Alex could determine.

Alex disagreed with Sera's assessment that the curse was solely her fault. He knew it was more complicated than that, and he felt a weight settle over him as he made his way back to the control room. Seating himself at the console, he appeared visibly drained, catching the attention of the technician from earlier.

"Are you alright?" Jeff asked, his concern evident in his voice.

Half-aware of his surroundings and lost in his thoughts, Alex turned to Jeff as if emerging from a daze. "Huh?" he mumbled at first, then added, "Yeah, I'm okay."

Turning back to face the console, Alex stared blankly at the knobs and dials, his mind elsewhere. "I think we're done for the day. Let everyone know they can leave," he said softly, his voice distant.

Jeff glanced at the digital display above the console. "It's only just past noon. We still have the studio booked until six thirty."

"It's fine. I'll deal with it later," Alex replied, still preoccupied. Turning to Jeff, he added, "Tell everyone they did a great job today. I'll lock up when I leave."

With a nod and a wave, Jeff left the studio, leaving Alex alone with his thoughts

Alex felt a cold, damp cloth wipe across his forehead. It was a memory—a very old memory from so far in the past as to be unbelievable. His temperature at that time was sky high, his body wracked with pain.

The memory flooded back with startling clarity: the burning fever, the agonizing joint pain, the overwhelming sense of helplessness as the disease ravaged his body. It was a time of fear and suffering, a time he had tried to bury deep within his subconscious.

Yet, here it was, resurfacing like a specter from the depths of his past, haunting him once again with its chilling presence.

Through the haze of the fever, he recalled the presence of Sera, nursing him. She, one of the twins destined to die and be reborn, had been there with him, a twist of fate bringing them together only to tear them apart as he suffered until his death. She never knew that.

Alex had never had the opportunity to tell her what he knew. Each time he reached her in a life, it was either before his death or hers. There had never been enough time to share his truth with her. This realization pressed down on him now. Seeing her months ago had triggered buried memories of past lives, reminding him of what had set him on this journey through multiple lifetimes: the love of one girl.

A deeper memory surfaced then. Hellena. His maternal grandmother. The hut was dark, and a knock on the door stirred him from sleep. He didn't fully awaken until the visitor had already departed. Alex, blurry-eyed and yawning, entered the main room of the house he shared with his grandmother.

"I heard voices. Who was that, Nanna?" he asked.

"Just a visitor who was lost for a moment," Hellena replied.

"It sounded like Sera, the girl from the market," Alex said.

"That was indeed her. Perhaps fate had brought her here for a reason. I recall your fondness for her, though she remains unaware of your existence," remarked Hellena.

Alex, still groggy but alert enough to grasp his grandmother's words, felt a blush creep up his cheeks. It was embarrassing to confide in his grandmother about his feelings for a girl who didn't even know he existed, only to be teased by her about it.

"Well, that'll change once I catch her attention. I'll marry that girl one day," Alex declared with determination. Hellena smiled gently, patting her lap as Alex approached to stand beside her.

"I have no doubt you will. Here, take this flower," his grandmother said.

With that, Alex was snapped back to the present, the memory of centuries past fading. The 12th century. He remembered it vividly, as he always did.

Unlike the cursed twins, he wasn't bound to a predetermined lifespan. Death could claim him at any moment, yet he would be reborn, destined to live through another age, another life, and tolerate the enduring ache for the one thing he loved with all his heart: Sera.

Meanwhile, Constance and Lynette were hard at work finishing their preparations for the upcoming display. In the gallery, they directed the setup, ensuring everything was perfect.

Lynette couldn't help but notice that Constance seemed distracted. While Constance completed her tasks, she often gravitated back to the photo of the strange man. It was the only piece featuring his image that had made the final cut, and now Lynette was worried about her friend.

"Are you alright? You seem pretty distracted, Constance," Lynette asked, stopping beside her.

Constance glanced at her, a half-smile playing on her lips, tinged with melancholy. "I'm sorry," she said. "I didn't mean to be so out of it."

"It's fine, girlfriend. The setup is going smoothly. We just need to make sure each piece is in the right place," Lynette reassured her.

Constance tore herself away from the photograph, turning fully towards Lynette. They began walking through the gallery for a final tour.

"I don't know what's wrong with me. It feels like I've forgotten something very important," Constance admitted, glancing over her shoulder, without thinking, at the picture once more.

Lynette wasn't blind to it. She noticed and worried about her friend. "If finding out who that guy is, is that important to you, maybe we can look online for facial recognition software."

"I've thought of that already," Constance admitted sheepishly. "Most of those websites either don't work as expected, are scams or require you to set up an account and pay for the service. I'm not willing to do that just yet."

"Then I guess it isn't that important," Lynette replied, walking ahead of Constance. "Keep up, you."

Constance smiled, her worries forgotten for the moment as she sped up to catch her friend. They spent the rest of the day working together until their task was completed. After bidding farewell to Lynette, Constance headed to her car, thinking about home. Just then, she got a call.

"Hi, William," Constance said, glancing at the caller ID before accepting the call. "I just finished work and was heading home."

"Great to hear you're off," William replied. "I was hoping you would be. Want to stop by for a bit? Maybe have dinner here with me? I'm cooking your favorite pasta."

Constance hesitated. She craved a nice shower and an evening of relaxation. A shower at William's place was fine, but relaxing there would be another matter. His presence would remind her of the looming decision about his offer to move in together.

Realizing she couldn't keep avoiding William just to dodge that conversation, she consented. She figured she could come up with something if he brought up the subject again. If he didn't, all the better.

"Yeah, I'll be over soon," Constance said. "When I get there, I'm going to take a shower first. Can I borrow one of your shirts?"

William laughed. "Of course you can. I'd love to see you in it."

Constance ended the call, a smile spreading across her face. She knew William enjoyed seeing her in his clothes. It wasn't overtly sexual, but it was intimate, and for now, that was enough.

By the time Constance arrived, William was busy in the kitchen. He took a moment to let her in after she rang the bell, then headed back to attend to the cooking, speaking over his shoulder.

"You know where everything is. Dinner will be ready shortly," William said.

Constance didn't immediately head to the back to take a shower. Instead, she gravitated toward the stools at the counter facing the kitchen. She watched as William buzzed around, tending to boiling pots and sizzling pans. He was good at what he did. Being with a professional cook was a blessing, if you didn't get fat because of it.

As she watched, she became absorbed by her phone, scrolling to the picture she had taken of the strange man. William, in his busyness, noticed that she was still at the counter and hadn't gone back to take a shower yet.

"Are you gonna take a shower?" he prompted.

Constance looked up from her phone. "Oh, yeah. Sure. In a minute. Just looking at something."

Intrigued, William dried his hands with a towel and walked around the counter to look over Constance's shoulder at her phone.

"Who's that?" he asked.

"Not sure. It's an image of a John Doe that's quite interesting," Constance replied.

William glanced at the picture again. To him, it looked like an ordinary guy. If he had been the jealous type, he might have confronted her, but he wasn't, so he didn't.

"I don't see what's so interesting about him," William said finally. "Looks rather ordinary to me. A bit handsome, but nothing special."

Constance put her phone down and rested her elbows on the counter, placing her chin in her hands. She looked at William, causing him to smile.

"Well, it's a mystery I'm curious to solve," she said. "I'll bet you'd find this guy interesting if you knew what I knew," Constance said with a smile. She then explained to William about the other images bearing a striking resemblance to the same man and how they couldn't possibly be the same person.

"That does sound odd," William replied as he returned to the other side of the counter. "But I'm sure it's just a coincidence."

He dismissed the incident from his mind, more focused on having Constance there and providing a good meal for her.

"So, are you interested now?" asked Constance.

William shook his head and chuckled and nodded toward the hallway. "Alright, Miss Detective. Go take your shower. Dinner will be ready soon."

Constance smiled back, finally heading to the bathroom. "Okay, okay. I'm going," she said playfully.

Dinner was spent catching up on their respective work details and the days they hadn't seen each other. William was attentive, giving Constance his undivided attention. However, it seemed she wasn't reciprocating. He noticed her occasionally glancing at her phone. Though it wasn't in her hand, her attention was clearly divided. Eventually, William had enough.

"Is finding out who he is that important to you?" William asked, his voice edged with frustration.

Constance, caught off guard by the abrupt shift, was at a loss for words. She opened and closed her mouth, trying to figure out what to say.

"You've been looking at that phone on and off for the last half hour. While I'm glad it's not in your hand, it's just as bad if you keep glancing at it," William said, disappointment evident in his voice.

His words tugged at Constance's heartstrings. She quickly realized her inattentiveness had caused him some grief and pain.

"I'm sorry, William," Constance said, setting her utensils down and leaning back in her chair. "I have to admit, I've been more than a bit curious about that guy since I first saw him. It's like I know him. No...," she paused, searching for the right words. "It's like he's a missing piece of me."

William was silent for a few minutes, struggling to understand how a person in an old photograph could have such an effect on Constance. "It's not like you know him. What's so special about that guy?"

Constance couldn't find the right words. All she knew was that the connection felt profound, almost inexplicable. It was as if the person in the picture held a part of her soul, and she, in this fragmented state, was waiting for him to come and make her whole again.

"I..." Constance began, but her words drifted into silence.

William leaned back in his chair, tossing his napkin onto his half-finished plate. It was clear he was done eating and more interested in understanding what was going on with Constance.

"Look," he began, his frustration evident. "I've given you time and space to figure things out. I asked you to move in, and you ghosted me at breakfast right after that. Now you're here, supposed to be spending time with me, and you're fixated on some guy who's probably a nobody and long dead by now."

He reached across the table and picked up her phone. With a quick swipe, the screen lit up, displaying that same image again.

"Look," he said, showing her the phone. "You didn't even close the picture app; you just left it open with his picture." William turned the phone back around, examining the image closely. He scrutinized the clothing, the aging of the picture, the tint—all signs that it was very old.

"If this guy were alive, he'd likely be well into his hundreds by now," William remarked, placing the phone back down and sliding it across to Constance.

"What's going on, Constance?" he asked, his tone laced with concern.

Constance, feeling flustered and not wanting to escalate the situation, responded quickly. "What do you mean, 'what's going on'? I'm here, aren't I? I mean, I'm here with you right now and not somewhere else."

"Your body might be here, but your mind isn't. You might as well be gone, somewhere else, because you obviously don't want to be here with me," William accused.

Constance had to admit, William was right. Things had been perfect between them, but since the day she saw that picture—saw that man—she knew she was missing a part of herself that William could never provide.

Despite this, she didn't want to hurt William. He was right; that guy couldn't possibly be alive. And even if he was, what did he really mean to her? She didn't have much time to dwell on these thoughts before William posed another question.

"Constance, I think I've been patient enough. I've gotta ask: Are you willing to move in with me and take our relationship to another level?" William's eyes pleaded with her.

Constance felt her heartstrings being pulled mercilessly. She winced, unable to find the words to respond.

"I understand," William finally interjected. He stood up, gathering the abandoned plates, and cleared the table before heading into the kitchen.

"If we're not that important to you, then what are we?" William's voice carried from the kitchen as he deposited the dishes in the sink and turned back to face Constance.

The wait felt interminable. Constance seemed reluctant to speak, but eventually, she broke the silence. "I don't know, William," she confessed, the words hanging heavily in the air. They seemed to reverberate, filling the room with a weighty stillness. The ambient city sounds, usually mere background noise, now intruded upon the tense silence.

Her admission hit like a thunderclap. It was a stark declaration, one that left them both reeling. Constance's mind raced back to the moment she first saw Tempus's picture, realizing then that she had become lost to William.

Without pausing to consider the consequences, she blurted out, "I think we need to break up."

The words seemed to echo in the room, shocking them both with their finality. As the reality of her declaration settled in, Constance rose from her seat and crossed the room to stand beside William, her heart racing as she took his hand in hers.

She felt the weight of her words, knowing they had wounded him deeply. Uncertainty gnawed at her, a stark contrast to the once unwavering resolve they promised to one another, to face whatever challenges lay ahead, united in their commitment to each other.

Constance wrestled with her inner conflict, battling the urge to end relationships in her relentless quest for that elusive missing piece. She had entertained the notion that perhaps settling down with William would suffice—he was, after all, the best option available. But now, she realized, she couldn't ignore the undeniable pull towards the man in the photograph. He represented a future she was fated to embrace.

Meanwhile, William stormed out of the kitchen, his heart throbbing with a tumultuous blend of anger and frustration. The dinner had unraveled into a disaster, his hopes of a future with Constance dashed by a mere photograph featuring a man of uncertain origins.

He scarcely registered Constance's hurried footsteps trailing behind him as he retreated to the bedroom. The cool night air seeping through the open window offered little solace, failing to quell the storm of disappointment and resentment raging within him.

William stood with his back to Constance, gazing into the void, his thoughts racing like a relentless storm.

"How could you be so callous? So indifferent to the future we talked about having together?" His voice, though soft and aimed away from her, carried the sound of hurt—of betrayal.

Constance lingered in the doorway, torn between the urge to console William and the instinct to flee the turmoil of their argument. Her chest burned with conflicting emotions, but she had resolved to confront the truth about her relationships, even if it meant facing the pain with William.

"I'm sorry, I—" she began, but William's raised hand silenced her before she could continue.

"Don't. Just—don't." His voice was barely a whisper as he turned to meet her gaze, tears tracing a path down his cheeks. "I think you should go home. I need to rest for work in the morning." With measured movements, he began the mechanical ritual of undressing, each motion stiff and devoid of its usual grace, his inner turmoil evident in his strained demeanor.

Constance hesitated, her heart heavy with the weight of their shattered bond, before venturing deeper into the room to gather her belongings. She avoided meeting William's eyes, fearful of the pain she might find mirrored there—the pain she had inflicted with her thoughtless words, severing the threads of their once vibrant relationship. Doubts about their future, once mere whispers, now thundered in her mind as she realized she had once again sabotaged a connection, driven by an elusive longing she could never define, let alone satisfy.

With her clothes and bag gathered in her arms, Constance paused at the doorway, unwilling to look back and confront the devastation etched on William's face. She feared the temptation to retract her words, to offer hollow reassurances that it was all a mistake, but deep down, she knew it wasn't.

"I'll have your shirt dry-cleaned and sent back to you," she murmured as she made her exit.

William offered no response, his silence a poignant farewell as he watched her depart, leaving behind the wreckage of their relationship, and his life to be painstakingly rebuilt.

From the shadowed corner of the living room, Sera observed her sister Constance's return home. Her heart clenched with a bittersweet mix of sorrow and resignation as she remained seated in the dimly lit room, her feet tucked beneath her in an armchair.

Tempus's affections lay with Constance. Witnessing their love unfold before her eyes, through all the lifetimes, served as both validation and a painful reminder of her own emotions. However, over the years, across those countless lifetimes, Sera had come to realize that her feelings for Tempus were not as profound as she once believed. She wasn't as in love with him as her sister was. Their connection ran deeper than the fleeting infatuation she had once mistaken for love, especially as destiny careened down its reckless path.

Now, Sera grappled with the purpose behind their enduring suffering. What was the point of enduring endless days and lifetimes if fate's supposed intervention was meant to lead her to her true love? It seemed that fate's design was far from the idyllic outcome she had envisioned.

Sera had lost count of the many lives she and Constance had shared. Never did she imagine they would endure such trials, nor did she foresee Tempus condemned to an eternity of loneliness, haunted by the untimely deaths of herself and her sister each time they met. Yet fate intervened, weaving a path to reunite the three once more.

Tears welled in Sera's eyes, but she swiftly brushed them away, unwilling to reveal her inner turmoil to her sister. With a heavy heart, she rose from the armchair and made her way toward Constance, momentarily forgetting the weight of unspoken emotions and shattered dreams.

"Hey, Connie. What kept you out so late?" Sera's voice trembled slightly as she spoke.

Constance's initial surprise at seeing her sister alone in the dark quickly gave way to a somber realization. She sighed softly, her gaze falling to the shirt she still wore from William's apartment, a painful reminder of their recent breakup.

"I... I was at William's for dinner," Constance admitted, her voice tinged with sadness. "We ended things tonight."

Sera's lack of surprise was evident as she swiftly closed the distance between them, offering a comforting embrace to her sister. She didn't anticipate Constance shedding tears over the breakup, nor did she believe her sister would be deeply affected by it. Sera recognized that Constance's emotional turmoil likely stemmed from the gradual return of her suppressed feelings, the realization that something essential was missing from her life. Tempus.

In Sera's mind, she knew that Tempus would soon reappear, triggering the relentless cycle once again. With his return, their time would be limited, and their lives would be in jeopardy. If nothing changed, their existence would soon come to an end following Tempus's arrival, only to be reborn and restart the cycle anew.

Despite the burden of her own memories resurfacing, Sera refrained from disclosing the truth to Constance. With her sister's memories still sealed, attempting to explain the situation would only lead to confusion and frustration. Sera understood that Constance needed her memories restored before she could comprehend the complexities of their predicament.

Constance wasn't oblivious to her sister's demeanor; she sensed a palpable unease emanating from Sera. Despite grappling with her own issues, she couldn't ignore the subtle signs of distress in her sister.

"Are you okay, Sera? You seem to be dealing with some troubles of your own," Constance inquired, her concern evident in her voice.

Sera paused, contemplating her sister's observation. She acknowledged the truth in Constance's words but hesitated to burden her with her own troubles, at least not yet. Motioning for Constance to join her on the sofa, Sera decided to confide in her sister, sharing at least a portion of her concerns.

"Do you remember the director of the film I'm working on?" Sera began tentatively.

Constance furrowed her brow in thought. "Alex, right? Is something going on with him?" she asked, recalling her brief encounter with the director during Sera's work on the film.

"Yeah," Sera responded, her tone tinged with uncertainty. "He recently confessed that he likes me. I'm not sure what to do."

Constance's excitement bubbled to the surface, momentarily overshadowing her own concerns.

"That's fantastic news," Constance exclaimed. Yet, upon closer observation of her sister's expression, she couldn't help but notice the underlying unease. "But why does it seem like it's not bringing you joy?" A hint of worry crept in as she observed Sera's unsettled demeanor.

"It's complicated," Sera replied simply, her gaze distant.

Constance's surprise was evident as she probed further. "What could possibly be complicated about a good-looking guy liking you?

It's not like you've got anyone else knocking down your door. You stay so cooped up away from people it makes me worried."

"It just is. There's a lot going on right now, and dealing with his confession is the last thing I need," Sera explained, her voice tinged with frustration.

Constance regarded her sister, sensing there was more to the story than Sera was letting on. "Is there something you're not telling me?" she probed gently.

Sera shook her head adamantly. "No," she insisted. "I just have a lot on my mind, and I don't know if I have the energy to navigate Alex's feelings right now."

Constance narrowed her eyes, detecting a hint of evasion in Sera's response. However, she decided to respect her sister's boundaries and give her the space she needed to address her own concerns. She understood that Sera would confide in her when she was ready.

"Well, enough about that," Constance interjected, steering the conversation away from Sera's dilemma.

She rose from her seat and made her way to the kitchen, where she skillfully prepared two bowls of ice cream. Returning to the living room, she settled beside her sister and handed her a bowl.

"Let's forget about our problems with a nice rom-com," Constance suggested, a hopeful glint in her eyes.

Sera's smile brightened at the suggestion, the familiar routine serving as a comforting escape from their troubles. They settled in to enjoy the movie, the flickering light of the television casting a cozy glow over the room. However, their respite was short-lived as Constance's phone rang, interrupting their movie night.

Lynette's voice crackled with excitement on the other end of the line, prompting Constance to request a slower explanation of the news she was eager to share.

"Slow down, Lynette, and start from the beginning. I barely caught any of that," Constance requested, her tone laced with patience.

Sera observed with mild curiosity as Constance engaged in conversation with Lynette over the phone, her spoon hovering halfway to her mouth.

"I saw a recent picture of that guy you were so fixated on. Someone who looks exactly like him, in the flesh," Lynette exclaimed excitedly.

Constance's shock was palpable. "Where?" she inquired eagerly, her curiosity piqued.

On the other end of the phone, Constance could hear Lynette fumbling before she spoke again. "I just sent you a picture," she announced moments later. "My friend was going on her honeymoon with her new husband, and they took a picture at the Atlanta airport. In the background, you can clearly see that guy."

Constance lowered the phone and tapped her way to the text message with the attached photo. Sera leaned in, curious to see what had captured Constance's attention.

The picture appeared on the screen, but it was too small to make out the details clearly. With deft movements of her fingers, Constance enlarged the image, focusing on the man in the background. As his face came into view, she uttered a single word.

"Tempus," Constance said slowly, realization dawning on her as memories flooded back all at once, filling the void in her life.

Sera, in shock, dropped the spoon she had been holding. "It can't be," she whispered, disbelief evident in her voice.

Chapter 10: "The Black Death II"

14th Century - Versailles, France

In the grip of the plague, love faces its ultimate test.

It had been nearly a week since Tempus and Alexander arrived at the De Montford château. During that time, finding a moment of solitude with Constance and Sera had proven challenging. Pierre's watchful presence made it nearly impossible for the sisters to have a private word with Tempus.

However, on this day, Constance, Sera, Tempus, and Alexander strolled through the gardens of the De Montford château, the girls ostensibly guiding their guests around the green space encompassing the house. It was the only excuse they could conjure to secure a moment alone for a private conversation without their father, Pierre, looming over them.

However, even in this secluded setting, open dialogue remained elusive. With Alexander present, the girls and Tempus found themselves unable to speak freely. The issue wasn't whether Alexander might overhear their conversation; rather, it was the delicate nature of the subject they needed to discuss.

Tempus trusted in his bond with Alexander, believing him unlikely to betray their confidence to Pierre. Yet, discussing matters as weighty as immortality and reincarnation in the presence of Alexander remained a daunting prospect. Tempus doubted Alexander's capacity to comprehend such extraordinary truths.

That being said, Sera had taken it upon herself to accompany Alexander during their stroll in the garden. This decision allowed at least Constance and Tempus the opportunity to engage in a private discussion, free from prying ears. Sera trusted that her sister would later fill her in on the details of their conversation. However, by choosing to spend time with Alexander, she forfeited the chance to pose her own questions, relying instead on those asked by Constance.

As they walked, the girls cast furtive glances back at the house, where their father watched over them like a hawk. In their earlier, pre-memory-renewal days, they cherished Pierre's protective gaze, but now, with their recollection of past lives and knowledge of Tempus, his presence felt stifling. There was so much to discuss now that they were reunited.

Pierre, standing conspicuously at the window, made no attempt to conceal his disapproval of Tempus and Alexander's influence over his daughters. He harbored a deep distrust of Tempus, despite inconclusive evidence regarding his claims of a servant telling him the names of his wife and daughters. Pierre believed there was more to the trio's relationship than met the eye, and he was determined to stay vigilant.

His wife, Luviet's, voice calling from somewhere in the house drew his attention. After a lingering moment watching the quartet in the garden, he turned and left, granting the younger ones some semblance of privacy on their walk.

Back in the garden, Constance glanced over her shoulder at Sera and Alexander, who were trailing behind. She turned back to Tempus, her cheeks flushing when their eyes met, causing her to look away with a shy smile. Having Tempus back in her life felt surreal, even more so with the memories of past lives trickling back. The sensation of déjà vu was overwhelming; she had experienced this reunion multiple times across different lifetimes. Yet, in this moment, with Tempus beside her, nothing else seemed to matter.

Tempus, too, was nervous. The last time he saw Constance was over thirty years ago, and he lost her a year later. For her, it was another life; for him, it was a continuation of the same painful existence. Each loss was a wound that never fully healed. He had learned to cope with the grief as best as he could, without succumbing to it entirely.

By the time he had reunited with the twins for the second time, Tempus had only just begun to understand the cyclical nature of their lives. Just before their first rebirth, he came to the realization that he was immortal, a revelation that felt more like a cruel cosmic joke than a blessing. The cycle of reunion and loss was a relentless torment. Each reunion brought hope, but the inevitable loss that followed was a heavy burden on his heart. It was a punishment, not a gift, to repeatedly find and lose the ones he loved.

Constance could see the pain and stress in Tempus's eyes in that singular glance before she turned away, blushing. Yet, she also saw the strength she remembered from her very first life—the first time she saw him, the first time she knew she loved him. In this universe, she had been blessed to find someone who cared for her without measure, without holding back, willing to stand as her personal sword and shield against the cruelties of the world. Tempus made her feel like a princess, whole and complete.

She wondered what held him back now. She waited patiently for him to speak, though thousands of questions raced through her mind. What had he been doing with his life since they last parted? Where had he gone? What had he endured? Who had he met? Among all these questions, one stood out most: Had you thought about me?

Tempus noticed Constance's curiosity and the way she glanced at him with unspoken questions. He was hesitant to break the silence, burdened by the weight of his own emotions. Every reunion brought with it the joy of rediscovery, but also the inevitable dread of future loss.

Taking a deep breath, he finally broke the silence, his voice tinged with both relief and sorrow. "Constance, I've missed you more than words can express. These years have been long and filled with many trials. But finding you again... it gives me a reason to keep going."

Constance blushed, then turned back to look at the house to make sure her father wasn't at the window. Satisfied that Pierre was no longer watching, she took Tempus's hand, a shiver running through her at the familiar warmth of his touch. Without a word, she hurried through the garden, leaving Sera and Alexander behind. She knew she needed to find a secluded spot where they could speak freely, away from prying eyes.

They wove through the meticulously kept paths of the château's garden, the flowers in full bloom around them. The scents of jasmine and roses filled the air, mingling with the fresh scent of earth after a recent rain. Constance's heart pounded in her chest, not just from the brisk pace, but from the anticipation of the conversation to come. She finally led Tempus to a secluded gazebo, hidden by tall hedges and overhung with wisteria.

As they entered the gazebo, she released his hand and turned to face him. The sunlight filtered through the wisteria, casting a dappled pattern on Tempus's face. She took a moment to collect her thoughts, then spoke, her voice barely above a whisper.

"Tempus, I have so many questions," she began, her eyes searching his face for answers. "What have you been doing all these years? Where have you been? And... have you thought about me?"

Tempus took a deep breath, his eyes filled with a mixture of sorrow and relief. "Constance, It's been hard." He paused, gathering his thoughts. "I've traveled Europe, trying to find some meaning, some way to break this cycle. But every time, I find myself back here, with you."

Constance nodded, her heart aching at the sadness in his voice. "I've remembered bits and pieces of our past lives. The feelings always come first, then the memories. It's overwhelming, but I can't deny what I feel for you."

Tempus stepped closer, his hand reaching out to gently touch her cheek. "I never stopped thinking about you. Every day of my life, every moment, you're always in my heart. But this cycle... it's unbearable. Losing you over and over again..."

Tears welled up in Constance's eyes as she felt the weight of his words. She leaned into his touch, her hand covering his. "I feel the same way. Every time we meet, it's like finding a piece of my soul that was missing. But the fear of losing you again... it's always there."

Tempus pulled her into a tight embrace, his voice trembling. "I've been trying to find a way to end this cycle, to find a way for us to stay together without losing each other. But it seems like fate has other plans."

They stood there for a moment, holding each other, their shared history pressing down on them. Finally, Constance pulled back slightly, looking up into his eyes. "Do you think there's a way to break this curse? To finally be free?"

Tempus sighed, his brow furrowing. "I don't know. I've consulted with scholars, mystics, anyone who might have an answer. But it's always the same. They speak of fate, of destiny, but no one knows how to change it."

Tempus took a few steps to the other side of the gazebo. He gazed out across the lawn at the meticulously cared for garden. His thoughts ran round his head like the circular pathways through this garden. He turned back to Constance, afraid of what kind of effect his answer might have had on Constance.

Constance frowned, frustration bubbling up inside her. "There has to be a way. We can't just accept this. There must be something we can do."

Tempus nodded, stepping closer until he stood before her. "I have no idea where to start anew. I know nothing of how or why this has happened to us."

Constance felt a tightening in her chest but forced herself to stay calm. "Together. We can at least look back on our lives together and try to figure out where this all began," she offered, her voice steady. "We'll find a way."

For a moment, they simply stood there, holding each other, drawing strength from each other's presence. Then Constance took a step back, taking his hand in hers. "We should get back before they start wondering where we are," she said, a hint of worry in her eyes.

Tempus held onto her hand, stopping her from leaving. "You're right. We don't want to give your father more reasons to dislike me, but we need to make sure we can speak again in the future."

She smiled, a hint of mischief lighting up her eyes. "I can find a way to get past my father," she said. It felt strange to call Pierre her father, knowing that in a previous life, he had been no such person.

Tempus's eyes softened at her determination. "I trust you, Constance. We'll find a way to break this cycle."

They walked back through the garden, hand in hand, their hearts a little lighter. As they approached the house, Constance could see Sera and Alexander by the fountain, engaged in conversation. As they approached the others, Constance squeezed his hand, a reassurance of her presence.

While Tempus and Constance were deeper in the garden talking, Sera took the opportunity to lead Alexander to one of the fountains. They sat on the stone wall enclosing the pool, initially saying nothing, simply comfortable in the shared silence.

Alexander admired the view of the garden, but his eyes frequently strayed to the girl beside him. He stole surreptitious glances in her direction, trying to ensure his interest in her went unnoticed.

Sera ran her hand through the cool water, watching the sunlight reflect off the surface she disrupted. Her thoughts were a tangled mess, much like the disturbance in the water. She was thinking about Tempus and Constance.

Her initial feelings for Tempus had evolved; she no longer felt romantic love for him. Instead, it was more familial. Recognizing her sister's feelings for Tempus tempered her own emotions. She understood that the care she had felt for Tempus in the past was tied to how he had protected them.

A sudden movement from Alexander, as he covered his mouth to cough, brought her back to the present.

"I'm sorry, I was distracted," Sera said, feeling guilty for being a poor host.

Alexander smiled gently. He didn't mind her distraction; he would have been content to simply sit there and watch her play in the water. His sudden cough had interrupted the spell of her beauty as she played distractedly.

"No need to apologize," he replied, his voice soft. "It's a beautiful day and a beautiful garden. Easy to get lost in thought."

Sera smiled, grateful for his understanding. "It is, isn't it? This place has a way of making you reflect."

Alexander nodded, his gaze lingering on her. "And sometimes, reflection is exactly what we need."

They shared a moment of quiet understanding before Sera spoke again. "Do you think Constance and Tempus will be alright?"

Alexander thought for a moment before answering. "I believe so. They should be fine. I have no doubt Tempus will be a gentleman."

Sera felt a warmth in his words and nodded. "I hope you're right."

As they sat there, the bond between them grew stronger. In their quiet moments together, a new connection began to form.

Sera began to notice things about Alexander that she hadn't paid much attention to before. His pale expression troubled her; he seemed unwell, yet despite his pallor, he appeared to remain strong.

There was also something familiar about him that tugged at the edges of her memory.

"Have we met before?" Sera asked gently.

Alexander glanced down at his lap, taking a moment before looking back up into her eyes. "No, I've never met you before, Sera De Montford," he answered, offering only a partial truth. He had never met her in this lifetime, but he knew exactly who she was.

Sera wasn't convinced by his answer. There seemed to be a haziness in her long memories of past lives, a part that refused to come into focus. It was like trying to grasp wisps of intangible smoke.

She peered at Alexander through squinted eyes, her head tilted as if that would give her a clearer view. "I swear I recall meeting a boy that looked like you before. I can't place where, though," she said slowly.

She continued to stare at Alexander, hoping for some reassurance that her memory wasn't playing tricks on her. Alexander wanted to reassure her, to tell her the truth, but he felt it wasn't the right time. He opened his mouth to speak but was interrupted by the return of Tempus and Constance.

Tempus and Constance's expressions were a mixture of relief and lingering tension. Constance's cheeks were flushed, and Tempus seemed more grounded, as if their conversation had given him some much-needed clarity.

Sera and Alexander's conversation had halted as Constance and Tempus approached but Sera had not completely given up on the thought of continuing it at some later time. Sera raised an eyebrow, a knowing smile playing on her lips. "Did you two have a good talk?"

Constance nodded, her eyes sparkling with a newfound determination. "Yes, we did.

Sera's smile widened, and she stepped forward to hug her sister. "I'm glad."

"Sera, Alexander," Constance called out, her voice bright but slightly strained. "We should head back inside. Father might start wondering where we are."

Sera nodded, her curiosity about Alexander momentarily set aside. She brushed off her dress, having not done so when she stood. "You're right. We wouldn't want to worry him."

Alexander, who had been watching the exchange with curiosity, nodded. He stood as well and joined the small group.

Tempus smiled gratefully. "Thank you, Alexander for giving me time to speak with Constance alone. Your support means a lot."

"If there's anything I can do to help, just let me know," Alexander responded.

With a sense of purpose and unity, the four of them headed back toward the house. Tempus walked beside Constance while Alexander took a position next to Sera as they made their way back to the house. Sera couldn't shake the feeling that there was more to Alexander than he was letting on. She glanced at him occasionally, trying to piece together the fragments of her memory that danced just out of reach.

Alexander, for his part, walked beside her in silence, his mind racing. He knew he couldn't keep his secret forever, especially not from someone as perceptive as Sera. But for now, he would have to maintain the facade and hope that when the time came, he could explain everything.

When they reached the house, Pierre was waiting for them at the door, his expression a mixture of concern and irritation. "I was starting to think you all got lost out there," he said, his tone light but his eyes sharp.

"Just enjoying the garden, Father," Constance replied with a smile, trying to ease his worries. "It's a beautiful day."

Pierre nodded, his gaze shifting from his daughters to their companions. "Well, come inside. Lunch is ready, and we have guests arriving soon."

As they entered the house, Sera cast one last look at Alexander, her mind still buzzing with unanswered questions. She resolved to find out more about him, convinced that there was a connection between them that went beyond this lifetime.

Constance and Tempus shared one last glance before parting as well, a silent vow passing between them. For the first time in a long while, Constance felt a change in her life that she welcomed. Her heart breaking free from the cold that had wrapped it until this day.

Inside, the atmosphere was warmer, filled with the aroma of a home-cooked meal. The tension of the garden was left behind as they settled in for lunch. Conversation flowed easily, but Sera's mind remained partly in the past, searching for the missing pieces of her memories.

Throughout the meal, Sera stole glances at Alexander, noting the way he interacted with her family, the subtle way he seemed to fit in yet stand apart. There was a depth to his eyes that spoke of lifetimes of experience, a familiarity that she couldn't shake.

After lunch, as the guests began to arrive and the house filled with the hum of conversation, Sera found herself drawn to Alexander once more. She approached him as he stood by the window, looking out at the garden they had just left.

"Alexander," she began softly, "I know there's more to your story. I can feel it. When you're ready, I want to hear it."

Alexander turned to her, a shadow of a smile on his lips. "And when the time is right, Sera, I promise you'll know everything."

Sera's curiosity about Alexander grew stronger. She gave him a warm smile, then went to find her sister. They needed to prepare for the dinner later that evening, now that the guests had arrived. She also wanted to discuss what Constance and Tempus had talked about in the garden.

Constance retreated to her room, her mind a whirlwind of thoughts, especially about Tempus. She needed to delve into memories of their past lives to uncover what had transpired between them all. Sera's help would be crucial, and she welcomed her sister's company. With Tempus back in their lives, Constance hoped they might finally uncover the key to understanding their situation and breaking free from this cycle.

Constance sat at her desk, her thoughts heavy, while Sera took a seat nearby. They had faced countless trials, but through it all, they had each other. Together, they delved into their shared past, discussing the relentless cycle they were trapped in, Tempus's return, and how they might finally free themselves from the shadow of fate.

Meanwhile, Tempus sought solace in a quiet corner of the château, reflecting on his recent conversation with Constance. Their reunion had been brief but meaningful. The pain of past losses lingered, yet the hope in Constance's eyes rekindled his own resolve. He vowed to protect her, to find a way for them to be together without the looming threat of separation.

As the sun set over the De Montford château, casting long shadows across the garden, a sense of calm settled over the house. The path ahead was daunting, but for the first time in many lifetimes, they felt a glimmer of hope. United in purpose, they were determined to unravel the complexities of their existence. Together, they would strive to break the cycle and finally achieve freedom.

The air in the grand dining hall of the De Montford château was thick with conversation and the scent of roasted meats. Candles flickered, casting long shadows on the tapestried walls. Alexander's face was pale, his eyes hollow as he tried to focus on the conversation at the table. He had been feeling increasingly fatigued, but he had attributed it to the stress and demands of their journey. Now, he felt a gnawing sense of dread.

Tempus leaned over, whispering, "Are you alright, Alexander? You look worse than this morning."

"I'm fine," Alexander replied, forcing a weak smile. "Just tired."

Pierre De Montford looked suspiciously at the two young physicians. His father's condition had improved slightly under Tempus's care, but Pierre remained wary.

"I hope your friend is not bringing illness into my home," Pierre said, his tone sharp. "We have enough to worry about without the Black Plague."

The rest of the guests turned their attention to Pierre, drawn by his words. Luviet leaned toward her husband, her voice gentle but firm. "You worry too much, dear. I'm sure the physicians would not have brought any danger to our doorstep."

Alexander opened his mouth to respond, but a sudden fit of coughing overtook him. He doubled over, clutching his chest, and the violent spasms racked his body. Blood spattered his handkerchief, and gasps echoed around the table.

"Alexander!" Tempus exclaimed, rushing to his side. "We need to get him to bed."

Pierre's face turned ashen. "You brought the plague here!" he shouted, his voice trembling with a mix of fear and anger. "You've condemned us all!"

Tempus, struggling to maintain his composure, gestured for Sera and Constance to help. "We need to move him now," he said urgently.

Sera, her face pale but determined, nodded. "Come on, Constance, help me with him."

The sisters supported Alexander between them, his weight heavy and cumbersome. Tempus followed closely, his mind racing. As they reached the guest bedroom, Sera and Constance carefully lowered Alexander onto the bed.

"We need to assess his condition," Tempus said, more to himself than anyone else. He looked at Sera. "Please fetch some hot water and clean cloths."

Sera hurried out, leaving Constance standing nervously by the door. She glanced at her father, who had followed them, his face a mask of worry.

"Father," Constance said softly, "Tempus is a skilled physician. He won't let this disease spread."

Pierre shook his head. "How can we be sure? The plague is merciless, Constance. We cannot take any chances."

Sera returned with the water and cloths, and Tempus set to work, wiping the sweat from Alexander's brow and cleaning the blood from his mouth. Alexander's breathing was shallow, each breath a struggle.

"Tempus," Alexander rasped, his voice barely audible. "I... I'm sorry."

"Save your strength," Tempus replied, his voice tight with worry. "You're going to get through this."

Sera watched, her heart aching for the young man lying before her. She had seen sickness before, but nothing like this. "Is it really the plague?" she whispered.

Tempus shook his head. "I don't believe so. His symptoms... they don't match entirely. It's something else, something we might still manage."

Constance moved closer, her hand resting gently on Alexander's arm. "You'll get better," she said softly, more to reassure herself than him. "You have to."

Pierre stood at the doorway, his resolve hardening. "If he does not improve by morning, we must isolate him. For all our sakes."

The room fell silent, the gravity of Pierre's words hanging heavily in the air. Tempus continued his work, determined to save his friend. But deep down, he knew the battle against this illness was far from over.

Tempus watched resignedly as Luviet guided Pierre away from the door. Their exit was followed by Constance and Sera, whom Tempus assured that their assistance was no longer needed. "I'll take care of Alexander from here," he said, determination in his voice. The sisters exchanged a worried glance but complied, leaving Tempus alone to tend to his friend.

Tempus spent the night at Alexander's bedside, tending to his needs as best he could. Upon further assessment, Tempus became convinced that his friend's symptoms were not indicative of the black plague ravaging the world outside the walls of the De Montford château. While Alexander slept fitfully, Tempus's thoughts raced, consumed by worry for his friend's health and the complex situation involving Constance and Sera.

Pierre had already cast doubt on Alexander's condition, fearing that the persistent cough, now producing bloody sputum, and fever were signs of the plague. As Tempus observed Alexander, he noticed the onset of night sweats. Gently, he took a cloth and mopped his friend's forehead.

Tempus's reverie was interrupted when Alexander reached out, clasping Tempus's forearm. "I'm sorry I caused such a commotion," Alexander said weakly.

Tempus, concern etched in his eyes, placed his hand over Alexander's. "It's alright. We'll get you through this," he reassured, though the worry in his voice was unmistakable. Alexander could see the concern clearly written on Tempus's face, adding to the heavy silence between them.

"You don't have to say anything," Alexander began, struggling to sit up in bed. Tempus swiftly moved from his chair to assist, helping him into a more comfortable position.

Exhausted from the effort, Alexander managed a weak smile. "I know already. It's consumption."

Tempus opened his mouth to respond but then closed it, his eyes drifting away from Alexander's. He stared at his hands in his lap, now that he had reseated himself. It took a moment before he could gather the courage to ask the questions weighing heavily on his mind.

Tempus had noticed Alexander's constant fatigue and weight loss but was certain it wasn't the black plague gripping his friend. While plague symptoms did include severe respiratory issues like a cough with bloody sputum, fever, chills, and severe malaise, Alexander's condition seemed different.

In the context of the black plague outbreak, any severe illness with fever and respiratory symptoms could easily be mistaken for the plague due to the widespread fear and high mortality associated with it. Limited medical knowledge and diagnostic tools made distinguishing between diseases with overlapping symptoms a challenge.

Tempus knew that with Alexander's worsening respiratory symptoms, additional fever, and coughing up blood, his condition could be mistaken for the plague. This misinterpretation could lead to their expulsion from the De Montford household.

After a thorough examination, Tempus found no evidence of swollen lymph nodes, a key indicator of the plague. Yet, this did little to ease his mind. The pervasive fear of the plague caused panic, and the high mortality rate made people quick to assume the worst. Without a clear diagnosis, any respiratory distress could easily be misattributed to the plague by those lacking medical knowledge.

"How long has it been?" he asked gently, his voice barely above a whisper. Deep down, he knew he had noticed the signs months ago, but admitting it aloud would mean confronting his own powerlessness to help his friend.

Alexander gave a heavy sigh. "I've known for about a year now. I originally got into medicine for this reason. To see if I could find a cure. But life...," he trailed off. not finishing the sentence that would validate the truth of his mortality. The truth that his lifespan had been cut short by the disease which had now reared its head in a final outburst to let him know it had a grip on his body.

"I don't have long to live, do I?" Alexander asked slowly. He hoped that Tempus might know something. Might be able to do something that could help him but he knew for certain that the chance was slim at best.

"I should think that with the symptoms you're displaying now, you don't have much longer to live. Maybe a month or two at best," offered Tempus.

"Ah," intoned Alexander softly. He turned his head upwards to gaze at the ceiling, coming to grips with the truth he had always known: his time was running out. "And here I just met her again," he murmured, mostly to himself, unaware that Tempus had overheard.

Tempus glanced at Alexander, his brows furrowing with curiosity. "Just met who?" he asked gently.

Alexander turned slowly towards Tempus. "Nothing. I said nothing." With that, he slid back into the comfort of the bed. Turning away from Tempus, he soon fell into a fitful sleep.

Constance stood in the wide hallway, her gaze fixed on the door to Alexander's room. Her concern seemed out of place—she had only recently met him, and their brief interactions hadn't warranted such emotional investment. Her primary focus had been the return of her memories and Tempus, not this guest of his. Yet, the worry persisted.

With her head bowed and her fist clenched to her chest, Constance remained unaware of the door opening until she heard the soft click of the latch. Looking up, she met Tempus's eyes, caught between her scattered thoughts and the present reality. Her smile was hesitant, a silent question hanging in the air: Was Alexander feeling better?

Tempus, still holding the door handle, turned halfway to face her. He was surprised to see her; he hadn't expected either her or her sister to stay or return. Having been with Alexander all night, he wasn't sure if Constance had left and come back. It didn't matter now; she was here.

As Tempus began to speak, Constance interrupted him. "I was worried. I came back to see how he was doing and..." She trailed off, uncertain why she had returned so early. Awake even before the house staff had begun their morning routines. In all honesty, she was more worried about how Tempus was doing with all of this.

Tempus sighed, releasing the breath he had been holding. He let go of the doorknob and faced her fully. "He's doing better than last night," he said softly. Placing a hand on the door behind which Alexander rested, he added, "He's asleep now."

Tempus's hand fell from the door as he turned back to Constance. "Are you worried?" he asked, tilting his head slightly. He stepped closer, placing his hands gently on her shoulders. "Thank you for caring about my friend."

Constance looked up into Tempus's tired eyes. Dark circles underlined his once vibrant cheeks, which had lost their usual glow. Leaning into his chest, she felt his arms encircle her.

"Yeah, I was worried," she murmured. After a brief pause, she disentangled herself from Tempus's embrace. She looked somewhat demure, her eyes cast downward as she continued, "If someone saw us like this, my father would be furious."

Tempus managed a weak smile and rubbed the back of his neck. "I know. It wouldn't be good."

Constance asked, "So, can anything be done for Alexander?"

Tempus's expression grew somber. "I've identified the problem, but unfortunately, effective treatments for consumption are scarce." He hesitated before finishing the sentence, reluctant to admit that such treatments were, at best, ineffective and, at worst, worthless. "I'm planning to ask your father if there's a place in the house where I can prepare some medicine to alleviate his symptoms."

Constance considered this, her gaze drifting to the door of Alexander's room. "There is a scullery in the house you could use. I can ask for you if you'd like," she offered.

Tempus's smile became more sincere. "I'd appreciate that. I didn't sleep well in that chair beside Alexander all night. With your help, I can rest and you can get an answer from your father without me having to find him and wait."

Constance nodded, a sense of relief washing over her as she prepared to assist. Tempus and Constance went their separate ways: Tempus to rest and Sera to find her father and request access to the scullery.

It wasn't until just past noon that Tempus awoke, dressed, and went to find Constance. She shared the news: her father had agreed to the use of the scullery.

Upon hearing this, Tempus asked Sera, who was with Constance, to update her father on Alexander's condition. He needed to assure him that Alexander's illness was not the plague. It was crucial to clarify this for two reasons: first, Tempus was still treating Pierre's father, and second, he wanted to avoid the risk of Alexander being evicted. Finding alternative shelter in the district was impossible, and returning to Paris was too arduous given Alexander's weakened state.

With the scullery issue resolved, Tempus could now focus on obtaining the herbs needed for Alexander's treatment as well as the medicine required for the senior De Montford. Ensuring both patients received proper care was paramount.

Over time, a routine took shape: Tempus spent most of his days in the scullery, busily preparing medicines. Meanwhile, Sera took on the responsibility of caring for Alexander, while Constance lent invaluable assistance to Tempus. The cycle of care and preparation became a steady rhythm in their days.

Although the senior De Montford's health showed a slow but steady improvement, Alexander's condition took a sharp turn for the worse, which deeply troubled Tempus. Fortunately, with the family head's recovery allowing him to focus solely on his friend, Tempus could now dedicate more time to Alexander's care. He immersed himself in the sparse medical texts he and Alexander had brought, desperately searching for any clues that might alleviate the consumption threatening his friend's life.

Despite his efforts and hopeful intentions, the reality proved harsh. The disease stood as an impenetrable barrier, highlighting Tempus's helplessness in the face of Alexander's worsening condition.

Tempus felt a deep sense of weakness and powerlessness as he confronted the daunting task of treating two individuals; one of whom was his dear friend. The enormity of the situation left him feeling as helpless as he had when his parents first announced Constance and Sera's marriage arrangements in their previous lives.

To make matters worse, Tempus had ordered herbs for making medication from the apothecary in the nearby village, hoping they would provide some relief for Alexander's suffering. However, when he received the shipment, it was far from what he had anticipated—barely enough to meet his needs. Frustrated and anxious, Tempus decided to confront the issue directly. With

Constance accompanying him for support, they made their way to the apothecary.

A carriage ride eventually brought the two to the desired location. Tempus stared out of the carriage window, his expression dark. "It's infuriating. I was explicit in my order. How could they send such a pitiful amount?"

"They might be struggling with supplies, Tempus," Constance said softly. "The plague has caused shortages everywhere."

Tempus clenched his fists. "That's no excuse. Alexander needs those herbs. His condition worsens by the day."

Constance placed a comforting hand on his arm. "It'll be alright. We're going there now to see if we can fill the missing items, aren't we?"

He sighed, his frustration evident. "I know. But it's not just about Alexander. It's... everything."

Constance's voice was gentle. "You're worried about Sera and me, aren't you?"

Tempus avoided her gaze. "How can I not be? Every time I see you, I fear it will be the last."

"We've been through this before, Tempus. Many times. Nothing will change immediately so see about Alexander first and we'll figure out something else for our situation later."

Tempus's voice rose, tinged with desperation. "A solution? Every lifetime we search, and every time I lose you both. How can I face that again?"

"Then let's focus on the present, like I mentioned," Constance said, her tone firm yet soothing. "Alexander needs us now. We'll handle the curse when we must."

Taking a deep breath, Tempus nodded. "You're right. I'm sorry. It's just... the herbs, the plague, the curse... it's all too much."

"One step at a time, Tempus," Constance reminded him. "Let's deal with the apothecary first. We need those herbs."

"For Alexander. For all of us," Tempus agreed, a note of resolve returning to his voice.

Despite the reassurances from Constance, Tempus stormed into the apothecary, his frustration barely contained. The narrow shop was dimly lit, shelves lined with jars of various dried herbs and powders. He approached the counter, where an elderly pharmacist was carefully arranging a set of scales, his movements deliberate and measured. Tempus's frustration was palpable. The elderly pharmacist looked at the two upon noticing their entry into the shop.

"I did not receive the entirety of the herbs I requested?" Tempus's voice was strained, his eyes darting around the shelves, searching for the expected quantities.

The pharmacist looked at him, his expression somber. "I'm afraid the supply is quite limited, Maître Tempus. The plague has ravaged our stock, and many herbs are in short supply."

Tempus's frustration boiled over. "This is unacceptable! I need these herbs to make medicine for a dear friend who is suffering terribly. The quantity you've provided is barely enough to make a difference!"

The pharmacist's eyes widened with concern. "I understand your distress, but we are facing shortages everywhere. The plague has taken its toll on our supplies and made it difficult to procure new ones."

Tempus's anger intensified. "You don't understand! Every moment I waste is another moment my friend suffers. This is not just about herbs; it's about saving a life!"

Constance, following Tempus into the shop, saw the strain on his face. Her brows furrowed, and the corners of her mouth turned downward. She felt overwhelming grief for the stress that Tempus was under. She placed a calming hand on his arm. Her voice was soft but firm. "Tempus, we need to keep perspective. The world outside these walls is suffering just as much as we are. The apothecary's limited stock is a reflection of the broader crisis."

Tempus, impetuous and angry, turned to face Constance, a thoughtless word forming and hanging ready to escape his lips. Fortunately, he was able to catch himself before he said something unthinkable to the woman he loved. He took a deep breath, his anger beginning to subside. He looked at Constance, her supportive presence helping to calm his frayed nerves. "You're right. It's just—"

The pharmacist cleared his throat, trying to offer some assistance. "There are some alternative herbs that might work in place of those you need. They won't be as effective, but they could still provide some relief."

Tempus's shoulders slumped slightly. "What alternatives do you have?"

The pharmacist gestured to a shelf at the far end of the shop. "We have a few herbs that are not as potent but could still help. You might consider using a combination of these."

Constance squeezed Tempus's arm gently. "Let's look at these alternatives. It's not ideal, but we can make do with what we have," she smiled.

It was enough. The anger slipped from Tempus like water from a melting icicle. He nodded, his resolve strengthening as he followed Constance's lead. Turning back to the pharmacist he said, "Alright. Show me what you have."

The pharmacist began pulling jars from the shelf, and Tempus examined the herbs with a critical eye. Constance stood beside him, her presence a steadying influence. As they selected the herbs, she whispered, "We're doing what we can. We'll get through this. And remember, we have each other to rely on."

Tempus nodded, a small smile of gratitude forming on his lips. "Thank you. I don't know what I'd do without your calming presence."

With their selection of herbs packed, Tempus and Constance left the apothecary and made their way back to the De Montford château. The streets were eerily quiet, the plague's shadow casting a pall over the city.

In the carriage, the silence was tense. Constance finally broke it, her voice trembling with a mix of shock and anger. "Tempus, what were you thinking? You can't just lash out at people like that."

Tempus looked down, regret evident in his eyes. "I know, Constance. I'm sorry. I just—seeing you and Sera again, knowing the curse will eventually take you away... it terrifies me."

Constance sighed, her anger softening into concern. "I understand your fear, but we can't let it control us. Right now, we need to focus on Alexander. We can confront our own issues afterward."

Tempus nodded, his voice barely above a whisper. "I'm just so scared of losing you again, that's all."

Constance's heart ached at his words. She, too, was silently battling the same fear. '*Every moment with Tempus feels fleeting, like sand slipping through my fingers,*' she thought. '*How much time do we really have left? I just want to make the most of it before fate tears us apart again.*'

She reached out and took his hand, squeezing it gently. "We will take care of Alexander first. And whatever comes next, we'll face it together."

Tempus looked at her, his eyes filled with a mix of gratitude and sorrow. "Together," he echoed, finding some solace in her words despite the storm raging inside him.

Back at the château, Tempus headed straight to the scullery, ready to begin the laborious process of preparing the medicine. Constance followed, her concern evident in her every step. She knew that while Tempus struggled with his own grief and frustration, the task at hand remained crucial.

Tempus stood by the large wooden table in the scullery, his hands methodically grinding herbs into a coarse powder. The rhythmic motion of the mortar and pestle was a small comfort in the midst of his mounting anxiety. His mind was far from the task at hand, consumed by the dire state of his friend, Alexander, who lay suffering from consumption in another room within the château.

Constance worked beside him, her hands methodically preparing additional ingredients. She observed Tempus in silence, her concern growing as she noticed his deepening despondency. The quiet of the scullery was punctuated only by the soft sounds of their labor and the occasional sigh from Tempus.

After a while, Constance decided to break the silence. "Tempus," she said gently, her voice laced with concern, "you seem lost in thought. Are you alright?"

Tempus looked up from his task, the burden in his eyes evident. "It's just... Alexander. He's suffering, and it feels like there's nothing more I can do. This disease is so sinister."

Constance's heart ached for him. She knew well the pain of loss, having experienced it repeatedly across their many lifetimes. But now, seeing Tempus in this state, she was reminded of her own anguish. Each time she regained her memories and was reunited with Tempus, she knew it was only a matter of time before fate would wrench them apart again. For her, the cycle of loss was unbearable enough when viewed from her brief moments of awareness; for Tempus, it was an unending torment, each wound reopening as soon as it healed.

As Tempus continued, Constance's thoughts turned inward. *'Every reunion brings a semblance of hope, only to be followed by excruciating separation. I remember our past lives and the pain of losing him again and again. It's a cruel fate to live with this knowledge, to understand that while I experience the suffering once, Tempus endures it perpetually. Each time we part from him, he is left to carry the pain of that loss, a wound that never truly heals.'*

Despite her inner turmoil, Constance maintained her outward composure. She reached out and placed a gentle hand on Tempus's arm. "I can see it's more than just Alexander's condition that troubles you. It's everything you've faced up until now, isn't it?"

Tempus's gaze met hers, a mixture of frustration and resignation evident. He quickly turned away from her, his brows furrowing as his eyes clinched shut. A crease appeared between his eyes, above the bridge of his nose. "It's hard to bear. Each time I'm reunited with you and Sera, it feels like a fleeting glimpse of hope. But then the inevitable happens, and the loss is even more profound because I've had the chance to care deeply all over again."

Constance nodded, her own heart heavy with the knowledge of what was to come. *'I can't share this pain with him. Not now. He's focused on Alexander, and he needs to be. But inside, I'm terrified of the future too. I fear the day I'll be taken from him again, the uncertainty of when that might happen, and the inevitable grief that will follow. I only have to endure this once in each life, but he bears it all, unceasing. I can only see that there is comfort in the oblivion of lost memories Sera and I have as we enter a new life before it all comes back when we meet up again. Unlike us, he has no such relief.'*

She took a deep breath, her voice steady despite the storm inside. "Tempus, I understand the burden you carry. While you've faced so many losses, each one seems to cut deeper. But remember, even in the face of such relentless sorrow, there's strength in the love and care you've given."

Constance reached out a gentle hand and cupped Tempus's face. She turned his gaze towards her.

Tempus's expression softened slightly. "Thank you, Constance. It's hard to see past the immediate despair, but I appreciate your words." Tempus was partially lying to himself. The despair only served to further drag him down into the abyss each time he lost the twins. Nothing relieved him from that. He had too much time to reflect on the lost, knowing only that fate would make him suffer through it yet again.

Constance continued, her tone reassuring. "We can't change the past or control the future. But we can make a difference in the present. We'll continue to care for Alexander, and we'll support each other through this."

Tempus nodded, though his eyes remained troubled. "I just wish there was more I could do."

Constance's heart ached for him. '*I wish I could tell him how deeply I feel this loss too, how every moment with him is a precious gift that will eventually be torn away. But for now, I'll be here, supporting him as best I can.*'

In an unexpected show of emotion, Constance leaned closer and brushed her lips against his before leaning away again. Tempus, surprised by the gentleness of the kiss, could only respond with a loving smile.

As they resumed their work, Constance's thoughts were a mix of sorrow and resolve. The scullery, once a place of routine, now felt like a space where they confronted their deepest fears together. For Constance, the knowledge of future separation weighed heavily, but in that moment, she chose to focus on the immediate task at hand and the comfort she could provide Tempus.

Their shared understanding and unspoken connection deepened, a bittersweet reminder of the cyclical nature of their fate.

Later that evening, Alexander was being tended to by Sera. He was at least responsive, though he was enduring the physical toll of the consumption raging within him.

Sera, dutiful in attending to his needs and honoring the promise she made to Tempus to help care for his friend, found herself caught between her confusion about the connection she felt toward this man and the knowledge that she had only just met him.

The window in the room was open enough to let in fresh air from outside. The curtains were drawn back, revealing a sparkling night sky. Sera adjusted the thin blanket over Alexander, her movements tender but deliberate. The room was quiet except for the occasional creak of the old wooden floors and the distant murmur of the household. As she worked, she couldn't shake the sense of confusion that had settled over her since she began tending to him.

Her eyes turned from the open window as she noted Alexander's gaze fall upon her as she worried the blanket.

"Alexander," she began softly, trying to break the silence, "have you ever wondered about the stars? What they might be like if we could see them up close?"

Alexander's eyes, dimmed by fatigue, flickered open. He glanced at her with a faint smile. "The stars?" he murmured. "I suppose I have. It's difficult not to wonder about such things when one is confined to a bed."

Sera nodded, her gaze drifting to the window where the dim light of dawn seeped through. "I've always thought the stars were like the promises of things beyond our grasp. Like a distant hope."

Her words hung in the air, heavy with unspoken meaning. Alexander's heart ached at the thought of what might be lost. He wanted to tell her everything, to confess his love and the truth of their intertwined destinies, but the weight of his impending death and the burden it would place on her kept him silent.

"I suppose hope is a valuable thing," Alexander replied, his voice barely more than a whisper. "It helps us endure even the hardest trials."

Sera's brow furrowed as she adjusted the pillow beneath his head. "Do you have any hopes? Any dreams you've held onto?"

Alexander's thoughts turned inward. *'I wish I could tell her of out past lives and how deeply my heart has always been hers. But it's too late for such confessions now. I must protect her from this burden, even if it means hiding my true feelings.'*

"I've always hoped to see a world where suffering is no longer a constant companion," he said, carefully choosing his words. "A place where we can find peace, even if only in fleeting moments."

Sera met his gaze, her eyes searching his face. There was something in his expression that unsettled her—a depth of emotion she couldn't fully understand. *'Why do I feel this strange pull towards him? Why does it seem like there's an insurmountable chasm between us?'*

"I think we all long for that," she said softly. "A place where we can be free of our struggles. It's a dream worth holding onto."

Alexander's hand reached out, his fingers brushing against hers. "Yes, it is," he said, his voice trembling slightly. "And sometimes, it's the small moments of connection that remind us of that hope."

Sera felt a warmth spread through her as their hands touched. *'What is this feeling? It's as though our brief touch has made me question everything I thought I knew about myself. It's both comforting and disorienting.'*

She pulled her hand away, her cheeks flushed. "I suppose that's true. Even in the midst of hardship, these small connections can mean everything."

Alexander watched her, his heart breaking. *'If only she knew how much I want to share my heart with her, how much I want to be with her in this lifetime and beyond.'*

As the conversation drifted to safer topics—local events and the latest news from the château—both of them were lost in their private thoughts. For Sera, it was a sense of inexplicable connection and concern that she couldn't quite place. For Alexander, it was the sorrow of knowing he would soon have to let go of the one person who had unknowingly been his constant through countless lives.

Within a few days of that exchange, Alexander departed this world. He left behind a deeply hurt Tempus, who felt the sting of his powerlessness to help his friend, and a confused Sera, who felt as though she had lost something she couldn't fully comprehend.

Tempus remained at the château for another two weeks after Alexander's passing, but the atmosphere grew increasingly somber. The curse that had long tormented him, Constance, and Sera manifested once more.

Tempus, already fractured by Alexander's death, faced a new torment. The once bustling halls of the château now felt hollow. The black plague, brought by an infected servant, claimed Sera the day before Constance's own final moments.

Tempus had been with Sera through her last breaths, offering her whatever comfort he could as she succumbed to the illness. The deep sense of loss that filled him then was a harbinger of the pain to come with the inevitable loss of Constance.

As the sun dipped below the horizon, Constance, gravely ill, lay in her death bed with the cries of anguish ringing through the halls of the De Montford château as the plague took its toll. Constance, weakened but resolute, lay in bed, her face pale and eyes filled with a sorrow that transcended the physical pain.

Tempus sat by her side, his heart a roiling tempest of despair and defiance. He had advised her parents to stay away from the twins during the illness to prevent them from succumbing to the disease.

The room was dimly lit by a single flickering candle, casting long shadows across the walls.

"I can't bear this, Constance," Tempus said, his voice cracking with raw emotion. "It's as if fate itself has conspired against us every step of the way, mocking our every hope and dream."

Constance reached out a trembling hand to grasp his, her touch a feeble comfort. Despite her own growing weakness, her gaze remained steady, a flicker of determination shining through her pain.

"We've faced this before," she said softly, her voice barely more than a whisper. "And we will face it again. Our bond is stronger than this momentary darkness."

Inside, however, Constance's mind was a storm of fear. *'What if this time is different? What if there's no more chance to find each other again?'* She fought to keep her fears hidden, not wanting to burden Tempus further, but the terror of dying—of leaving him alone, gnawed at her heart.

She took a deep, shuddering breath. "We've always come back together, haven't we? Sera and I? This isn't the end. It's a pause—a mere interlude in a story that's far from over."

Tempus, barely able to comprehend her words through the haze of his own sorrow, clenched her hand tighter. "I don't want to lose you, Constance. Not now, not ever. I grow weary of this never ending cycle."

Constance managed a faint, sad smile. "I know. And I don't want to leave you. But remember, even if we're separated, our love and our memories will endure. They always have. This is just one of many cycles."

As the night deepened, Constance's strength waned. Her breaths grew shallower, and the light in her eyes dimmed. Tempus remained by her side, his tears mingling with hers, a silent testament to the depth of his love and his helplessness in the face of her impending death.

When Constance finally succumbed to the plague, her hand still clutched in Tempus's, it was as though a part of him had been irrevocably torn away. The room, once filled with the echoes of their shared history and hope, now felt like an empty, haunted shell.

Tempus sat in the darkness, his mind a maelstrom of grief and disbelief. The void left by Constance and Sera's passing was unbearable, and he was left alone, grappling with the weight of their loss and the cruel irony of their curse. He found himself haunted by memories of Constance's final moments, her reassurances now a bittersweet echo in his heart.

As he awaited the distant possibility of their reincarnation, Tempus knew that the curse was far from over. The pain of losing them would stay with him, a constant reminder of their transient lives and the enduring cycle of love and loss. The story of their bond was far from finished, but for now, it was a story he would endure alone yet again.

(This is a question for you, Daniel, as my beta reader. Should I entertain the notion of showing the aftermath of the death of the girls due to the plague since Pierre had an outburst where he said that Tempus had brought the plague into their home?)

Chapter 11: "Fates Entwined"

Present Day - Atlanta, USA
The bittersweet nature of unrequited love and the burden of past mistakes.

Sera watched as the color drained from Constance's face after her call with Lynette. The silence between them was heavy, a silence that screamed of unspoken fears and buried truths. She saw the realization dawn in Constance's eyes—Tempus had returned to their lives. Constance's grip on the phone went slack, her gaze distant as she was lost in a whirlwind of memories and emotions.

Sera took a deep breath, her mind racing. She could no longer keep the truth hidden. The moment had come, the moment she had dreaded for so long. The curse binding them together—the endless cycle of reincarnation and death—it all hinged on her.

"What the hell is this?" Constance muttered, her voice barely more than a whisper as she grappled with the flood of memories crashing into her mind.

Her thoughts felt like a tumultuous sea, with waves of memories crashing against the shore of her mind. She felt a strange completeness, a sense that the emptiness she had long carried was somehow filled by the realization that Tempus was the man she had always felt incomplete without.

Yet, along with this revelation came a deep, gnawing despair. She knew all too well the cruel cycle of their existence—the brief moments of reunion followed by inevitable tragedy. The knowledge that their time together was always fleeting left her with a bittersweet sense of fulfillment, tinged with the certainty of imminent sorrow.

Constance turned to Sera, her eyes pleading with a mix of relief and anguish. She felt guilty for finding joy in Tempus's return, while being terrified of losing him—and her sister—again.

"Why?" Constance's voice broke as she spoke, not truly seeking an answer but questioning the cruel destiny that seemed to bind them. "Why us? Why does this keep happening?" Her gaze became distant as she drifted into memories, her mind wandering through echoes of their past.

Sera, understanding the depth of her sister's pain, felt the weight of her own guilt pressing heavily upon her. The endless cycle of tragedy had taken its toll, and she knew that the time had come to reveal the truth she had kept hidden for so long.

"Constance," Sera began, her voice shaking with a mix of fear and resolve. "There's something I need to tell you. Something important."

Constance snapped out of her trance, her eyes locking onto Sera with a mixture of confusion and wariness. "What is it, Sera? What's going on?"

Sera looked away, struggling to find the right words. "The curse, Constance... it's my fault."

Constance's eyes widened, her face flushing with anger. "What do you mean, it's your fault?"

"It's true," Sera continued, her voice cracking. "I made a wish a long time ago. I wished for Tempus to love me, to change our fate. And because of that wish, we're cursed to live and die over and over again. We're trapped in this cycle."

Constance's face hardened, her emotions boiling over. "You did what? You wished for that? And you never thought to tell me? To warn me? This entire time, we've been suffering because of your selfish wish?"

Sera recoiled, the sharpness in Constance's voice cutting through her like a knife. "I was desperate," she pleaded. "I didn't *know*... no, I didn't *understand* what it would mean."

Constance's eyes flashed with hurt and fury. "Well, now *I* understand. And I can't *believe* you kept this from me. All these centuries, I've been dragged into this hell because of *you!*"

Sera flinched, the weight of Constance's anger almost too much to bear. "I know. I was wrong to keep it from you."

Constance's mind swirled in chaotic disarray. She had barely processed the tumultuous end of her relationship with William earlier that evening. The breakup had been a storm of emotions, leaving her exhausted and raw. And now, as if fate hadn't been cruel enough, she was hit with the staggering revelation that Tempus had returned to their lives. The weight of it all felt like a crushing tide, dragging her under.

Her thoughts raced, the images of Tempus mingling with the recent pain of how William looked when she decided that there was nothing more between them. How could she have faced such an overwhelming mix of heartache and confusion in one night? It was as if the universe had conspired to test her limits.

Her feeling of betrayal was from the fact that Sera had kept the truth about the curse hidden for so long. Constance felt a searing anger, not just at the curse itself, but at her sister for withholding the truth. All those years, the endless cycle of pain and loss—it had been driven by Sera's desperate wish.

Sera's eyes were filled with regret, her voice trembling as she struggled to find the right words.

When Sera's voice attempted to break the silence, Constance's anger flared. "What is it, Sera? Is there more you haven't told me?"

Sera shook her head. "I'm sorry, Connie..." began Sera. Her voice trailed off into silence under the intense stare of Constance.

"It's been over thirty lifetimes! Don't you get it? It's been *centuries*. That's a goddamn long time to keep this from me!" Constance shot back.

Constance's emotions churned in a tempest of grief and fury. The realization that her sister's wish had bound them to an endless cycle of pain hit her with overwhelming force. The thought of Tempus's return mingled with the recent breakup with William, creating a whirlwind of confusion.

As Constance grappled with the revelation, her gaze remained distant, her thoughts spiraling through echoes of their past and the relentless sorrow of their cursed existence. Her voice, tinged with both anger and hurt, broke the silence. "Can you forgive me?" Sera's voice trembled.

Constance's face hardened. "I don't know. I need time, Sera. I need to process this." Her voice cracked as she continued, "I can't deal with you right now."

Without another word, Constance turned and headed for her room, her steps heavy with the weight of her turmoil. The door closed behind her with a finality that left Sera alone in the corridor.

Sera stood motionless, the enormity of the confrontation sinking in. She knew she needed to give Constance space, but the sense of isolation and regret was overwhelming. With a deep, shaky breath, she pulled out her phone and dialed Alex's number.

"Hey, Alex," she said softly when he answered. "I need somewhere to go. Can I come over?"

Alex's voice, warm and accommodating, offered a brief respite. "Sure, I'm not busy. You know where the hotel is, right?"

Sera nodded instinctively, despite Alex's inability to see her. "Yeah, I'll be there soon," she replied, trying to muster a hint of confidence.

As Sera hung up, she glanced back at the closed door of Constance's room, a pang of sorrow gripping her heart. She stepped out into the cool night air, the city lights a blur as she made her way towards the hotel, her actions and the fractured relationship with her sister sitting heavily on her shoulders.

Sera arrived at Alex's hotel room, her face pale and her eyes red from sleeplessness and tears. Alex opened the door, his expression shifting from surprise to concern as he saw her.

"Sera?" he asked, stepping aside to let her in. "Are you okay?"

Sera shook her head. "I need a place to stay," she said, her voice barely above a whisper. "I had a fight with Constance. You were the first person I thought to call to find a place to go."

Alex nodded, leading her into the apartment. "Of course. You're welcome here." His feelings for her made turning her away impossible. That wasn't an option for him. The fact that she came to him instead of seeking others made him wonder if she felt something deeper for him—perhaps a need for comfort and support that only he could provide.

As Alex looked at Sera, his heart ached with the weight of his secret. The depth of his feelings for her was a constant struggle, a battle between wanting to protect her and the overwhelming desire to share the truth. He knew he had to tread carefully, to be there for her without overwhelming her. He kept his expression gentle, but inside, a storm of thoughts raged.

'*How long have I waited for this moment? Centuries upon centuries, each life slipping away before I could find her again, each death a bitter reminder of our cursed existence. And now, here she is, so close and yet so far. Can I really keep this from her?*' Alex thought.

'*She looks so fragile right now, so lost. How can I burden her with the knowledge that I've loved her through countless lifetimes, that I've seen her die more times than I can bear to remember? But this lifetime is different. I've been with her, even if only for a few short months, without either of us fully knowing our shared past.*'

Eventually, Alex stepped aside. He allowed her in and gestured towards the only available chairs in the room, next to a small table.

As Sera settled into a chair, trying to compose herself, Alex made them both tea. The warmth of the drink offered little comfort as her mind remained tangled in the turmoil of admitting to Constance her culpability in their shared curse.

Sera realized that she sat in a hotel room with the man that had only just recently confessed his feelings for her. She didn't have time to dwell on the awkwardness of the situation, especially since she hadn't yet responded to his feelings. Other matters took precedence. The evening's revelations were pressing on her heart. She looked at Alex, who had been so kind and understanding, but inside her, a storm of conflicting emotions raged.

There he was, gazing at her gently, his presence a source of comfort. She felt a sting in her heart and instinctively brought her hand to her chest. Instead of dwelling on that, she decided to explain to Alex what had brought her to his doorstep.

"I told Constance that it was my fault about the curse," Sera said after a lingering silence. Her voice sounded tiny and fragile as it cut through the quiet that had engulfed them since Alex had given her the tea and sat across from her.

Alex nodded, his concern deepening. "That must have been incredibly difficult for you."

Sera stared into her cup, the steam rising like ghosts of her past mistakes. "She was so angry, Alex. I've never seen her like that."

Alex reached across the table, his hand resting gently on hers. "You did the right thing, Sera. She needed to know the truth, even if it hurts."

Alex reflected on his own struggles with reincarnation, the same as Sera's. *'I remember every single life. The pain, the loss, the endless searching, so I can understand how Constance feels. But this time, I got to hold Sera, to see her smile, to hear her laugh. I got to love her in the simplest, most beautiful way. I've cherished every moment, knowing how fleeting it might be.'*

'What would she think if she knew that I was the same as she? Cursed with reincarnation. Would it comfort her, or would it only deepen her sorrow? Could she even begin to comprehend the depth of my feelings, the centuries of longing and heartache?'

He shook off these thoughts as Sera's voice broke through.

Sera's eyes filled with fresh tears, her voice trembling. "But what if she never forgives me?"

Alex's grip tightened, his gaze steady. "Give her time. She loves you, Sera. She just needs time to process everything."

The warmth of his hand and the kindness in his eyes offered a glimmer of hope amid her despair. As she sipped her tea, Sera allowed herself to believe, if only for a moment, that things might eventually be okay.

However, things weren't that simple. She felt the immense guilt of her actions crushing her spirit. *'Tempus... I've spent centuries trying to come to terms with my feelings for him. It was a love born out of desperation and a selfish wish, and it hurt the people I cared about most. Constance and Tempus had a love that was deep and true, and my actions shattered their lives repeatedly.'*

Her thoughts spiraled, condemning her past self as she stewed in regret over the mistakes and pain caused by her decisions.

The silence between them was comfortable, a quiet space where Sera could gather her thoughts. The weight of her confession hung in the air, mingling with the steam from their cups. She knew she had to face the consequences of her actions, but the path ahead seemed shrouded in uncertainty.

"I hurt them, Alex," she whispered, her voice breaking. "I hurt Tempus and Constance with my selfish decision. I thought I loved Tempus, but now I realize it was a mistaken emotion that led to all of this. I just wanted to change my fate, to feel loved."

Alex's heart ached for her, but he kept his own feelings hidden. "Sera, we all make mistakes. You were trying to find happiness in a life that seemed to offer none. It's human."

Sera looked up at him, her eyes searching his face for reassurance. "Do you really think that? If that's true, then how can I make it right between me and Constance?"

Alex wasn't certain. Despite that, he didn't want her to give up hope. He squeezed her hand gently. "I'm not certain how you can do that but I believe you can. But first, you need to forgive yourself. Only then can you start to mend the broken pieces." He figured that if she started with forgiveness for herself, just maybe she might be able to find a way to ask for forgiveness from her sister.

Despite the worry on Sera's face, Alex's thoughts drifted to how much he wanted her in his life. *'Every time I've found her, it's been a struggle to keep going,* he mused. *But this time, the universe gave us a reprieve, a chance to be together. How can I not be grateful for that?'*

Yet, the thought of losing her again was unbearable. *'I need to tell her, but how? How do I reveal a truth that spans lifetimes, that carries so much pain and yet so much love?'*

"Sera—" he began, but she interrupted him.

Sera nodded slowly, the weight of his words settling over her. She took a deep breath, trying to steady her racing thoughts. "I don't feel the same about Tempus anymore. I realize now that what I felt was more about escaping my own loneliness. And in doing so, I caused so much pain."

Alex's heart pounded in his chest. This was the moment he had been waiting for—the chance to tell her how he felt. But he knew he had to tread carefully, to be there for her without overwhelming her.

'I see her looking at me, so full of confusion and hurt. She needs me now more than ever, but I have to be careful. I can't burden her with the weight of my confession. She needs time to heal, and maybe, just maybe, there will be a time when she's ready to hear the full truth,' he thought.

"Sera," he began softly, his voice tinged with hesitation. "I need to tell you something."

He paused, his thoughts pressing on him. 'Is it fair to burden her with this, knowing everything she was already carrying?' But after a moment of contemplation, he decided the truth couldn't be held back any longer.

"I really do love you," he finally confessed, the words escaping him like a breath he'd been holding for far too long.

Sera's eyes widened in surprise, her mind struggling to process his words. "You love me? But why? We've only known each other for a few months. We've barely gone on dates or anything, except that one time we went to Stone Mountain."

'How can I even think about falling in love again? After everything I've put Constance and Tempus through, how can I deserve happiness?' she thought to herself. The thoughts whirled through her mind, but she managed to ask aloud, "How can you be so sure?"

Alex looked down, gathering his thoughts. "I know it sounds strange, but sometimes you just know. Being with you, even in these few months, has made me realize how deeply I care for you. You're always in my thoughts, and I can't imagine my life without you."

He chose not to mention the other lifetimes they had experienced together. That truth, he felt, could wait for another time.

Tears welled up in Sera's eyes as she looked at him, the sincerity in his voice touching her deeply. "Oh, Alex... I don't know what to say. I've been so lost, and now... I don't know how to feel. With everything that's going on... I just don't know."

Alex leaned forward, his eyes locked onto hers. "You don't have to decide anything right now. Just know that I'm here for you, whatever you need."

Sera felt a sense of relief wash over her, a glimmer of hope in the darkness. Having time to think allowed her to sort through her thoughts. She reached out, taking his other hand in hers. "Thank you, Alex. I don't think I deserve your love, but I'm so grateful for it."

He smiled softly, his heart swelling with love and determination. "You deserve all the love in the world, Sera. And we'll find a way to fix things with your sister."

'*For now,*' he thought, '*I'll be here for her, loving her quietly, supporting her through this storm. And when the time is right, I'll find the words to tell her everything. Until then, I'll cherish these moments, knowing that in this lifetime, I've had the privilege of loving her once again.*'

Alex took a deep breath. He squeezed Sera's hand gently. He smiled softly. For now, he would be her rock, her support. And when the time was right, he would reveal the truth and pray that their burgeoning love could withstand their shared past.

Sera, however, was caught in a spiral of doubt. She couldn't shake the feeling that she didn't deserve love—not after the pain she'd caused. The misguided love she thought she had for Tempus had led to so much suffering, and the wish she'd made had torn two people who truly loved each other apart.

'*I can't risk it,*' she thought, a cold resolve settling in. 'I can't risk hurting him the way I've hurt Constance and Tempus. I have to protect him, even if it means pushing him away. It's the only way to break this cycle.'

She searched Alex's eyes, desperately trying to discern the truth behind his words. He looked at her with so much hope, so much care, that it broke her heart. But she knew what she had to do.

Taking a deep breath, Sera braced herself for the heartbreak she was about to inflict. "Alex," she began, her voice trembling, "I just want to make things clear. For now... I can't be in a relationship with you. I hope you understand."

She saw the hurt flash across his face, but she pressed on, needing to explain. "I've only just come to terms with my feelings for Tempus.

It took centuries for me to understand that my love for him, though deep, was fleeting. It wasn't grounded like the love between him and Constance. And my wish... my selfish wish caused so much harm to them both."

"I don't deserve your love. I've caused so much pain, and I can't risk hurting you too. The curse... it's always there, waiting to tear us apart. Even if I wanted to, I can't subject you to that."

Tears welled up in her eyes as she continued, "I'm grateful for your kindness, for your support. But I can't do this. I can't let myself love again, knowing the pain it might bring. I hope you understand."

Alex's face softened with understanding, though the hurt was still evident. He reached out and took her hand gently. "Sera, I understand your fears. But you don't have to go through life alone."

Sera nodded, grateful for his admission but resolute in her decision. She squeezed his hand, feeling a mix of relief and sorrow. She knew it was the right choice, even if it broke her heart to make it.

They sat in silence for a while, each lost in their own thoughts, the weight of the evening hanging heavily between them.

Eventually, Alex felt the need to break the silence. He looked across the small table between them. "So, do you have any plans to stay somewhere else tonight?"

Sera glanced around the room. There was only one bed, just like the last time she'd stayed with Alex. The memory of that night made her blush, even though nothing had happened between them. The idea of staying alone in a hotel crossed her mind, but the thought of being by herself didn't appeal to her.

She looked back at Alex, then quickly lowered her gaze to the cup of tea in her hands. The hopeful expression on his face made her heart flutter.

"Well..." she began, then hesitated.

"It can be just like the last time," Alex offered, trying to reassure her that there was no pressure. He wanted her to know the decision was hers alone.

Sera glanced at the bed again before making her choice. "I'll stay here with you, if you don't mind."

Her voice was quiet, but Alex heard her clearly. He stood, went to the bed, and pulled back the covers before turning back to her. "If you're ready, I'll go ahead and get some rest. It's been a long day for both of us."

Sera hesitated, then nodded. She stood and started toward the bed but changed course to the bathroom instead. There, she removed her jeans, leaving herself in just her undergarments and the t-shirt she had on. When she returned to the room, the lights were off except for the soft glow of the bedside lamp. Alex was already in bed, his back turned toward her.

Sera climbed in beside him and reached out to turn off the light, the room settling into a comfortable darkness around them.

The quiet stretched between them, the room filled with only the distant hum of the city and the soft whir of the air conditioning. Sera lay still, staring at the ceiling, her heart pounding in her chest. She felt the warmth of Alex's presence beside her, but the space between them felt like an ocean. Every beat of her heart seemed to echo in the silence, her thoughts a tangled mess of yearning and fear.

She swallowed, her throat dry. The words she wanted to say clung to the back of her mind, refusing to come out. Finally, she gathered the courage to break the silence. "Alex," she whispered, her voice barely audible above the soft hum of the room.

There was a pause, just long enough for doubt to creep in. Had he fallen asleep? But then, his voice came, soft and with a touch of amusement. "I haven't even been in bed long enough to sleep," he said, his tone light but carrying an underlying concern.

Sera let out a small, nervous laugh, her fingers twisting in the sheets. She could feel the heat rising in her cheeks again, and she was grateful for the darkness that hid her face. "I... I was just wondering if..." Her voice trailed off, the words sticking in her throat. How could she ask him to hold her? It felt like too much, yet not enough.

There was a shift beside her, the sound of fabric rustling as Alex turned slightly in the bed. "Do you need something?" he asked gently, his voice closer now, filled with a patient warmth that made her heart ache.

Sera hesitated, biting her lip as she stared into the darkness. She wanted to say it, to ask for the comfort she craved, but fear held her back. Instead, she just shifted slightly, pulling the blanket up closer to her chin as if it could shield her from the vulnerability she felt.

Asking for comfort from someone who had just professed his love felt wrong—especially since she had just turned him down. The awkwardness of her desire only intensified, making the request even more difficult to voice.

Alex waited, sensing her turmoil. The silence stretched on, but it wasn't oppressive. It was more like a fragile thread connecting them, waiting to be pulled tighter or to snap. When she didn't answer, he spoke again, softer this time. "Sera... It's okay. You can ask me anything."

His words were a lifeline, and she clung to them, taking a deep breath before finally letting the words slip out. "Can you... would you... mind holding me? Just while we sleep?"

The request hung in the air between them, and for a moment, Sera was terrified that she had overstepped, that she had asked for too much. But then, she felt the bed shift as Alex rolled over without a word. His arms encircled her gently, pulling her close against his chest.

The warmth of his body seeped into hers, and she let out a breath she didn't realize she'd been holding. Her head rested just below his chin, and she could hear the steady rhythm of his heartbeat, a soothing counterpoint to the chaos in her mind.

"Is this okay?" Alex murmured, his breath warm against her hair.

Sera nodded, her face pressed against his chest. "Yes," she whispered, her voice trembling with a mix of relief and emotion. "Thank you."

He tightened his hold slightly, just enough to let her know he was there, without overwhelming her. "Anytime," he whispered back, his voice soft and full of unspoken promises.

The tension in Sera's body slowly began to melt away, replaced by a sense of safety she hadn't felt in a long time. She closed her eyes, allowing herself to relax into his embrace, the steady rise and fall of his chest lulling her into a state of peace.

For the first time in what felt like forever, the thoughts that had plagued her were quiet, replaced by the simple comfort of being held by someone who cared. As she drifted towards sleep, she realized that this was what she had been yearning for all along—a connection, a reassurance that she wasn't alone.

And in the quiet darkness of the room, held close in Alex's arms, she found that comfort.

Constance went to work despite feeling emotionally shaken from her breakup with William and the revelation from her sister that she was the cause of their curse. She didn't even think to ask her sister when her memories of the past had returned; it was a haunting uncertainty. Sometimes her memories resurfaced before Sera's, and other times they returned simultaneously. But this time the truth felt like a crushing weight.

She was poor company for Lynette, who patiently waited for her friend to open up. Finally, having had enough of the gloom that seemed to envelop Constance, Lynette put her work aside and called out to her.

"What's bothering you, Constance? You've been acting distracted and in a foul mood all morning. Is it something I can help with?" asked Lynette.

Emerging from the fog of her thoughts, Constance shook her head. She realized she hadn't been attentive to her tasks and that her distracted, somber mood had likely made her unbearable company for the past few hours.

Constance set aside the things in her hands and sat back in her chair with a heavy sigh. "I broke up with William last night. If that wasn't enough, my sister dropped a bombshell secret on me. It has me reeling, and I just don't know how to feel about it."

Lynette looked shocked. "Hold up, back up. You broke up with William?"

Constance gave Lynette a dumbfounded look. She wondered why Lynette would focus on that tidbit of information first before asking about what was really bothering her. She was about to say something but paused, realizing Lynette might not understand why she was so upset with her sister.

"Does that even matter right..." she began, then stopped herself. With a heavy sigh and a dismissive wave, she said, "William isn't the real problem here."

"Really? But you guys have been together since—forever. Why isn't that a big deal to you? It seems like you don't really care about that," said Lynette as she stood from her desk and moved closer to Constance.

With Lynette standing, Constance had to look up at her. She thought about what Lynette had just said. It was true that, in the past, she had been reasonably content with William. He was the best partner she had found so far. That was even after knowing deep down that she wasn't sure he was the one she was meant to be with.

"I never felt truly complete with William," she admitted, her voice trembling as she looked down at the cluttered surface of her desk, which mirrored the chaos in her mind. "There was always this lingering doubt in my mind that I couldn't shake. It was like that with every guy I'd ever dated, ever since high school."

Lynette looked confused. She sat down on the edge of Constance's desk. "I thought you were happy with William," she stated softly.

Constance turned to face Lynette, a melancholy look settling uneasily on her face. With a half-smile, she looked at Lynette before speaking. "I wasn't happy. I tried to be, but..." she trailed off, tears beginning to form in her eyes. She hastily wiped away the dampness before the tears could actually fall.

Lynette looked on for a moment longer, desperately wanting to comfort her friend. She longed to pull Constance into her arms but realized it might not be the right approach while sitting on the desk. Instead, she reached across the space between their desks, pulled her chair closer, and moved close enough for Constance to lean into her arms.

"Just let it out," Lynette said softly as Constance buried her face into her shoulder.

Constance didn't cry about William. She didn't want to. She was surprised that she felt no reason to be sad about the breakup with William. Instead, she buried her head in Lynette's shoulder, suffering not from the breakup but from the fear that knowing the truth revealed by her returned memories might mean her life was forfeit soon.

Eventually, she leaned back and wiped her eyes with the back of her hand. "It's not that I'm upset about the William thing. I'm upset because my sister, who I love beyond measure, has been hiding something serious from me for years," she said instead of revealing her true fears.

"Alright, I'll let the issue with William slide... for now. But what kind of secret could your sister have kept to affect you like this?"

Constance felt the need to confide in someone about her problems but realized she couldn't talk to Lynette about this matter. She wasn't sure Lynette would believe or understand what she was going through. Besides, she didn't want to burden her friend with a truth that couldn't be undone.

She shook her head and decided to downplay the issue. "It's not so much what she kept from me but the fact that she did. I felt so betrayed, like my own flesh and blood—the closest relative one could have—would keep something from me."

"Maybe she had her reasons," Lynette offered gently.

Constance gave a weak smile. "Yeah," she said softly. "Maybe that's it."

Lynette sensed that Constance didn't want to delve deeper into the matter. She decided not to press further, though she remained wary and worried for her friend.

Trying to lighten the atmosphere, Lynette glanced at the clock on the office wall. "Hey, it's lunchtime. Let's go grab a bite to eat and you can decompress," she suggested, hoping a change of environment might help Constance.

Constance wiped her eyes again. "Okay," she agreed. As she stood up, she worried her eyes might be puffy from crying earlier. "I'm sorry about all this. I probably look a mess right now."

Lynette smiled, tucked a stray hair behind Constance's ear, and gently rubbed her cheek with her thumb. "You look fine, girl. Let's go take a break."

Morning arrived for Alex and Sera while Constance had already been at work for a few hours. Soft sunlight filtering through the partially open curtains, casting a warm glow across the dim room. Dust motes floated lazily in the beams, adding a quiet stillness to the space.

Alex had been awake for only a few minutes, his eyes tracing the gentle rise and fall of Sera's breath as she remained nestled in his embrace. He marveled at how he had managed to hold onto her throughout the night, given his usual habit of shifting to find comfort.

Yet here she was, still in his arms. The woman he cared for so deeply hadn't pulled away; she hadn't vanished like she had so many times in his dreams. In this moment, he could savor the fleeting victory of holding her close, even if only for a night.

His thoughts were interrupted as Sera stirred, her eyes fluttering open to meet his. A blush crept across her cheeks, and she instinctively pressed her palms against his chest, as if to create space. But something felt right in his arms, so instead of pulling away, she slipped her arms around him, drawing him closer.

"Good morning," she murmured, a shy smile curving her lips as she tucked her head against his chest.

Sera couldn't bring herself to meet Alex's gaze, the weight of her own emotions making it too difficult. Alex, sensing her discomfort, decided to tread carefully, not wanting to add to her embarrassment.

"Maybe we should get out of bed," he suggested, though the reluctance in his voice was unmistakable. His arms, however, didn't loosen their hold on her. He wanted nothing more than to stay like this all day, to keep her close, but he knew that wasn't likely. He was aware she was still unsure of her feelings, and the last thing he wanted was to pressure her. The decision was hers to make.

Sera glanced at the clock on the nightstand, surprised to see that it was nearly lunchtime. She hadn't realized how late they'd slept. It was clear that Alex didn't mind—they could have stayed wrapped up in each other for hours more. But as much as she longed to remain in his arms, the contrast between her desire to stay close and her insistence the previous night that they couldn't be together began to gnaw at her, leaving her feeling increasingly conflicted.

"Uhh... I think we should get up," Sera said, her voice tinged with the lingering hesitance of the morning. She slowly pulled herself from his embrace, the warmth of his arms replaced by the cool air of the room as she slipped out of bed.

Alex nodded, though his gaze lingered on her as she moved across the room. The soft morning light filtered through the partially closed curtains, casting a gentle glow around her as she reached for her jeans. To him, she looked breathtaking, the light catching in her hair, framing her face with an ethereal beauty that made his heart ache. He couldn't tear his eyes away as she pulled on her jeans, her movements graceful in their simplicity.

As she stood, adjusting her shirt, he finally spoke, trying to keep his tone casual. "Do you want to go out and get some lunch?"

Sera, focused on fastening the button on her jeans, didn't notice the way his eyes traced her every movement. But she felt his presence—steady, warm, comforting. There was something in his voice, a hint of care that wrapped around her like a gentle embrace. She glanced up briefly, meeting his gaze with a small smile. "Yeah, that sounds good."

They continued getting dressed in a comfortable silence, the room filled only with the soft rustle of clothing and the distant hum of the city outside. Alex quickly pulled on his own clothes, but his eyes kept drifting back to Sera, captivated by the way the morning light played across her features, highlighting the delicate curve of her cheek, the soft lines of her neck.

Sera, unaware of his admiring glances, finished dressing and slipped on her shoes. She ran a hand through her hair, smoothing it down before turning back to him. "Ready?" she asked, her voice a little more sure, a little less hesitant.

Alex smiled, feeling a surge of affection for the woman standing before him. "Ready," he replied, his voice warm with a mixture of fondness and something deeper.

They left the room together, stepping out into the bustling world beyond. As they walked side by side, the morning's awkwardness slowly dissipated, replaced by a quiet understanding. There were still uncertainties between them, but for now, they were content to simply be together, sharing a moment of peace in the midst of all the things left unsaid.

As Alex and Sera strolled down the lively street, the sunlight cast dancing shadows on the pavement. They walked in comfortable silence, occasionally exchanging small smiles that spoke of a budding connection. The chatter of the city surrounded them, blending with the distant clamor of traffic.

Sera glanced around, her mind still preoccupied with the internal struggle of her feelings. The city's vibrant pulse seemed to mirror the conflicted rhythm of her heart. "I've been craving something different," she said, breaking the silence. "How about we try that new bistro around the corner? I heard they have amazing reviews."

Alex, feeling a bit more at ease, nodded. "Sounds perfect," he said, extending his hand out. "It's your city, since you know the way, then lead the way."

They turned the corner, approaching the quaint bistro with its charming outdoor seating area. As they neared, Alex's gaze was drawn to a reflection in a window in front of him. A familiar figure walking towards them from behind caused his heart to skip a beat. "No way," he murmured under his breath, his eyes widening in disbelief.

After a second more, Alex said in a hushed voice, "It can't be..."

Sera, noticing his reaction, followed his line of sight. Her brow furrowed in confusion. She couldn't see what Alex was staring at—*a reflection?*

In the glass before him, Alex had already begun to vanish into memory.

Unaware of the image that held him, she scanned the area, trying to spot what had drawn his attention.

"What is it?" She asked softly.

Before Alex could respond, a voice called out from behind them, causing both of them to turn. "Alexander?" Tempus murmured in quiet reverence.

Alex flinched at the name.

Sera's eyes widened as she saw Tempus, standing there with a look of stunned recognition. The connection between them was instant and electric, though none of them understood what was happening. Tempus's gaze locked with Alex's, his expression a mix of shock and disbelief.

Alex's mouth opened, but no words emerged. The air was charged with confusion and an unspoken history that seemed to hang between them. Time felt suspended, with Alex caught in the midst of an unexpected and disorienting reunion.

Sera's gaze darted between the two men, her disbelief palpable. She had been startled when Tempus called out Alex's name, but the reaction from Alex was even more perplexing. It seemed as though their encounter was not the first as she had thought.

"Alexander?" Sera whispered in stunned recognition.

As Sera's mind raced, fragments of past memories began to resurface with alarming clarity. She stared at Tempus and Alexander, her thoughts tumbling over each other. "The Black Plague...? De Montford...?" she murmured, her voice trailing off as the weight of her revelations began to settle in.

Sera would have been stuck in those thoughts if not for recognition of a voice calling out from beyond where Tempus stood. A voice that drew all of their attention, causing Tempus to turn around.

Constance and Lynette walked out of their office, the tension from their earlier conversation beginning to dissipate with each step. The midday sun was bright and warm, casting a cheerful glow over the city. Constance, still feeling the burden of her unspoken troubles, tried to focus on the simple pleasure of sharing a meal with her friend.

As they strolled down the street, Lynette chatted about lighthearted topics, trying to lift Constance's spirits. Constance smiled weakly, appreciating Lynette's effort to ease her mood. The familiar buzz of the city provided a pleasant backdrop as they approached the corner that would lead to the bistro that Lynette had suggested.

As they strolled halfway down the block, Constance suddenly came to a halt. Her gaze was fixed on a figure who had just rounded the corner—a tall man in a dark suit. Her heart skipped a beat as recognition dawned on her. "—Tempus?" she murmured, her voice tinged with both longing and surprise, her eyes following the man as he moved away.

Lynette, sensing the abrupt shift in Constance's demeanor, looked in the direction her friend was staring. "What's wrong?" she asked, concern evident in her voice. Internally, Lynette thought, *'I've never seen her like this before.'* By the time Lynette's eyes caught up with where Constance was looking, the man had already disappeared around the corner.

Without waiting for an answer, Lynette noticed Constance's pace quickening, driven by an urgent, unspoken need. "Where are we rushing to?" Lynette called out, hurrying to keep up with her friend's sudden haste.

Constance didn't answer, her eyes were fixated on something—or someone—in the distance. Someone that Lynette had missed.

Constance rounded the corner a step ahead of Lynette, coming to a sudden stop. Lynette, caught off guard, nearly collided with her friend's stationary figure.

Panting and slightly out of breath, Lynette looked around, trying to grasp the scene before her. A few unfamiliar faces stood ahead, adding to her confusion. "What had you rushing?" she huffed.

Constance, barely able to contain her emotion, called out, "Tempus?" loud enough to be heard by those standing in front of her.

Lynette blinked, her confusion deepening. "Who? Are you talking to me, Constance?"

Before Constance could reply to Lynette, Tempus's gaze locked with hers. His expression shifted from surprise to recognition, and he froze, his face a complex mix of emotions. "Constance?" he uttered, his voice thick with disbelief.

Constance's breath caught in her throat, overwhelmed by the unexpected encounter. Lynette glanced between Constance and Tempus, her own confusion evident in her expression.

Adding to the confusion, the door of the bistro swung open, and a man stepped out, stopping abruptly as his eyes locked on Constance. "Constance? Is that you?" William's voice broke through the chaos, tinged with both surprise and familiarity.

"What the hell is going on?" Lynette blurted out, her frustration finally spilling over. As she took in the scene around her, pieces began to fall into place. She recognized William, who had just emerged from the bistro, and then noticed Sera standing beside an unfamiliar man. In the center of it all was the rather striking figure Constance had called Tempus.

The moment was a swirl of confusion and disbelief. Everyone stood frozen, unsure of what to say or do. Tempus, caught off guard, had never expected to see Constance or Sera here.

He had left Europe precisely to avoid this, believing their paths wouldn't cross again—at least not in this lifetime. Their reunions had always happened on the other side of the ocean, and he had hoped that distance would protect them.

But the reality was undeniable. There they were, Constance—the woman he loved with every fiber of his being—and her sister, Sera, standing before him. The past he had tried to outrun was now staring him in the face, both behind and in front of him.

What unsettled Tempus most was the sight of the man he recognized—someone he had long believed lost to history. Alex, who had appeared as vibrant and alive as he had been just days before tuberculosis claimed his life during the Black Plague, was standing right before him.

A whirlwind of emotions—frustration, relief, ecstasy, and sheer confusion—surged through Tempus. He raised both hands, signaling for silence, halting the flurry of questions swirling around them. His voice, though steady, carried the weight of disbelief. "What the hell is going on here, Alex?"

Though seeing Constance and Sera again stirred a mix of gratitude and a thousand other emotions, one question burned above all others. He needed to know—'*how was Alexander still alive?*'

Alexander's chest tightened as Tempus's cold, accusing words cut through the air. He had always known that this moment would come—that he would one day have to face the man who had been an important part of one of his past lives. But the reality of it was far more harrowing than he had anticipated.

Tempus's anger was palpable, a force that seemed to press down on him, demanding answers he wasn't sure he could give. Memories of their last encounter flooded back—of a friendship once forged in the pursuit of knowledge, now reduced to bitter ashes, especially given his death by tuberculosis in that past life.

The sight of Constance and Sera standing beside Tempus only deepened his guilt, reminding him of all he had lost back then. Of continually losing Sera through each lifetime. His mind raced, searching for the right words, but all that surfaced was a profound sense of inadequacy, his mouth working spasmodically to answer. How could he explain his return, his presence here, when he barely understood it himself? The weight of Tempus's expectation bore down on him, and for the first time in centuries, Alexander felt truly vulnerable.

Sera looked at Alexander, her eyes full of questions. Her memories from the De Monford lifetime brought clarity about who Alexander was, yet, like Tempus, she couldn't comprehend how he was still alive.

Constance, meanwhile, was caught between giddiness and fear. The emptiness she had felt for so long was suddenly filled with the sight of Tempus. Her heart swelled, almost to the point of bursting, as she fought the overwhelming urge to rush forward and throw herself into his arms.

Lynette and William, on the other hand, stood as bewildered onlookers. They had no idea where they fit into the unfolding drama. It was clear that the four others shared a deep history—one that left Lynette and William feeling like outsiders, desperate for answers to make sense of what was happening around them.

Lynette's heart pounded in her chest as she tried to make sense of the chaos unfolding around her. The intensity in Tempus's eyes, the way Constance and Sera seemed so deeply entangled with him, left her feeling utterly disconnected from her friend's life. This was a side of Constance she had never seen before—a world where ancient ties and secret pasts seemed to hold more sway than the reality they shared. The more she observed, the more she felt like an outsider, her presence reduced to that of a spectator in a drama that was far beyond her comprehension.

Besides her, William's confusion mirrored her own, but his was laced with an unspoken fear. He had no idea how he had become part of this web, and every instinct screamed at him to walk away. But his feelings towards Constance kept him rooted in place, even as he questioned whether he truly belonged here at all.

Tempus turned slowly, his gaze settling on Alex and Sera once more. Constance felt a pang of disappointment as he seemed to disregard their reunion for something she initially deemed unimportant. Her mind was solely fixated on being with Tempus again, not on who else was present. But as she listened to Tempus's measured questioning and took a closer look at Alexander, recognition dawned. The chaotic emotions of their encounter had clouded her memory, but now she could see—this was someone from their distant past.

Tempus's voice remained calm, a product of the one lesson he had learned over the eons: patience. For someone with an endless life, patience wasn't just a virtue—it was a necessity. But even infinite patience had its limits, especially when it was laced with the cold anger he now felt. This anger was born from the sense of betrayal, from feeling deceived by someone he had once mourned deeply. Losing Constance and Sera in every lifetime had been agonizing, but losing Alexander—one of the few people he had truly cared about—had left a bitter scar on his soul.

"What the *fuck*, Alexander?" Tempus's voice was edged with ice. "How are you alive, and why are you with Constance and Sera?"

Alex and the others couldn't suppress the shiver that ran through them at the sound of Tempus's voice. There was an unspoken energy radiating from him—an aura of power that seemed to ripple through the group, making the air thick with tension.

Before Alexander could respond, William broke the silence. He looked toward Constance and took a tentative step forward, but Tempus's icy glare froze him in place. "What the hell is he talking about, Constance?" William demanded, his voice tinged with confusion and fear.

Constance turned to William, ready to explain, but Tempus cut her off sharply.

"You," Tempus said, pointing a finger at William. "Shut your mouth."

William looked like he wanted to protest but thought better of it. The force behind Tempus's command left little room for argument, and William reluctantly held his tongue. The oppressive tension was finally broken by the sudden ring of Tempus's phone, shattering the silence like glass.

Tempus pulled the phone from his pocket, glancing at the caller ID. Only a select few people on the entire planet even knew that number existed, and he knew he had to take the call. Yet, as he answered, his mind was already set—he wouldn't let this conversation drag on. Not when there were more pressing matters at hand.

Before answering the call, Tempus issued a command that brooked no argument: "Don't speak. Don't move," his gaze sweeping over everyone present.

He brought the phone to his ear and spoke quietly, "What is it, Elias? I'm *occupied* right now." He glanced over the others quickly before his gaze swept away.

Elias, accustomed to his employer's extraordinary nature, didn't take the comment as a rebuke. Instead, he adjusted his tone accordingly. "I'll be brief, sir. It seems the situation has escalated. We're in danger close."

Tempus recognized the coded message instantly. Without another word, he ended the call and slipped the phone back into his pocket. He glanced up at the sky, drawing in a slow, steadying breath before scanning the faces around him. Each person watched him intently, their expressions a mixture of curiosity and apprehension, silently waiting for his next move.

Surveying the growing crowd, Tempus knew that this was neither the time nor the place for the answers they all needed. Too many ears were nearby, and the tension in the air had already attracted more attention than he liked.

Taking another deep breath, he tucked his hands into his pockets and made his decision. "We're leaving. All of us. Follow me," he instructed, his tone leaving no room for debate.

Constance, Sera, and Alexander exchanged brief glances, a mutual understanding passing between them. They nodded in silent agreement, prepared to follow Tempus without hesitation.

William and Lynette, however, hesitated. They exchanged uncertain looks, unsure of their place in this unfolding drama but unwilling to abandon their friends. Though they didn't fully grasp what was happening, they were determined to see it through. At least for Constance and Sera's sake.

Chapter 12: "A Wish's Consequence"

Present Day - Atlanta, USA

Under siege and buried in turmoil.

Tempus's day, which he had intended to spend leisurely exploring the city, had turned into an utter catastrophe. What was supposed to be a peaceful morning at the bistro had spiraled into chaos, courtesy of fate's cruel twist.

He had left Europe deliberately, thinking that by putting distance between himself and the continent, he could escape the relentless cycle of the twins' reincarnations. It had never occurred to him that they could be reborn elsewhere—an oversight that now felt painfully naive.

He had occasionally left Europe after losing the twins, never daring to venture far, he would eventually return. Now, he realized how foolish he had been to believe that distance alone could sever the ties that bound him to Constance and Sera.

And as if their sudden reappearance wasn't enough, the unexpected presence of Alexander had only compounded his problems, adding another layer of complication to an already impossible situation.

"I feel like a fool," Tempus whispered to himself.

As they walked, Tempus cast a quick glance over his shoulder at the man who had once been his most trusted friend. "Damn," he muttered under his breath, frustration tightening his chest. Swallowing his words, he turned back around, determined to focus on leading the group forward.

'What the hell is happening now?' Tempus's thoughts churned, frustration simmering beneath the surface. *'It wasn't enough that I'm stuck in this immortal mess and the girls are trapped in their own cursed cycle? Now Alexander's somehow tangled in all of this. What the hell is going on?'*

Unease gnawed at him as he risked another glance back at Alexander. The uncertainty of Alexander's presence weighed on him, yet, in some inexplicable way, seeing him alive brought a sliver of comfort. The grief that had haunted Tempus for decades eased, just a little, at the sight of his old friend, even as the confusion deepened.

Alexander walked silently beside Sera, both trailing just behind Tempus. Constance, Lynette, and William followed closely, with Constance choosing to stay near them. It was obvious that they knew no one else well enough but her. And having no one else, she felt her presence would be comfortable enough to be next to. The atmosphere was thick with tension, making their proximity feel forced and awkward.

Sera glanced back to check on Constance and the others. She needn't have worried—Constance seemed determined never to let Tempus out of her sight again. The desperation in her sister's eyes was palpable, her need to be near him almost radiating off her. Sera was struck by how much self-restraint Constance was managing to muster by staying with William and Lynette while they walked.

Reassured that everyone was where they needed to be, and avoiding the effort of trying to read Tempus's mood, Sera turned her attention to Alexander. He seemed lost in his own world, anxiously gnawing at his thumbnail. Concerned, Sera reached over and gently tapped his hand, hoping to draw him back from whatever thoughts were troubling him.

Alexander snapped out of his daze, dropping his hand to his side and offering Sera a weary smile. His heart felt heavy, a deep sense of displacement gnawing at him. He had planned to reveal things to Sera gradually, but with Tempus's sudden arrival, those plans had crumbled, leaving him to face the uncertain aftermath.

He had no idea how Sera would react to the truth he needed to share. Though he cared about what Tempus might think, it was Sera's response that truly concerned him.

"Are you alright?" Sera asked softly, her voice drawing Tempus's brief attention. Tempus glanced back, his eyes meeting theirs for a moment before he returned his focus to leading the way.

Sera, lowering her voice even further, asked again, "Are you alright?"

Alexander's eyes flicked to the back of Tempus before he replied. "I think we should hold off on any discussion until we get to wherever he's leading us, don't ya think?" he suggested, gesturing subtly toward Tempus.

Sera looked away from Alexander, crossing her arms with a huff. "Alright. See if I care to check on you ever again," she muttered, her voice laced with frustration. She was upset that her concern had been dismissed so easily, all because of Tempus's brooding presence.

Her gaze drifted to Tempus's strong back, memories of his occasional grumpiness from their childhood resurfacing. Back then, it had been easier to handle—just a fleeting mood. But this time, it was different. His demeanor was far darker, and the weight of unspoken words hung heavily between them, made worse by the fact that they were surrounded by others, unable to talk freely.

Sera's arms slipped from their defensive position as her shoulders sagged, a silent acknowledgment of the tension that now permeated their once familiar bond.

Tempus led the group to a parking lot adjacent to the bistro. He pulled out his cellphone and dialed a familiar number. "Yes, this is Tempus. I need a ride back now."

Within minutes, a stretch limousine emerged from the parking garage and pulled up to the curb. Tempus ushered everyone inside, the plush interior a stark contrast to the crisp air outside. The silence inside the limo was heavy, punctuated only by the occasional rustle of clothing and the low hum of the air conditioning.

As the cityscape of Atlanta slipped by outside, the tension inside the vehicle was palpable. The brief ride ended quickly, and they arrived at the Waldorf Astoria Atlanta Buckhead.

Tempus got out the limo and came to a halt before the grand entrance, his eyes scanning the group before he simply said, "We're here." Without waiting for a response, he strode through the revolving doors, the others following with expressions of confusion and apprehension.

Inside the opulent lobby, the grandeur was overwhelming. Marble floors gleamed under soft lighting, and the scent of fresh flowers filled the air.

Constance took the opportunity to subtly push past William and Lynette, her eyes fixed on Tempus as she moved forward. There was an almost desperate urgency in her steps, her gaze never leaving his back.

William, wary and protective, reached out to gently grasp Constance's forearm, his fingers tightening around her as she attempted to pull away. "Wait, don't go—" he began, but his voice faltered as Tempus suddenly appeared beside him. With a calm yet menacing grip, Tempus wrapped his hand around William's wrist, applying just enough pressure to make his point clear.

"Don't put your hand on her ever again," Tempus warned, his voice low and dangerous. William's face drained of color, and he quickly released Constance, rubbing his wrist as Tempus let go.

Before anyone could react further, a well-dressed man approached, his demeanor respectful yet cautious. "Is there a problem, Mr. Auerelius?" the hotel manager inquired, his voice polished and professional.

Tempus didn't bother to look at the man, his gaze still locked on William as he protectively slid Constance behind him. "No. There's no problem here. *Is* there?" he asked, his tone leaving no room for dissent.

William shook his head, too stunned to speak. At the same time, both Constance and Sera exchanged shocked glances. They had never heard anyone use Tempus's real family name so openly before. It was a name from a time long past, one that he had kept hidden for centuries, always adopting different identities to avoid drawing attention. The fact that the manager knew it—and used it so casually—sent a ripple of unease through them both.

Tempus continued speaking to the manager over his shoulder as he moved toward the elevators. "We'll be heading up to my suite."

"The presidential suite is already prepared for you, sir. We've finished our morning services." The manger looked over the others who had accompanied Tempus, unsure if they should be considered as guests that would be staying as well. "Shall we send up any bags?" the manager replied, maintaining his professional tone.

Tempus finally turned to face the man, his expression unreadable. "No. But send up a chef," he instructed, brushing past the manager without another word. Constance and Sera fell in step behind him, their movements almost synchronized, as if drawn by an invisible force.

Alexander lingered for a moment, catching the unsettled look on William's face. He hesitated, then offered an apologetic smile, trying to convey understanding without words. After a brief pause, Alexander turned and followed the others toward the elevators.

William and Lynette exchanged a glance, both feeling the weight of the situation. Without needing to speak, they silently agreed to follow, trailing after the group with a shared sense of unease.

As they stepped into the elevator, the tension seemed to thicken in the confined space. The elevator ascended smoothly, and when the doors finally slid open, they were greeted by a room that epitomized luxury and grandeur.

Tempus opened the door to the presidential suite with a sweeping gesture, his voice carrying the sharp edge of authority mixed with a veneer of forced calm. "Make yourselves comfortable. I'll be at the bar." He stepped inside, the opulence of the suite starkly contrasting with his grim demeanor.

Constance, unable to ignore the pull of Tempus's presence, trailed closely behind him. Her eyes, filled with a mixture of concern and frustration, followed his every move as he headed toward the bar.

The others entered hesitantly, their eyes widening at the luxurious surroundings. The suite's grandeur seemed almost too vast for their unease. Sera glanced around, her heart pounding with the weight of old memories now mingling with the present.

The presidential suite was a vast expanse of elegance, with floor-to-ceiling windows offering a breathtaking view of the Atlanta skyline. The living area was adorned with plush, oversized furniture in rich fabrics, accented by gleaming hardwood floors and intricate rugs.

A grand piano stood in one corner, its polished surface reflecting the soft, ambient lighting. The walls were tastefully decorated with modern art, and the ceiling boasted a sparkling chandelier that cast a warm, golden glow throughout the room. A marble fireplace added a touch of classic sophistication, its mantel adorned with ornate carvings.

To the side, a dining area featured a long table surrounded by high-backed chairs, perfect for hosting an intimate gathering. Beyond that, a set of double doors led to the master bedroom, where a king-sized bed with a luxurious canopy dominated the space. The suite also boasted a fully equipped kitchen, ready for a private chef to prepare an exquisite meal.

As the group entered the suite, the atmosphere was heavy with unspoken questions and unresolved tensions, each of them acutely aware that the answers they sought might be waiting just beyond those doors.

"I... I think I'll sit over here," Sera murmured to herself, her gaze darting between Alexander and the couch. She moved cautiously, the uncertainty of their changed relationship hanging heavily on her. Settling at the far end of the couch, she stole occasional glances at Alexander, her internal conflict evident in her furrowed brow.

Alexander, seated at the other end of the couch, shifted uncomfortably. The sight of Sera's tentative approach and her subsequent retreat to the opposite end only deepened his unease. He was acutely aware of the awkwardness between them, the once-familiar bond now strained by the weight of their shared history.

William and Lynette, their expressions reflecting a mix of discomfort and reluctant curiosity, chose seats along the periphery of the room. William still clutched a takeout bag from the bistro, the bag crumpled and slightly greasy. He glanced at it occasionally, as if it might provide some form of solace or distraction.

Constance watched Tempus with barely concealed impatience as he rummaged through the assortment of bottles behind the bar. Her fingers drummed against her thigh, her eyes narrowing as she waited for him to acknowledge her.

Tempus finally turned, a glass in hand filled with a rich, amber liquor. "Since we all ended up at the same bistro without so much as a meal, we'll be having brunch here," he announced, his tone clipped. The statement, though practical, did little to diffuse the underlying tension in the room.

William cleared his throat, trying to mask his discomfort. "I... um, I still have this from earlier," he said, holding up the takeout bag as if it were a peace offering. "Not sure if anyone wants it."

Lynette shot William a look that blended irritation with sympathy, clearly caught between feeling out of place and the awkwardness of the situation. "Maybe we can just... wait and see what Tempus has planned," she suggested softly.

Tempus poured himself a generous amount of liquor, the clink of the ice cubes against the glass punctuating the silence. He took a deep sip, his eyes scanning the room.

Constance's patience finally snapped. "Tempus," she began, her voice taut with frustration, "do you have any idea what's going on here? What's the plan?"

Tempus shot her a sidelong glance, his expression impassive. "Brunch," he replied coolly, provoking Constance's irritation further.

Her eyes narrowed in exasperation. "I'm talking about the *goddamn elephant in the room*, you jerk."

Tempus's tone grew clipped. "We'll discuss it all soon enough. For now, let's just settle in."

Constance's gaze flickered to Sera, who was still seated at the far end of the couch, her shoulders tense. She then looked at Alexander, who had his gaze fixed on his hands, lost in thought.

"*Fine*," Constance said, her voice softening but still laced with a hint of irritation. She moved to a nearby armchair, her eyes lingering on Tempus as if hoping for some sign of explanation.

As the group settled into their chosen spots, the tension in the room was palpable. The luxury of the suite seemed to do little to alleviate the discomfort that hung between them. Each person's silence spoke volumes, the grand surroundings a stark contrast to the personal dramas unfolding within.

Tempus poured another glass, this time for Constance, and handed it to her with a curt nod. "Here. Might help ease the waiting."

Constance accepted the drink with a nod of thanks, but her gaze remained fixed on Tempus, her impatience and concern barely masked. The stage was set, and the unresolved issues simmered beneath the surface, waiting for the right moment to be addressed.

The room, while splendid, seemed small under the weight of their collective uncertainty. And as the minutes ticked by, the promise of answers loomed, casting long shadows over the suite's opulent furnishings.

Tempus sank into a large, overstuffed chair, a throne that seemed made for someone in control—though he was anything but. Inside, his mind raced in a frantic loop: What the hell? What the hell? What the hell? The uncertainty and confusion were relentless. Externally, he tried to maintain a calm facade, but it was clear he was falling apart.

Constance, meanwhile, moved from irritation to outright fury. She perched on the arm of the chair, a position that, while physically close, felt unbearably invasive to Tempus. Her gaze was unrelenting, piercing through him as he struggled to sip his drink and collect his scattered thoughts. This is madness, he mused, feeling the weight of her frustration.

The room was thick with silence, punctuated only by the shifting glances of those present, each person reluctant to fixate on any one face. Finally, Constance had had enough. She stood abruptly, marched over to the coffee table, and slammed her tumbler down with such force that Tempus flinched, half-expecting the glass to shatter. Her anger was palpable as she stopped a mere foot from him, hands on her hips, her eyes blazing.

"You owe me a fucking apology, you jerk," Constance demanded, her voice cutting through the tension like a knife.

The shock was evident on every face in the room, but none more so than Tempus's. His mouth fell open, and the glass he held wobbled precariously. He tightened his grip, struggling to keep the liquid from spilling, as he shifted uncomfortably in his seat.

"What... what do you mean?" he stammered, his voice barely above a whisper.

"Centuries!" Constance cried, her voice breaking as tears streamed down her cheeks. "I haven't seen you for so goddamn long, and now you're here, and all you've done is call my name. You haven't said a single word since. What the hell?"

Tempus quickly set his glass aside and rose to his feet. He wrapped Constance in his arms, pulling her close as if to shield her from the rest of the world. "I'm sorry, my love. I... I was just..." he mumbled, his voice filled with regret.

Constance struggled against him, her fists pounding weakly against his chest. "You were just what? Sorry to see me? Sorry you had to face this all over again? What was it?"

Tempus drew her back into his embrace, gently rubbing the top of her head. "It was unexpected. I know it always is, but this situation... it's more intense than usual."

"Like war or disease is any better?" she retorted, her voice trembling with emotion. "At least we're not in the midst of the War of the Roses again. Or in the Holy Roman Empire during the Great Peasants' War. This time, we're all healthy." She pulled away slightly, gesturing towards Alexander. "Even Alexander," she pointed out.

Tempus's mind reeled. Alexander's presence was a shock he hadn't anticipated. He should have been dead—long dead, a memory from a distant past. But here he was. "Let's set aside Alexander's situation for now," Tempus suggested, his voice firm but soft. "We can deal with that later. First, let me make it up to you."

Tempus began to lead Constance away, but their moment was abruptly interrupted by a voice calling out.

"Hey, who are you?" William demanded, his frustration evident. "Constance, who is this man? Is he the reason you wanted to break up with me? Have you known each other since we were together?" His anger was palpable, but it quickly faded against Tempus's fierce response.

"I don't know who you are," Tempus snapped, his voice a low, dangerous growl, "but I've loved this woman long before your family name even existed. For over a thousand years, I've loved her, and I won't tolerate you questioning her fidelity in that tone."

Constance turned to William, her face a mix of shock and disappointment. "Is *that* what you think?" she asked, shaking her head in disbelief. "That I cheated on you? I *told* you I felt *incomplete*. That something was missing from my life. *Tempus* is what I was missing. I'm sorry if that *bruises* your ego."

William sank heavily into a chair, defeated. He slumped forward, his anger giving way to resignation. The breakup was final, and he had no right to control her choices. Whether she was his girlfriend or not, she was free to pursue whatever made her happy.

Tempus reconsidered the idea of taking Constance away for a private conversation. Instead, he sank back into the chair, and with a surprising touch of childlike defiance, he pulled Constance into his lap.

Before anyone could react or voice their objections, he began recounting their intertwined histories. His tale unfolded slowly, revealing who he was, who Constance and Sera were, and the profound connections between them. His words wove a tapestry of loneliness, despair, intense anger, and fear. They spoke of abandonment and other indescribable emotions that seemed to hang ponderously in the air.

When he finished, the room fell silent once more, each person lost in their thoughts as they processed the weight of the story.

The silence was eventually shattered by a sudden burst of laughter. William lurched forward, hands covering his face as he laughed uncontrollably. "You expect me to *believe that*? It sounds like something out of a bad romance novel!" He turned to Lynette, searching for support. "*You* don't believe any of that, *do you*?"

Lynette averted her gaze, leaving William to flounder for validation from someone else. He briefly considered turning to Constance but quickly discarded the idea; she was clearly entangled in the story and wouldn't offer any objective perspective. The same was true for Sera.

Desperate, William turned to Alexander, the only other person he didn't recognize. "You're not part of this group, right? You can't honestly believe what he just said is true, can you?"

Alexander opened his mouth to respond but caught sight of Sera's face. With a mechanical motion, he shut his mouth and turned away from William, leaving him isolated and uncertain.

"Great. Just great," William muttered, his frustration evident.

In a burst of anger, he stood up, clutching his bag tightly. "Alright. You can all go on your crazy ride together, but I'm done." He started towards the door but paused near Constance. "You really had me. I loved you and thought we'd build a life together." He turned to the rest of the group, waving dismissively. "If this is what you want, then you can have it."

As William spoke, Constance felt Tempus trying to rise beneath her. She deliberately shifted her weight to prevent him from gaining his footing, then leaned closer and placed a gentle hand on the side of his face. "This is my mess to clean up," she said softly. Turning back to William, she added, "If you don't believe, that's your choice. There's nothing more between us anyway. If you want to leave, then you can."

William hesitated, casting a final glance at the group before letting out a dismissive snort and heading for the door. He likely intended to slam it behind him, but the door's design thwarted his attempt at a dramatic exit.

Following coincidentally behind William's exit, the chef Tempus had asked the hotel manager to send entered the suite. He closed the door carefully behind William before he moved close enough to Tempus to speak without seeming impolite. "Sir, I'm here to prepare brunch." He looked over his shoulder at the closed door then surveyed the room. "Will there only be five of you?"

Tempus nodded. Constance leaned forward and placed a tender kiss on Tempus's forehead. "Well done. You didn't lose your temper like you did at all those damn dinners."

Tempus growled in response, but he allowed Constance the satisfaction of having the last word.

The unspoken decision to postpone any further discussion of the past seemed to settle over the group as soon as the chef entered. It was as if everyone silently agreed to leave those heavy conversations for another time.

Gradually, without a word exchanged, the group began to disperse. Alexander was the first to rise. He moved toward the bar, pouring himself a drink with practiced ease before slipping out onto the expansive patio that stretched along the entire length of the suite. The door slid open with a soft thud, allowing the warm, unconditioned air to wash over him. He took a deep breath, feeling the tension in his shoulders begin to ease as he exhaled.

Leaning against the railing, Alexander gazed down at the stream of traffic below. His mind was blissfully blank, savoring this brief moment of calm before the inevitable discussions that loomed ahead. He raised his glass to take a sip, but a faint sound behind him made him pause. He turned, curious to see who had followed him outside.

"Sera?" Alexander asked, his voice tinged with surprise. He had expected her to keep her distance until he was ready to reveal the secrets he was holding from them all.

Sera stood hesitantly in the doorway, one arm crossed over her body, gripping her opposite elbow. When their eyes met, she quickly averted her gaze, unable—or perhaps unwilling—to meet his eyes just yet.

"Did you want to be... alone?" she asked softly, her voice trembling with uncertainty.

Instead of answering, Alexander instinctively took a step toward her. Sera looked so fragile in that moment that all he wanted was to wrap her in his arms and shield her from everything. But when she took a small step back, glancing nervously over her shoulder at the partially open door, he stopped.

The unspoken distance between them suddenly felt like a vast chasm, created by the secrets he had yet to share. He longed to bridge that gap, to make her feel safe again, but now was not the time. With a heavy heart, he stepped back, allowing the space to remain, knowing it was what she needed for now.

Sera hesitated for a moment, letting what felt like an eternity pass before she reached behind her and quietly slid the door shut. Without glancing at Alexander, she moved toward the railing, carefully keeping her distance as she passed him. She stopped at the edge, her eyes fixed on the blue sky, where soft white clouds drifted lazily across the warm Atlanta summer horizon.

Alexander, reassured that she wasn't about to flee, joined her at the railing, though he kept a respectful distance, not wanting to frighten her away again. Sera began speaking softly, so softly that at first, Alexander wasn't even sure she was talking.

"I thought I was getting to know you," she murmured, her voice barely above a whisper. "And I was okay with that. I didn't know where things might lead, but I was fine with you being there for me when I needed you, even if I didn't realize it at the time." She paused, crossing her arms tightly over her chest as her gaze dropped from the sky to the ground. "But now... I'm scared, Alex."

Alexander's heart clenched painfully. "Of what? Of me?"

Sera shook her head slowly. A few more moments passed in silence as Alexander waited, watching the breeze play with her hair. He resisted the urge to reach out, to tuck a stray strand behind her ear, just for the excuse to touch her, to reassure her with a gentle caress.

"Is it because I didn't tell you my secret?" Alexander asked when the silence between them stretched on, realizing Sera wasn't ready to speak first.

Sera turned to him slowly, her eyes glistening—she would have blamed the wind if asked. She shook her head. "It's not just that. I mean, that's part of it, but not everything." Her gaze drifted over her shoulder, back toward the suite, where Constance and Tempus sat together. "I have my own secrets to reveal to Tempus," she admitted, acknowledging her role in their shared curse.

When she turned back to Alexander, her eyes were soft yet piercing, making his breath catch. "I have a secret I've been reluctant to tell you too," she confessed, her voice barely above a whisper as she dropped her head, avoiding his eyes.

Alexander let out a small, humorless chuckle. "It can't be bigger than mine, I'm sure." He cautiously stepped closer to her. Though she didn't move away, the tension between them made it clear that one step was all she would allow for now.

"Is it something you need everyone to hear?" he asked gently.

Sera shook her head, finally lifting her eyes to meet his. "No," she whispered. "Just you."

Alexander took a chance and stepped closer, now just a small movement away from her. He lifted his hand, resting it lightly on her elbow. That simple touch seemed to dissolve the last of Sera's hesitation. She moved forward on her own, close enough for him to wrap his arms around her. She rested her head on his shoulder.

"Do you know when I realized I wasn't really in love with Tempus? That it was just..." she paused, searching for the right words. "I cherished him so much because of everything my sister and I lost. And because he was always there for us."

She hadn't said she loved him—not like that—but she also hadn't not believed it. For too long, she mistook the ache in her chest for longing, the quiet he left behind for emptiness. But now, watching him smile at her sister with a kind of stillness no storm could shake, she did not feel envy. She didn't even feel the absence of envy. Whatever she thought she'd felt—it was never this. And that, more than anything, told her what it wasn't.

"Yeah," Alexander sighed, memories of his own time with Tempus flooding back. "He's like that."

A moment of silence passed as Sera shifted even closer to him before she spoke again, her voice barely above a whisper. "I knew the truth when I lost you back then. When... you died."

Alexander stiffened, his breath catching in his throat as a wave of vertigo washed over him. He stepped back from the railing, instinctively pulling Sera with him. His hands settled on her shoulders, and he tried to gently move her away, wanting to see her eyes. But Sera resisted, tightening her grip around him.

"Don't!" Sera's voice trembled with urgency, and Alexander froze, sensing the weight of the moment. He remained still, his arms falling to his sides as he waited, knowing she needed to finish what she had started. Slowly, he wrapped his arms back around her, a silent promise to listen.

Only when Sera was sure he wouldn't force her to look at him did she find the courage to continue. "I remember that time vividly," she began, her voice soft but steady. "I fell in love with you at first sight, but I didn't recall any of it—not a single memory from that past life with you—until Tempus reappeared."

Alexander swallowed hard, his voice rough when he finally spoke. "What are you trying to say, Sera?"

"I'm saying..." She hesitated, gathering her thoughts. "I'm saying that I do love you. Last night, when I said I wasn't ready or whatever nonsense I used to push you away... I was wrong. I know it now. I love you, Alexander."

With those final words, Sera abruptly broke the embrace and rushed back inside, leaving Alexander standing there, stunned, as he tried to process what he had just heard.

Meanwhile, inside the suite, Constance, Tempus, and Lynette remained as Alexander and Sera talked on the patio. Lynette, feeling like a third wheel, refused to let the unexpected reunion and its accompanying awkwardness isolate her. Determined to break the silence, she considered how to approach Constance about the recent revelations, careful to choose her words so the chef—or anyone else listening—wouldn't pick up on the deeper meaning of their conversation.

However, finding the right moment proved challenging. Constance and Tempus seemed lost in their own world. Constance was nestled comfortably in Tempus's lap, her hands gently held in his, their eyes locked in a silent exchange. To anyone observing, it was clear that words were unnecessary between them; their connection transcended speech.

Lynette cleared her throat, finally drawing Constance's attention. "You do realize we're ditching work, right?" she said with a playful smile, half-joking but mostly trying to break the spell that seemed to hold Constance and Tempus in a bubble of their own. She knew the day's work was long forgotten, but wasn't sure if Constance was aware of anything beyond Tempus at that moment.

Constance's face flushed a deep red, her embarrassment clear. She quickly slipped her hands from Tempus's grasp, bringing them up to cover her mouth. "Oh. Oh!" she exclaimed, her eyes darting between Lynette and Tempus. Tempus merely shrugged, a hint of amusement playing on his lips.

As the initial shock gave way to irritation, Constance balled her fist and playfully struck Tempus on the chest.

'Again with the violence, woman?' Tempus mused with a smile, wondering what challenges she had faced growing up in this lifetime.

Flustered by the realization that she had walked out on her job, Constance turned to Lynette. "What do we do? I'm not—"

Lynette raised a hand to calm her. "Don't worry, girl. We don't have to clock in, and there's no supervisor breathing down our necks. Just the director. He'll understand. Whatever we were working on can wait."

Constance let out a breath she didn't realize she'd been holding, her shoulders relaxing as the tension eased. Tempus seized the moment, pulling her closer to him.

"You beast," she laughed, her voice lightening.

Tempus grinned, his eyes softening. "I haven't seen you in centuries. I'm not letting you go again, even if I did try to stay away by leaving Europe." He had come to terms with the inevitable—fate had reunited them, and there was no point in resisting it anymore.

Lynette's voice cut through the lighthearted moment. "So..." she began cautiously, glancing toward the kitchen to make sure they were still alone. "Is he the one? The guy from the images? You know, the lithograph, the photo, and the painting?"

Tempus's eyebrow shot up at the mention of these items. "What lithograph? What painting? What photo?" he asked, turning to Constance with clear curiosity.

Constance smiled, adjusting herself in his arms before rising to smooth out her clothes. She took a seat beside Lynette, realizing they had been a bit inconsiderate of her friend. As much as she longed to stay wrapped in Tempus's embrace, she knew there would be plenty of time for that later.

She recalled the strange, fuzzy feelings she'd experienced just before discovering those items—memories resurfacing, no doubt. Fate was at work again, intertwining their lives. "It seems destiny had pulled us together once more," she said. "Lynette and I work at the High Museum of Art, and we were sorting through thousands of items for a display. I happened to come across those three pieces—each one bearing your image."

Tempus leaned forward, now perched on the edge of his chair, his curiosity piqued. "Are you sure?"

Constance nodded and looked to Lynette, seeking her confirmation. Lynette gave a firm nod in agreement, her expression serious.

Lynette spoke up, her tone tinged with disbelief. "Yeah, it was pretty freaky seeing the same guy in three different time periods. At first, I thought it was just a coincidence, but then..." She trailed off as she pulled out her phone, scrolling to the image she had shown Constance earlier. She handed the phone to Tempus, who could clearly see his image in the background. "My girlfriend was at the airport when this photo was taken. You must have just arrived because there you are, right behind her. I was stunned, but I still couldn't wrap my head around the idea that it could actually be the same person. It just seemed too bizarre."

Tempus studied the photo, recognizing himself immediately. He leaned back, lacing his fingers together in his lap as he tried to recall the moment. Yes, he did remember a flash going off as he passed by a couple at the airport. "I see," he murmured, his voice thoughtful.

Constance's curiosity sparked. "So, do you think those other images were of you too? Maybe my mind was just making the connection as my memories were coming back."

Tempus shook his head slightly, still deep in thought. "I wouldn't know without seeing them myself. But I don't think you were mistaken. I've spent my life trying to stay low-key, but there might have been times when I slipped up—when a photo was taken, or a painting made. I've always tried to keep out of the public eye, but it's not foolproof."

Lynette glanced around the luxurious suite, raising an eyebrow. "If this is you keeping low-key, I'd hate to see what high-profile looks like."

They all shared a laugh, the tension easing as humor lightened the mood.

"While I don't flaunt my means overtly, I do take some liberties where it's safe to do so. I have... resources that keep me protected," Tempus said.

He glanced over his shoulder as the patio door swung open and Sera stepped in, dabbing at her eyes with the back of her hand. Tempus's anger flared momentarily as he looked past her at Alexander. It took a conscious effort to suppress his irritation. Despite considering Alexander a brother, his patience had limits when it came to Constance and Sera. Tempus reminded himself that he didn't fully understand what had transpired outside, and though his initial reaction was to blame Alexander, he knew better. If this Alexander was anything like the old one, he wouldn't intentionally hurt Sera. Still, people—and circumstances—change.

Tempus stood abruptly, excusing himself. "I'm sorry, ladies. I need to step outside for a moment." He pulled a cigar from his inner pocket and flashed it with a quick smile before walking out towards the patio, not waiting for a response.

The focus then shifted back to Sera. Both Constance and Lynette noticed her red eyes and immediately began to comfort her, chatting softly and asking about what had happened.

Before Tempus could step outside, the chef interrupted him. "Sir, brunch is served."

Tempus hesitated, torn between confronting Alexander and joining the others for the meal. Deciding to defer the conversation for now, he knocked on the window and signaled Alexander to come in.

"It's time to eat," Tempus said with a welcoming smile as Alexander stepped through the sliding door. Turning to Constance and Lynette, he added, "Brunch is ready."

The chef guided everyone to the dining room, setting plates on the table as they settled into their seats. Once he had finished his task, he turned back to Tempus. "Will you be needing anything else?"

Tempus, accustomed to being served yet keen to maintain politeness, waved a hand dismissively. "Thank you for the meal. I'm sure it will be excellent. I'll arrange for someone to clean up afterward. Your work is much appreciated."

The chef nodded and took his leave, leaving the five of them gathered for their meal. The mood remained a bit uneasy, though less tense than before. There was a palpable awareness that important discussions lay ahead, now that they were alone and free to speak openly.

Tempus turned to Alexander, the anger and confusion he had felt earlier melting away. Instead, a sense of camaraderie and brotherhood settled in his chest as he met Alexander's gaze.

"Alex," Tempus began, his voice tinged with emotion. "Seeing you again was a surprise, but I'm really glad we have this chance. I..." His voice faltered, and he cleared his throat. "I missed you."

Alexander's smile was warm and genuine. "I've missed you too, Tempus. You've always been the closest friend I've ever had."

Tempus nodded, the weight of the reunion settling on him. "So, can you tell me what's happening? How are you here now, when you passed away during the Black Plague?"

Alexander set his fork down and picked up his napkin, dabbing at the corners of his mouth before letting it fall back into his lap. He glanced around at those seated at the table, his expression thoughtful. "It's a long story—very long," he began, giving a nod toward Constance and Sera. "Just as long as yours and theirs."

"Go on," Tempus encouraged, leaning in.

Alexander paused, searching for the right place to start. He began with a story about his grandmother, who had raised him and whom he had known as his only family. He described how women from the city, both single and married, would seek her advice or request love potions. The girls smiled and giggled at the mention, while Tempus, catching their amusement, shared a smile before turning his attention back to Alexander.

Continuing, Alexander spoke about how their fates had become intertwined. "I can see that none of you really remember the first time we all met."

Tempus looked at Sera and Constance, both of whom shrugged in response. Curious and open to what Alexander would reveal, Tempus turned back to him. "If it wasn't during the Middle Ages, then when was it?"

"Hellena," Sera suddenly murmured, drawing all eyes toward her. She sat with her gaze fixed on her plate, her fork suspended mid-air as the memory halted her. Looking up at Alexander, she asked softly, "Your grandmother was Hellena?"

"Yes," Alexander confirmed quietly. "Hellena was my grandmother. She was the one who gave you the flower."

Tempus, Constance, and Lynette exchanged glances, their heads moving left and right as if caught in a tennis match.

Constance was the first to break the silence. "Who was Hellena? What flower?"

Alexander slid his chair back, the room filled with an expectant silence as he moved to Sera's side and placed his hands gently on her shoulders. "I met all of you at the market—just one day. I fell in love with Sera that day. A few nights later, Sera came to my house and spoke with my grandmother."

Constance's attention snapped from Alexander to Sera. "When was this?"

Sera shifted her gaze between Tempus and Constance, her unease palpable. She hesitated, unsure if revealing this would reignite Constance's anger from the night she confessed her wish to alter her fate, or what Tempus might think, considering he was not yet aware.

"It was the night you confessed your love to Tempus," Sera began, her voice trembling. She paused, taking a deep breath. "Remember that night? I came back to our room late, and you asked where I'd been." She looked at Constance, her eyes filled with regret. Gently placing her hands over Alexander's on her shoulders, she continued, "I had left the house and gotten lost in the city. I met an old woman who gave me directions. I told her about how I loved..."

Sera hesitated, her gaze dropping to her lap. She struggled with whether to reveal that she loved Tempus as well. Instead, she said softly, "I told Hellena that I loved someone who didn't love me back."

Constance's eyes widened as she absorbed the revelation. "Who did you love that you couldn't tell..." Constance began then stopped. Her heart ached as she looked from her sister to Tempus, realizing the depth of Sera's pain. Reaching out, she pulled Sera into a comforting embrace. "I'm so sorry, sweetie. I never knew. I didn't see it," she murmured, feeling the weight of her sister's unspoken suffering.

Sera clung to Constance, tears streaming down her face. "I'm sorry. I'm so sorry," she sobbed. "I thought I was in love with Tempus. It wasn't jealousy of you, Connie. I just wished to be seen by him the way you were."

Tempus cleared his throat, visibly unsettled by the new information. "I didn't know either, Sera. Why didn't you tell us?"

Sera's voice cracked as she continued to weep, taking shallow breaths between sentences. "How could I? I didn't want to cause any trouble between you two. You were so in love with each other. Who was I to come between that?"

Everyone waited in silence as Sera took a moment to calm herself. After a few deep breaths, she finally spoke, her voice steadier. "It's my fault we're in this mess. I made a wish to change my fate."

Constance's eyes widened with concern. "When did you make this wish? Years had passed since then and..." She trailed off, her gaze drifting to Tempus. The girls had tragically passed away in a carriage accident a few years after Constance's confession to Tempus.

Sera wiped her tears, her voice trembling as she continued. "Hellena told me that the flower I had could grant a wish to change my fate. I held onto it, hoping things would improve on their own, but they didn't." She glanced at Tempus, not with accusation, but with a resigned acknowledgment of his role in the unfolding events. "When your parents announced their plans to marry us off that month, I made the wish. The next day, we... were in that accident."

Tempus absorbed her words slowly, his face reflecting the gravity of the situation. "So that's how all our fates changed," he said quietly. He looked up at Alexander. "But if that's the case, why did Constance and Sera keep reincarnating while I remained immortal? And where do you fit into this?"

Alexander shrugged, a hint of frustration in his eyes. "I'm not entirely sure myself. That night Sera came to my house, my grandmother gave me a flower—one very similar to the one she had already given Sera. I had just told my grandmother about falling in love with Sera. I was young and naïve, and I didn't fully understand what I was doing, but I had already wished for Sera to be in my life. That's when I became entangled in all of this."

Tempus frowned, trying to piece the information together. "If that's the case, why did we only encounter each other once before? During our time at the De Montford château and at the medical school in Paris?"

Alexander shook his head. "I don't know. Sometimes I'd run into Sera, but she wouldn't recognize me. Until recently, I didn't try to engage with her—I was still trying to make sense of my own situation. My memories of past lives were fragmented and didn't come back to me until it was almost too late."

Constance and Sera nodded in understanding. They were familiar with the same patterns from their own reincarnations.

Lynette, struggling to keep up with the conversation, finally interjected. "Wait a minute. I'm a bit lost here. Can someone clarify a few things for me?"

Tempus, sensing the group's collective uncertainty, finally spoke up. "What do you want to know, Lynette?"

Lynette exhaled slowly, gathering her thoughts. "First of all, are you saying that all of you were born in the twelfth century?"

Tempus looked around at the others, who gave subtle nods in confirmation. "Yes, that's right," Tempus confirmed.

Lynette turned to Constance, her eyes wide with disbelief. "So you've loved this man through multiple lifetimes, only to die and face the same heartbreak over and over?"

Constance offered a sad but understanding smile and nodded.

Lynette then shifted her gaze to Sera. "And you, Sera, wished for a different life, which somehow cursed all of you?"

"That's about the gist of it," Sera replied softly.

Lynette's eyes drifted upward to Alexander, who stood behind Sera's chair. "And you were drawn into this because you wished to be with the girl you loved?"

Alexander leaned forward and gently kissed the top of Sera's head. "Yes, that's right," he said with a smile. Sera patted his hands on her shoulders before awkwardly turning in her chair to give him a sideways hug. Though it was a bit uncomfortable, it conveyed her affection as Alexander wrapped his arms around her as best he could.

Lynette then turned to Constance. "And what about you? What is your wish?" Her gaze then shifted to Tempus. "And you?"

Tempus and Constance exchanged a loving look. Tempus, his voice thick with emotion, said, "I always wished to be with her forever."

Lynette nodded thoughtfully, taking in their responses. "It seems clear that Sera and Alexander's connection is tied to that flower," she said. Turning to Tempus, she continued, "You likely became part of this because you wished to be with Constance forever. That might explain why you became immortal. But that's just my guess."

Tempus pondered Lynette's theory, finding it surprisingly plausible given everything they had experienced. It made sense, in a strange way—his wish for eternity with Constance might have been the key to his immortality. Yet, he knew he hadn't possessed the flower that Sera and Alexander had spoken about.

"So how exactly am I connected to this?" he asked. "I can grasp that my wish for forever with Constance might explain my immortality, though it sounds far-fetched. What does that have to do with me specifically? And what about Constance?"

Lynette shrugged. "I'm only speculating here," she admitted. She then turned to Sera. "Sera, can you tell us exactly what you wished for?"

Sera took a moment to reflect. More than a few lifetimes had passed since then, yet the memory was vivid, as if it had happened just yesterday.

"I remember Tempus's parents telling us that Constance and I were to be married in a month. I think I wished to change 'our' fate," Sera said slowly, her eyes shifting to her sister. "Not just mine," she added, her tone laced with surprise. The revelation shifted her perspective on their predicament.

"So, to protect both you and your sister, you wished to alter both of your fates," Lynette clarified.

Sera nodded. "That's right."

A heavy silence settled over the room as everyone absorbed this new information. Lynette's sharp instincts led her to turn to Constance for the next question. "What about you, Constance? What did you wish for?"

Constance opened her mouth, then closed it, struggling to recall. *'What* did *I wish for?'* she thought, but found no clear answer. She looked from Tempus to Alexander and Sera, her expression uncertain. "I... don't think I wished for anything. I honestly don't know."

Constance felt a wave of distress. It was as if a crucial piece of the puzzle was just out of reach—an elusive idea or hint that she couldn't quite grasp. She had a sense that a solution, a way to end the cycle of rebirth and tragedy, was near but remained frustratingly out of focus. Before she could pursue this thought further, Lynette's next question interrupted her train of thought.

"Why didn't you look for the flower again, Sera? Maybe it could have helped you change things, turn things around?" Lynette asked.

Sera glanced at Alexander, who answered on her behalf. "She did. In every lifetime, she searched for the flower." Alexander's gaze fell, his eyes downcast. "When she told me about it, I consulted a botanist friend to see if he knew anything about the flower," he continued, his voice trailing off.

"And?" Tempus urged.

Alexander looked up at Tempus who offered a look of reassurance. Alexander's expression darkened to a look of resignation. "He told me the flower went extinct a long time ago."

"What kind of flower is this again?" Lynette asked, her curiosity piqued. "I'd like to see it."

Sera smiled, reaching into her bag and pulling out her phone. "I painted it from memory," she said, swiping through her gallery until she found the image. She held the phone out to Lynette, who leaned in, intrigued.

Alexander glanced at the phone and then at Sera. "The flower... it was only ever in existence in San Marino," he said, his voice tinged with a hint of sadness.

"Let me see," said Tempus softly.

Sera hesitated, the phone hovering between her and Lynette. She pivoted the screen toward Tempus. He studied the image with intense focus, his brow furrowing in concentration. Beside him, Constance leaned in, mirroring his scrutiny.

"I don't really recall seeing a flower like this," Constance said, her voice thoughtful. She leaned back, breaking her gaze from the phone. Her admission drew Alexander's attention, and she let out a light, almost self-deprecating laugh. "I was so preoccupied with everything happening at home that I didn't really notice the flowers around us."

Her laughter carried a trace of regret, hinting at embarrassment over her past preoccupations. The memories of her youthful concerns—her love for Tempus, her desire to stay out of his parents' way, and the struggle to feel welcome in their home—were a reminder of challenges she had no desire to revisit.

Alexander turned to Tempus, who had been quietly observing the photo on the phone. "Tempus, have you ever seen this flower before?"

Tempus leaned closer, his eyes narrowing in thought. "Not in recent times," he admitted. "But I remember seeing something like it back when we were all together in the twelfth century. Not since then."

As Tempus spoke, Lynette had taken the phone from Sera's hand, her eyes widening as she examined the painting. The gasp that escaped her lips was barely contained. "Oh my god!" she exclaimed, her voice catching the attention of the others at the table.

Constance looked at Lynette, her expression a mix of confusion and concern. "What? Have you seen this flower before?"

Lynette's eyes were wide with amazement. "Yes, I've seen it—well, sort of. I think this was in basement of our museum."

Constance's confusion deepened. "You mean the painting?"

"No," said Lynette, shaking her head. "I mean the actual flower. It was so vivid, and I remember thinking it looked like something out of a fairy tale."

Constance's gaze flicked between Lynette and Tempus. "For real?" she asked, her mind racing. She turned back to Lynette. "Are you serious?"

Lynette shook her head slowly, still processing. "I don't know. I believe it is, but I couldn't make sense of this. That flower just... showed up with some other miscellaneous stuff that came in last week."

Tempus's gaze softened as he looked at Constance. "Perhaps there's more to this flower than just its beauty. If it's the same flower, it might be a clue or a link to breaking this cycle."

Constance's curiosity and apprehension deepened. "Do you know where that shipment came from?"

Lynette furrowed her brows as she thought. "I believe it was from Italy."

Tempus's mind raced. Goods from San Marino would have to pass through Italian customs, unless transported by air. "If the flower is indeed from San Marino and it's showing up at the museum... it might be connected to something significant. That's where both of you work, right? It feels like fate has been toying with us for a long time." He reflected on his attempts to avoid meeting the twins in Europe, only to find himself encountering them in the United States. "Even now, when I thought avoiding you both in Europe would be best, fate brings us together here."

Constance nodded slowly. "I have to admit, it sounds crazy. But considering everything we've been through, maybe it's not that far-fetched. Who lives multiple lives and remembers each one so vividly?"

Tempus spoke softly, his voice heavy with unspoken pain, his words meant for himself alone. He had no inkling that the others were listening. "Who the hell lives forever and endures constant loss?" he murmured. His gaze was fixed downward, his chin resting on his steepled hands. It wasn't until the silence stretched and he felt the weight of others' attention that he realized they had heard him.

"I'm sorry," he said, offering a weak smile. He waved his hand dismissively and leaned back in his chair. "Just some thoughts. What else is there to say?"

Alexander leaned back, his eyes contemplative. "We should investigate further. There might be a reason this flower is surfacing now."

"That's if it's the same one," Constance interjected, her tone pragmatic.

Lynette, her mind racing with possibilities, looked between them with determination. "I'll help however I can. We can head to the museum right now, find the flower, and see if it matches."

As Sera pondered the flower's significance, the conversation around her seemed to blur. The flower was weaving a new thread into their tangled lives. She snapped out of her reverie when Lynette mentioned going to the museum. "Can I come with you? Maybe I can tell right away if it's the same one."

Before Lynette could respond, Alexander added, "I'll join you as well. I remember the flower pretty clearly."

Lynette hesitated, her mouth opening and closing as if searching for words. Constance noticed her discomfort and asked, "What's wrong, Lynette?"

"Well, the thing is..." Lynette paused, glancing at Tempus. "We don't have a way to get there without calling a cab or rideshare."

Tempus smiled and pulled out his cell phone. "I'll arrange transportation," he said, swiftly making the necessary arrangements.

Chapter 13: "Breaking the Cycle"

Present Day - Atlanta, USA

A love reborn, free from the shadows of the past..

Constance and Tempus watched silently as the others left the suite. The door clicked shut, leaving a quiet stillness between them. Tempus stood close behind Constance, his presence palpable. As the silence stretched, she asked softly, "Are you sure you don't want to go with them? To the museum, I mean. To see if it's the same flower?"

Tempus stepped closer, his arm slipping around her waist, pulling her gently against his chest. The warmth of his body and the undeniable strength in his embrace sent a shiver down her spine. She became acutely aware of him—of the years they had been apart and the weight of their shared history pressing down on this moment.

His free hand brushed softly against her cheek, tucking a stray strand of hair behind her ear. Constance's breath caught as she lifted her hands to hold his, turning slowly in his arms to face him. The intimate gesture, his hand lingering against her skin, made her mind wander to thoughts she had long suppressed. Thoughts that surged to the surface now that they were finally alone, after lifetimes of separation.

Tempus's voice broke the silence, filled with a tenderness that made her heart ache. "I wanted to spend some time with you alone. You know, as a way to make—"

"What? To make it up to me for ignoring me this whole time?" Constance asked, her tone a mix of playful teasing and genuine accusation, her smile barely masking the hurt underneath.

Tempus chuckled softly, trying to deflect the moment by turning away, but Constance quickly placed a finger on his lips, halting both his movement and his words.

"You totally ignored me," she continued, her eyes narrowing as she searched for the right words. "You kept me at... way more than arm's length until you pulled me down into your lap. What was that about? Asserting your dominance in front of William?" Her attempt at a witty retort fell a little flat, but she took satisfaction in the flicker of guilt and awkwardness that crossed Tempus's face. Her smile widened.

Tempus hesitated, clearly searching for the right response. It was true—seeing William with Constance had struck a nerve. The idea of someone else, especially William, claiming a place in her life as her boyfriend had been hard for him to stomach. He couldn't deny that it had triggered something deep within him.

"I needed to make sure I got to spend time with you, that's all," he finally admitted, his voice quieter. "And then..." He hesitated again, his gaze dropping before he met her eyes once more. "I guess I did kind of get pissed at him. It was probably childish of me to respond the way I did."

Constance studied him for a moment, reading the sincerity in his eyes. The tension between them softened as she recognized his honesty, his willingness to admit his faults. She let out a small sigh, her fingers still resting lightly against his lips before she gently pulled them away.

Constance smiled, relieved to see that the old, protective Tempus was still very much present, even after all these centuries. It warmed her to know that he still cared, despite everything they had been through.

"But why the cold shoulder when I found you?" she asked, her smile fading slightly as the memory of their reunion resurfaced. There was still a hint of hurt in her voice. "You seemed to have a lot to say, and a need to exert control when we met up. You made the rest of us feel like kids."

Tempus paused, then took a step back. He reached for her hand, his grip firm yet gentle, and led her back to the seating area. Settling into the chair he had occupied earlier, he pulled Constance down into his lap, holding her close.

"Look," he began, his tone softer now. "It was chaotic out there. I didn't know how to respond, and I fell back on old habits—taking charge, trying to get the situation under control until I could figure out what was happening."

Constance's brows knitted together as she studied his face. "So taking charge is an old habit?" she asked, a hint of skepticism in her voice. "I don't remember that Tempus from our past."

Tempus sighed, running a hand through his hair. "Maybe you're right," he admitted. "I wasn't always like this. But after everything that's happened, it's become second nature. I've had to keep it together for so long, to make decisions... and I forgot that things are different now with your return."

Constance softened at his words, understanding the burden he had carried for so long. She rested her head against his chest, listening to the steady rhythm of his heartbeat. "Things are different now," she echoed, her voice gentle. "But you don't have to carry it all on your own anymore."

Tempus looked up into Constance's eyes, and she could see the loneliness etched in his gaze—a deep, ancient sorrow that had settled into his soul over the eons. She leaned forward and pressed a gentle kiss to his forehead, then rested her cheek against his head, holding him close until he began to speak.

His voice was barely a whisper, heavy with the weight of centuries. "You don't know what it was like, Constance."

He spoke of the countless years that had spanned his life, the relentless ache of loss that had repeated over and over again. It wasn't just a few hundred times—he had endured the heartbreak of losing someone dear to him thousands, tens of thousands of times. The years had become a ceaseless cycle, an unending torment.

"That never-ending yearning for it all to stop," he continued, his voice faltering. "Sometimes I just couldn't handle it. Other times, I had to... change. Become someone cold-hearted and..." His words trailed off, the pain too overwhelming to articulate.

Constance, feeling the depth of his despair, wrapped her arms around his back and gently pulled him closer, his face resting against her chest. She kissed the top of his head, her touch tender and full of love, offering him the comfort he so desperately needed—the promise of an end to his suffering, right there in her embrace.

"I know," she whispered, her voice soft and understanding. "I can't imagine what it was truly like for you, but I know about the pain."

For Constance, the pain had been different, but she understood that his ran deeper. She couldn't fully grasp the extent of his suffering, but she offered him the only thing she could—her acceptance, her love, and the reassurance that he wasn't alone anymore.

Constance eventually leaned back, though the urge to comfort Tempus lingered. She longed to reconnect with him, but there were questions she needed to ask—questions that had been nagging at her since their reunion.

"You mentioned leaving Europe to avoid meeting us in this lifetime," she began, her voice laced with a hint of hurt. "Why did you do that?" The memory of his words felt like a pinprick in her heart, and she almost winced at the thought. As she waited for his response, she traced her hand gently down his chest, seeking reassurance.

Tempus knew he couldn't hide the truth from Constance. It wouldn't be fair to her, and he had never intended to deceive her. He started to turn his face away, but Constance's hand came up, cupping his cheek, guiding his gaze back to hers. Her deep eyes held him, urging him to be honest.

With no escape from her penetrating gaze, he confessed, his voice heavy with regret. "I thought if I stayed away, I might save you from what always happens after we reunite—your and Sera's deaths. I thought... maybe I could spare you that heartache. You know how it goes. We meet, your memories return, and then, not long after..."

"I know, Tempus," Constance interrupted softly, her voice gentle but firm. "I know." She leaned in and kissed him, a brief, tender touch that conveyed both understanding and pain. As she pulled back, she let him continue, though she held onto her right to be angry later, depending on what else he had to reveal.

"I thought maybe you and Sera could have this lifetime—live it out to old age," Tempus said, his voice tinged with uncertainty.

Constance's response was immediate, catching Tempus off guard. "And you think that would have been fair to me?"

Tempus was stunned. *'Why shouldn't she have the chance to live to old age?'* he wondered, but before he could voice his thoughts, Constance continued.

"You would have left me alone? To live the rest of my life feeling incomplete? Un-whole? I don't think I would have liked that," she said, her tone firm yet tinged with the pain of the thought.

Tempus tried to explain, his words almost defensive. "I didn't want to cut short your chance at a full lifetime. Not this time."

Constance's eyes narrowed as she responded, "That's an asshole, selfish way to look at it."

Her words struck him like a blow. He grimaced, realizing how his intentions might have come across. He had been trying to protect her, but now he saw how misguided that attempt might have been. He struggled to find the right words, desperate to make her understand that his decision wasn't about selfishness—it was about them, about trying to spare them both more pain.

"Constance, I—" Tempus began, his voice softening as he searched for the right way to bridge the gap his words had opened.

"Did you really think I'd need or want that?" Constance's voice was soft but insistent, her eyes searching his.

Tempus shook his head, his uncertainty palpable. "I don't know. I just don't know anything," he admitted, his voice heavy with the weight of his internal struggle. He was lost, caught between what he thought was right and the overwhelming fear that his presence might bring harm to the woman he loved more than anything. It didn't make sense to him, but he would choose her happiness over his own, always, no matter the cost.

But Constance saw it differently. The idea of living a life without Tempus, especially after regaining her memories, felt like no life at all. The thought of spending years feeling incomplete, knowing something essential was missing—it was unbearable. She wasn't entirely sure how to articulate it, but she knew she couldn't accept the idea that he would willingly stay away to spare her.

Suddenly, Constance stood up, determination in her movements. She swung one leg over Tempus's outer thigh, straddling his lap. Her skirt hiked up, but she didn't care. Knees tucked on either side of his hips, she wrapped her arms tightly around him, burying her face in his shoulder. The tears she had been holding back finally spilled over.

"I wouldn't want that," she said, her voice choked with emotion. "I wouldn't want to live a life without you. Ever."

Tempus, stunned by the depth of Constance's emotion, tightened his embrace, pulling her closer into his lap. "I'm sorry," he whispered, his voice thick with regret. "I didn't mean to make you worry. I thought I was considering what was best for you, but it seems, once again, I didn't think things through. I had no idea your life felt incomplete until we met in each lifetime."

Constance sniffled, her voice half-muffled against his shoulder. "That's because I never had the chance to sit down and talk to you like this, you jerk."

Tempus sighed, guilt washing over him. "I'm sorry," he repeated, his hand gently circling her waist while the other cradled the back of her head. He began to rock her softly, hoping to ease the ache in her heart.

Constance allowed herself to be soothed by his rhythmic motion. Her mind, swirling with a mix of emotions, gradually began to settle. The reality of their situation took root, and as she calmed, a new awareness surfaced.

She became acutely aware of the man beneath her, the way her body pressed against his, the solidness of him. His scent filled her senses—a subtle cologne mingled with the clean fragrance of his shampoo and conditioner. Her nostrils flared as she nestled her head into the curve of his neck, the scent of him enveloping her, warm and heady. She couldn't quite place what she was feeling, but the closeness of him stirred something deep within her, an ache building with each subtle sway of their bodies.

The gentle rocking motion only intensified Constance's internal turmoil. Her heart pounded as the friction between them stirred sensations she hadn't anticipated, making her simultaneously wish he would stop and desperate for him to quicken the pace. An unexpected thought pierced through her confusion—'*I've never been intimate with Tempus.*' The realization sent a shiver through her, which Tempus misinterpreted as lingering sadness, prompting him to continue rocking her gently in his arms.

As the weight of that realization settled, a cascade of emotions and thoughts overwhelmed Constance. Her mind drifted back to the love she had always believed she felt for Tempus, but now, that love seemed tangled with new, unsettling questions. She recalled Sera's confessions about how she came to understand her own love for Tempus, and doubt began to creep in.

'*Do I really love Tempus?*' The question echoed in her mind. '*Is my love different from Sera's?*' The realization that they had never shared true intimacy made her question the depth and nature of her feelings. Were they rooted in something genuine, or were they simply a reflection of Sera's unfulfilled desires? The uncertainty gnawed at her, leaving her unsure of what she truly felt for the man holding her so close.

Constance's mind cleared in an instant as a single thought took hold: 'I want this man. I *want* this man. I want *this man*.' The words echoed endlessly, a relentless chant reverberating through her. She couldn't escape it, and she didn't want to.

A low moan escaped her lips, breaking the rhythm of their embrace. Tempus immediately paused, concern flashing across his face. He began to shift back, but she caught his shirt in her hand in a firm grip.

"No. Don't," she whispered, her breath quick and uneven. Her heart raced, and she fought to steady herself, to regain control over the emotions and sensations that had overwhelmed her. She realized, with a mix of shock and embarrassment, that she had just orgasmed. The realization made her cheeks burn, and she couldn't bear to meet Tempus's eyes.

"Are you alright?" Tempus asked gently, his voice laced with concern.

Blushing fiercely, Constance abruptly stood, breaking free from his hold. She averted her gaze, taking a step back to put some distance between them.

Tempus rose as well, worry etched on his face. "Are you alright?" he repeated, stepping towards her.

Without thinking, Constance extended her hand, pressing it firmly against his chest to stop his advance. She ducked her head, praying he wouldn't realize what had just happened.

"I, um..." she stammered, her voice barely above a whisper. She took another step back, trying to compose herself. "I need to go to the bathroom. I'll be back."

Without waiting for a response, she turned and quickly made her way to there, her heart still pounding in her chest.

Tempus watched Constance leave, a swirl of confusion and concern churning within him. He was left alone with his thoughts, unsure of what had just transpired and anxiously waiting for her return. He settled back into his chair, feeling helpless and unsure of what else to do.

When Constance returned a few minutes later, her cheeks were still faintly flushed, and she avoided meeting his gaze. Tempus stood up and extended his hand toward her as she approached. She took it slowly, and he guided her to a nearby sofa instead of their original seat, sensing her reluctance to return to the previous spot.

"Are you feeling better?" Tempus asked, his face etched with worry.

Constance quickly turned to him with a forced smile, her hands lightly patting her cheeks. "Yeah, I'm fine," she said, then muttered under her breath, "just hot as hell."

"What?" Tempus asked, not quite catching her words.

"Nothing," Constance replied, turning back to face him. "I was just thinking if there's something we could do while we wait for the others."

Tempus raised an eyebrow. "I thought we were going to wait here for them to come back?"

Constance shook her head. "You're new to Atlanta. From here, at this time of day, it'll take them at least an hour both ways. We've got time to kill," she said, silently adding to herself, '*and I can't stay alone with you right now. The only thing on my mind are some very inappropriate thoughts.*' She gave Tempus a hopeful smile as he considered her suggestion.

"Well, I guess we could head to the mall next door and wander around a bit. It'll help pass the time," Tempus suggested.

He stood and offered his hand. Constance gratefully accepted it, her relief palpable. "Yeah, that's a good idea," she said. Leaving the room felt like a breath of fresh air. She was eager to escape the space where her feelings for Tempus had been overwhelming her, and she needed a distraction from the confusing emotions that had surfaced.

Tempus and Constance exited the hotel elevator, ready to make the short walk to Lennox Square Mall. As they stepped into the expansive lobby, Tempus couldn't shake the unsettling feeling that something was off. The luxurious space, usually a haven for high-class residents, seemed unusually populated with unaccompanied men in a variety of sharply tailored suits. The stark contrast between these suits and the bespoke attire typical of the hotel's clientele struck Tempus as peculiar.

He brushed off his initial unease, attributing it to his distraction by Constance. Her presence, while comforting, made it difficult for him to focus on anything else. Despite a nagging sense of discomfort, Tempus tried to remain in the moment, appreciating their leisurely stroll.

Once they reached the mall, Tempus and Constance wandered through the bustling shops, window-gazing and occasionally stepping into stores. Constance's enthusiasm led them from one boutique to the next. At one point, she held up a blouse and asked Tempus for his opinion. His phone buzzed with an incoming call, but he slipped it back into his pocket, giving her his full attention.

As they left the store with a purchase in hand, Tempus's sense of unease intensified. His nerves, previously on edge, were now screaming at him. He noticed that they were being followed by several men who seemed to be moving deliberately and discreetly. One of them was speaking into the cuff of his sleeve—a subtle signal that they were equipped with sophisticated radio devices, unlike the special police who used clear tubes and earpieces.

Tempus's heart raced as he made a quick decision. He gently but urgently guided Constance towards the nearest exit, masking his anxiety with a calm demeanor. "Let's head back to the hotel," he suggested. "I need to check on something."

Constance looked at him, puzzled but trusting. "Is everything okay?"

Tempus managed a reassuring smile. "Everything's fine. It's just a precaution. I want to make sure we're back at the hotel before the others return."

Constance gave a casual shrug. "Alright," she said, her tone light. She hadn't anticipated the shopping spree in the first place, so cutting it short didn't bother her much.

Once they were outside and heading back to the hotel, Tempus's mind was racing. He feared for Constance's safety and was determined to resolve the situation quickly. He knew that he needed to contact someone who could handle the situation with the discretion and authority required. His primary concern was keeping Constance out of harm's way, and he hoped that by returning to the hotel, he could get the situation under control before things escalated further.

As Tempus and Constance walked back toward the hotel, a van suddenly pulled up beside them, blocking their path. Tempus's senses sharpened. He glanced behind and saw the men who had been tailing them in the mall, closing in from the rear.

His instincts screamed at him, but he maintained a calm exterior. Tempus moved Constance behind him, subtly guiding her away from the street and into a safer position. The van's engine rumbled ominously as it stopped, its presence adding a layer of foreboding to the already tense situation. He could discern the outline of the men's profiles through their suits, the distinct shapes of weapons subtly suggesting their intentions.

The van's passenger, a man with a steely gaze, leaned out and made eye contact with Tempus. "Is there something I can help you gentlemen with?" Tempus asked, forcing a polite smile.

The man's expression didn't change. "Can you get in the van and come with us?"

Tempus glanced over his shoulder at Constance, her eyes wide with confusion and fear. He turned back to the speaker, maintaining his smile but allowing a hint of concern to seep through. "Sure, I could do that, but I don't think the lady would appreciate it. I should escort her back to the hotel first."

The man's hand moved subtly towards his jacket button. Tempus sighed, recognizing the potential escalation. "Alright, we'll take the ride. Where are we headed?"

The man dropped his hand and motioned toward the van's interior. He glanced behind as car horns blared at the sudden halt of traffic caused by the van. Turning back to Tempus, he said, "You'll find out when we get there."

With a resigned nod, Tempus and Constance climbed into the van. The man who had spoken got out of the passenger seat, closing the door behind him, and slid into the back of the van in the seat behind them, his eyes never leaving the pair as the side door shut with a heavy thud. The van lurched forward, picking up speed as it left the hotel area behind.

As the van rolled smoothly through the city streets, Tempus couldn't help but note the surprising opulence of their ride—a high-end limousine van, complete with a well-stocked beverage bar. The irony of being kidnapped in such comfort wasn't lost on him. He glanced back at the man seated behind them, who was keeping a close watch, and nodded towards the bar.

The man, recognizing the silent request, leaned forward and spoke over the hum of the road and the soft elevator music drifting from the speakers. "Help yourself, sir. We won't be long. There are snacks below, as well."

Tempus nodded appreciatively, then turned his attention to the bar. He selected a bottle of liquor and poured a generous measure into a crystal glass. He passed the glass to Constance, who took it with trembling hands. "I'm sure you'll need this," Tempus said gently, hoping the alcohol would offer her some relief.

Constance downed the shot in one swift motion, her face contorting as the liquor burned down her throat. She handed the empty glass back to Tempus, her voice sharp with anxiety. "What the hell is going on here? Where are we going? Who are these people?"

Tempus took the glass and poured another shot, his mind racing to piece together the situation. He could feel the weight of Constance's fear and confusion pressing against him, and he knew he needed to keep her calm. "I'm not entirely sure of the details yet," he said, handing the glass back to her. "But I promise we'll find out soon enough. For now, just try to stay calm."

Constance accepted the glass gratefully, her eyes searching Tempus's face for answers. As she took another shot, her breathing began to steady, though the questions and tension remained.

The van glided to a smooth stop after about twenty minutes, its motion ceasing with a finality that made the hairs on the back of Tempus's neck stand up. The sliding door opened, and Tempus and Constance were guided out and led toward a small, five-story office building. A faded "For Lease" sign hung in the front window, and the building appeared forlorn and neglected.

As they entered, the interior confirmed their expectations: an empty office space with a vast, open floor plan. The only remnants of its previous occupants were a few scattered chairs and stray pieces of paper, which lay abandoned amidst a thin layer of dust. It was clear the place had been untouched for months, if not years. The late afternoon sun filtered through the dirty windows, casting long shadows and bathing the space in a soft, orange glow that accentuated the building's desolation.

They made their way up to the third floor, their footsteps echoing in the vacant building. The dim lighting added to the eerie atmosphere as they reached the center of the floor, where they were instructed to wait. The absence of artificial light left them in a twilight haze, amplifying their sense of unease.

Constance, her nerves on edge, pressed close to Tempus. She was visibly shaken, her eyes darting around the empty space, unsure of what was about to unfold. Tempus's mind was racing, trying to piece together the situation when a familiar voice cut through the quiet. It was a voice he recognized all too well.

"Victor," Tempus said with a tone of disgust, turning sharply in the direction of the voice.

Victor, stepping into the dim light, greeted Tempus with a cold, calculating stare. His presence was a jarring contrast to the otherwise lifeless surroundings. Tempus's face hardened as he faced the man, his anger and frustration barely contained. Constance clung tighter to Tempus, sensing the tension in the air. The building seemed to close in around them as they awaited the next move in this unsettling game.

Tempus looked at Victor in anger. Constance stood behind Tempus, shivering. She was unsure of what to expect at this point with Victor threatening violence against them with the use of the gun in his hand. Constance tried to shrink behind Tempus as best she could. Even though she was afraid for her own safety and was using Tempus as a shield, it wasn't strictly at her own choice. Tempus was working to move himself between her and the gun and pushing her back with his hand simultaneously.

"Are you going to shoot me now, Victor," Tempus asked a little too calmly. He was want to look behind him to reassure Constance but he didn't want to take his eyes off of Victor. Specifically, he didn't want to take his eyes off of the gun in Victor's hand.

Tempus's attention got divided by the movement of the para military personnel Victor had brought with him but it never wavered from the gun. Tempus breath got slow and shallow, taking an actual breath way longer than a normal person could.

Victor glanced to his left and right as the men moved into position beside him. He turned back to Tempus and smiled. "Would it matter if I shot you? You're immortal, this I know because every ancestor I had, up to Harlon, has known this and has came after you."

Tempus noted the relaxed stance that Victor had taken as he started speaking, even if Victor himself hadn't noticed that he had relaxed his vigil. Tempus's eyes traced the minute movement of the barrel of the gun as it swayed back and forth. Tempus shifted, imperceptibly. He noticed when Constance, still being behind him, tensed up even more.

Tempus's focus returned to Victor. The man had clearly let his guard down, thinking that he had won in this situation due to Tempus and Constance being cornered in the warehouse and the number of men he had.

Constance's hand was on Tempus's shoulder, so she noticed when Tempus's muscles spontaneously coiled up like a tight spring. Her gaze moved from Victor to Tempus's back in wonder.

Outwardly, Tempus seemed to have gotten relaxed. He had straightened up his back, having moved from a guarded position from Victor. His shoulders seemed to rise and fall as if his breathing was normal, not where it should have been given the excitement and danger of this situation. For all intents and purposes, anyone would have assumed that Tempus had given up on opposition.

Even Victor noticed it. He too interpreted it as Tempus accepting his fate. But, that wasn't the case. Tempus was angry but it wasn't the hot anger of action, no, it was the cold calculating anger that was excessively dangerous. Tempus was angry because Victor had pointed a gun at him, and in doing so, had threatened Constance's life.

Tempus crossed his arms and just from his stance, seemed to be looking down on Victor as if he were nothing. To Victor, it continued to look like Tempus had given up on fighting back and accepted his fate.

"I was wondering if you would come to your senses or continue to fight," said Victor. He was now totally relaxed. The gun lifted up as he shrugged his shoulders, the barrel pointing haphazardly around the room as he finished the gesture. "I guess you're smart enough to know you're outnumbered and cornered."

"What do you really want from me, Victor," Tempus asked slowly.

"Your secrets. Immortality. I want it all," said Victor. "You kept telling my family, through the generations, that there was no secret, that you know of, to grant anyone immortality?" Victor questioned. He waited for Tempus to answer but it seemed Tempus wasn't going to play into his little game of power dynamics.

Victor looked over his shoulder at the man that was in charge of his mercenaries. Tempus's gaze followed Victor's towards the lieutenant. As Victor passed the gun to him, Tempus smiled.

Victor turned back to Tempus and moved towards him. He poked his finger into Tempus's chest as hard as he could. "You might not know the answers that we wanted for all these years but guess what. Medicine these days has advanced a lot. If I can't get the answers from your mouth, I'll have my scientists dissect you and get the answers to immortality from your body. It's all about power and once I strip down your body to the cellular level, I'll have that secret and all the power."

Tempus brushed Victor's hand from his chest and dusted off his shirt absently. He looked over Victor's shoulder and nodded. Victor, in confusion, turned to look back at the mercenaries he had bought and brought to help him track down Tempus. One of the men was approaching the pair of them with a chair in his hands.

Victor looked at the man questioningly and then in confusion when the man passed him and went to stand behind Tempus as he positioned the chair behind Tempus.

"What are you doing?" Victor asked. He turned around and looked back at the lieutenant. "Elias, get your man under control."

Elias looked back at Victor as if he were air. Insignificant and worthless. Too insignificant to even deign to hold in contempt.

Tempus's voice brought Victor's head around, hard and quickly. "You know, you do your job a little too damn well, Elias. Every time I got settled in, your guys would find out my new identity within a few years."

"Sorry, sir. You wanted the best. I trained the best," said Elias.

Elias was right. While he was ultimately the one responsible for providing identities to Tempus, he never once gave this information to the men under him who, based on orders from Victor, worked to find out where Tempus was. The fact that they actually worked for Tempus was not known to Victor.

"What's going on here?" Victor asked, confusion evident in his face. He looked like he would break into a hysterical fit from the frustration and the feeling of helplessness at controlling the situation. It had all evaporated like steam—dissipating into nothingness.

"Don't you know already?" asked Tempus. "Do you know what your problem is?" Tempus asked softly. "You assumed I was weak.

You see weakness as a sin but I don't think it's necessarily so. To me weakness isn't a sin, instead I think that being weak... and not knowing it, is a bigger sin."

Tempus reached behind him and pulled a hesitant Constance around to stand in front of him before he coached her to sit on his knee. Complying to Tempus's prompts without any resistance, Constance seemed to be in the same state of disorientation that Victor was in. Once she was as comfortable as she could be, Tempus turned his attention back to Victor.

"You wanted power. I'll show you power," Tempus said. He snapped his fingers. Immediately, the sound of men turning on heels resounded in the empty warehouse. This was followed by the sound of the armed men as they began filing out of the area, leaving just the three of them alone.

"Let me ask you something, Victor. Did your family think I was stupid? Did you think I was weak? Did you think I was... powerless?" Tempus waited until Victor seemed on the verge of tears from his confusion. "I have lived well over one thousand years. Did you think I was idle in that time?"

Tempus wasn't expecting a response from Victor but he waited patiently just because. "You wanted power?" he finally asked the obviously confused and distraught man.

Tempus guided Constance to get up so that he could stand up. He shifted her and let her sit in his vacated seat. Tempus, after ensuring that Constance was seated, turned and approached Victor. He stopped within a hair's breadth in front of Victor, topping Victor's shorter height by four inches. Tempus leaned forward, over Victor's shoulder, until his lips were close to Victor's ears.

"You think because your family has money that you have power. Let me tell you something. You have no idea what power is. For me, it is as natural as breathing," Tempus whispered. He leaned back until he was standing straight in front of Victor, gazing down his nose at the man.

"I'll tell you this so you can get an idea of what power is. If I wanted a child I had to be baptized, the Pope himself would willingly do it without question. If I wanted a mountain moved, I'd have countries fighting to the death for the chance to do it for me. And *that* is not a lie. You can gain a lot of things if you've lived a thousand years," Tempus said.

Tempus turned and took the few steps back towards Constance. He reached out his hand towards her, and taking her hand, he guided her to her feet and began to lead her from the warehouse. Before he was gone, he called out over his shoulder.

"Oh, by the way, your family might be rich, but I personally own every bit of the debt of your family. I think I'll call in what's owed when I leave here," said Tempus. With that, he and Constance left the warehouse and a befuddled Victor, standing alone, in their wake.

Tempus and Constance stepped out of the building into the fading light of late afternoon. The air was cool, but the tension from inside still clung to them. As they approached the van, Tempus's calm exterior remained intact, though Constance could sense the anger simmering just beneath the surface. He opened the door for her, and she climbed in, still feeling the weight of everything that had transpired.

As the van pulled away from the desolate building, Constance settled into the seat beside Tempus. She couldn't shake the feeling of disorientation, as if the world she had known was suddenly tilted on its axis. The quiet, domestic life she had once cherished now seemed impossibly distant, shattered by the looming threat of violence and the reality of who Tempus truly was.

She glanced at him out of the corner of her eye, his profile sharp against the dimming light. His face was composed, betraying nothing of the emotions she knew were churning inside him. It struck her then, with a clarity that felt like a punch to the gut: she didn't really know Tempus, not the way she thought she did. Their lives had been intertwined for centuries, yes, but her experience of those centuries was fragmented, while his had been continuous, unrelenting.

'*What had that time done to him? Who had it made him into?*'

She turned her gaze to the window, watching the city blur past as her thoughts spiraled. The van's interior felt too small, too enclosed, as if the weight of her realizations might crush her. She had always believed in the bond between them, the love that had transcended lifetimes. But now, for the first time, she wondered if there was something else she should fear more than the inevitable end that came after every reunion with Tempus.

The man beside her had lived for centuries, surviving countless losses, battles, and betrayals. How had those experiences shaped him? Was he still the man she had loved in those past lives, or had time and suffering turned him into something else—someone she could no longer fully understand, or perhaps even trust?

The thought sent a shiver down her spine. She knew Tempus loved her, but she also knew that love alone couldn't erase the toll of centuries on his soul. The encounter with Victor had rattled her, not just because of the immediate danger, but because it had revealed a side of Tempus she wasn't prepared for—a side that had seemed almost too powerful, too distant from the man she thought she knew.

Her thoughts were interrupted when Tempus spoke, his voice breaking through the silence. "Are you alright?" he asked, his tone soft but carrying the weight of his concern.

Constance turned to him, forcing a smile that she hoped would mask the turmoil inside her. "I... I think I need a drink," she replied, her voice unsteady.

Tempus nodded, understanding the need for a moment of reprieve. He leaned forward and reached for the bar in the van, selecting a bottle of liquor. Pouring a generous measure into a glass, he handed it to her with a gentleness that contrasted starkly with the events of the day.

As she accepted the drink, their fingers brushed, and she felt the familiar warmth of his touch. Yet, as she raised the glass to her lips, she couldn't shake the lingering questions that haunted her. What had centuries of unending life truly done to him? And in the end, what would it do to her?

"Weren't you afraid that Victor could have gotten violent and used the gun before he gave it away?" asked Constance.

Tempus's gaze lingered on her for a moment before he turned away from her. He couldn't let himself fall into the well of her eyes, lest, through his own silence, he cause her distress to increase.

As Tempus turned away, prior to speaking, his hand moved up to just below his neck. There, beneath the silk shirt, lay the locket of the twins. His fingers absently brushed against the fabric, causing the locket to rub against the bare skin of his chest. Almost unconsciously, his mind had already drifted to other thoughts, a response to Constance lingering just out of reach, before he even realized the gesture.

His words came slow and measured. "It could have gone wrong, but it didn't. *Real* power rarely, if ever, needs violence in order to be effective."

The drink burned as it went down, but it did little to calm the storm inside her. Constance leaned back into her seat, her gaze returning to the window. The city lights flickered past, a blur of motion, but all she could see was the shadow of the man beside her, and the uncertainties that now stretched out before them.

For the first time in a long while, she wasn't sure what scared her more: the threat of dying after their inevitable reunion, or the reality of living with a man shaped by centuries of survival, someone who might have become a stranger without her ever realizing it.

Elias, sitting in the front seat, glanced back at Tempus, his voice low and apologetic. "I'm sorry about that, sir. I tried to call you and warn you that we were near."

Constance, lost in her swirling thoughts, was jolted back to the present by Elias's words. She turned her head to watch the interaction, sensing the tension that still lingered between Tempus and the man who had just helped him orchestrate the unsettling confrontation.

Tempus waved a dismissive hand, his gaze fixed out the opposite window. "It needed to be finished. It's alright now," he replied, his tone flat and emotionless. The casual finality of his words sent a chill down Constance's spine, but what came next was worse.

"Make sure to bankrupt his family," Tempus added, still not looking at Elias. His voice was cold, as if he were discussing a routine task rather than the destruction of an entire family's livelihood.

Constance shivered involuntarily. The man beside her, the one she had loved across lifetimes, suddenly felt like a stranger—a force of nature that she could barely comprehend, let alone control. She hesitated, watching the city lights flicker past outside, before gathering the courage to tap his shoulder.

He turned to her, his expression softening as he saw the glass she held out. Without a word, he took it and refilled it, the amber liquid catching the light before he handed it back to her. Constance accepted it with a nod, her fingers brushing his in a fleeting touch that felt both comforting and foreign at the same time.

As she sipped the drink, she felt the warmth spread through her, giving her the courage to voice the question that had been gnawing at her since the encounter with Victor. She knew she needed to ask—needed to understand. The man beside her was more than just the Tempus she had known; he was something different, something... more.

"Who are you, Tempus?" she asked quietly, her voice barely above a whisper.

Tempus sighed, the weight of centuries pressing down on him as he folded his hands in his lap. He stared down at them, the silence stretching between them, thick with unspoken fears. He knew that answering her honestly could mean losing her—that the truth of who he had become might be too much for her to bear.

But he couldn't lie, not to her.

"I'm just a man," he began slowly, his voice tinged with resignation. "A man that will not allow the world to run over me."

He finally turned to face her, his eyes filled with a vulnerability she hadn't seen before. Tears glistened on the edge of his lashes as he continued, "I am just the man that loves you."

Constance said nothing, the weight of his words hanging between them. She could see the depth of his love, but she could also see the immense power and control he had accumulated over the centuries—a power that both drew her in and terrified her.

Without a word, she downed the rest of her drink, the burn of the liquor doing little to ease the turmoil inside her. She turned back to the window, watching the city blur by as the van sped toward the hotel. The silence between them was heavy, filled with the echoes of everything that had been said—and everything that hadn't.

As the hotel loomed closer, Constance's thoughts swirled with uncertainty. She loved him, but could she live with the man he had become? Could she accept the darkness that time had woven into him, even as he tried to shield her from it?

The van slowed as they approached the entrance, but the questions in her mind only seemed to quicken, racing ahead to a future that now felt more uncertain than ever.

Constance walked silently beside Tempus as they made their way through the lobby of the hotel. The plush carpet muffled their footsteps, and the soft lighting cast a warm glow on the marble floors and opulent decor. Everything around her screamed wealth and power, and she realized with a sinking feeling that this was probably just another day in Tempus's life. This level of luxury, the effortless control over people's lives—it was all second nature to him.

As they approached the elevator, Constance stole glances at the intricate details of the hotel's interior. With her new perspective, she saw them differently. These surroundings weren't just a testament to his wealth; they were a manifestation of the authority he wielded—authority that had likely been built over centuries.

She couldn't help but think back to their previous reunions, the fleeting moments when they were together in past lives. She had been so caught up in the joy of seeing him again, in the whirlwind of emotions that came with their meetings, that she had never truly stopped to ask him about himself. She had basked in his attention, letting him shower her with love and affection, without once considering what he might be going through or what his life had been like in the years they were apart.

The realization hit her like a punch to the gut. She had been so naive, so foolish. Each time they met, she had allowed herself to be the center of attention, thinking that was love. But now she saw it for what it was—a childish, selfish way of holding onto him without really understanding him.

As they stepped into the elevator, Constance's thoughts darkened. If she had truly loved Tempus as deeply as she believed, shouldn't she have asked him about his life, his struggles? Shouldn't she have done everything in her power to support him during the brief time they had together? Instead, she had let him direct the focus toward her, basking in the comfort of his love while remaining ignorant of the burdens he carried.

Her hands clenched into fists at her sides as the elevator ascended. She couldn't shake the feeling of anger that welled up within her—not just at herself, but at Tempus as well. He had orchestrated it that way, hadn't he? Always keeping the attention on her, shielding her from the weight of his reality. Was it to protect her, or was it to keep her from seeing the truth of what centuries had done to him?

By the time they reached the suite, Constance's emotions were a tangled mess of regret, anger, and a desperate desire to understand. Tempus opened the door, and as they stepped inside, the familiar scent of the room washed over her. She paused just inside the doorway, taking in the sight of Alexander, Lynette, and her sister, Sera, who had already returned from the museum. The air in the room was filled with the quiet hum of their conversation, but it all came to a halt as Tempus and Constance entered.

Alexander looked up first, his sharp eyes immediately scanning Tempus's face, searching for any sign of what had happened. Lynette, sitting beside him, glanced between the two of them, concern etched on her features. And Sera—Constance's heart tightened at the sight of her sister. Sera's gaze met hers, and in that moment, Constance felt the weight of everything she had just realized pressing down on her even harder.

"Hey," Sera said softly, breaking the silence. "Everything okay?"

Constance forced a smile, the expression feeling strained on her face. "Yeah, we're fine. Just... tired."

Tempus didn't say anything as he crossed the room, heading straight for the small bar in the corner. Constance watched him go, her thoughts still churning as she followed more slowly. She could feel the eyes of her Lynette and sister on her, but she couldn't bring herself to explain. Not yet. Not when she was still trying to make sense of it all herself.

As Tempus poured himself a drink, Constance joined the others, sinking into a chair beside Sera. The warmth of her sister's presence was comforting, but it also served as a reminder of how little she had understood about the man she loved—how much she had taken for granted.

For now, she pushed the thoughts to the back of her mind, knowing that there would be time to confront them later. But even as she did, the questions lingered, unanswered and unspoken, between her and Tempus like a shadow that refused to fade.

Constance forced herself to push aside the turmoil in her mind. The weight of centuries of mistakes, doubts, and regrets lingered, but there was something more pressing now—something they had been waiting for. She glanced at Sera, who sat quietly on the couch, and then at Alexander and Lynette. The tension in the room was palpable, and Constance knew why.

"Did you find it?" Constance asked, her voice steady despite the storm brewing within her.

Sera looked up, her eyes meeting Constance's with a mixture of hope and fear. She reached into her bag and slowly pulled out a small, delicate flower. The petals were a deep violet, almost shimmering in the light. The moment Constance saw it, her breath caught in her throat.

"This is it," Sera whispered, holding the flower out for Constance to see. "The flower that started everything."

Tempus moved closer, his gaze fixed on the flower. The usually composed immortal looked momentarily shaken as his eyes flicked between the flower and the two sisters. Alexander, standing beside Sera, stared at the flower intently, his brow furrowed in thought.

"That's the same as the one my grandmother gave me," Alexander said, breaking the silence.

Sera nodded, her voice barely audible. "Yeah, me too."

Constance felt a shiver run down her spine as she looked at the flower, the small and unassuming thing that had caused so much pain and suffering across lifetimes. She glanced at Tempus, searching for some kind of reassurance, but his face remained unreadable. Turning back to her sister, Constance hesitated before asking the question that hung heavily in the air.

"So... what do we do now?" she asked, uncertainty lacing her words. "How do we use this to break the curse? Will it even work?"

The room fell into a tense silence as they all contemplated her question. Constance could feel her doubts gnawing at her. After everything they had been through—lifetimes of suffering, dying, and being reborn—could this fragile flower really undo it all? Could they finally be free from the curse that had bound them to this endless cycle?

"I don't even know where to start," Constance admitted, her voice wavering slightly. "I mean, we have the flower, but what if it's not enough? What if we're missing something? What if—" She stopped herself, realizing that her fear was taking over. She looked at Sera, Alexander, and Lynette, searching their faces for answers.

Sera gently placed the flower on the table between them, her fingers trembling slightly. "I don't know either, Constance," she said softly. "But... we've come this far. Maybe... maybe we just need to make a new wish."

"A new wish?" Alexander echoed, his gaze still fixed on the flower.

Sera nodded slowly. "It's what started all of this, right? Maybe it can end it too."

Constance stared at the flower, her mind racing. A new wish. It sounded so simple, but she knew it wouldn't be. Nothing about their lives had ever been simple. She glanced at Tempus, who remained silent, his eyes still locked on the flower.

"What do you think?" Constance asked him, her voice barely above a whisper. She wasn't just asking about the flower; she was asking about everything—about their lives, their future, and whether this small, delicate thing could really change the course of their cursed fate.

Tempus finally looked up, his gaze meeting hers. There was a depth of emotion in his eyes that she hadn't seen before—fear, hope, and something else she couldn't quite name. "I think... we have to try," he said quietly. "It's all we can do."

Constance nodded, feeling the weight of his words settle over her. It wasn't much, but it was a start. And in that moment, surrounded by the people she loved and the flower that had haunted their lives, she knew that trying was all they had left.

Constance held the flower in her trembling hands, its fragile petals brushing against her fingers. The weight of the moment pressed down on her as she looked around the room, searching for answers in the faces of those she loved. But when her gaze met theirs, they all seemed to avoid her eyes, each of them uncertain and afraid of making the wrong choice.

"Who should make the wish?" Constance asked, her voice barely steady.

Lynette spoke up, breaking the silence. "From what we found out earlier, Sera made a wish using one of these flowers," she explained, her eyes darting to Alexander. "And Alexander made one without even knowing it, I guess. So I think... you need to make the wish."

Constance's heart skipped a beat as she absorbed Lynette's words. She looked down at the flower, feeling the delicate stem between her fingers. The thought of making a wish—one that could either end their suffering or make things worse—was overwhelming. She hesitated, her mind spinning with the possibilities and the fears that came with them.

She glanced over at Tempus, who stood silently, his expression unreadable. "But what about Tempus?" Constance asked, her voice trembling. "He didn't use a flower, and he's trapped in this too."

The room fell silent again, and Constance could see the uncertainty in their faces. No one seemed to know the answer. The reality of the situation hung heavy in the air—there was no clear path forward, no guarantee that any wish would free them from the curse.

"I don't know, honey," Lynette finally said, her voice soft and filled with empathy. "Let's just go with you making the wish and see if that changes anything."

Constance looked around the room, seeing nods of agreement, though the tension and uncertainty were still palpable. She turned her attention back to the flower, the weight of the decision pressing down on her. This wasn't just about ending the curse; it was about understanding what she truly wanted—what her love for Tempus meant and how far she was willing to go to free them all.

She closed her eyes for a moment, trying to center herself. Memories of past lives flooded her mind, moments of joy and pain intertwined. She thought of the times she and Tempus had shared, the love that had sustained them through centuries of suffering, and the weight of his immortality that had always loomed over them. She wondered what would change if she made the wish—would it free them, or would it only bring more heartache?

What did she truly want? Did she want to break the curse, to finally end the cycle of death and rebirth? Or did she want something more—something that could give them a chance at a life together without the shadow of their past hanging over them?

As she opened her eyes, Constance looked at Tempus, who was watching her with an intensity that made her heart ache. She knew he was afraid—afraid that whatever wish she made might change everything, and not necessarily for the better. But she also knew that they couldn't stay like this, trapped in a cycle that had no end.

Taking a deep breath, she tightened her grip on the flower, feeling its soft petals against her palm. The time had come to decide, to make the wish that could either save them or condemn them to more suffering.

But what should she wish for? What would truly free them from this curse, and what would that freedom look like?

Constance stood there, the flower still cradled in her hands, feeling the weight of the decision pressing down on her. She knew the wish she made would define the rest of their lives—hers, Sera's, Tempus's, even Alexander's. But the truth was, she wasn't ready. The enormity of it all—the curse, Tempus's true nature, the depths of her own feelings—was too much to process in this moment.

Slowly, deliberately, she placed the flower back on the table. The delicate petals seemed to shimmer in the dim light of the suite, as if taunting her with the power they held. Constance tore her eyes away from it and looked at Tempus. His face was a mask of calm, but she could see the tension in his posture, the way his hands were clenched at his sides.

"I think I need more time to wrap my head around... things," she said quietly, her voice barely steady.

But even as she spoke, her mind churned with thoughts of what "things" truly meant. It wasn't just about the wish or the curse—it was about Tempus himself. Who was he, really? What did her love for him mean? Was it something pure and eternal, or had it been twisted by centuries of suffering and loss? And what would happen once she made the wish, whatever that wish turned out to be?

The room remained silent as the others absorbed her decision. She could feel the weight of their expectations lifting slightly, replaced by a sense of uncertainty that matched her own.

"You've got time. Take it, honey. We won't rush you," Lynette said softly, her voice filled with understanding.

Constance nodded, grateful for the reprieve, but she couldn't shake the sense of foreboding that lingered in the air. She glanced at Tempus again, and this time, the hurt she had been trying so hard to hide slipped through. The pain she felt—the confusion, the fear—it all stemmed from him, from the man she had loved for so long but who now felt like a stranger in many ways.

Tempus must have seen it too, because he reached into his inner pocket and pulled out a cigar. Without a word, he turned and walked out to the balcony, his movements stiff, controlled. Alexander followed him, leaving Constance alone with Sera and Lynette.

The quiet of the suite settled over them like a heavy blanket, and Constance could feel Sera's eyes on her. "What's going on?" Sera asked gently, her voice laced with concern.

Constance looked out at Tempus, his silhouette framed against the evening sky. The memory of the day's events flashed through her mind—the unexpected intimacy with Tempus, the terrifying encounter with Victor, the revelation of just how powerful and distant Tempus had become over the centuries.

"A lot happened," Constance said, her voice hollow. "But I don't want to talk about it right now. Maybe later."

Lynette, sensing the depth of her distress, placed a comforting hand on Constance's shoulder. "We're here for you, whatever you need," she said softly.

Sera, though clearly worried, nodded in understanding. She glanced out at Tempus on the balcony, her brow furrowing as she tried to piece together what could have happened in the short time they had been apart. But Constance remained silent, unwilling—or perhaps unable—to share the details just yet.

After a few moments, Lynette stood, stretching slightly as she glanced at the clock. "I think I'm going to head home. It's been a long day."

Alexander reentered the suite as Lynette made her way to the door. Sera turned to her sister, then back to Alexander, a thoughtful look crossing her face. "Yeah, a lot has happened," she said quietly, her eyes on Alexander. "And I think I've got some things I need to talk about with someone."

Alexander offered her a gentle smile, one that seemed to hold a promise of understanding. Sera smiled back, her expression softening as she stood to leave.

The sisters and Lynette exchanged hugs, lingering for a moment in the warmth of their connection before stepping out into the hallway. Constance watched them go, feeling a pang of loneliness as the door closed behind them. The room felt emptier now, quieter, the weight of her unspoken thoughts pressing in on her from all sides.

She turned back to the balcony, where Tempus still stood, his back to her as he looked out over the city. The distant glow of the lights reflected off the glass, casting long shadows across the room. Constance took a deep breath, knowing that the time had come for another conversation—one she wasn't sure she was ready for, but knew was inevitable.

As she walked toward the balcony, the sound of her footsteps seemed to echo in the stillness, a reminder that, for better or worse, they were in this together.

Constance stepped out onto the balcony, the cool evening air brushing against her skin as she approached Tempus. He turned to face her, and for a moment, her breath caught in her throat. The sight of him—tall, composed, with that undeniable aura of authority—sent a wave of conflicting emotions crashing over her. He was undeniably handsome, but it was more than that. She could feel the power emanating from him, a power that excited, thrilled, and terrified her all at once.

As their eyes met, the tension between them seemed to ease, if only slightly. In a surprisingly gentle moment, Tempus broke the silence. "Do you want to eat dinner?" he asked, his voice soft and almost tentative, as if he knew how fragile the moment was.

Constance, at a loss for anything else to do and unwilling to dive into the complexities of their situation, simply nodded. The prospect of dinner felt like a welcome distraction, a way to avoid the weight of the conversation that loomed between them.

Tempus pulled out his phone, dialing a number with the ease of someone who had done this countless times before. Constance watched him, curious but silent, as he waited for someone to pick up. A moment later, a woman's voice responded on the other end of the line.

"I need an evening dress sent up to the suite," Tempus said, his tone calm and authoritative. He then proceeded to give the woman Constance's exact measurements, much to her surprise.

When he hung up, Constance stared at him, her eyebrows raised in astonishment. "How did you—"

Tempus glanced at her, a small smile playing on his lips. "You learn a lot with a long life," he said, his voice tinged with a mix of humor and sincerity. He hoped she would see it for what it was—an attempt to be considerate, to make her feel special, even in the midst of everything that was happening.

Constance found herself smiling back, a little taken aback by the gesture but appreciative nonetheless. She nodded, understanding the sentiment behind his words. For all his power and authority, he was still trying to connect with her, to show her that he cared.

A short time later, there was a knock at the door. Tempus retrieved the package, handing it to Constance with a nod. She took it and made her way to her room, her heart pounding as she carefully opened the box. Inside was a beautiful evening dress, its fabric shimmering in the soft light of the suite. It was elegant and perfectly suited to her—another reminder of how much Tempus knew, even when she hadn't expected it.

She slipped into the dress, smoothing the fabric as she looked at herself in the mirror. For a moment, the curse, the doubts, and the fears seemed to fade away. She could almost imagine that this was a normal evening, that they were just a couple going out to dinner, free from the burdens of their past.

When she emerged from her room, Tempus was waiting for her. He stood there, looking immaculate in his tailored suit, his gaze sweeping over her with an intensity that made her heart skip a beat.

For all the centuries he had known her—through lives, through echoes, through names half-remembered—he had never seen her like this. Not truly. The dress didn't just accentuate her beauty; it revealed the distance between what he thought he understood and what stood before him now.

His breath caught, an involuntary reaction that startled him, not because she was beautiful—he had always known that—but because something primal and unbidden stirred in him, quiet and fierce. He had spent lifetimes mastering restraint, carving walls around certain kinds of want

And yet here she was, radiant and real, and every hard-won barrier in his mind softened in an instant. It was not lust that shook him—but awe, edged in something dangerously close to hunger. He hadn't meant to speak, not aloud, but the words slipped through before he could stop them.

"My god, you look beautiful," he murmured, his voice filled with admiration.

The dress clung to her like memory—soft where it needed to whisper, taut where it meant to linger. Midnight blue, it shimmered with the subtle sheen of starlight, tracing the slope of her shoulders and dipping just enough at the back to suggest something unspoken.

The fabric hugged the gentle curve of her waist before flowing down like water over the lines of her hips, each movement turning her into something almost too perfect to behold. Her bare arms caught the low light, and the delicate slit at her thigh revealed not just skin but poise—every inch of her composed and devastating.

She didn't look dressed; she looked *deliberate*, like the world had conspired to sculpt her into this exact moment.

Constance felt a warmth spread through her at his words, and she smiled—a genuine, heartfelt smile. She walked over to him, her movements graceful as she took his arm. For the first time in what felt like an eternity, there was a moment of peace between them, a brief respite from the storm that had consumed their lives.

Together, they made their way down to the dining room. The evening felt almost surreal, as if they had stepped into a different world—one where their love, their connection, was all that mattered. The candlelit ambiance of the dining room only added to the sense of calm that settled over them as they sat down to dinner.

As they began their meal, the conversation flowed easily, focused on light topics that kept the weight of their situation at bay. Constance allowed herself to be present in the moment, savoring the food, the atmosphere, and the man beside her. For now, at least, they could pretend that everything was normal—just two people enjoying a quiet evening together.

But beneath the surface, she knew the questions, the decisions, still lingered. Yet for tonight, she chose to push them aside and simply be with him, finding comfort in the familiar warmth of their connection.

As dinner progressed, the conversation eventually turned toward the topic that had been hovering between them all night—Tempus himself. Constance had been content to keep things light, but she could sense that he had something he needed to say. His expression grew more serious as he set down his fork and looked at her, the candlelight casting shadows across his face.

"Constance," he began, his voice soft but weighted with emotion, "I think it's time I told you... everything."

She held her breath as he began to speak, recounting the long, lonely years he had endured. Tempus didn't spare any details. He spoke of the centuries of isolation, of watching the world change while he remained the same. He told her of the countless times he had tried to live a normal life, only to see it slip through his fingers like sand. He explained how, over time, he had built walls around himself, becoming the man she saw before her now—powerful, detached, but always longing for the connection he once had.

As he spoke, Constance felt her heart ache for him. The loneliness he described, the endless years of watching people he cared about die, and the weight of immortality—it was almost too much to bear. Tears welled up in her eyes, and she had to blink them away as she listened to his sorrowful tale.

But despite everything, Tempus made one thing clear. "No matter what any of that means," he said, his voice steady, "I am still the man you professed your love to so long ago. Nothing will ever change that."

Constance felt a sense of peace wash over her as his words sank in. She realized then that she didn't need to reconcile the man he had become with the one she had loved in the past. Instead, she could accept things as they were—embrace the present and the future, rather than dwell on the past. She would take the time to truly get to know Tempus now, without the burden of who he once was.

With that resolve, Constance felt a weight lift from her shoulders. She looked across the table at him, her heart full of acceptance and understanding. "I think... I'm ready to let go of the past," she said quietly. "And just live in the moment. With you."

Tempus smiled at her, a genuine smile that softened the hard edges of his face. They finished their meal in a comfortable silence, a new understanding forming between them.

After dinner, they returned to the suite. Constance felt a little nervous as she prepared to take a shower, unsure of what to wear afterward. But when she opened the closet, she found that Tempus had already arranged for clothes to be provided for her. She slipped into a simple t-shirt and her underwear, feeling both surprised and grateful for the thoughtfulness he had shown.

When she emerged from the bathroom, she found Tempus waiting for her by the fireplace, a glass of wine in his hand. He looked up as she approached, his eyes warm and inviting. She joined him on the couch, and they sat together in a comfortable silence, the crackling of the fire and the soft clinking of their wine glasses the only sounds in the room.

No words were needed. They simply enjoyed each other's company, the connection between them stronger than ever.

As the evening drew to a close, Constance began to wonder where she would sleep. But before she could ask, Tempus turned to her, his expression gentle. "Would you sleep with me tonight?" he asked, his voice low. "I promise... nothing but my company."

Constance felt a rush of warmth at his request. She had been thinking the same thing—how she couldn't imagine being away from him now, not after everything they had shared. "Yes," she replied without hesitation, grateful that he had asked.

Together, they made their way to the bedroom. But just as they were about to settle in, Constance paused, her gaze drawn to the small flower on the table. "Wait," she said softly, crossing the room to retrieve it. She held the flower delicately in her hand, then followed Tempus to bed.

As they lay down together, Tempus wrapped his arms around her, pulling her close. Constance felt his warmth against her back, his steady breathing comforting her as she clutched the flower in both hands. The weight of the day, the weight of the past, seemed to slip away as she let herself relax in his embrace.

As she drifted off to sleep, her thoughts began to blur, and she whispered softly into the darkness, "I wish... I wish..."

The words lingered in the air, unfinished, as sleep claimed her. The flower remained in her hands, a symbol of both their past and the unknown future that awaited them.

Chapter 14: "Eternal Bloom"

Years Later - Atlanta, USA

In the garden of time, love blooms eternally..

Constance thought it a good idea to share some quiet time with Tempus after all they'd been through. Six months had passed. A gentle bump curved beneath the sash at her waist, the growing child a sign of peace finally won.

She hadn't been easy to live with—her mood swings ran from laughter to tears in seconds. Neither she nor her sister had experienced pregnancy in their past lives. It was a journey full of unknowns. Tempus bore the brunt of it and still cherished every moment. To him, it meant permanence.

They wandered the Atlanta Botanical Garden, bathed in golden light. The wind danced through blooming flowers, and sunbeams slanted through the canopy above. It was a rare kind of quiet.

"This is what life should be," Constance murmured. Her fingers found his, grounding her in a present unshackled from their past. "Calm. Beautiful. Uninterrupted."

Tempus gave her hand a soft squeeze. "I've spent lifetimes waiting for this. I used to wonder if it would ever come."

She stopped by a still pond, her reflection rippling as petals drifted across the water. "We're free now," she said, turning to him. "No more fear. No more running from fate."

His arm slid around her waist. "It feels like a dream."

"I can't believe real. But it is real. It's right here, right now," she replied, her hand settling over her stomach. "All that time brought us here."

They sat on a nearby bench, the breeze stirring the leaves as twilight fell. The curse was broken. The cycle had ended. At last, they had each other, whole and unthreatened. Fate would never take them apart arbitrarily again.

Tempus watched her silently, awe in his eyes. "Every time I found you, it felt like I'd been holding my breath for centuries."

Constance looked at him, her eyes glistening. "In every life, I felt something missing. I didn't always know it was you... but I always knew something wasn't whole."

He nodded slowly. "I kept hoping that the next time would be *our forever.*"

"Well, you don't have to worry about that anymore," she said, "we've made it our's now."

He reached out and tucked a strand of hair behind her ear. "I was afraid—still am. How do I love you without fearing the end?"

She placed her hand over his heart. "We're here. Together. I've lived through so many endings, but this one's not the same."

His voice dropped to a whisper. "I'll hold you forever, if that's what it takes."

"And I'll stay," she said. "I've loved you across lifetimes. Now, I get to love you in the one that really matters."

They sat together in silence, the world fading around them.

Years had passed. Tempus and Constance found themselves at the Atlanta High Museum of Art, visiting the place where she once worked.

Tempus turned and smiled at Constance. Their children tried to hurriedly huddle their own children and keep them from running ram shod through the corridors of the museum. Moving around them, other family units moved gracefully across the marbled floors on their survey of the walls of history.

"How many lifetimes has it been?" asked Tempus as he took his wife's hands. Her thin and translucent skin crinkled as she slipped her hand into his.

A gentle smile graced Constance's face. Her eyes slowly drifted closed as she shook her head. "I could say *too* many but I won't."

Tempus turned his head to the side, curious to know why she wouldn't declare it as such. "Why won't you say that?" he asked softly.

Constance leaned over and kissed Tempus's cheek. His leathery skin folding to encompass the shape of her lips. Laugh lines presented themselves at the edge of her eyes, a gift from living a fulfilling life. "I'd rather not say that because I think it's been... *just enough.*"

Author's Reflection

(On Writing a Love Story Without Love)

How do you write a love story that has no *love* in it?

How do you write about a love that has never been allowed to develop into intimacy?

A love that has lasted so long, that God himself may have forgotten it?

You just begin.

I'll give you the key.

A key—not to unlock the door before you, but to understand why it's always been locked.

You pick up the pen, the pencil—open the laptop.

The questions you ask are the love story.

A love story without love isn't *hollow*—it's *haunted*.

It *breathes* in the space between *what could've been* and *what never was*.

It *echoes* in the *absence*, in the *ache*, in the *waiting*.

To write a love story that has never been allowed to develop into intimacy,

you must master restraint.

Show the gravity of a touch that never lands.

Let longing become the language.

Let the nearly, the almost, the not yet

carry more weight than consummation ever could.

You write about:

– Eyes that don't linger—but want to.

– Letters never sent—but have a stamp.

– Dreams remembered—by only one of them.

– Moments interrupted—by the lived lives of longing.

– Choices made too late—when it was never clear a choice was present.

– One holding on. One forgetting. Both enduring.

And when you say the love is so old

that even God may have forgotten it—

then you're writing something mythic.

A love that outlasts religion, flesh, even death.

A love not written in hearts and flowers,

but in erosion, reincarnation, and ruin.

To write that story,

let silence be your syntax.

Let time be your antagonist.

Let the never quenched desire be the lines between the paragraphs.

Let the lovers never quite align—

but make sure they always almost certainly do.

Let the reader hope.

Let them despair.

Let them carry that unanswered ache

with them after the last page closes.

Because that's what a love story with no love in it really

is:

A love story that hurts to believe in...

and hurts more not to.

—*J. A. Springs*

Also by J. A. Springs

Chronicles of Cosmic Realms
Shadows of the Forgotten Void

elctrcsheepdrmwrks (Electric Sheep Dreamworks)
Blurred Vision
Fractured
Zero One

Essays in Systems and Being
Essays in Systems and Being

The Absurdities Anthology
How Not to Find Your Local Weed-Man

The Gifted
The Untamed Force
Next Exit

The Shepherd Series
The Bad Shepherd
The Good Wolf

Standalone
Sundrops
Behind the Red Door
Boundless Fragments: A Collection of Novellas and Short Stories
Fragments of Forever

Watch for more at https://authorjasprings.com.

About the Author

I'm J. A. Springs.

Father of six wonderful children. I served twenty years on active duty, living around the world and experiencing things I never imagined I would. I spent time in societies and countries I once couldn't have envisioned as part of my future. I've done a lot—and still not enough.

These days, I live quietly, accompanied by my cats, music, and an interest in writing that consumes me. I've been writing seriously since 2021. I never set out to write in a particular genre—it made more sense to write around them instead. As for goals? There aren't many. Enjoy the first cup of coffee in the morning and see what the day brings.

Read more at https://authorjasprings.com.

About the Publisher

LLC. Lancaster, PA

www.writingfortheworldpress.com

Read more at https://www.writingfortheworldpress.com.

www.ingramcontent.com/pod-product-compliance
Lightning Source LLC
Chambersburg PA
CBHW030241030726
47493CB00023B/347